1-2022

Wait For It

Center Point
Large Print

Also by Jenn McKinlay and available from
Center Point Large Print:

Better Late Than Never
About a Dog
Barking Up the Wrong Tree
Death in the Stacks
Every Dog Has His Day
Hitting the Books
Word to the Wise
Paris Is Always a Good Idea
One for the Books

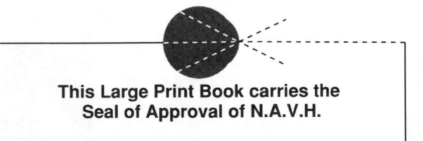

**This Large Print Book carries the
Seal of Approval of N.A.V.H.**

JENN McKINLAY

CENTER POINT LARGE PRINT
THORNDIKE, MAINE

*For Susan Norris McKinlay,
the most remarkable woman I've ever known.
Our family couldn't ask for a stronger,
wiser, or more loving matriarch.
We are lucky to have you,
and I'm so proud that
you're my mom.*

Annabelle

"Annabelle, please tell me you are not meeting Jeremy at the Top of the Hub for your annual un-anniversary celebration," Sophie Vasquez, my former college roommate, life partner in all shenanigans, and best friend forever, said.

"Fine, I won't tell you," I muttered into my cell phone. My breath came out in a plume of steam in the freezing February air.

I was walk-jogging because I was late. Little-known fact, I, Annabelle Martin, am always late. As my father liked to say, "Sunshine, you were born late." He's not even joking. According to my mother, I was two weeks late and wouldn't leave the womb without an eviction notice. Having since learned that life is hard, I think in utero me was onto something.

In my defense, my lateness is not on purpose. I'm not trying to be rude, it's just that my comprehension of the human construct of time is marginal at best. Like, I know that it takes at least twenty minutes to walk to the Prudential Center from my studio apartment on Marlborough Street, and while I had every intention of leaving twenty-five minutes ahead of time, I got sidelined

7

by an idea for a sketch because of the way the moonlight shone through my windowpane, making patterns on the floor.

As an artist, I'm constantly distracted by the details that most people can filter out. Shapes, light, shadows, the subtle nuances that make up the world around me, I'm in their thrall. Naturally, my quick sketch made me late, and now it was fifteen minutes until I was supposed to be at the restaurant, and I was running through Back Bay in the frigid winter cold, in high-heeled boots, with my thick wool coat flapping behind me, no doubt looking like a crazy person.

"Belle, this is such a bad idea," Sophie said.

"Why? We do it every year. It's tradition." My tone was defensive because I knew how Sophie felt about my relationship with my first ex-husband.

Yes, you read that right. *First* ex-husband. And yes, I am only twenty-eight and have two ex-husbands. I've had a few people give me side-eye over this fact, and I even had one woman accuse me of taking all the men. Yes, she did! I told her she owed me a thank-you for vetting them for the rest of womankind. Honestly.

I mean, it's not like I wanted to be a twice-divorced twenty-something. It's just that life stuff happened—big bad life stuff—and my coping skills in my early twenties had not been awesome. Besides, I'm impulsive, and when I'm in love, I'm sooooo in love, I lose all sense of reason. Clearly.

Considering her tone, I supposed I should have let Sophie's call go to voicemail, but when your bestie calls from Arizona, you answer even when you know she's going to challenge your life choices. I heard the distinct sound of water in the background.

"Soph, if you're calling me from a swimming pool, I'm hanging up on you," I said.

Laughter greeted me. "I'm not," she said. "I swear I'm not."

A suspicious splash punctuated her words.

"You are such a liar," I accused. I hurried down the sidewalk, feeling the bitter wind sweep in from Boston Harbor.

"Technically, it's a hot tub. What gave it away?"

"Splashing."

"Sorry," she said. She didn't sound a bit sorry. "How's the weather there? Another blizzard on the way?"

"It's Boston in February," I said. "Cold, gray, and sad. It's just horribly sad. In fact, I think I have a case of seasonal affective disorder brewing."

"Aw, that is SAD, poor Belle," she said. "You should come visit me in Phoenix. It's a delicious eighty-two degrees without a cloud in the sky."

It was two hours earlier in Phoenix. While

she enjoyed daylight, I was navigating the early dark on one of those painful thirteen-degree days where your snot freezes solid before you can blow it out your nostrils.

"Why, yes, I'll have another margarita," Sophie said, obviously not to me. "Thank you."

"I hate you. You know that, right?" I asked. I adjusted the purse strap on my shoulder as I jogged the final stretch to the Prudential Center, known locally as The Pru.

"Well, I think you'll hate me less when you hear why I called," she said.

I stepped on a patch of ice, and my heel slid out from under me. I fought to keep my balance, pulling a hamstring in the process. "Ow! Shit!"

"How about I explain before you start swearing?"

"Sorry, that wasn't meant for you. I slipped," I said. Now I was limping, which I'm sure was a fabulous look for me. "I'm almost at the building. I might lose you in the elevator."

"Then I'll be quick," she said. "I'm calling to offer you a job as the creative director in our company."

"But your company's in Phoenix," I said. Sophie and her husband, Miguel, owned a graphic design firm that was quickly gaining national attention. This was no small offer.

"Yes."

"You want me to move to Phoenix?" I stopped

10

walking. The bitter wind pushed me up against the side of the building.

"Yes."

"Phoenix, Arizona?"

"Yes."

"But . . ."

"Just hear me out," Sophie said. "You're the most talented graphic designer I've ever known, an absolute trend visionary, and we desperately need you here. Phoenix is in a boom, and we can top the money you're currently making as a freelancer. Think of it as an opportunity to shake up your life a little bit."

"I wasn't aware that my life needed shaking," I said. It did, but I didn't want to admit it because . . . pride.

"Oh, come on, Belly, come to Phoenix."

For the record, Sophie is the only person on the planet allowed to call me "Belly," because when we were roommates at the Savannah College of Art and Design, she held my hand when I got my belly button pierced. We shared a bond of bad decisions that was stronger than steel.

I tried to picture myself in the Southwest. Couldn't do it. She used my stunned silence to press her point.

"You've been freelancing for five years," she said. "Don't you want more stability?"

"No." *Yes.*

"A pay raise?"

"Maybe." *Definitely.*

"Retirement? Benefits? Paid vacation?" *Check, check, check.*

I sighed. It came out as a limp jet of hot breath in cold air. She was making solid points. I had no rebuttal. I went for avoidance. I pulled my phone away from my ear to check the time. "I have to go. I'm going to be *sooo* late."

"You're always late."

"I'm trying to be better," I protested. "It was my New Year's resolution."

"And how's that going?"

"Shush," I said. "You're not helping here."

"I am helping. You just don't want to hear it. Are you going to get back together with Jeremy?" she asked.

"No!" I cried. "Why would you even think that?"

"Because he's your social fallback plan, and you spend an awful lot of time together for people who are no longer married," she said.

"We're friends with benefits," I said.

"You don't need him as a friend, and you're not doing him any favors by offering him benefits. You're keeping each other dangling. It's not healthy for either of you."

"We're not dangling," I said. "We agreed that we can date whoever we want."

"And yet neither of you do," she said.

"You don't know that," I protested.

"Please," she said. "I've been on this ride before. Neither of you is seeing anyone else, but you don't belong together and you know it. You need to stop picking the lowest-hanging fruit."

"Did you just call Jeremy an apple?" I asked.

"I think of him as more of a peach, easily bruised," she said. "Your entire relationship was spent with you protecting him by doing everything for him because he's so socially inept, albeit lovable. You were like a lawnmower wife, moving every obstacle out of his way. Do you really want that for the rest of your life?"

"I didn't—I'm not—" I protested but she interrupted.

"Yes, you did and you are," she declared. "You've run interference for him his entire adult life, even when you were married to the big disappointment, who also used you to prop himself up. And then what did the BD do? He left you—just like Jeremy did when his mother stamped her foot hard enough. Time to break the pattern, my friend."

"I . . ." I slumped against the wall. Is that how she saw it? How she saw me? I didn't know what to say.

"Come to Phoenix," Sophie insisted. Then she made a weird burbling noise. "Do you hear that? That's me motorboating a margarita as big as my head. Come. To. Phoenix."

I heard another splash and decided, since I

could no longer feel my toes, the tips of my ears, or my fingers, that I really did hate her.

"I love that you're asking me," I said. "But—"

"Don't say no!" she ordered. So bossy! "Promise me you'll at least think about it."

"Fine, I'll think about it." I wasn't going to think about it. "Now I *have* to go. Miss you. Love you."

"Miss you. Love you, too," she echoed. "Say 'hi' to Jeremy for me, you know, before you tell him you're leaving him for me."

"Will do," I said. I wasn't leaving him for her. I mean, creative director? That was a huge job. Sure, as a one-woman operation, I was essentially doing that already, but this was a large firm and the position would require supervising—I couldn't even supervise a house plant—the art director and being in charge of the overall creative concepts and not doing the actual designing, which quite frankly was the fun part.

I ended the call and ran into the building, realizing I was entering the danger zone of lateness where Jeremy was going to be peeved with me for making him wait, especially given that it was our un-anniversary and all. Damn it!

The Top of the Hub sits on the fifty-second floor of The Pru. It's a white tablecloth, fine china, heavy silverware sort of restaurant, which boasts outstanding views of the Charles River, Boston Harbor, and the surrounding city. Jeremy

14

and I had been coming here to celebrate our un-anniversary ever since he landed in Boston a few years ago, shortly after I divorced Greg DeVane, aka the big disappointment, or the BD for short. Yes, he was a disappointing husband, but that's a story for another day, preferably accompanied by a shot of three wise men with an IPA chaser.

Jeremy Pettit and I met in Georgia when I was attending the Savannah College of Art and Design and he was at Savannah State studying engineering. I spotted him at a coffee shop on Broughton Street and had been a smitten kitten on sight. He was everything a college girl looked for in a boyfriend—shy, sweet, attentive, as snuggable as an oversized teddy bear, and it certainly helped that he looked like he'd just walked out of the Patagonia catalog wearing their fjord flannel.

Jeremy had the distracted air of a guy with one foot in childhood and the other in adulthood, uncertain of which direction he wanted to go. I figured he just needed a good woman—i.e., me—to give him a solid shove in the right direction. I had not accounted for the realities that I was no readier to be an adult than he was, his mother hated me, and he had a host of issues that didn't even start to appear until after we were married, which was a month after graduation.

If I closed my eyes and listened, I could still

15

hear my older sister Chelsea's shriek of outrage echoing on the airwaves to this day. Our mother had passed away six months before I met Jeremy, and in hindsight, I could see that our relationship and subsequent marriage was an attempt to fill the gaping hole left by my mother's passing, but what twenty-one-year-old has that sort of insight? Not me.

I'd thought Jeremy was my soul mate sent to comfort and keep me just when I needed him most. I truly believed we'd be together forever and ever. Amen. We didn't last two years. By the time he was finishing his master's degree in biomedical engineering, the ink was drying on our divorce papers, which had been drawn up by his mother's attorney. The only time she ever smiled at me was the day she came to collect Jeremy and his things from our apartment.

Now five years later, we were in the same city, celebrating our un-anniversary at the Top of the Hub, while enjoying an "exes with benefits" relationship of which absolutely no one in my life approved. You'd think that would be more of a deterrent for me. Nope.

The elevator opened and I strode into the lobby, pretending I wasn't panting for breath and trying not to look sweaty. Jeremy, in a navy suit with his hair cut high and tight and sporting a blond bruh beard, was standing beside the hostess station waiting for me. He looked mildly panicked so it

16

appeared dinner was going to start with tension. I decided to sink that battleship right away.

I dashed across the lobby and threw myself at him. He caught me and I kissed him full on the lips, knowing it would melt his brain and make him forget he was mad.

"Sorry, sorry, sorry," I panted when we came up for air. Then I shrugged and said, "Artist."

To my relief, his shoulders dropped from around his ears, the tight lines around his mouth eased, and he laughed. Then he hugged me. "I suppose I should be used to it by now."

Well, yeah, you should, I thought. After all, my tardiness was one of the many reasons we'd divorced. Wisely, I did not say this out loud. Instead, I checked my coat and then curled my hand around his elbow while we followed the hostess to our table.

She led us through the rows, to a table tucked beside a tall window. To my surprise, it was strewn with pink rose petals, and a bottle of champagne was in a bucket with two glasses already poured and waiting for us. I gave Jeremy a side-eye.

"You went all out this year," I said.

He shrugged. "It seems like a special un-anniversary, doesn't it?"

His pale green eyes met mine, and I felt a prickle of alarm. Had I missed a memo? What did he mean by "special"? My heart started to

17

pound in my chest like warning shots being fired. I could feel my flight-or-fight response, okay, mostly flight, kick in.

Jeremy and I had celebrated our un-anniversary ever since he moved to Boston three years ago. It was always low-key and fun right up until last year, when, in a bout of deep loneliness, I invited him to spend the night. He'd been "spending the night," if you get my drift, a couple of times a month ever since.

I knew Sophie was right that the relationship wasn't doing either one of us any good, rather like glazed doughnuts, the occasional cigarette, or a three-day-long video-game-playing binge, but I didn't want to give it up because then I'd have to go out there and find a real relationship, which felt like entirely too much work.

He pulled out my chair, and I slid onto my seat. I felt out of step, like I was clapping on the down beat, and couldn't quite get the rhythm of the room. I noticed that people at surrounding tables were covertly watching us. This was bad.

The hostess put our menus on the corner of the table and stepped back. She was younger than me by a couple of years. She had that fresh-faced enthusiasm that could only be found on a person who hadn't been paying their own rent for very long.

She glanced between us, and then with a soft squeak, she stepped back, turned on her heel, and hurried away. The early warning system inside of me grew insistently louder.

Jeremy picked up the two champagne glasses and handed me one. I debated downing it, sensing that liquid courage was going to be required. He lifted his in a toast. I wished he'd sit down. It felt as if he was looming over me.

"Annabelle, you're my best friend," he said. Oh dear, this sounded like the opening of a speech. That couldn't be good. Usually we just said, "Look at us," clinked glasses, and down the hatch the beverage went. We didn't do speeches.

"And you're mine," I said. I lifted my glass, indicating the toast was over. But he didn't get the message. In fact, he looked as if he was just warming up.

"I know," he said. "Despite the fact that we got married too young and you had that episode with what's his name, we're still each other's plus one."

I stared at Jeremy. That "episode" was my second marriage. Jeremy knew the BD's name, but even now, three years after my divorce, he still refused to say it. I knew he'd been in denial about the whole thing, but it seemed significant at the moment that he couldn't say his name or mention my marriage.

"You mean my marriage to Greg?" I asked. I blinked innocently.

He made a face as if a fly had just flown into

his mouth. He waved his hand dismissively and continued on.

"Yeah, even then I always felt like we were meant to be together, you know."

I didn't know. I had thought we were done except for the friendship and fringe benefits. The cold feeling in the pit of my stomach began to harden into a block of ice. If he was headed where I feared, we were not going to come out of this as friends, never mind friends with benefits.

"I always believed we'd grow old together and end up on a porch somewhere in matching rocking chairs," he said. His smile was adoring when he tilted his head and stared into my eyes. He was going to propose. I could see it coming as if it had the bright blaze of a meteor breaking through the atmosphere.

I had to stop him. I didn't want to marry him again, and I didn't really believe he wanted to marry me. It would ruin everything if he asked because I'd have to say no and he'd be so terribly hurt. He did bruise easily just as Sophie said. I jumped to my feet. I clinked my glass with his and said, "Are you about to congratulate me?"

He paused. He looked confused. I forged ahead, taking advantage of his surprise.

"Sophie told you, didn't she?" I asked.

"Sophie?" He shook his head. "Told me what?"

"She offered me a job as creative director for her company, and I accepted," I said. "Isn't it amazing? I'm moving to Phoenix. Promise you'll come and visit."

His mouth hung open for a moment, then he cleared his throat and said, "Actually, I didn't know. This was—"

"So incredibly thoughtful of you," I said. My voice was high pitched, a little manic, and my smile brittle. I felt as if I were throwing a drowning man a life preserver and he was refusing to take it. "Here's to new beginnings!" I cried, hoping he'd get with the program and let go of his misguided plan to propose. "Bottoms up."

His eyes went wide as I put my glass to my lips and upended the champagne into my mouth. The stress of the moment had me chugging the fizzy beverage, hoping to ease the tension. Instead something hard hit the back of my throat and got lodged in my windpipe. Just like that, I couldn't breathe. I dropped my glass and clutched the front of my neck, trying to get some air. I made horrible gasping noises and staggered. Everything went gray and I started to see spots.

"Annabelle!" Jeremy cried. "Oh my god, you're choking on the ring!"

Ring? I would have asked for more details but instead, I blacked out.

2

"This, too, as they say, shall pass," Dr. Curtis said. He glanced from the clipboard in his hands to me.

I was lying in a bed in the emergency ward of Boston Medical Center. My hospital johnnie was bunched up beneath my back and my throat was raw. This is what happens when you choke on a one-carat cushion cut solitaire in a platinum setting and then instead of spitting it up, you swallow it.

"What does that mean?" Jeremy asked. "Is she going to be all right? No permanent harm?"

To his credit, he seemed more concerned about me than he was the engagement ring.

Dr. Curtis was a tall man, very thin, with a shiny dome for a head and glasses that perpetually slipped down his nose. He pushed them back up and smiled at me. He had a gentle smile that made me feel cared for, which helped exponentially, given the current ambiance of the woman in the bed on the other side of the curtain who kept moaning and the random profane shouts of some guy down the hall who sounded like he was being waterboarded.

"I suggest a high-fiber diet, some prune juice, and patience," he said. He unclipped a picture from the front of his board and handed it to me. It was a print copy of the X-ray. I glanced at it. Sure enough, there was a diamond ring in my belly.

"If I make myself throw up, will that dislodge it?" I asked.

"No, don't do that," Dr. Curtis said. "It could damage your esophagus on the way back up, and trust me, you don't want that."

"So she'll have to—" Jeremy began but stopped as if he couldn't finish the sentence.

"Poop it out," I said. I figured I'd best be blunt so we were all on the same page. "Once it has, um, reappeared, I'll get it cleaned and get it back to you."

I glanced away from Jeremy. While a part of me felt that I had every right to be annoyed that he'd put the ring in my drink—*who does that?!*—another part of me was well aware that I was rejecting his proposal in front of an emergency room doctor, as if I needed a witness, and his feelings were likely going to smart a bit. Okay, more than a bit.

"Yes, well." Dr. Curtis started edging away from the bed as if he didn't want to be present when I crushed Jeremy's plans under my bootheel once and for all. "If you have any questions or complications, be sure to follow up with your personal doctor."

"I will," I said. "Thank you."

He shook Jeremy's hand and then patted my

arm in a gesture of sympathy. I wasn't sure if it was for what was to come with Jeremy or my upcoming colon cleanse, but I appreciated the kindness either way.

Dr. Curtis drew the curtain shut as he left. Suddenly the circle of cloth that separated us from everyone else in the emergency room seemed thick enough to suffocate. I smoothed the thin sheet that covered my legs.

I could feel Jeremy staring at the side of my face. I knew I was being a coward by not looking at him, but the truth is I hate conflict, I despise making people feel bad, accidentally or on purpose, and he was my best friend. But there was no way to avoid hurting him because I was absolutely not going to agree to marry him again no matter how bad I felt.

We both knew he'd been about to propose marriage when I'd tried to slap it down by announcing a move to Phoenix. I supposed the mature thing would be to tell him that I wasn't going to take the job Sophie offered, that I had caught on to his proposal and had cowardly tried to avoid hurting him instead of being honest. Fortunately, I am not known for my maturity, and weirdly, once the words *I'm moving to Phoenix* had flown out of my mouth, the idea had taken root in my winter-bundled soul, and now the thought of being in a swimming pool, sucking down a margarita in February, was blooming inside me with all the fervor of an early spring.

Did they make prune juice margaritas? Sign me up! But first, I had to hash this thing out with Jeremy and try not to lose our friendship in the process.

"So Phoenix, huh?" he asked.

I glanced up and my heart squeezed tight. Jeremy, with his precision-cut blond hair, bearded jaw, and kind eyes would always be my first love. Of that there was no doubt, but I imagined that would be cold comfort to him now.

"Yeah," I said. I slid my hand across the bed and put it over his. He didn't pull away. I took that as promising. "A ring, huh?"

He shrugged. "It was just an idea, unless . . ."

I shook my head. He looked crushed and it took everything I had not to take it back and swivel my head into a nod. It was killing me to see his look of deep disappointment, but marriage between us hadn't worked the last time and I sincerely doubted we'd changed enough for it to work now.

I was an artist and he was an engineer. To him, on time was late, while I aimed for *ish,* as in if my appointment was at seven, I aimed for seven*ish,* which was a built-in buffer of fifteen minutes on either side of the appointed arrival time, and hoped for the best. He had a place for everything and everything in its place, and I had already lost years of my life looking for my house keys. We simply didn't suit beyond friendship, and Sophie was right, I hadn't been doing us any favors by pretending we could sleep together and just be friends.

"What am I going to do without you?" he asked. He sounded plaintive, like a lost kitten, and my resolve started to wobble like a table with one short leg, but then his tone changed and became accusatory. "I came to Boston for you."

The wobbling stopped. I had never asked him to come to Boston. In fact, I had been shocked when he left Georgia, and his mama, behind. Suddenly, Sophie's words rang true. I was a lawnmower! I had been making his life easier, going to functions with him, charming his superiors to compensate for his social awkwardness, clearing my calendar for him when he needed someone to talk him through his moods and his mother wasn't available. Enough.

"I have to go, Jeremy," I said. I put every bit of resolve I had into my voice. Mercifully, it worked. He met my gaze for a moment and then glanced away.

"I'll leave you to get dressed," he said. He slipped his hand out from under mine and walked to the curtain. "I'll take you home when you're ready."

It took three days for the blasted ring to pass. I won't go into the details because . . . ew.

Suffice to say, upon its reentry, I had the ring professionally cleaned and delivered to Jeremy. I simply couldn't face him.

During the three days I spent afraid to leave the close proximity of my bathroom, I noshed on more prunes than was healthy, sublet my apartment to an eager grad student and his Labradoodle, packed and repacked my bags five times, and arranged for my other things to be stored in my dad's basement.

When I called Soph to accept the job and explained about the proposal giving me a change of heart, she told me I'd made the right choice, after she laughed herself stupid at the ring debacle, of course.

My family was amazingly supportive, mostly. My dad was thrilled to have me in Arizona; I suspect it was because the golfing is exceptional there, and who doesn't want to get away from winter in Boston? Sheri, my stepmother, was more in tune with my abrupt need to flee the city—and more accurately, Jeremy—and she came over to help me pack, along with my older sister, Chelsea, who, having just had her own life-changing adventure, was full of words of encouragement and support.

Here's the thing: Nothing makes me doubt my own decisions more than other people telling me that I'm doing the right thing. It's as if their approval is a red flag warning me away from logic and reason. I think it's my freewheeling impulsive nature that rejects positive reinforcement, as if because people approve of what I'm doing, then surely I must be making a mistake. My plane ticket had been bought, however. I was paddling in the rapids now.

Sophie and her husband, Miguel, met me at Sky Harbor International Airport. I'd left Boston before the sun was up and it chased us all the way across the country, catching up and passing us before we landed. It was midday when I stepped off the plane, wearing my thick knee-length wool coat and stylish black leather boots. Within minutes, I was sweating. It was glorious.

When I passed the security checkpoint, I spotted Sophie immediately. She is blond and blue-eyed, petite but muscled in the way only a former cheerleader who was always on the top of the human pyramid could be. She bounced on her toes, scanning the crowd, and I thought she'd leap into an air split when she saw me. I was not completely wrong. She began to jump and clap and then she ran at me. I had only a second to brace myself for impact.

"You're here, you're really here," she cried as she locked me in a hug that strangled.

I laughed and hugged her back, feeling the rightness of my decision to come here sweep through me. It had been years since Sophie and

I had lived in the same city. No matter how this turned out, it was going to be great to spend time with my best friend again.

"Babe, you're going to choke her out." Miguel chuckled from behind us.

Sophie let me go and stepped back to study my face, making sure I was still breathing.

"Hi, Annabelle," Miguel said. He reached over his diminutive wife and hugged me.

Miguel was the poster boy for tall, dark, and handsome. He was Phoenix born and bred with a large family who had embraced Sophie as one of their own. The two of them had met during a post-college internship at a graphic design firm in Los Angeles. He'd asked Sophie to marry him within three months of their first date, and she'd said yes and moved to Phoenix to be with him. They'd been together ever since, building their business and their life together. They were relationship goals for me.

"Hi, Miguel," I said. He was a few inches taller than me and a good hugger. Strong and solid, with an affectionate pat on the back that let you know he really liked you.

He took my carry-on and led the way down to baggage claim. Sophie looped her arm through mine and pulled me close as if she was afraid I'd get away.

"So how was the flight?" she asked.

I laughed. "That's not what you want to know."

She blinked at me. "I'm trying to be mature and ease into the good stuff."

"Please, this is me," I said. "No easing required. You want to know if I've talked to Jeremy since having his ring returned via a messenger."

"Don't *ass*ume I only want the gossip," she said. She emphasized the first syllable of the word.

"I see what you did there," I said. I sent her a mock scowl.

"Cheeky, isn't she?" Miguel asked. There was a wicked twinkle in his eye.

"Okay, get all your butt jokes out now," I said.

"I think the moment has passed," Sophie retorted.

"Much like the ring," Miguel quipped.

They exchanged a super-annoying high five.

"Remind me again why I agreed to come work for you two nerds," I said.

"Because you're fleeing the shitstorm you made out of your life," Sophie said. She blinked at me. "Oops, I did it again."

I sighed. "I'm never going to hear the end of this, am I?"

"Oh, I'm sure we'll stop making cracks about it." Sophie paused to snort. "In a year or two."

"Why, oh why, did I buy a one-way ticket?" I asked no one in particular.

"Come on, now," Sophie said. "Look on the bright side, you don't have any exes here."

"Your past has been wiped clean," Miguel chimed in. They both cracked up.

I rolled my eyes. This was the problem with good friends—they knew all of your damage and were not afraid to abuse you with it. Repeatedly.

I followed the laughing idiots down the escalator to baggage. While we stood by the carousel, waiting with the other passengers from my flight, Sophie described the place they'd found for me to live. We'd arranged it while I was still in Boston, and I'd signed the rental agreement and paid first and last months' rent and a security deposit.

"Nick Daire, your new landlord, was a member of Miguel's entrepreneur group before he, well, retired. Your place is a sweet little guest house on his property that he is happy to rent out to you for six months while you decide if Phoenix is the perfect fit for you—which it is," Sophie said.

Miguel made a pained face and I studied him, trying to figure out what that meant. Was his look of doubt about Mr. Daire or me?

"I take it 'happy' isn't exactly the word to describe how he feels about leasing his guest house?" I asked, trying to gauge what he was thinking.

Miguel shrugged. "He offered so we accepted."

I got the distinct impression there was much more to this than he was telling me, but I decided to see the place before I panicked.

"Rents in Phoenix, while not as bad as Boston, are insane," Sophie said. "This place is perfect because it's right down the street from the office. You won't even need a car."

That seemed promising. My bags appeared, and Miguel hauled them off the carousel. I had three big rollers so we each took one and headed for the parking garage. As soon as we stepped outside, I felt the desert warmth engulf me. I had a feeling I'd be packing my winter coat away for the duration of my stay. Not a hardship.

As we drove out of the garage, the midday sun—bright beautiful sun!—was blinding, and I dove into my handbag for my sunglasses. We were in their SUV, and I had taken the back seat. Sophie turned around to face me, pointing out the features of the area—Camelback Mountain, which really did look like a camel lying down; Tovrea Castle, a crazy wedding cake–looking building that some guy had built for his wife; and Tempe Town Lake, yes, an actual man-made lake in the middle of the city—as we cruised toward our destination.

I'd been to the desert only once before, for their wedding, and while I remembered being awed by the red mountain vistas and humungous saguaro cacti, I'd mostly been in a frenzy of wedding prep, which meant a lot of spa time and poolside margaritas, so my memories were shrouded in a lime-infused tequila haze.

We drove through the sprawling city, passed tall apartment buildings, offices, and restaurants. I gawked at the bushes and trees and planters overflowing with blossoms, some of which I recognized, such as petunias and pansies, and others I did not. How long had it been since I'd seen a flower blooming? Months. It made my heart sing.

"How about some dinner before we get you settled into your new place?" Soph asked. "There's a great Mexican food joint in the neighborhood, unless you'd rather I make you a home-cooked meal—"

"No!" Miguel and I said together with matching tones of horror.

Sophie frowned. "What? I can cook."

"Of course you can," Miguel said. "But we'd miss you too much if you spent your evening in the kitchen."

"Exactly," I jumped in. "I mean I just got here."

"All right then, Blanco Tacos and Tequila it is," she announced.

I don't think I was imagining the look of relief on her face. The truth is that Soph is not at one with the culinary arts even though she would like to be, and I imagined she wanted my first meal to be one that was actually edible.

Dinner was amazing. Shrimp fajitas to die for chased down by a margarita on the rocks with the salt on the rim just as the good lord intended. We reminisced a little, talked about their business, and autopsied the sad remains of my personal life. The consensus was that I needed to get back out there, but I was unconvinced.

It was early evening when we arrived at my new home. Judging by the size of the houses, we were in an exclusive neighborhood in the Biltmore area. This particular road was small and tucked away, camouflaged by enormous olive trees, which lined the quiet street. Miguel punched a code into the keypad in front of the massive wrought-iron gate, and with a lurch it slid open.

Instead of driving up the main driveway to the massive modern structure ahead of us, he took a narrow road that ran parallel to the main drive before veering off to the right. Tucked under a line of olive trees was a petite version of the big house. Small and square, it was a block of modern glass, steel, and concrete with wooden accents. I liked its austerity and the way the gray of the concrete blended with the silvery leaves of the olive trees that surrounded it.

When we climbed out of the car, there was a scuffle in the neatly trimmed oleanders beside us, and a pair of Gambel's quail squawked and scurried deeper into the bushes as if fleeing certain death. They seemed comically overwrought, which made me laugh. I didn't get this sort of wildlife in the center of Boston, so this was definitely a check in the plus column for Phoenix.

I glanced up at the trees, wondering what else was waiting to be discovered, but my attention was diverted by the sky. I moved away from the overhanging branches to see it better. The sunset over the city was a spectacular swath of deep burnt orange streaks and dusty splashes of purple. I stopped to stare at it, and Sophie noticed my rapt expression.

"Arizona has the best sunsets in the world," she said.

"It makes me want to paint again." I wasn't sure if I was talking to her or myself because I was preoccupied with the itch in my fingers, a feeling I hadn't had in years, that used to mean I was eager to get to a canvas and play with colors.

"Excellent," Sophie said. "You're a brilliant artist. It's past time for you to get back in the game."

I turned my head and grinned at her. I felt lighter, as if by coming here and starting over, I'd buried my troubles in a snowbank in Boston and left them there.

Miguel unloaded my bags out of the back of the SUV and hauled them up the wide concrete steps to the front entrance of my house. It had thick glass double doors done in a swirled pattern that made them opaque. Gorgeous. They were bookended by two square bronze metal planters that were overflowing with trailing asparagus ferns and spiky lavender stalks. Miguel turned and handed me the keys to the house.

"I'm going up to the main house to let Daire know you've arrived," he said.

"Shouldn't I come with you?" I asked.

He and Sophie exchanged a look. Then he shook his head. "Nick Daire is a bit reclusive. I'm sure you'll meet him eventually, but I'd wait for him to take the lead on that."

He walked down the steps and took a side path that cut through the olive trees and led to the front of the main house. I watched, taking in the very large house that perched behind my baby house like a mama hen hovering over its chick.

I turned to Sophie. "So what's wrong with him?"

"Miguel? Nothing!"

I frowned. Why would she think I was asking about Miguel?

"No, Mr. Daire," I said. "What's wrong with him? Because *reclusive* seems like code for weird, odd, or possibly pervy."

She took the keys from my hand and unlocked the glass doors.

"Belly, I am shocked. *Shocked* that you think I would put you up with a pervert," she said.

"Just sayin'," I said. "Spill it. What's his damage?"

Sophie opened her mouth and then closed it.

She looked me right in the eye and said, "Listen, I think it's best if you just steer clear of the main house. Nick Daire is fine, seriously, but you don't need to meet him, befriend him, or know him in any way other than to send him your rent check on the first of every month, okay?"

"Do you even know me?" I asked. I pointed to myself. "Extrovert. I like people. I like to be friendly."

"Yes, I know," she said. "And since I do know you better than most people do, for once, listen to me. Steer clear of your landlord and all will be well."

Clearly, she did not know me as well as she thought she did if that was her idea of keeping me away from my mysterious landlord. Now I was irrationally curious to meet him.

She turned on her heel and led the way into the small house. I was about to continue my interrogation, but I caught sight of the interior and completely forgot about my new landlord, the fact that I was exhausted, or that I needed to call home and check in.

The place was perfection. The glass front doors opened up into a large living room that had two squared-off couches in a pale blue-gray with black and white accent pillows, and a large-screen television was over the glass-enclosed gas fireplace. I could absolutely picture myself under a chenille throw with the fire blazing, a glass of wine in one hand, and a book in the other.

A door on the right led to a compact kitchen with granite counters, stainless steel appliances, and a matching sink deep enough to bathe a golden retriever. I wasn't much of a cook, but this setup would certainly do.

The far wall was made up of floor-to-ceiling windows, which bracketed a set of French doors that led out to a divine patio. The wall of windows let in the natural light, which came from the north, making it perfect for painting. I took it as another sign that it might be time to revisit the fine arts. I crossed the room and gasped as I took in the stunning backyard full of lemon and lime trees, which circled an in-ground azure pool and hot tub. Both of which looked so inviting, I almost grabbed my swimsuit and forgot all about unpacking.

Beyond the pool was the backside of the mansion I had glimpsed. Like my little house, it was very modern with loads of glass and squared edges framed in steel and concrete. I wondered if the interior was decorated the same, because the one thing I noticed about my little house was the lack of art or color of any kind. The walls were painted a soft creamy white but were completely devoid of any pictures. At all. There wasn't even any cheap motel art on the walls. It felt barren and bereft. Where was the art?

A door to the left led to a large bedroom

and bathroom. Like the kitchen, they were immaculate. A king-size bed with a black frame, more blue-gray for the bedding, and a matching black dresser took up half the room. A small writing desk with a black leather office chair had been placed in front of the window. It was cozy and perfect, and I knew I could work quite happily here as soon as I hung up some pictures or bought some colorful pillows or possibly a throw.

Soph and I wheeled my bags into the bedroom and then headed back to the kitchen to take stock of what I would need to survive.

"The place comes with dishes and cookware, and I put some supplies for you in the cupboard this morning," she said. I opened the surprisingly deep pantry and noted there was stuff in there.

"Oh, you didn't have to—" I began but she interrupted.

"Please." She held up her hand in a stop gesture. "I've lived with you. I know your essentials. Coffee, sugar, and your breakfast granola are in the pantry; milk, yogurt, and wine are in the refrigerator; and a couple of frozen pizzas are in the freezer just to get you started. We can hit the grocery store this weekend for a bigger supply run."

I tipped my head as I gazed at my sister from another mister in surprise. "Look at you, momming me."

"No. Nope. Nuh-uh," she said. "I am not mom material. Not yet at any rate. I am merely being a fabulous boss because I don't want you to regret coming here, and I know if you wake up without coffee first thing tomorrow, you will examine your life choices in a fit of insufficient caffeine and regret everything."

She knew me so well. I supposed it came from years of drowning our sorrows in cheap booze and pints of ice cream after bad breakups, followed by holding each other's hair out of the toilet while we threw up, which we then topped off by sharing the greasiest breakfasts we could find in the wee hours of the morning at some fairly sketchy city diners.

Ours was a once-in-a-lifetime sort of friendship, forged in dubious choices, heartache, drunken texting, and the complete acceptance and understanding of our individual gifts as well as our flaws. I'd take a bullet for Soph without question, and I knew she'd do the same for me.

"So work tomorrow, huh?" I asked.

She met my gaze. "Yes. You don't have to work the whole day, but I am just so excited for you to see the office and meet everyone."

She was dancing on her tiptoes again, and I was afraid a high kick of excitement was headed my way.

"I was just confirming," I said. "Of course I'll be there bright and early."

She hugged me tight, pulling me down to her level while she hopped up and down.

"Is she trying to choke you out again?" Miguel asked as he strode through the kitchen door.

Sophie released me and turned to him. "I think I have been remarkably self-contained, given that having Annabelle here is a dream come true for me."

"Yes, I know." His smile was tight as he slid his arm around her back and gave her a half hug. When he looked down, I noticed his smile was not reflected in his eyes when he asked, "And you always get your way, don't you?"

Sophie blinked at him. A look of hurt flashed across her face, but she visibly shook it off. I didn't know if I was just overtired from the long day I'd already put in, topped by margaritas, and was being oversensitive, or if my feeling that there was something wrong between them, and that something appeared to be me, was accurate or not.

I forced a laugh, because, as I've mentioned, I hate conflict and will always try to laugh it off, but then Miguel held out an envelope to me, stifling my awkward attempt to keep things light. The letter-size envelope looked thick, like something the IRS hand-delivers to your house if you forget to pay your taxes.

"What's this?" I asked.

He blew out a breath. "Daire's rules for the renter."

I looked at him and then at the envelope. I weighed it in my palm. It had some heft. I glanced back at Miguel. "How many pages is it?"

He shrugged and said, "I don't know. Feels like fifty-eleven."

Soph frowned at the envelope. "I thought we hashed all that out when she signed the rental agreement."

"Apparently, Daire got to thinking about it, and he has some additional house rules that he'd like Annabelle to follow," Miguel said.

"Like what?" Soph asked. She sounded annoyed on my behalf. "She paid her first and last, put down a security deposit, and signed the lease. What more could he want from her?"

Miguel sighed. "It's details. He has too much time on his hands. It makes him overthink things. I don't think these are hard-and-fast rules but more like suggestions for peaceful neighbor cohabitation."

"Oh, in that case," I said. I tossed the envelope onto the counter to be ignored with all the other junk mail that was sure to find me within the week.

"Don't you want to look at it?" he asked.

A big jaw-cracking yawn slid out of me. "Not tonight. I'm going to shower, put on my jams, and pass out. The 'rules' can wait until tomorrow."

"Fair enough," he said. "But you will look at

them just so that there's no misunderstandings, right?"

"Sure." I squinted at him, suddenly suspicious. "Question."

"Shoot," he said.

"Why is some old retired guy, who lives in a huge house and is clearly not hurting for money, willing to rent his guest house to a complete stranger?"

"Uh," Miguel stalled. I'd obviously caught him off guard.

"Because Miguel saved his life," Soph said. "He collapsed and Miguel happened to be the one who found him and called an ambulance. Daire doesn't like to be indebted to anyone, and he's been badgering Miguel for a way to make things square. When we couldn't find a reasonably priced apartment for you nearby, we suggested the use of his guest house for six months as his payback. Daire jumped on it."

I jerked my thumb at the envelope. "Do you think he's reconsidering?"

"No," Miguel said. "He's just a pain in the ass."

"Ah," I said. "Well, I'll do my best to abide by his rules."

"Perfect," Soph said. She grabbed me in another hug. I yawned. Miguel hugged me, too. I yawned again. They shared an amused look and left me to my new home, promising to pick me up on their way to the office in the morning. My eyes were slamming shut as I locked the door after them.

In the quiet after their departure, I took another look at my sparsely furnished abode. Whoever had put it together had minimalist taste, which was perfect because it gave me enough room to make the place my own.

I picked up my phone and texted my family that I had arrived and all was well. I glanced at the envelope on the counter, thinking maybe I should read the letter now. The neat script on the front read *Tenant*. As a graphic designer who had a special place in my heart for fonts and the feelings they could evoke, like the global loathing for Comic Sans, I tended to look at people's handwriting with the same critical eye. Mr. Daire's handwriting was very square, very neat, and almost painfully precise. It's not that it spooked me exactly, but it certainly didn't give off a happy, carefree vibe. No, it was more like a "drop and give me twenty" feeling of military precision.

I decided to ignore it just like I would a spider in the pantry, because maybe it was a good little bug eater or maybe it would bite me. Yeah, I could absolutely wait until tomorrow to open that letter and find out what I was dealing with because, judging by the handwriting, I was guessing my landlord was the bitey sort.

Nick

3

"You know what you should do, Nick?" Jackson Popov asked.

"Nothing good has ever been said after that opening question," I replied, taking a quick inhale as I lowered the 275-pound barbell to my chest. I could feel the bunch and clench of my pecs and biceps, and it grounded me. With a soft grunt, I dug deep into my core and lifted the weight to a full extension while exhaling.

"I'm going to tell you anyway, you ingrate," Jackson said. He held his hands wide as he stood at my head, getting ready to grab the bar if I maxed out.

Jackson was a big burly man, a walking wall of muscle mass, with a shaved head, pale gray eyes, and an improbable goatee that came to a wicked point, like he was the villain in a silent film.

He was the youngest of many siblings—I could never keep track of them all—which had crafted him into a person who talked too much, laughed too loud, and was stubborn as fuck. I supposed he had to be all those things to get any attention being raised in such a crowd. I didn't particularly like him, but he'd come into my life after my world imploded, and I hadn't had the wherewithal to get rid of him, especially since I'd gone through four physical therapists before he showed up. It seemed some of them found me difficult to work with while I found them to be incompetent. Whatever.

I racked the weights on their holder and used the barbell to pull myself up to a seated position. Jackson tossed me a towel, and I wiped off the sweat that was pouring down my face and neck.

"By all means, tell me what you think I should do," I said. "I'm as giddy as a schoolgirl to hear your thoughts."

Jackson shook his head and pointed one beefy finger at me. "That attitude right there. You need to lose that shield of sarcasm."

"It's not a shield," I said. "It's who I am. It's who I've always been. You just don't appreciate my cutting wit."

"Cutting?" he scoffed. "Cutting what exactly? Farts?" He smelled the air as if checking for a rogue funk.

I pressed my lips together, refusing to laugh. "I'm sorry, whose name is on your paycheck?" I asked. I didn't care if I sounded like an asshole.

He should have been duly chastened; instead he laughed. It boomed against the walls of my home gym. I glowered. Why had I fired all of my previous trainers? Even Dougie, the wake-and-bake potato head with the weed problem, seemed preferable to Jackson right now. Maybe I should fire him.

Oblivious to my dark thoughts, Jackson tossed me a bottle of water just far enough out of reach that I had to lunge for it. Prick.

"Get up, Daire," he barked. He always used my last name when he was about to torture me.

"No," I said. "I don't feel like it."

"I'm sorry, who is the physical therapist in this room?" he asked.

I ignored him. His eyebrows went up and he crossed his arms over his chest while he waited. I stalled, taking a long drink of water.

"If you're going to reach your goals, you have to stick to the workout, brother." His gaze was steady on mine. I knew he wasn't going to stop badgering me until I did as he asked.

"Don't call me that," I said, for the millionth time. "We're not related."

I put down the water and rose from the bench. I stood for a moment, checking my balance and getting a feel for the floor beneath my feet. I hated this. I'd never felt weak a day in my life until it all came crashing down nine months ago. I moved my weight from side to side. I felt off, which gave me a burst of panic, but I forcibly shook it off and decided to power through it.

"Let's do some balance exercises," Jackson ordered. We'd been doing these for a few months. I hadn't seen that they'd made any difference, but I dutifully began to work through the yoga positions he'd taught me.

When I was warmed up, he gestured to the treadmill. I wanted to balk. I hated getting on that thing. It made me feel vulnerable, but since the docs hadn't been able to pinpoint what precisely was wrong with me, there was really no reason not to give it a go.

We started slow with Jackson hovering. I walked. He upped the incline. I could feel my anxiety rising, but I pressed on. One foot in front of the other until I had a rhythm going. I was feeling pretty good about it. I upped the speed, and Jackson sent me a considering look. I pushed on, keeping my hands suspended over the rails in case I needed to catch myself.

I increased the incline again and upped the speed some more. Now I was breathing heavily but it felt good. I felt whole and strong. I broke into a light jog. Jackson moved in closer. I thought I might be making him nervous. I wanted to laugh but I was too winded and it was taking all of my concentration to keep the pace. This was the best I'd felt in months.

A memory of that horrible day flashed through my mind. The feeling of complete helplessness, being unable to speak or think clearly while they'd slid me into the MRI machine. I could feel my heart rate picking up, and I was sweating harder than I should have been from just jogging on a treadmill. Suddenly, I couldn't get enough air and I thought I might throw up.

Bam! Just like that, I was falling, crashing into the handrail before I could grab it, my muscles limp and unresponsive no matter how hard I tried to control them.

Two big burly arms grabbed me around the middle and Jackson hauled me off the treadmill as if I were no bigger than a child. And wasn't that just the humiliation cherry on top of the shit sundae?

I wanted to push him off but that was stupid as I'd only succeed in falling on my face. Jackson pulled my left arm over his behemoth shoulders and dragged me back to the bench. He turned so I could sit and then he went back to the machine to shut it off.

I sat there, feeling a level of anger and frustration that I had never felt before, not even during my most desperate days as a kid, and believe me, I'd had more than my share of those.

"I told you I didn't feel like it," I snapped.

"You did," he agreed. He handed me my water bottle. "You also managed to go longer and harder on the treadmill than you ever have before. I call that progress."

"Progress?" I scoffed. I gestured to my body. "I collapsed—again. How is my life ever supposed to be normal if I keep collapsing?"

Jackson raised his hands. "You have to talk to

your doctors about that. I am a trainer. I know how to make you strong. I don't know how to fix what's broken on the inside."

"It's not broken *on the inside,*" I insisted. I knew what he wasn't saying—that he thought the issue wasn't with my body but rather my mind. We'd had this argument before. But as I'd told him, repeatedly, that was a load of horseshit. I was in here, wasn't I? Wouldn't I know if I was mental? "How am I supposed to live like this?"

"I don't know," he said. His gaze was full of sympathy, which made my stomach turn. I glanced away. Shame at my own weakness bubbled up in the back of my throat like bile, and I desperately wanted to punch something until my knuckles bled.

As if he knew I needed a minute, Jackson strode over to the windows that overlooked my backyard. He stood there, looking out over the lawn and the pool, while I collected my shattered sense of self and reined in my temper. It took a minute or ten.

These episodes didn't usually last very long, five to ten minutes but sometimes more; still they freaked me out all the same, because I never knew when or where they were going to happen or if they would be a precursor to something worse. The anxiety I felt anticipating these episodes ate at me day in and day out and was almost worse than my body betraying me. Almost.

When I felt my strength return, for the most part, I glanced at Jackson, preparing to call him back. Even though I'd had an episode, I knew he wouldn't let me shirk the rest of my workout. Which was fine. I wasn't a quitter, and I wasn't giving up on myself. Not today.

As he gazed out the window, a small smile turned up the corners of his mouth. He must have felt my stare, because he turned to me and said, "She's out there."

He didn't need to tell me who *she* was. I lifted the water bottle to my lips and drained half of it. "So what?"

He turned back to the view and let out a low whistle.

"She's a looker." He glanced over his shoulder at me, and one of his eyebrows quirked up in challenge before he returned to the window.

"Right, your idea of a good-looking woman is whether or not she can bench-press a car," I said. "If you think she's good-looking, then she's definitely not my type. I don't go for women who wrestle hogs for fun."

"If you say so," he said. He didn't turn away from the window but kept staring, clearly enjoying the view.

I sat impotently—which, for the record, is not a word I liked to use in reference to myself in any way, shape, or form—on the bench. Oh, sure, I could try to get up and walk to the window. In fact, I suspect that's exactly what Jackson was trying to goad me into doing. Jerk.

It would take a lot more than the promise of a good-looking woman for me to give up the security of my safe seat, especially after an episode. Still my curiosity was yammering at me to get a look at the woman Miguel Vasquez had foisted upon me.

"All right, all right, I'll take a look," I said. I waved my hand at Jackson. He understood the unspoken command and yet chose to ignore it.

"Walk," he said, and turned back to the window.

"No," I said. It was the voice I'd used on construction guys who were slacking and bank loan officers who were weasels. It was supposed to make the person I was speaking to fall in line. Jackson was impervious.

"You need to—" he began.

"Dut dut dut," I interrupted him. "I didn't hire you to tell me what *I* need. I hired you to train me and to be around as *needed*."

"You don't need me right now," he said.

He didn't even bother turning around to speak to me, so riveted was he on the woman he could see from the window. My new tenant. What was her name? I couldn't remember. Fuzzy brain, damn it, another gift from that horrible day. No wonder I never left my house.

I gauged the distance from where I was sitting to my wheelchair parked beside Jackson at the window. I could get there, spotting myself on the line of equipment in my personal gym if I was so motivated. Jackson was still staring outside, ignoring me. All right, my curiosity was most definitely getting the better of me.

I pulled myself to my feet. The fatigue that occasionally clobbered me, also without warning, made me inch my way to my wheelchair beside the window. I absolutely did not want to slide to the floor in a hcap. I'd had enough humiliation for one morning. I felt my heart rate accelerate as I got closer. My nerves werc snapping just beneath the surface. Being picked up by Jackson twice in one day was more than my ego could bear. I tried to distract myself.

As I got closer, I asked, "Scale of one to ten, with one being my great-aunt Madge with the long chin whisker and the faint odor of mothballs about her, and ten being Scarlett Johansson, where does she rank?"

Jackson glanced over his shoulder at me with an assessing stare then he shook his head. "I don't rate women."

"What?" I cried. "You're the one who just called her a 'looker.' "

"Just an observation, not a rating. I can objectively notice that a woman is very attractive without diminishing her as a person by assigning her a number based on society's arbitrary standards of beauty."

"Dude, you need to give me your man card," I said. "You're one of those 'woke' males, aren't you?" Truthfully, I respected that Jackson wasn't a dick about women, bucking the misogynistic stereotype of most muscle heads, but I would rather swallow my tongue before I'd admit it.

He stared at me with his unnerving gray gaze, and I got the distinct feeling I didn't fool him one little bit. I definitely needed to fire him.

"An eight-point-five," he said. "She's a little scrawny for me."

In spite of myself, I laughed. Then I choked on it, realizing that having a hot tenant was not good. In fact, it was bad, very bad. I did not want any distractions during my recovery, and Annabelle Martin—*that was her name!*—my unwanted renter, was an eight-point-five. Shit! Then again, maybe Jackson graded on a curve. Maybe his hotness meter would register as a five for me.

I took four steps, keeping my hand out to grab the rack of barbells I passed if I started to crumble again. It wasn't necessary. I reached the wheelchair, turned, and lowered myself onto the seat with the familiarity that had come from the past nine months of hauling myself around in the stupid thing. I hated it. I hated that I needed it. I hated what it represented. But mostly, I hated that I was afraid to be without it.

I put my feet on the footrests and spun the chair so that I faced the floor-to-ceiling windows, which were curtained by heavy drapes. I cast Jackson a dark look, at which he wagged his eyebrows. He moved the curtain aside just enough to let me see out, too.

My tenant was seated on her patio in one of the two cushioned chairs that faced the pool. She was wearing a long-sleeved black shirt over a pair of black-and-white-plaid pajama bottoms. There was nothing sexy about the outfit and yet the sight of her in her sleepwear, with her painted pink toes peeking out beneath the hem of her pants, felt oddly intimate.

I watched as she lifted her coffee mug to her lips. She was pale, as if she hadn't seen the sun in months, with long dark hair, and average features that were neither stunningly beautiful nor hideous. Compared to the women I'd dated back in the day, she was plain with a side of pretty, but nothing I would have looked at twice.

"Meh," I said. "I've seen better."

I felt Jackson's gaze on the side of my face, but I ignored him, not wanting to get a lecture about my Neanderthal tendencies toward the female gender. As I watched my tenant, her sleeve rolled back and I could see a tattoo on the inside of her wrist. I squinted. Was she one of those girls who got the ubiquitous butterfly tattoo on her arm? Probably.

There was an effortless grace to her movements, and when she puckered her lips to blow the steam away before she sipped, I found myself watching her mouth a little too closely. I glanced away. My first assessment about her had been correct, and I wasn't going to change it.

"She's just average," I said. I tried to sound dismissive, but my voice dipped a bit lower than normal and Jackson didn't look like he believed me.

"Average for what?" he asked. "A goddess?"

"Goddess?" I choked. "Sure, if you're sight impaired."

Jackson laughed, that annoying booming laugh that came up from his belly and encompassed anyone in a hundred-yard radius. "If you say so," he said.

He turned away to go grab more of his gear. He was whistling as he gathered several resistance bands, or as I thought of them—implements of torture. I turned back to the window and took just another quick peek at the woman who was going to be living in the little guest house on my property for the next six months.

All right, so with that long mane of curly dark hair and heart-shaped face, she was actually quite pretty. Since I had no intention of ever interacting with her during her time here, it wasn't relevant to me in the least. As I watched, she opened an envelope and a sheaf of papers fell into her lap.

I felt my face grow warm. Those were the additional rules I'd had Miguel deliver to her yesterday. Why I felt a sudden surge of embarrassment, I had no idea. Probably because in my mind I had pictured Annabelle as a nerdy, man-hating graphic designer, with glasses, improbably dyed blue or green hair, who dressed from neck to knee in too big, secondhand store cardigans, ironic T-shirts, and old-school lace-up sneakers.

Instead, I watched this unexpected—What? What was she? A girl? A woman? The words swirled around my head, not quite locking into my fuzzy brain. The only word that clicked was Jackson's. *Goddess*. I watched as this unexpected goddess—I rolled my eyes—read my rules with a smile tucked into the corner of her mouth, as if she thought I was joking. I wasn't. Not even a little.

Annabelle

4

I brewed a pot of coffee in the oh-so-high-tech coffee maker, which had a cool milk frothing doohickey built into the side. I could foam up my morning cup of joe? Fancy. I might never leave.

I took it and the envelope Miguel had given me last night out to the patio. I found a sunny spot in the corner and pulled one of the padded wicker chairs over to it. I sighed, feeling the sun warm the top of my head and shoulders while a cool breeze scented the air with something delicately sweet. After I'd slugged back half of my coffee, I used my thumb to open the envelope. Ten pages fell into my lap. Ten.

I would like to report that it was a friendly, chatty, getting-to-know-you missive. It was not. It had bullet points. Seriously. And suddenly the term *bullet points* seemed very on target, so to speak.

The language was unapologetically terse as if the person issuing the rules felt that this would preemptively halt any argument coming from the recipient of the letter, i.e., me. Hmm.

I scanned the pages, looking for any hint of warmth or apology for not including these rules in the original lease. There was nothing, just rule after rule, belabored to the point of exhaustion. I glanced back at the first page and began to read, while the froth on my coffee deflated much like my spirits.

Tenant *[as if he didn't know my name from all the paperwork I'd submitted]*

Be advised *[I wondered how hard it was for him to use the word* advised *instead of* at my command*] that the following is a list of rules I encourage you to follow *[I suspected there had been a punishment— such as lashings or banishment—that had been listed here but he forced himself to reconsider, given that he'd missed his opportunity to put "the rules" in the legally binding lease]* for the benefit of all residing on these premises.

- The pool is for the exclusive use of the homeowner. *[I noted he did not mention the hot tub.]*
- No noise, such as loud music, is allowed after 9 PM. *[9??? Good grief, he must be old enough to remember life before motor vehicles.]*
- No pets, of any kind, are allowed. *[Did that include dragons? I wondered. I*

suddenly quite desperately wanted a fire-breathing dragon.]

- Trash pickup is Tuesday morning. You are responsible for putting your bins at the curb and must bring them in before nightfall the same day. *[He really did have too much time on his hands.]*

On and on it went. By the end, I was only surprised that he didn't specify which way I put my toilet paper, over or under, on the holder. Honestly, it was clear Mr. Daire needed a hobby. Well, nagging me was not going to be it.

I glanced at the clock and realized that Soph and Miguel would be here to pick me up for my first day of work soon. I carefully folded "the rules" and stuffed them back into the envelope. Mercifully, I wasn't going to be here most of the time so Daire's rules shouldn't impact me overmuch. I had only signed a six-month lease, so if it became unbearable, I could always leave.

I glanced at the big house across the yard. I wondered if Mr. Daire was up and about. It was a beautiful home, and yet it had an air of orneriness about it like a man sticking out his chin and asking for a punch. The windows, like mine, were floor-to-ceiling, but whereas I kept my draperies open, his were drawn, blocking any light that might have gotten inside the big house.

I saw one of the drapes twitch. Was my landlord

looking for a peek at me like I was for him? I glanced down. I was still in my pajamas, which were unassuming to say the least. My long, curly dark hair was an unbrushed straggly mess, and I had no makeup on. I was surprised I didn't hear a shriek of horror from the main house. I sipped my coffee and stared at the curtain. It didn't move again. Huh.

Despite lingering over my coffee, I met Miguel and Soph at the curb at the appointed time. Yes, I was actually on time, surprising everyone, mostly myself.

I climbed into the back seat, and Soph turned around with a big grin.

"Are you ready for your first day?" she asked. I would have answered but she forged on. "How did you sleep? Is the house okay? Is there anything you need? You're not homesick, are you?"

Miguel reached across the console and grabbed her hand in his while he steered the SUV out of the drive and into the traffic. "Breathe, babe."

Soph took a quick breath and then smiled at me. "Sorry."

I laughed. "It's fine. And to answer your questions. Yes, yes, no, and no, at least not yet. And before you ask, let me assure you that I did read the rules from my new landlord."

"And what did you think?" Miguel asked.

His gaze met mine in the rearview mirror, and I smiled at his look of concern.

"You're right," I said. "That guy has entirely too much time on his hands, and while his list was incredibly exacting and detailed, I think it's fine. And if it's not fine, I'll just move out in six months when the lease is up."

"So you think you'll be leaving in six months?" Miguel asked. He sounded almost perky at the prospect. Hmm.

"No, that's not what she said," Soph argued. "She meant she'll find a new place in six months, isn't that right?"

"Yeah, something like that," I said. Again, I felt like there was a weird power play happening between my friends. I decided to change the subject. "Am I supposed to get in touch with him with a confirmation of the rules?" I asked. I was hoping for a yes, because I really wanted to get a look at this guy who could be so highly pedantic about his dos and don'ts.

"No," Miguel said. "I think if you just take the rules to heart and avoid any interactions with him, you'll be much happier."

Drat! My curiosity about Mr. Daire was not to be appeased. When I pictured him in my head, I saw a skinny, slump-shouldered, bald-headed, hook-nosed, steely-eyed eagle of a man à la Mr. Burns from *The Simpsons*. I figured he was the kind of guy who sent his food back to the kitchen just because he could, you know, a real "Get off my lawn!" sort of old man.

I usually had decent success with charming those codgers. Mostly, I'd discovered their anger came out of feeling displaced by a society that was moving on without them, making them feel powerless, obsolete, and left behind. A little attention went a long way toward mitigating the grumpiness.

Despite Miguel's advice to leave Mr. Daire be, I figured if my path ever crossed my landlord's, I'd go out of my way to be positive and bring him some cheer. It's what I do. I'm a people pleaser, which is why I was able to be a freelance designer for so long. I know how to get a person to yes.

Miguel turned into a multistory attached parking garage, and I looked out the rear window. We had driven only half a block from my house to here. Soph had not been kidding when she said I could walk. Sweet!

We wound up the ramp to the second floor, and Miguel parked in a spot by the elevators. I slid the strap of my large bag onto my shoulder as I exited the car.

I'd worn a black flared skirt and green knit top today with a pair of utilitarian black pumps with a heel that was slightly too high. My feet already hated me, and I had no idea how an eight-hour stint in grown-up shoes was going to go. Working at home, it was oversized T-shirts, yoga pants, and socks all the time, which was great because I frequently struck a downward dog or warrior pose when my creativity got stuck, but I figured with it being my first day and all, I should at least try to look professional.

Vasquez Squared was located on the fifth floor of the attached office building. We rode the elevator up, and the closer we got, the more excited Soph became. She started bouncing on her toes, and Miguel smiled down at his petite wife as if he knew she was barely reining herself in and he was charmed in spite of himself. It reassured me that whatever was happening between them wasn't serious.

"What is it?" I asked.

"Can't say," Soph said. "It's a surprise."

I lifted my eyebrows. I love surprises. It's weird, I know. I mean who really wants fifty people to jump out at them and shout "Happy Birthday!"? Me. I do. I can admit it. But given the recent surprise of Jeremy's proposal, which ended with me examining the contents of my toilet bowl closer than anyone should ever have to for a matter of days, yeah, I wasn't feeling the whole gotcha thing at the moment.

Miguel must have been able to read the trepidation on my face, because he said, "It's okay, really."

I followed them off the elevator and into a

very upscale lobby, as in there was a real live receptionist, with leather furniture, a view of the city from the big picture window, and potted plants that didn't look as if they were seeking an escape route. Frankly, capped off by the stylized V^2 logo, representing Vasquez Squared, done in copper and hanging off the pale teal textured wall, the place reeked of success.

I turned to Miguel and Sophie with my mouth slightly agape. "Ah-mazing!"

"Right?" Soph clapped her hands with that girl squad enthusiasm that I loved. She grabbed my hand and dragged me forward. "Annabelle Martin, I'd like you to meet Nyah Vanderberg. She is the cornerstone of this operation."

Nyah rose from her desk. She had dark brown skin, dark eyes that sparkled, and a luxurious cloud of black curls that reached past her shoulders. She was built curvy and walked with a decided flirt in her stride. She put off great energy as her wide smile was bracketed by two deep dimples.

I shook her hand and said, "Nice to meet you."

"You too. Sophie has been so excited for you to arrive," she said. "I'm really looking forward to hearing your side of all the tall tales she's been telling."

I glanced over my shoulder and looked at Soph. "What have you been saying?"

"Nothing but the truth," she said.

"That's what I'm afraid of," I said.

Nyah laughed, which made me like her even more. "If you need anything, come to me. I'm the details gal."

"Thanks," I said. "I will."

"Come on, come on." Soph grabbed my hand and led me through a glass door that opened into a large meeting room. It was empty at the moment, but the wall boasted a huge smart board, and I surmised this was where the big meetings took place. We passed through another glass door on the opposite side, stepping into a large communal work space.

My artist's heart did a pitter-pat as I surveyed what could only be described as graphic designer nirvana. There were drafting tables; workstations with iMacs, Macbook Pros, iPads with Apple Pencils; shelves full of paper and art supplies. On a large table, I saw mood boards with color swatches, sketchbooks, Pantone color books, paper samples, and a fat stack of design annuals.

And, oh, my heart. There was artwork on the walls! Great big pieces of hand lettering, and poster designs from famous designers I recognized—Milton Glaser and Seymour Chwast—as well as some fine art prints from Keith Haring and Andy Warhol.

"It's great, right?" Soph asked.

"So great," I agreed.

No one was using this communal space at the

moment, and we plowed through the room to a row of offices, situated all along the exterior of the floor, giving each one floor-to-ceiling window views. Sophie passed two of them and then paused. She held up her hands like a game show model, and it was then that I realized the frosted glass door had an engraved nameplate. Etched into the brushed copper was *Annabelle Martin, Creative Director*.

"Oh, wow," I said. I ran my fingers over the letters. They'd been done in an original font exclusive to Vasquez Squared. Somehow, seeing my name on the door made my being here seem more real. I wasn't sure how I felt about that, but I knew how Soph wanted me to feel, and I cried, "This is the best!"

"Isn't it?" She did jump, just a little one, this time. She reached past me and opened the door, pushing it wide.

I walked in feeling as if I'd crossed over some mythical threshold into adulthood. This was not a space to be inhabited by a woman who wore yoga pants and T-shirts. I felt an itch in the middle of my back and wondered if I was developing a rash. I'm not allergic to full-time work, I swear. I am a little skittish about working for other people, even best friends, however.

"We'll leave you to get settled," Miguel said. "Staff meeting in the conference room at ten."

"I'll be there," I promised.

Soph hugged me tightly about the neck. "I'm so glad you're here. This is going to be fabulous."

I had no words so I hugged her back and hoped really hard that I did not screw this up. Six months. We'd agreed that I'd try this for six months. Surely I could behave like a proper professional woman for a mere six months.

After pacing the room to get the feel of the space, while contemplating my new job, I sat down and adjusted my ergonomic chair. Then I began to zip through the programs preloaded on my desktop computer. There were some I had never utilized before, which was both thrilling and terrifying but definitely more thrilling. At ten ten, I glanced up from the Adobe Illustrator program I was using on my sweet new setup with the massive screen. *Ten ten!* Shit! I was late.

I popped up from my desk, toeing on the shoes I'd kicked off. I fluffed my hair and straightened my clothes as I hurried to the door. I shot out of my office, not bothering to close it, and hustled down the hallway to the meeting room. As I drew closer, I could hear the low rumble of voices and was afraid the meeting had started without me. Damn it.

I tried to slip unnoticed through the door but my skirt pocket got snagged on the door handle and what would have been a quiet entrance became a scuffle of me versus the door. I won but it was dicey for a moment, and when I glanced up from unhooking my pocket from the door handle, the entire room had gone quiet while everyone watched me. So much for going unnoticed.

"Annabelle, you're here. Fabulous," Sophie cried.

"Sorry I'm late," I said. "I lost track of time."

"No problem," she said. "Start times are flexible here since everyone is on one deadline or another."

"Oh, okay." That was a relief. The one job I'd had at a company after college had been super stressful with late nights, crazy deadlines, and no forgiveness for missed meetings. Frankly, it was one of the reasons I preferred to freelance. My experience with working for others had been demoralizing at best and borderline abusive at worst.

"Is this the new kid?" a voice asked from behind me.

I turned and found myself gazing up at a startlingly handsome man, who looked to be about my age. He had short, light brown hair that was stick straight but side parted to make it more interesting, a wide forehead, sharp cheekbones, caramel-colored eyes, and a square jaw. He wore a pale blue dress shirt and creased gray trousers. He had a congenial air about him that was welcoming, as if he didn't take life too seriously and was always looking for the laugh.

"Carson West, this is our new creative director, Annabelle Martin," Sophie introduced us. "Carson is our senior art director."

We shook hands, and I noticed, before he released my hand, that his grip was firm and warm. I liked that.

"Pleasure to meet you," I said.

"You must be loving the change of climate," he said. "Miguel said you hail from Boston?"

"It wasn't a hardship to pack away the sweaters and coats," I agreed.

"Carson's been in Phoenix for—how long now?" Soph asked him.

"Fifteen years. Since my time with Miguel at ASU." He glanced at me. "We go way back."

My quick mental math put him at thirty-three-ish. I did a visual scan of his hands and noted there was no wedding ring. I wondered if he was single, oh, not for me. Nope, nope, nope. I wasn't anywhere near ready for anything like that. I was just trying to placeholder him, you know, guy who could be a friend, potential guy for dating way, way down the road, possible gay best buddy if he swung that way, and so forth. It was the curse of being single, always trying to figure out the potentiality of anyone you happened to meet.

"Soph, can I talk to you for a sec?" Nyah waved to Soph from across the crowded room.

"Sure." She nodded. "Carson, can you introduce Annabelle around? We'll try to get started in the next five minutes."

"Happy to," Carson said. He smiled as he watched her walk away, but when he turned back to me, his expression was devoid of anything even remotely friendly. Instead, his lip curled up in one corner and his eyes were cold. "Just so we're clear, in six months, your office becomes mine like it should have been all along."

5

"Excuse me?" I asked. I needed him to repeat what he'd said just to make certain I'd heard him right.

His handsome face relaxed and he smiled his big wide welcoming grin, but this time I noticed it wasn't reflected in his eyes. "Because you'll obviously be getting promoted, Ms. Big Shot. Everyone here knows you're on the fast track to partnering with Sophie and Miguel. That's why they brought you in, right?"

This was news to me. Is that what everyone thought? "I—"

"Trent, have you met Annabelle yet?" Carson cut me off and called to another man, who had just entered the room.

This abrupt shift in direction gave me whiplash, but the one thing I did recall very well was the feeling in my gut when he'd said my office should have been his. That hadn't been the friendly comment he'd tried to twist it into. No, this guy was pissed, and I was his target, so now I was on my guard.

"Nice to meet you, Annabelle." Trent extended his hand. "Trent Brockton. I'm the guy you want to see to get your paycheck."

"So you're the one I bring the Friday doughnuts to," I said.

"Yeah, I'm that guy. And just for the record, the jellies are my favorites." He patted his belly and pushed his glasses up on his nose. His smile was the real deal. He was older, in his fifties, with a buzz cut and square glasses, making him look like a scientist from the atomic age. He was wearing a plaid shirt and khakis with a loosely knotted tie and comfortable shoes, which only added to the look. I liked him immediately.

Carson walked away, and I felt my tension ease as he went. He took a seat at the large table, leaving it to Trent to introduce me to the rest of the staff. Okay, then. Ultimately, it was better this way but it felt like a slight, and I didn't for one second buy his bologna about me being promoted. What I had on my hands, I was quite certain, was a man with some entitlement issues and bullying tendencies who reported directly to me. Oh goody.

Meeting the rest of the staff was a blur of handshakes and good wishes. I didn't get any weird vibes from anyone else, so that was reassuring. But I did catch myself giving Carson a cursory glance every now and again.

The meeting was primarily so that everyone could meet me, plus there was cake. One of those luscious white chocolate raspberry Bundt cakes with the cream cheese frosting piped in thick stripes from the center, over the top, and down the sides. Delicious. Personally, I don't trust people who don't like Bundt cake, and I noted that Carson was the only staff member who abstained. Just sayin'.

Back in my office, I sat down with Booker Stevenson, assistant creative director. I was hoping we'd click as he was essentially my right-hand man. Black, tall, lithe, with close-cropped hair, rectangular black-framed glasses, and wearing a tweed sport coat over a white dress shirt and black jeans, Booker had a soothing professorial energy about him that I liked.

"Favorite designer?" he asked by way of greeting.

" 'Bridge the gap between seeing and understanding,' " I quoted.

"Milton Glaser," he said. "Nice."

"And you?" I asked.

" 'Beige is the color of indecision,' " he replied.

"Paula Scher," I said. I lifted my fist, and he gave me a knuckle bump. "So you're a type guy."

"It's all about the font."

"Booker, I think we're going to get along just fine," I said.

He grinned at me and we spent an hour chatting about our work histories and the various projects in play at V² and my vision for the team.

I then set up a schedule to meet each of our

designers to find out what they were working on, when it was due, and the current status of the projects. On the one hand, I felt very grown-up and responsible, but on the other, it felt like carpool mom drudgery. I'd run my own business for so long, I wasn't used to having to direct people. During the two-year stint I'd done before going solo, I'd only been a designer, never a director, art or creative, which suddenly made my acceptance of the creative director position much more daunting, especially with a direct report like Carson cruising around me, undoubtedly watching for me to make a mistake.

"Knock-knock." Soph's voice broke through my concentration. I felt as if my eyes were beginning to roll in different directions. "Hey, you, are you ready to grab some lunch?"

I glanced at her over my computer screen. "I don't know, I'm kind of—"

"There's an awesome restaurant up on the top floor, and they have an amazing Caesar salad," she said. "Not to try and influence you or anything, but you're not used to keeping regular hours and you need to fortify yourself if you're going to make it to quitting time."

"Fair point," I said. I shoved my feet back into my shoes. Ouch. Ouch. Ouch. The toes pinched and my heels were scraped raw. Tomorrow I was wearing ballet flats or sneakers and I didn't care how it looked.

We walked together to the elevator. I scanned the office as we went, checking out the graphic designers and copy editors I'd be working with, which still felt weird. I'd gone over the accounts currently in progress, looked at the creative briefs, and I had questions. One of the main roles of the creative director was to question everything. I was skilled at questioning my own work because I rarely took offense at myself, but this was going to be a stretch for me, asking other designers to answer how their design met the goals of the client.

I already had a few ideas to tweak the logos and ads they were working on to make sure the deliverables were what the client was asking for, but I had to figure out how to do that without appearing as if I was just the new gal determined to get my sticky fingers on things. I was new but I wasn't interested in laying claim to anything. I genuinely saw some areas for improvement, but my delivery had to be executed flawlessly. My job was to mentor and motivate. I planned to grill Sophie over our salads about how best to approach my team. I also wanted to get a sense of Carson's role at Vasquez Squared.

My inner alarm had not stopped clanging after I watched him work the room at the staff meeting. He seemed to have an excellent rapport with everyone so why had he been so off-putting with me? Was it me? Was I being oversensitive?

Was I just insecure because I'd never been in a supervisory position before? Maybe he really was the cool guy he seemed to be. My gut was shaking that off hard. No, there was something not quite right about Carson West, and I wanted to know what it was.

The restaurant offered casual cafeteria-style dining, but I had to admit the chicken Caesar salad was amazing. Also, there was a patio for outside dining. Soph carried her tray and led the way. We found a table in the sun, which felt heavenly, while the cool breeze kept it from being too hot. I took a moment to enjoy the view of Camelback Mountain, and the potted bougainvillea plants with their magenta blooms, which decorated the terrace.

"So let me have it," Soph said.

"Have what?" I asked. My heart lurched in my chest. Was she asking for my resignation? I'd only been employed for a matter of hours.

"Whatever is bothering you," she said. She sipped her sweet tea and pointed at me with her fork. "You get that one deep groove in between your brows when you're overthinking something."

I resisted the urge to rub my forehead. "Just trying to navigate the office dynamics."

"What do you think of the setup?" she asked.

I wasn't sure what to say. I'd been there for only a few hours, but I sensed Sophie's need for some positive feedback, so I went with vague impressions.

"From what I've seen so far, everyone is very talented and enthusiastic," I said. This was true. I decided this was my moment to ask about Carson, so I went for it. "But I have a question."

"Shoot," she said.

"Was Carson in line for my job?"

Soph coughed on the bite of chicken she'd just consumed. She held her napkin to her mouth as she tried to clear her throat. She blinked against the tears that filled her eyes, and she looked at me in confusion. Her voice was gruff when she asked, "Why would you assume that?"

Here's the thing with Soph. She is a terrible liar, as in the worst ever. And I knew, as her longtime BFF, that her tell was to widen her eyes and tip her head ever so slightly to the right, which she did right now.

"Soph, it's me," I said. "It seems pretty clear that Carson thought he was in the running for the job and is not happy about my arrival."

She leaned forward. Her mouth was a thin, tight line. "Did he say anything to you?"

"Only that he expects my office will be his in six months," I said.

"What?" she cried. "He didn't."

"He did, and when I called him on it, he said it was because I was clearly up for a partnership

78

with you and Miguel and would be moving up," I said.

"But that's—he's—ugh." Soph slumped in her chair.

"Also, I couldn't help but think it was very interesting that he said that he and Miguel go back to their time at ASU together, and yet Carson was not at your wedding. I would have remembered. So want to tell me what's going on?" I asked.

She looked like she was about to. She even opened her mouth to speak, but then she shook her head. "I'll have Miguel talk to him. If he ever says anything that makes you uncomfortable, please let me know immediately."

I studied her for a moment. "Uncomfortable how?"

"Oh, not in a sexual harassment sort of way," she said. "He's not like that, but he can be . . . I don't know how to describe it."

"Hard to pin it down, full of backhanded compliments that really aren't, and insults that are passed off as jokes?" I asked.

"Exactly," she said. She glanced around the room and leaned in closer. "It's like he doesn't say things that are in my face mean and yet I still get a negative vibe from him. And he wasn't at our wedding because I planned it for a weekend when I knew he had to be in his brother's wedding."

"Genius," I said.

"Well, I couldn't have that sort of negativity on my big day," she said.

"I get that," I said. "Any idea what it is he wants? Other than my job?"

She was quiet for a moment and then said, "Maybe. Listen, I don't want to put you in a tough spot, but could you do me a favor and document anything that seems significant, particularly in regards to the work?"

Anxiety flitted across her face like the shadows made from fast-moving clouds. I wanted to tell her she could talk to me, but I didn't want to push her. Hopefully, she and Miguel could resolve whatever issue Carson had and we could all move on.

"Yeah, I can do that," I said.

"Thanks." She smiled and I could tell she was relieved, knowing I'd have her back.

I tucked into my salad, feeling marginally better about things. My instincts about Carson had been correct, and I knew this meant I needed to be cautious around him.

When I resumed work in my office, I wondered why it felt as if the clock were moving backward. I was so used to structuring my workdays around working out at my gym, lunching with friends, or taking in a midday movie that this straight shift was a shock to my system. Sure, I used to regularly work until midnight, but I was in control of how I spent my time.

At six o'clock, quitting time, Nyah appeared at my door as I was slipping on my shoes. *Ouch.* She was wearing a fabulous pair of brown boots, which I hadn't noticed earlier when she was standing behind her desk. They were low-heeled and hand-stitched works of art. Seriously, I had absolute boot envy happening. Especially since my toes were cramped, my arches ached, and I was certain I had a blister on each heel.

"Annabelle, a few of us are going for happy hour after work on Friday," she said. "I wanted to invite you before you made other plans."

That made me smile. I had to admit, despite the lack of post-lunch naps, I had missed the social aspect of working in an office. I knew going to happy hour was probably mandatory for me in order to build a rapport with my colleagues, but I still hesitated before I agreed.

"Who all is going?" I asked. I tried to sound casual.

"Just a few of us, the singles mostly," she said. "Me, Luz, Christian, Booker, Shanna, oh, and Trent, even though he's married. His wife has him on a strict diet so he mainly goes for the appetizers to fortify himself for his salad-only weekends."

I laughed. I could totally see Trent loading up a napkin with mini tacos. And no Carson. That worked for me. "I'd love to," I said. "Thanks so much."

"Great." She grinned and her dimples deepened. "I'll collect you after work on Friday."

She left with a wave and a flash of her awesome boots, and I shut down my computer, feeling as if I should stay longer but also painfully aware that I was going to give myself gangrene if I didn't get out of these horrible shoes. I was going to burn them when I got home.

I poked my head into Soph's work space. She and Miguel had adjoining offices at the corner of the building.

"Hey, I'm heading out, if that's okay?" I asked.

Her blond hair was up in a French twist on the back of her head, held in place by two pencils. She looked pale and tired, and I wondered how long she planned to stay at work. I felt guilty for leaving, but she smiled at me and said, "I'm sorry. Miguel and I have a . . . a meeting. Otherwise I'd give you a ride."

"Seriously?" I asked. I tried not to think about my poor feet. It was my own fault for trying to be all fancy and wear my big-girl shoes. "I'm embarrassed you gave me a ride this morning. It's so close. I can walk home in five minutes. In fact, I can't wait to get to my sweet new pad."

Soph smiled. It was her pure one hundred percent happy smile. The one she busted out when everything was working according to plan.

Soph always had a plan. She plotted her life with the intricacy of a novelist; even her subplots had subplots. I, on the other hand, tended to live my life by the seat of my pants, letting the universe fill in my blank pages as it would. Truly, I sometimes marveled that we were so close, given that my modus operandi was so completely different from hers.

"See you tomorrow," I said. Then I felt compelled to add, "Bright and carly." Making me want to kick my own ass. Early? I hated early. On time was about as good as I could get and even that was a stretch for me.

"Belly, I'm so glad you're here," Soph said. There was an entire unspoken conversation in that sentence, but I got it. Everything in my long day shifted into place at the sincerely relieved expression on her face. My friend needed me, and I was here for it.

"Me too."

On that sweet note, I left. My feet hurt so bad, I debated using a ride service, but I didn't want anyone in the office to see me and think I was lame, so I began the trek home, forcing myself to keep my shoes on and trying not to limp.

I crossed Camelback Road and strode up Twenty-fourth Street. My side street was tucked on the west side of the road. I turned and walked past the secluded mansions that sat back on the quiet two-lane road. The yards were so vast,

I almost forgot I was in the heart of the city.

Daire's estate was halfway down the street on the right. I let myself limp the final stretch, almost sobbing in relief when I got to the security gate. I punched in the code and it slid open. I hobbled up the drive to the right that led to the guest house. I used my key to enter, noting that it was getting dark and I hadn't left a light on.

I dropped my bag and kicked off my shoes as soon as I stepped into the cool interior of the house. My feet were throbbing. I glanced down and noted that my heels did, in fact, have blisters. Well, hell. I knew the best thing I could do was to soak them, but I just didn't have the energy to fill up the tub right now. I glanced out the back window. The pool was lit up with a blue glow in the early twilight. The attached hot tub also glowed but with purple. I knew that hot water would feel so good on my aching feet.

I stared up at the big house. The drapes were drawn. I couldn't see light coming from any of the massive windows. Hmm.

The list of rules sat on the counter where I'd left it. I reread the part about the pool. It did not mention the hot tub. I poured a glass of wine into a plastic cup, not because I'm classy like that, but because deep down my decision had already been made. I was going to sneak into the hot tub.

It's not that I'm a rule breaker by nature. I just look at rules, like this list, more as guidelines.

And technically Daire had not mentioned the hot tub specifically as being for the homeowner's exclusive use, so I figured it was fair game.

I twisted my hair into a knot on the top of my head, slipped on my bathing suit and bathrobe, and grabbed a towel from the bathroom. I opened the door to the backyard and felt the cool night air wash over my skin. I clutched my glass of wine and walked the perimeter of the yard to the far end, where the hot tub sat. Its jets were already whirring, water was bubbling, and steam was rising up into the night. It would be a tragedy to let it go unused.

I slipped off my robe and dropped it and my towel onto a nearby lounger. Then I tiptoed over to the edge of the hot tub, placing my wine on the surrounding ledge. I slipped into the water like a crocodile disappearing into a marsh. It took everything I had to stifle the moan that rose up in my throat as the hot water embraced every aching sore muscle in my legs and feet. Even the sting of the hot water on my blisters quickly faded into bliss.

I sat on the built-in bench, keeping my head just above the water. It was getting chilly out, and I knew it was going to be invigorating when I stepped out, but I wanted to get my body to optimum hot before I left the tub. I sipped my wine, pondered the few stars I could see amid the city's light pollution, and glanced at the big house, repeatedly, wondering if anyone could see me and if they did, was I going to get busted?

Too bad so sad, I thought. Come what may, this was totally worth it. I stretched my legs, rolled my ankles, and flexed my toes. The hot water felt delicious. I put my feet right over two jets and let the force of the water massage the aches out of my soles.

I tipped my head back on the ledge and spread my arms and legs out wide. The hot tub was so big that I couldn't even reach each side. I let the water lift me up and I drifted off the ledge. I pulled my hairpins out and tipped my head, letting my long curls float on the bubbles. I closed my eyes and relished being enveloped in the heat. It felt delightfully decadent.

When I started to sweat, I knew it was time to get out. I would have loved to take a plunge in the cold pool, but that had been expressly forbidden in the rules, so instead, I sat up, finished my wine, and tried to climb out of the hot tub as quietly as I could.

The cold air was like a full-body slap and I shivered. I danced from foot to foot on the chilly stone deck while I slipped on my robe. Then I bent over and swiftly wrapped my hair in the towel. I grabbed my empty plastic cup and hurried to my house as stealthily as possible. I was just stepping into the door I'd left unlocked, when the sensation of someone watching me made the hair on the back of my neck prickle.

Hoping fervently that it was just my overactive imagination, I glanced over my shoulder at the big house. I saw one of the drapes on the second floor move as if someone was yanking it back into place. Well, hell.

Nick

6

"Jackson, what were you going to say?" I asked.

Jackson and I were seated in the small dining room, adjacent to the kitchen, which overlooked the backyard. Lupita, my housekeeper and cook, had set us up with a charcuterie board while she put the finishing touches on dinner. I loved that woman. If she wasn't already married to my groundskeeper, I'd propose to her for her carne asada alone.

"When?" Jackson asked. He looked confused. Small wonder since I was referring to our conversation this morning while working out.

"This morning, when I was bench pressing, you were about to tell me what you thought I should do," I reminded him. "But we got interrupted."

"Oh, right, by the hot tenant," he said. He wagged his eyebrows. I stared at him.

He scrunched up his face as if trying to remember. Then he snapped his fingers and pointed at me. "You should go meet her."

I glared. "That wasn't what you were going to say. You just made that up."

He shrugged. "So? The fact remains. She's your

tenant, and you should go meet her and welcome her to her new home."

"You mean her temporary lodgings," I corrected him. "She'll be leaving in six months if not before."

"Unless you like her and invite her to stay longer." Again, he wagged his eyebrows.

I shook my head. "That's never going to happen. I can't even imagine attempting to date anyone like this." I spread my arms wide to encompass my entire body.

Ironically, I was in the best shape of my life. At any other time, I'd be happy to be out there in the sea of singles, mixing and mingling, but no. I'd limited my alcohol intake to almost never, and given up sugar, almost all caffeine, and women, basically anything that made life worth living.

For the past few months, I'd worked out just about every day with Jackson. I was determined never to be as vulnerable as I was on that horrible afternoon, knowing something was wrong but unable to communicate as my body went weak, my face drooped, and my ability to form words evaporated. The mere memory of it caused me to break into a sweat as my heart raced, which scared the crap out of me and then made me furious. I hated feeling weak.

Of course, this was exactly why I put up with the big blockhead. Jackson took our workouts seriously. My goals were his goals. Straight up.

I trusted him even if he did end every workout by blasting Metallica's "Enter Sandman" on the sound system.

"What does Dr. Henry say?" Jackson asked, breaking the silence.

"That he's run every test he can think of and there's nothing wrong," I said. "I'm a medical anomaly."

Jackson tugged at his chin hair. I recognized it as his go-to gesture when he was thinking about something. Very slowly, his gaze rolled up to mine and he said, "I think you need a different sort of doctor."

"I already have a cardiologist, a general practitioner, a neurosurgeon, and a neurologist," I said. "I am ass deep in doctors. Who else could possibly help me at this point?"

He stared at me as if gauging my possible reaction to what he was about to say. He wasn't usually this circumspect so I felt myself prepare to be on the defensive.

"A therapist," he said. "I think you need a therapist."

I frowned. "*You're* my physical therapist."

He shook his head. "Not that kind of therapist."

"Then what kind . . ." My voice trailed off. I narrowed my eyes at him. "You think I'm mental."

He looked at me with one eyebrow raised. "I know you're mental." When I was about to tear into him, he added with a shrug, "We all are."

"You think my fatigue, fuzzy brain, and the weakness in my leg isn't real," I said. My voice sounded hurt and accusatory. That just pissed me off because I didn't want him to think I cared about what he thought of me, because I didn't.

"No." He shook his head. "It's real. I just think there's something else keeping you from a full recovery."

"That's stupid," I said. I picked up my glass of water, resenting that he was having a beer, and took a long sip. "I have done everything, absolutely everything, to recover. Why would I sabotage myself like that?"

"PTSD," he said. "Emotionally, you're just not ready. I saw a lot of it when I came back from Afghanistan."

"I didn't go to war," I reminded him. I took a breath, forcing myself to say the hated words that I usually tried to avoid. "I had a stroke."

When a thirty-five-year-old man says this, it usually stops people cold. Not Jackson.

"You think it's much different?" he asked. "In one case, you have unexpected IEDs blowing up in your face, possibly killing you or your squad. In your situation your entire body shit the bed on you without warning. Seems like both instances are pretty fucking traumatic."

I didn't know if he was trying to schmooze me into listening to him by comparing my medical misadventure to his time in the military. Right, make me having a fat blood clot in my head comparable to a guy putting his life on the line for everything our country holds dear. Sure. I'd have to be a complete asshole to buy that fantasy. Besides, the amount of self-loathing I would feel if this were just some neurotic response to the horrible event of nine months ago would be unparalleled.

"I don't have PTSD," I said. It had been suggested that I might have some complications like that before by my regular doctor, but I felt like a tool even considering that the weakness in my leg or my constant feeling of impending doom came from a flaw in my character.

"There's nothing wrong with being traumatized by what you went through," Jackson insisted. He took a chunk of meat off the cutting board and chewed with gusto.

"I know that," I said. "But that's not it. I know it isn't." I didn't know that but I wasn't ready to entertain the idea that I was broken emotionally from the hell of the past few months. "The docs just haven't figured it out yet."

"You need to look wider, Nick," he said. His voice wasn't judgmental but I heard it that way anyway.

"I'm sorry, where did you get your medical degree?" I asked. Now a normal person would have been pissed, cussed me out, or taken a swing at me. Not Jackson. He laughed. That annoying shake-the-bricks-in-the-wall cackle. I definitely needed to fire him.

"What is the ruckus in here?" Lupita Guzman, my housekeeper and cook, came into the room carrying two heaping plates of chicken enchiladas.

She was short and curvy with wavy black hair that she wore in a stylish bob, dark eyes that sparkled, and a smile that lit up the room. She always wore a neatly pressed dress shirt and slacks with comfortable shoes. Honestly, she was the mom I'd always wanted and never had.

I'd gotten lucky when I hired her and her husband just after I bought my house five years ago. The bonus being that they lived in one wing of the house, so I always had someone nearby in case of an emergency when Jackson wasn't around. He lived here, too, but also had other clients that he worked with in the afternoon and evening, which was a good thing. We'd likely kill each other if we were together all the time.

Lupita's husband, Juan, was my groundskeeper and driver, who felt more like a reserved uncle as he maintained a certain emotional distance. I knew he appreciated the work and he liked me just fine, but he had two grown children of his own and wasn't looking for another. Lupita did not have these boundary issues.

She crossed the room and clucked her tongue

as she put a plate in front of me. In her lightly accented voice, she asked, "You worked too hard today, didn't you?"

I could have tried to answer in the nanosecond she gave me, but she turned on Jackson instead. She put his plate in front of him. "What are you thinking? You know he has the weakness in his leg." Jackson opened his mouth to answer, but Lupita rolled right over him as she swung back to me. "I will make you a restorative smoothie. Mango with vitamins A and C. It's good for you." She added that last bit like I was going to argue.

"Do I get one, too, Lupita?" Jackson asked. She looked him over as if deciding whether he was worthy. Jackson leaned back in his chair. "I'm feeling faint."

Her eyes went wide. "Strawberry banana for you. Potassium." With that, she turned on her heel and left while we both shouted, "Thank you, Lupita," after her. She responded with a wave of acknowledgment.

Jackson turned to me. "How do I get her to adopt me?"

"Pay her an exorbitant salary to put up with you," I said. Like Jackson, I paid Lupita and Juan very well. Given that I had no family to lean on, they were worth every penny.

"I think she's out of my league," he said.

"Then make sure I don't fire you so you don't lose access," I said.

"You're not going to fire me," he said.

"Oh no?" I asked. I was surprised and a little impressed by his confidence. I could be a moody son of a bitch and had fired people for less.

"No one else will put up with you," he said.

"Says you," I countered. It was true, but I wasn't about to agree with him and lose my bargaining position.

After dinner, Jackson left to go and attend one of his evening clients. With envy in my heart, I watched him grab his bag of gear and jog out the door. That used to be me. I had believed I was invincible. If I set a goal, I could achieve it. Nothing could ever stop me. Until it had. And now I was a prisoner in my own body, afraid to leave my house, afraid to walk, afraid to run, afraid of everything, and man, I hated it. But more than that, I hated myself. I hated what I'd become but I didn't know how to change it.

I spent the evening like I always did, with no real sense of purpose. It was exhausting. I read every single page of the newspaper and watched television. For the first time in my life, I was caught up on every show I'd missed when I was busy having a life.

Before my life imploded, I'd had more life than I could handle. I'd been a thirty-five-year-old mogul on the rise. After my family unraveled when I was fourteen, I bounced around several foster homes and a group residence for boys. I'd escaped it all at the age of sixteen when I emancipated myself and started work as a carpenter, hanging drywall. I worked for local construction outfits in the brutal desert temperatures for two years. It didn't take me long to realize I wanted more.

I went back and got my GED, then I went to college at night. I studied business. I didn't finish. The degree had never been my goal. I wanted to know how business worked and how to get ahead, and once I had it figured out, I quit school and was in the game. I saved every damn dime that came my way and started buying properties in low-income neighborhoods that were on the brink of being gentrified and then I began flipping them.

The 2008 recession had destroyed my city, but it gave me my first out with a slew of foreclosed properties ripe for the picking. I knew the streets, the neighborhoods, and the zoning ordinances. I knew exactly how to leave one wall standing to be able to call it a historic preservation project and then build a cheesy McMansion around it. I scooped up all the tax breaks and then charged a fucking fortune for a place that wasn't worth the aesthetically pleasing yet cheap materials we loaded into it, except for location, location, location.

With the onslaught of rich Californians pouring into Arizona for the cheaper cost of living, there was money to be made in the housing industry, and I was determined to be one of the ones to make it. Soon, I was flipping entire neighborhoods, and my builders and I could hardly keep up with the demand. I made a fortune and was at the top of my game and then BOOM.

My body essentially gave me the big middle finger and crapped out on me. I hadn't been able to get my old self back since. When I looked in the mirror now, I didn't recognize the man with the shadowed eyes, who didn't sleep, who woke up drenched in sweat with his leg going numb, who never left his house, who was, for the first time in his life since childhood, not in control.

I thought about Jackson's suggestion that I see a therapist. My entire body went rigid. *Nope, nope, nope. They'll want to talk about your entire life, not just your post-trauma stroke issues. Do you really want to wade around in that cesspool? Oh, hell no.*

Looking for a distraction from these disturbing thoughts, I settled into my recliner by the fire, sipping the thimbleful of whiskey that I allowed myself on bad days while reading the latest Gray Man thriller from Mark Greaney.

I had just gotten my chair into the perfect recline when I heard a very soft splash. It was coming from the pool area. I waited. I heard another very soft sound. Someone was in the pool. I knew it wasn't Lupita or Juan. They'd already retired for the night. And Jackson was still out and wouldn't return for at least another hour.

My wheelchair was parked beside my recliner and I pushed myself to standing. I took a moment to check the feeling in my legs. Did they feel weak? Could I get to the window and back without falling? I didn't want to risk it. I lowered myself into the wheelchair and rolled to the window just to be on the safe side.

I pushed aside the curtain, just a few inches, to peer into the yard. My first glance was at the pool. It was lit up at night, a restful Caribbean shade of ocean blue. It was empty. My gaze swept the citrus trees that circled the pool. I didn't see anyone. Then my gaze was caught by a movement coming from the hot tub.

There she was. Annabelle Martin. In a tiny scrap of a bathing suit, with a plastic cup sitting on the ledge of the hot tub, while she floated in the hot steaming water with her hair streaming out around her. Her eyes were closed, her lips slightly parted. It hit me that this was what she'd look like during sex. The thought staggered me. Parts of my body that had been dormant to the point of me thinking they were broken reared to life. My breath was short and I had to close my eyes and try to think of something, anything, else. I thought of taxes and root canals and diarrhea. Nothing helped.

The sight of her, drifting in the steam, looking dreamy and sexy as hell, was now going to be imprinted on my brain forever. *Shit!*

I would never admit it to Jackson, but in this moment, the way she looked all honey skinned and wet from the water, *Goddess* was actually the perfect description. I shook my head. I blinked. I tried to rattle reason back into my brain.

This could not stand. I'd given her carefully detailed rules, pages of them. I had specifically said that the pool was for the exclusive use of the homeowner—i.e., me. And yet there she was, flaunting the rules and herself and—dayum!—she was a sight to behold. I was riveted.

I knew I should move away, punch myself in the face if necessary, but I didn't do either of those things. Instead, I watched as she floated, finished her beverage, and then finally climbed out. This was a mistake. The sight of the water sluicing off her body in the violet light of the hot tub made my mouth dry, and I was making a weird raspy breathing noise in my throat. Not to mention the fact that I was essentially being a pervy Peeping Tom and I knew Jackson would slap me upside the head for it.

Sorry not sorry. I couldn't move. She hopped from foot to foot and I suspected the cool decking was freezing under her bare feet. She shrugged into her robe, wrapped her hair, and grabbed her plastic cup. I saw a flash of the tattoo on her wrist but still couldn't make it out. She dashed to her house and then stood perfectly still for just a moment. That should have been my warning, but I was too enthralled to look away, and that's when she turned and faced the house. As if sensing my stare, her gaze zeroed right in on me. I rolled back, dropping the drapes.

A hot blush of shame heated my face, and my heart was galloping in my chest. I was terrified for one crazy moment that this debacle might cause me to have another episode. I pulled my phone out of my pajama pocket, getting ready to call Lupita and Juan. But nothing happened. The panic eased. My heart slowed. I was okay.

I didn't dare look out the window again, but I knew what I had to do. Such flagrant disregard of the document I had sent her simply could not be tolerated. I rolled over to my desk and grabbed a piece of paper and an envelope. Clearly, my tenant needed a refresher on the rules.

Annabelle

7

I waited for a shout. There was nothing. I thought maybe a shaking fist would appear. That didn't happen either. Instead, the grounds between my little house and the big house grew very quiet as if I wasn't alone in waiting for something to happen, but nothing did.

I closed and locked my door, wondering if I'd imagined the whole thing. Wouldn't be the first time I'd gotten carried away. I decided to forget about it and preheated the oven to cook the frozen pizza Soph had put in my freezer. This was best friend love in its purest form.

While the pizza cooked, I took a quick shower and put on my pajamas. Several times I walked back to the windows that overlooked the yard. I stared at the curtain that I was certain I'd seen move but there was nothing. No movement, no light, no indication that anyone lived in the house at all. Maybe I had imagined it. Hmm.

I took my pizza into bed—because, why not—fired up my laptop, and watched some reruns of *The Office*. Since I was now working in an actual office again, it resonated. I glanced around my bedroom during the opening credits, noting again the lack of art. It was positively savage to have nothing but barren walls. Art, in my opinion, was a window to an alternate world of imagination, emotion, and truth.

That's how I'd always viewed it at any rate. Ever since I was a kid, museums to me were like amusement parks, where every painting was a portal to another dimension of the artist's creation. It was why I initially wanted to be a fine artist, but I didn't believe I had the purity of talent, plus I wanted to eat, move out of my parents' house, pay my own bills, and so forth.

I considered the plain white wall across from me. What would I hang on it? It would have to be big, huge in fact, to cover so much real estate. A landscape? Something that felt like I could step right into it and smell the sun-warmed wildflowers or the new-fallen snow or the damp darkness of a forest at night. Should it be desert mountains in all their bronze and purple glory? Or maybe a seascape to counteract the arid climate, something with big blue-green waves crashing on a rocky shore? Perhaps, a still life? A bowl of lemons so vibrantly yellow that the blistered rind seemed like it could be plucked right out of the painting and the one lemon sliced open made the viewer pucker at the potential bite of its tart juice. Yes, I would like that.

I woke up with a gob of cheese stuck to my face. I'd fallen asleep on my pizza. My computer battery was dead, and—I glanced at the clock—I was late. Later than late. I should be walking into the office *right now!*

My phone was on my nightstand, and I picked it up and glared at it. Why hadn't the alarm gone off? Oh, the betrayal! I ran into the bathroom. One glance in the mirror, and I screamed. My hair was a rat's nest, I had a pimple sprouting on my forehead, and I kept burping pepperoni.

I combed out my hair and twisted it into a topknot. I washed my face and brushed my teeth. I dashed to my suitcases, which I had tossed into the closet, where they remained unpacked as I hadn't had the motivation to deal with them yet.

I riffled through the first one and found my underwear. I yanked it on and then flipped the lid on the second one, which was full of acceptable work clothes. I grabbed the ubiquitous black knit dress and a zebra print scarf. I pulled it over my head, minding my hair. Then I grabbed a pair of thick socks and my beat-up black high-top Converse sneakers, which were more scuffed than not. I didn't care. My feet were still tender and these shoes would not cause any more harm. I grabbed a yogurt out of the fridge and a granola bar from the pantry, dropped them into my bag, and raced for the front door. I was killing it! If I kept up this pace, which meant running all the way to work, I would only be fifteen minutes late.

I thought about texting Soph and making an excuse, but our friendship was too valuable for me to treat it like that, plus she was my boss now. I was going to have to take my lumps for being late and just make certain it didn't happen again. Of course, it might have been easier if I hadn't said I'd be there bright and early. Ack!

I grabbed my jean jacket—it was cold in the morning—and yanked open the front door. Taped to the middle of the double doors was an envelope. I snatched it off and stuffed it into my bag, barely taking time to lock the door behind me as I ran down the driveway for the street.

By the time I got to the office, I was panting and sweaty and even my comfortable kicks were chafing my feet. As I stood waiting for the elevator, I shrugged off my jacket and pulled the front of my dress away from my skin in order to get some air. I was just checking the messages on my phone when the doors opened and Carson stepped out.

He blinked at the sight of me, and a slow smile curved his lips. "Just getting in?"

"Early meeting with a client ran late," I lied. Although maybe it wasn't. Maybe the mysterious envelope on my door had been about a job and not someone trying to sell me life insurance. I could always hope, right? I lifted my phone to my ear to listen to the voicemail from my sister, Chelsea.

"Sure it was," he said. His voice was whisper soft and full of doubt.

Then he shook his head, dismissing me as he stepped out of the elevator and around me as if I were no more significant than a cautionary Wet Floor sign. I knew he was trying to rattle me, but I was not about to let him.

I tipped my chin up in the air and strode into the elevator. I lifted my phone to my ear and pretended to bc talking into my phone, and said, loud enough for Carson to hear me, "Hi! Yes, isn't it fabulous? So nice to have such a huge client come on board."

I saw a flicker of uncertainty cross Carson's face as the doors shut. Okay, great, now I just needed to bring in a huge client. No big deal.

I greeted Nyah and Trent as I hustled to my office. No one seemed to care that I was late, which I appreciated. I had a feeling Carson would be making a federal case out of it to Miguel, and I didn't really need anyone else to pile on.

I dropped my bag in a desk drawer and fired up my computer. I wanted to check my email and see if the meetings I'd set up had been confirmed. While my desktop booted up, I remembered the envelope taped to my door and retrieved it from my bag.

I used my thumb to break the seal and opened the note. I recognized the handwriting with its particular precision right away. The letters were squared off and thick as if the writer meant what he wrote and wrote what he meant—there was an air of authority about the handwriting that made me take notice. I quickly scanned the lines and the word *busted* leapt to mind.

> Tenant:
> At exactly seven o'clock last night, you were seen entering the hot tub with what appeared to be an alcoholic beverage. Per the list of rules that was delivered to you upon your arrival, the pool is for the exclusive use of the homeowner. It would be greatly appreciated if you could refrain from using the facilities during the duration of your stay.
>
> —Daire

So the curtain twitch had been the old guy. I stared at the note. I was torn between laughing my head off and crumpling the note up into a tight little wad in my fist and tossing it in the trash.

Tenant? Again, the crotchety old geezer didn't even use my name. Surely he knew it from where I'd signed the lease in at least seven different places. And the way he signed his name. *Daire.* I said it out loud with all the condescension I could muster.

I didn't crumple the note. Instead, I shoved it in the top drawer of my desk and contemplated what I should do. I thought about asking Miguel or Sophie for advice, but I didn't want to drag them into this. It was likely *Daire*—I said it in my head with a partial lip curl of annoyance—would tell them himself, which would be awkward enough.

No, my best line of defense here was clearly a strong offense. Maybe I could bring the old guy a pizza as a peace offering while I pleaded my case that the hot tub was a separate feature and therefore not covered by the rule stating no use of the pool. I had genuinely loved my time soaking in the tub and didn't want to give up access. I wondered if I could broker a deal with the inflexible curmudgeon.

Maybe I could convince him to give me use of the hot tub at certain times of the day, like at night when he was asleep. I could promise not to make any noise. I mentally scanned the evening before and wondered if I'd made any sounds, you know, like singing, whistling, or talking to myself. It happened sometimes. I doubted it as I had been determined to go undetected but maybe I'd blown it. It had been pretty great, soaking up the heat under the stars. I might have gotten carried away. Wouldn't be the first time.

Newly determined, I opened the file on my computer and began to work. I met with all of my team members and got up to speed on their projects. I made some suggestions, which were well received, so I felt like things were off to a good start. It was exciting to be working with other creatives again.

There was some righteous talent at Vasquez Squared. This didn't surprise me since Sophie had a real eye for talent, and Miguel was brilliant at pulling the very best out of his staff. They had an ambitious plan to be one of the top design firms in the country, and I knew them well enough to know they wouldn't quit until they got there.

Feeling guilty for arriving late, I ate lunch at my desk, working to make up the lost time. Soph popped in for a minute but she and Miguel were presenting a corporate identity proposal to an international soap company located in the Valley, so they were out of the office for most of the afternoon. Normally, I would have gone with them on a new business pitch, but they were giving me some time to get my sea legs, which I appreciated.

Throughout the day, I revisited Daire's note. While debating various responses, I found myself doodling on a fresh piece of paper with a fistful of random colored pencils that I'd taken from the supply cupboard. It was a simple drawing, depicting my version of a mighty saguaro cactus, framed by a variety of cactus blossoms. Beside the cactus was a small pond, an oasis, with a lone

fish, a koi type all flowing fins and shiny scales.
Below the picture, I wrote:

Landlord:
Please excuse the misunderstanding. I
would like to respectfully point out that
the hot tub was not listed in "the rules,"
and after a long day at work I couldn't
resist it. Please accept the enclosed
drawing as an apology but I would also
request that you reconsider the use of the
hot tub. If there is any time of day that
my use would be acceptable, it would be
greatly appreciated.
                              Annabelle Martin

I had no idea if he would take the salutation as
one of snark or not. I hoped the gift of the picture
would soften him up at least a little. I supposed if
he said "no," I would learn to live with it, but it
seemed awfully selfish of him. What good were
things like hot tubs if they weren't frequently used?
I found an envelope in the office to put the
picture in and stored it in my bag. I wasn't sure
how I was going to get it to him, but I'd worry
about that when I got home. Not wanting to eat
another frozen pizza, I called for a car to pick me
up and take me to the grocery store.
When I arrived home, I unpacked my groceries
and then moved to the doors to stare at the big

house that loomed across the yard. It seemed the protocol was to leave the note on the front door. Okay, then.

I found some tape in the utility drawer and took it with me. I walked briskly down the path that cut through the side yard and led to the front door of the big house. The sun had set, leaving a smoky blue dusk behind that shifted into darkness by invisible degrees.

The path was lined with short garden lamps, making pools of light that I strode through as I walked to the house. The night was chilly and I noted the lack of noise. No cars could be heard tucked away this far from the main roads, and the songbirds had obviously called it a day. I was right behind them. I could not wait to microwave my bowl of prepackaged ramen and put on my pajamas.

When I reached the house, I hesitated. There was a light illuminating the front door, but the windows on either side had the same heavy drapery as the back of the house. Truly, if I didn't know any better, I would think the place was vacant.

Quietly, slowly, cautiously, I approached the front door. No one popped out of the house to yell at me, so I assumed my presence had gone undetected. Cool.

I hurried forward and taped the envelope with my response to the door. Shoving the tape in my pocket, I dashed down the steps and jog-walked the length of the path as if I were fleeing a haunted house but trying to look cool about it. I didn't breathe properly until I was back at my place, where I quickly locked the door behind me and rested against it as if I'd just robbed a bank and was hiding from the law.

Per usual, after I've done something that was driven more by impulse than thought, I was deluged with a truckload of self-doubt. Did I do the right thing to try to gain access to the hot tub? Was Daire going to be angry that I called him "landlord"? It had seemed like an on-the-nose way to make my point at the time.

Oh man, I was going to get tossed out on my behind. I knew Miguel and Soph would take me in. But when they'd offered originally, I hadn't wanted to be an imposition, plus I'd feared being made creative director and living with the bosses wouldn't go over well with the staff I was supposed to supervise. And now that I'd met the throbbing nerve of resentment that was Carson West, I knew I'd made the right call.

I put my ramen in the microwave and crossed over to the windows to glance at the big house while my dinner cooked. No lights were visible. I wondered if my smartest play would be to sneak back and retrieve my stupid note. Probably not; he had to have gotten it by now. Damn it.

The microwave beeped and I took my soup out and put it on the counter. I debated having a glass of wine for about a nanosecond and then went ahead with a generous pour of chardonnay. I wasn't sure if this was the correct pairing with ramen, but whatever.

While the soup cooled, I retrieved my phone from my bag in the living room, planning to text my sister while I ate. I was halfway back to my seat when there was a knock.

I dropped low to the floor like someone had thrown tear gas through the window. I glanced in the direction of my bedroom. Could I get there without being seen? No. Unlike at the big house, I liked having all of my drapes pulled open and anyone could see in, because I didn't want to live feeling buttoned up to the neck. I might have to rethink that.

I stayed perfectly still. Maybe if I didn't move, the person would assume I wasn't home and they'd go away. I held my crouched position even though my back was beginning to spasm.

The knock sounded again. I didn't move. I didn't even breathe. What if it was Daire himself, coming to throw me out?

"Hello? Ms. Martin?" a voice, a man's voice, called through the door. *Gah!* It probably was Daire. I felt my entire body cramp. If I was capable of moving, I would have smacked my forehead with an open palm, but I didn't want to make a sound.

Despite my curiosity about my landlord, which

was like an itch I couldn't reach to scratch, this was not how I wanted to meet him. We needed neutral ground or something.

There was movement behind the glass doors, and a bald, bearded man peered at me through the narrow window on the side of the double doors. He blinked. I didn't move. Would he think I was a piece of furniture? A delightfully random sculpture, perhaps?

His gaze held mine, and he waved one big beefy hand. I realized he could see me quite clearly in my awkward frozen crouch, and I likely looked like an idiot. I waved back and then pretended to tie my shoe, yeah, because that was going to fool him. My heart was beating hard in my chest and I felt suddenly sweaty.

I rose and crossed the room to the doors. Steeling myself with a big breath, I unlocked the doors and pulled open the one on the right. "Hello," I said. I made my voice cheery and, I hoped, innocent sounding. Just me eating a bowl of ramen, nothing to see here.

"Hi, I'm Jackson Popov," he said. So he was not Mr. Daire. My spine relaxed and I drew a relieved breath.

"Annabelle Martin." I pointed to myself.

"I know. I work for Mr. Daire. He asked me to bring you this."

He held out an envelope. I didn't take it. His eyes went wide as if he didn't know what to do

113

with my nonparticipation. But really, why would I want to take what was likely an eviction notice? I felt like I was being served legal papers, and I wanted no part of them. He flapped the envelope at me. I kept my hands at my sides.

He pursed his lips and squinted one eye as if he was unclear on what to make of me, and it gave me a chance to study him. I guessed him to be in his early to mid-thirties, despite the bald head, which looked shaved rather than the result of hair loss. He was built huge in height and width; the T-shirt he wore strained to cover the muscles that rippled beneath his skin with every move he made—even in his neck. Impressive and fascinating.

I wondered what he did for Mr. Daire. Bodyguard? Personal trainer? Enforcer? The last one made me pause, but his friendly face didn't seem like the type to crack skulls for a living. Still, the possibilities were endless.

"Is he throwing me out?" I asked.

He shrugged his massive shoulders. Seriously, if he tried to come in, he'd have to turn sideways to manage it. He held the envelope out and said, "There's only one way to find out."

Reluctantly, I took it. I glanced at him and asked, "Scale of one to ten—with one being 'What infraction of the rules?' and ten being 'Let's stone her to death!'—how mad was he that I used the hot tub?"

Jackson's lips twitched. "Funny you should use the scale of one to ten."

"Just trying to get an assessment of the potential fallout," I said.

"Understood." He looked up at the dark night sky and then down at the ground while he considered his answer. "I'd say a solid seven. It's all he talked about today."

"Oh," I said. The envelope in my hand felt suddenly hot. "Sorry."

"No, trust me, it was a nice change from the usual," he said.

I wondered what "the usual" was but didn't ask. Instead, I said, "Do you want to come in? Can I get you a glass of wine?"

"You're stalling," he said. His pale gray eyes glinted with understanding.

Of course I was, but I did appreciate that he could see my BS for what it was. I glanced down at the envelope and saw the precise handwriting on the outside: *Ms. Martin.*

Was it a promising sign that I had been upgraded from *Tenant?* I wasn't sure.

A chime sounded and he took his phone out of his pocket and glanced at the display. "Gotta go," he said. "Nice meeting you."

Then he turned and walked down the steps. He didn't stay and wait to see if I had a reply for Mr. Daire, as if this were an Austen novel and he was the footman with a return message. I wondered if that meant this *was* an eviction notice. Clearly, in that case, there'd be no need to wait since there was only one way this was ending.

I closed the door and locked it as he disappeared from view. I turned and tossed the envelope onto the counter. It didn't feel as thick as the original rules. Was that a good thing or a bad thing? I had no idea.

As long as I didn't open it, then I could live in blissful ignorance. I went into the kitchen and picked up my spoon. I ate at the counter, staring at the envelope, trying to guess what was inside. I lifted it up to the light, wondering if I would see the words *Get Out* through the envelope. No such luck.

I put it back down and chewed on my noodles. The soup was spicy and I began to sweat. I refused to believe it was from nerves, and I took a fortitudinous sip of my wine. When the soup was gone, I washed out the plastic dish and put it in the recycle bin. I debated putting on my pajamas and going to bed. See? I can do avoidance like nobody's business.

I suspected I wouldn't sleep without knowing the contents of that stupid envelope. I picked it up and used my thumb to break the seal. One sheet of paper fell out. It fluttered to the counter like a bird with a broken wing. I scooped it up and read.

Ms. Martin:
The hot tub is a part of the pool and as such is off limits.

Daire

Well, that was coldly to the point, wasn't it? I sighed in disappointment, knowing that I should be grateful that he hadn't decided to kick me to the curb, given that this was my thirty-day probationary period and all. Still, I was a bit hurt that there was no acknowledgment of my drawing. My artist's pride was not taking it well. Daire had probably thrown it in the trash. One woman's art was another man's garbage, after all.

I wandered over to the window and glanced out at the pool, which was empty, and the hot tub, also vacant, and then turned my gaze to the house. The drapes were all drawn. Jackson had been the first sign of life I'd seen from the big house and now he was gone, swallowed back up into the cloaked abyss. In a weird way, the lack of life about the place depressed me. Much like the bare walls in this guest house.

Daire had probably already gone to bed. If he had a live-in caregiver, or whatever Jackson was, he must be in very poor health. I managed to dig up a little empathy for him, but it was a struggle as I gazed at the lovely purple glow of the hot tub and pondered how glorious a glass of wine would be while soaking under the stars. My sigh was as

117

gusty as a storm front that vanishes right before the rain.

There had to be a way to get Daire to give in, and I was just the woman to find it.

Nick

8

"What was she like?" I asked.

"Fine," Jackson answered. He lumbered into the room, catching sight of his reflection in the far windowpane and pausing to flex, just the pecs. I rolled my eyes. Jackson could never pass a reflective surface without checking out some part of his muscled physique.

The evening was on the cold side, and I had the fireplace turned on. He sprawled onto the couch beside me and picked up his controller. The large flat-screen TV fired to life as our video game came out of sleep mode.

We were playing a team game, real macho nonsense but stupid fun. We'd been dropped into the jungle and were seeking ancient treasure while fighting off other adventurers, giant spiders, wildfires, and a wraith who wanted us dead. We'd taken a break just before entering a sacred tomb so that he could deliver my note to my tenant.

Unsurprisingly, given how much rent-free space she was taking up in my head, I couldn't let it be and had to ask him about her.

" 'Fine' as in the slang way of saying she's

really hot, or 'fine' meaning she said she was fine, which is girl code for 'I refuse to talk about this because it's not fine but I haven't figured out how I am going to make you pay for it yet'?" I asked.

"My, dude." Jackson shook his head. "What sort of women have you been dating?"

"Recently? None," I said. "Before that? Expensive ones."

Jackson's mouth curved up on one side. He had very reluctantly been drafted to be my messenger boy. The only reason I even managed to get him to go was by threatening not to finish our quest.

"On your six!" he yelled.

I whipped my character around and took out an enormous arachnid with three blasts from my laser. *Zap!* I got it right in one of its big red eyeballs. It rolled over with its legs in the air and then turned to dust and blew away.

I glanced at Jackson. "So?"

"You really want to do this now?" he asked. "We're almost at the entrance."

I thought about playing it cool and pretending I didn't care what Annabelle Martin seemed like up close and personal. Yeah, no. Sometimes you just have to be at one with your curiosity, like a cat. Cats were curious and they were still considered cool. Right?

I assumed an indifferent pose and said, "I just want to know if she looks to be the type to have human sacrifices in my guest house living room or not?"

Jackson had started to take a sip of beer and sputtered, inhaling some beverage into his lungs. I paused the game while he coughed. When he could speak, he pointed at me with his beer bottle and said, "You have a dark soul."

"Don't I know it," I muttered.

"No, she's not having human sacrifices or anything else in her living room," Jackson said. "She seems . . . nice."

"Nice?" I asked him. I stared at him like he'd recently whacked his head and was now speaking in tongues. "I saw her. In the hot tub. In her bathing suit. She is *not* nice."

He rolled his eyes. "A woman can be attractive and still be nice."

"No," I said. "It's been my experience that those are mutually exclusive traits."

"Well, your experience is for shit," he said. He turned his attention back to the game. He was in the lead and I had his back as we navigated the jungle. "You need to raise your standards."

"My standards are fine. I just like my women to have a certain aesthetic," I said.

Jackson slowly swiveled to face me. He had one eyebrow raised higher than the other. "Like what? A big ass or something?"

"Not specifically, but I do like them to be super-model worthy," I said. I glanced at the screen of our game, trying to maintain a straight face. Why did I enjoy tormenting Jackson with my feigned misogyny so much? It was bad of me, I knew that. He was just such a Boy Scout about these things that I liked to get him all aggro with my knuckle dragger comments.

"So it's just about looks for you?" he asked. His expression was deeply disappointed. "Well, having seen her up close, I can assure you, she could give any model a run for her money with those big brown eyes, perfect skin, and a killer smile."

I frowned, annoyed. I used the machete my character carried to hack up some foliage. Totally unnecessary but it made me feel better. "Exactly how close did you get to her? I only sent you to deliver a message, not try to score."

Jackson's laugh erupted with a sonic boom. You'd think I'd be used to it by now. I wasn't. I jumped in my seat. I bit back the urge to slug him. Barely.

"Relax, she just invited me in for a glass of wine," he said. He pressed on through the jungle.

"She *what?*"

Jackson wagged his eyebrows at me. "What's the matter? You don't care if I hook up with her, do you? After all, she's clearly too nice to meet your 'aesthetic.' "

"I don't care," I scoffed. "It's not my business. It'd just make things awkward if I have to throw her out."

"For breaking your rules," he clarified.

"Yeah." I really hated that he'd managed to turn this around on me.

"What did your note say?" he asked.

"Why?"

"Because she was worried you were going to throw her out," he said. We'd reached a cliff and we were both clicking away at our controllers as our characters scaled the face of it. "You didn't, did you?"

"No, I just answered her question about the hot tub," I said. My thumb was starting to cramp as I tried to navigate the terrain.

"What question was that?"

"Whether it's off limits. It is."

Jackson shook his head. He reached the top of the cliff and paused to turn and look at me. "For a guy considered to be one of the sharpest businessmen in Phoenix, you are dumber than a bag of dirt."

"What?" I protested. My character reached the top, finally, and I turned to look at him.

"You have a beautiful woman, living on your property, wanting to use your hot tub and you tell her no," he said. "That takes a special kind of stupid."

I opened my mouth and then closed it. He had a valid point, which I didn't want to admit. Instead, I went on the offensive. "And I'm telling you, the hotter the woman, the crazier she is. It's a fact."

He shook his head and resumed playing. "Nick, I say this as your trainer and your friend, you have got to get out of the house. You're becoming the epitome of everything a woman does not like in a man these days."

"Bullshit. I never had any trouble before," I said. "They certainly seem to enjoy my picking up the check."

He pointed at me again. "That, right there, isn't cool. Besides, it sounds like you were dating the wrong sort of women."

"There's a wrong sort?" I turned my attention back to the game as Jackson led the way into the tomb. I knew better than to be the first man to enter. They were always sacrificed in these games but Jackson was a newbie, so it was his painful life lesson to learn.

"Of course there's a wrong sort—argh, damn it!" He turned outraged eyes on me. "You knew! You knew that zombie was hiding in the tomb. You knew he was going to lop off my head and you let me go in anyway."

"Maybe." I shrugged.

"Yeah, well, now you have to wait for me to respawn before we can continue," he said.

He tossed his controller onto the coffee table and I did, too, because, frankly, I was much more interested in getting all the intel on my tenant than I was in acquiring virtual nonbankable treasure.

"Just tell me this," I said. "Do you think she's going to be a problem?"

He frowned. "In what way? By using your off-limits hot tub? Why exactly is that, by the way? I just don't get it."

"Because it's disruptive," I said.

"Of what?" he argued. "I've been living here for six months, and the only time you use the pool is for exercise, and you only use the hot tub after a hard workout."

"Which is often. Listen, I never wanted to rent the guest house," I said. "You know this. I didn't want anyone around while I recovered, but I owed Miguel a favor, so—"

"Yeah, yeah, I know. You agreed so your debt would be square," he said. He took a long sip of his beer. "But I really don't see why—"

There was a knock on the door, interrupting whatever Jackson was going to say.

"Excuse me."

I whipped my head around half expecting to see Annabelle Martin, the subject of our conversation, standing there, but it wasn't her. It was Lupita. I was certain the flicker I felt wasn't disappointment but rather indigestion.

"Hi, Lupita. What is it?" I asked.

"There is someone here to see you, and I . . . I wasn't sure what to say," she said. She looked ill at ease, and I knew it was because I hadn't allowed any visitors inside the house in over nine months. I was like the proverbial wounded animal. I didn't want anyone to see me weak or in pain.

I wondered if it was Annabelle, coming to argue her case to use the hot tub. I felt my curiosity surge. At a distance, she was lovely, and I found I was eager to see her up close, especially after Jackson's description of her.

"Who is it?" I asked. I tried to keep my expression neutral in case Annabelle was standing in the hallway behind Lupita.

Nothing prepared me for my housekeeper's answer, however.

"She says she's your sister, Lexi."

My heart stopped, and for a stone-cold second, I was certain I was going to blink out again.

9

"I'm sorry," I said. "Who did you say was here?"

"Your sister," Lupita answered but another voice joined hers, and a woman stepped around Lupita and entered the room. "Hi, Nicky, it's me, Lexi."

Both Jackson and Lupita had comically slack-jawed expressions of surprise on their faces. I supposed it would have been funny if it wasn't such a gut punch to see my baby sister, standing in the middle of the room, looking at me expectantly.

I wanted to charge across the floor and scoop her up in a hug just like I used to when she was five and I was ten. But I couldn't get up. In an instant, my heart rate accelerated, my hands began to tingle, and my left leg went numb. I flailed around on the couch for a second, fighting for breath until coolness prevailed. I rolled my panic into a stretch and then slumped back into a relaxed pose, which likely appeared as a particularly unfriendly greeting to the sibling I hadn't seen since I had struck out on my own at sixteen, but what could I do? I was freaking out and *I couldn't walk*.

Mercifully, my wheelchair was parked in the

corner out of sight. It was stupid, but I didn't want to appear less than, not to her, not to the kid who used to follow me around in pigtails, carrying her favorite stuffed animal, a chicken no less, with a look of hero worship on her face like I made the sun come up every day. No, I couldn't bear to have her look at me with pity. I'd take hurt and anger over that every damn time.

"Look at you," I said. My voice came out wobbly, so I cleared my throat. I gestured to a nearby chair and said, "Have a seat."

"Can I bring you anything? A drink or a sandwich?" Lupita, clearly a much better host than I, asked Lexi.

"Um, no, thank you. I'm good," Lexi said. She crossed the room and sat down in the armchair nearest the couch.

I watched her, tried not to stare, and failed. She was thirty, soon to be thirty-one, and she looked so much like our mother that I felt my heart clutch hard in my chest. She had long light brown hair that curled on the ends, big hazel eyes framed by pale lashes, a stubborn chin, and even the same faint spray of freckles across her upturned nose. Her voice was just like our mother's, too. It wrecked me.

"You look well," Lexi said. Her voice was soft. I felt Jackson stir beside me, reminding me that he was there.

"Thanks," I replied. I was not about to divulge

the past nine months of sheer hell. Instead, I gestured to Lupita and Jackson. "This is my housekeeper, Lupita, and my . . . tra . . . friend, Jackson."

Jackson shot me a quick glance, and I knew he'd caught on that I didn't want Lexi to know he was my trainer or that he mostly lived here in case my body decided to flip me off again. Too much information.

"It's nice to meet you." Lexi and Jackson leaned forward and shook hands. Then she waved at Lupita, who hadn't left her position by the door but who waved back with a warm smile.

"If you need me," Lupita said, and I nodded. She closed the door softly behind her when she left.

Jackson half rose from his seat. "I'll just—"

"Stay," I said. It came out like an order. I softened my tone and added, "I'm sure Lexi won't mind."

My sister gave him a tiny smile and nodded. "Not at all."

Jackson settled back onto the couch. I could feel him glancing between us, confused. Not a surprise, given that I'd never mentioned having any family, because, as far as I was concerned, I didn't have any.

Lexi looked around the room, taking in the massive television, the video game still frozen on the screen where Jackson's character had had his head lopped off, and the oversized leather furniture and utilitarian coffee table. It was definitely a man's lair. The whole house was, in fact, and I suddenly wished I'd taken Lupita up on her offer to buy fresh flowers or plants to soften the place a little. It had seemed pointless to me at the time since flowers and plants always died.

The quizzical expression on Lexi's face, the pinch to her lips, and the tiny V between her eyebrows as she tried to reconcile this house as the home of the brother she'd once known reminded me so much of our mother, before everything went wrong, that for a second, I felt as if I'd been cast back in time and my mother was about to read me a story or teach me to tie my shoes. It was jarring.

I fought the memories off, digging into the pain and betrayal of my childhood to ward against any soft feelings that might bubble to the surface. I had no issues with Lexi, aside from not knowing her, not really, but our parents were another story.

"Well," I said. I wanted to get right to the bottom of her visit, even though I had a pretty good idea of why she was here.

"You look good," she said. She lifted a hand as if she'd reach out and pat mine, trying to connect. I moved my hand away from the armrest and her hand fell awkwardly back into her lap.

"So you said." I wasn't trying to be curt, honestly, but I could think of no reason why she'd be here right now save one.

"I did, didn't I?" she said with a laugh. It sounded forced and it clanged, a dissonant sound in the otherwise quiet room. "It's been a long time since I've seen you."

"Twenty years," I said. That wasn't entirely accurate, but she didn't need to know that. I had checked up on her over the years, enough to make sure she was well cared for and got a full-ride "scholarship" to the University of Pennsylvania's School of Design to study architecture. She didn't need to know that either.

"A lifetime," she said. Her eyes, one of the many traits we shared, met mine. At one time, she had been my person, my sibling, the only living being I'd walk through fire for without hesitation. Now she was a stranger. I glanced away.

"You look well, too," I said. My tone was grudging, but I didn't want her to think I was a complete asshole. My throat got tight when I added, "You look like her." I didn't need to say who. She knew.

"Do I?" she asked. She lowered her face and stared at her hands, clasped in her lap. Her thick curtain of honey brown hair fell about her face. She tucked it behind her ears, just like our mother used to do. "I don't really remember her. My memories of her and Dad are fuzzy."

"Lucky you," I said. The bitterness in my voice was like acid, and I was surprised it didn't burn a hole in my tongue. A flash of pain crossed her face, and I regretted the harshness of my words. What had happened to us as kids hadn't been Lexi's fault. I blew out a breath and, needing this surprise visit to end sooner rather than later, asked, "How much?"

She tipped her head to the side, looking confused. "What?"

I rolled my hand in a get-on-with-it gesture. "How much?"

She raised one eyebrow and stared at me. This was an expression all her own. "What are you talking about, Nicky?"

"It's Nick," I said.

"What are you talking about, Nick?" She emphasized the *ck*. I was only surprised she didn't swap out the *N* for a *D,* but it was implied.

I almost laughed in relief. There she was. This was the girl I remembered, who gave me hell when I wouldn't take her along on bike rides with my friends, who punched the neighborhood bully right in the eye when he was tormenting a pigeon, who had fought like a bobcat, all teeth and claws, when the system separated us so that she could have a family of her own while I was sent to a series of foster homes and then finally a group home for wayward—*Ha! More like unwanted*—teen boys.

"I think it's pretty obvious why you're here," I said. Despite being happy to see that she had retained some of her feistiness, I didn't want to play games about her purpose. We had been siblings once, but those days were long gone. There was only one thing anyone ever wanted from me now.

She leaned forward, resting her elbows on her knees. "Is that so? Do enlighten me."

"You need money," I said. "And since I have it, you've probably decided to pull your old connection to me as your big brother out of your back pocket and cash in."

I heard Jackson make a choking sound from beside me, but I didn't bother to look at him. I was too busy taking in the kaleidoscope of fury that was twirling in front of me in the form of my very pissed off sister.

She popped to her feet. She stretched her arms out wide. She opened her mouth to say something but then bit it back. She blinked several times.

"That's what you think this is?" she cried.

"Isn't it?" I asked.

"No," she snapped. "Did it ever occur to you that I've been trying to drum up the courage for years to come and see you?"

I put on my bored face. She was not going to bamboozle me. She could have approached me anytime over the past twelve years, when she was officially an adult, and yet she never had.

"Well, you're here now," I said. "So what do you want?"

"I want my brother back," she said.

We stared at each other. What was I supposed to say? We couldn't just erase a twenty-year absence of birthdays, holidays, vacations, and the day-to-day cap on, seat down, who ate my yogurt issues that were the bedrock of being a family.

"I can't help you with that," I said.

I heard Jackson hiss a breath. I could have drowned in the disapproval pouring off him. I opted to hold my breath.

"That's it?" Lexi asked. She began to pace the room.

She looked devastated, as if everything she had feared about approaching me had come to pass. Not gonna lie. It made me feel like shit. Still, I didn't say anything, which was fine as it turned out she wasn't done.

"You don't have anything else to say to me? No 'Hey, Lexi, I've missed you, too. Sorry I never reached out'?" She stopped pacing and planted her hands on her hips, staring down at me from across the coffee table.

"Reach out? Are you serious?" I snapped. I wished with everything I had that I could stand up. I couldn't risk it. The muscles in my leg still felt weak even as the tingling in my hands faded. I was not about to do a face-plant in front of her.

I didn't have a lot of the old me left, but I had my pride.

I supposed that was wrong, but that pride had gotten me through some very bleak times and kept me from following my parents into the quicksand of bad decisions. It also stoked the fire in my belly to prove myself, to be somebody to the foster dad who called me worthless and slapped me so hard, my ear rang for a week when I accidentally scratched the back bumper of his piece of shit ancient minivan with my bike. And to the foster mother who liked to call me into the bathroom when she "forgot" a towel, laughing when my adolescent body betrayed me and responded to the sight of her naked and wet. Yes, those were the "parents" I hoped choked on my success. But the ones I wanted to suffer above all others were my real parents, the ones who'd abandoned me and my sister to the system when they decided getting sober for their kids was just too hard.

I shook off the memories and stared my sister down. "Reach out?" I repeated. "You got placed with a family, a good family, and moved three thousand miles away to the East Coast. Exactly how was I supposed to reach out?"

I could feel Jackson's eyes on my face. He didn't know anything about my past, because I never talked about it. I was certain he was examining these pieces and trying to figure out how they fit into the puzzle that was me. I would have told him not to bother, but I was too focused on making my past, in the human form of my sister, go away. I didn't want anyone to see me in my self-imposed isolation, especially Lexi. The pity would flatten what little self-respect I had left. And believe me, I hadn't been operating at capacity for a long while.

"There's this crazy thing called the Internet. You could have found me. You could have stayed in my life," she argued. Her pointy chin was set at the stubborn angle I remembered so well when she didn't get her way.

"Is that what your new family told you?" I stared at her, incredulous. I didn't want to shotgun any positive feelings she had about her adoptive family, but they had made it very clear, painfully clear, when they moved that I was to stay far, far away.

"No," she said. She glanced down and then back, still brave even after all these years. "Mom admitted that Dad told you to keep your distance when we left Arizona. They were worried you'd be a bad influence on me."

It was jarring to hear her call her adoptive parents Mom and Dad. It's what I'd wanted for her when she left, but it made the chasm between us feel that much wider.

"He said it a hell of a lot more plainly to me than that," I corrected her. "When did she tell you?" Suddenly, it was very important for me to know how long she had known the truth.

"After he died last year," Lexi said. "Mom started to get worried that if something should happen to her, I'd have no one, and she told me I should find you. When I said I doubted that you were interested in me because I'd never heard from you after we moved to Virginia, she told me what Dad said to you." She looked sad. "You still could have reached out to me, you know."

I stared at her. Hard. She had no idea. That day, the day they packed up and left Arizona, taking my baby sister with them, had been the worst day of my entire life. It still was, ranking even higher than the day the bottom had fallen out on me, which was saying something.

Upon the Brewers coming to collect her, Lexi had worked herself into such a state, she had to be sedated for them to be able to take her from the foster home where we'd been since our parents had abandoned us. Lexi had been nine. I'd been fourteen, too young to be emancipated, too young to take care of us by myself.

Up until that moment, I'd thought having my parents decide they didn't want to be a family anymore was the most devastating thing that could happen to me. They were suburban junkies, hopped up on OxyContin after a car accident left my dad with a crushed vertebra and my mom a debilitating case of guilt since she'd been the driver. Their doctor tried to make it all go away by prescribing the wildly addictive narcotic painkiller. What he actually prescribed was the death of a family.

My father became an addict first, and he dragged my mother down the dark path with him. When they couldn't get their scripts filled anymore, they rolled over to street drugs until they were selling everything we owned to supply their heroin habit. Looking back, I was only surprised they didn't try to sell me and Lexi, instead of just handing us over to the state when parenting was cutting too deeply into their drug money. Still, none of that had cut as deeply as losing Lexi, the one person who understood how horribly awry our childhood had gone. The one person I loved, who loved me back unconditionally.

I shook my head. There was too much. Too much hurt and anger and grief to unbox from my past. I had moved on, pushed through, and I had no intention of backsliding now. I had enough on my plate, thanks.

"No, I couldn't reach out," I said. "If I did, your 'dad' was going to have me arrested and thrown in jail. I had to give you your best shot, so I did. Now we've both moved on. We've built lives for ourselves. There's simply no need to revisit the past."

Lexi ducked her head but not before I saw a

tear slide down her cheek. All of my old brotherly instincts rose up inside me. *Always protect Lexi.* I heard the voice inside my head as surely as I had when my mother said it while putting Lexi in my arms the day she came home from the hospital. Holding her swaddled in a pink blanket with her wrinkly red skin, scrawny fingers, head of downy hair, and milky blue eyes, my five-year-old self had experienced love at first sight for the very first time.

"But I need *you,* Nicky," she said.

Shit. I didn't have the reserves it would require to resist a plea from my sister. Why couldn't she just give me a dollar amount so we could be done with this?

"Why?" I asked. "You have a life of your own. Why do you want me in it now?"

Lexi swiped at her cheeks as if she was furious with herself for the display of emotion. She sniffed and glanced at the closed curtains and then back. "All right, I'll be honest. I'm only in Phoenix temporarily for a job and I'm in a jam. I need your help and your connections, Nicky. I need your power."

I stared at her for a beat and then I threw back my head and laughed. I had no power. It had all evaporated the day my body betrayed me. "I really can't help you."

"Yes, you can," she said. "Listen, I'm currently building a net-zero housing development that could revolutionize the industry, but I'm making enemies, Nicky. There are a lot of developers who want to see me fail, well, a few of them want to see me dead, but that's not why I need you."

I felt Jackson stiffen beside me. I could tell his protective instincts were kicking in just like mine. I'd rip anyone apart who harmed my sister, whether we were in each other's lives or not, even if I had to crawl to get to them.

"Who wants you dead?" I demanded.

"Relax, that was hyperbole," she said.

She didn't meet my gaze, however, so I suspected a death threat had been made.

"Bullshit. Tell me all of it, Lexi," I said.

"It's simple. I received a green building grant from the Environmental Protection Agency and the State Energy Program, to pair zero-emission designs with affordable homeownership on a vacant lot," she said. "Most low-income homes spend about ten percent of their income on utilities. With the alternate sources of energy we're putting in, the residents should have no utility bills. The goal is to create a cost-effective, completely self-sustaining housing development of twenty small homes on an abandoned lot in Central Phoenix. It's about the greenest build you could ever imagine."

"So what's the problem?"

"You mean aside from the utility companies who most definitely do not want housing developments to become self-sustaining? Or the construction companies who don't want me to upset their established practices by pushing through innovations that could slow them up if adopted into the building code? Or the investors who are suddenly panicking at the budget and want me to switch to cheaper non–environmentally friendly materials? And let's not forget the local politicians on the take from all of the above. I'm getting slammed with supposed building code violations that don't even make sense. And then there's a whole anti-gentrification group of protesters, who are ridiculous because I am literally building on an abandoned lot."

I grimaced. I knew all of these players. I knew exactly who and what she was talking about. These were not choirboys. There was a lot of money at stake in building, and they were not going to play nice with someone who was planning to change the game and cost them money, time, and potential projects.

"To be clear, what is it you think I can do for you?" I asked.

"I need public opinion on my side. I need the powerful dealmakers in Phoenix to get on board," she said. "And I need the politicians to want this for the city."

"That's a tall order," Jackson said.

She glanced at him. And I noticed that the sympathy in his gaze made the tension in her shoulders ease. Jackson was good like that.

"What's your plan to make this happen?" I asked. "And how do I factor?"

"I'm proposing that we have a gala," she said. She dropped back into her chair and leaned forward, obviously hoping to sell me on her idea. "Black tie, champagne, hors d'oeuvres, you know, all the good stuff, held at the Phoenix Country Club with photo ops galore. We invite anyone who is anyone in the city. We announce your comeback from early retirement to support your sister and we get them on board with Green Springs."

"*Green Springs?* That's what you're calling it?" I asked. "No wonder it's tanking. It sounds like the name of a cemetery."

She stuck her chin out and glared at me, crossing her arms over her chest just like she used to when she was six and wanted her way whether it was cake for breakfast or one more story. It felt like a punch in the chest to see it again.

I wanted to howl for all the years we'd missed, but I was a broken man and there was simply no way I could let Lexi back in my life again. Not like this.

"I appreciate that you think I can help you with this," I said. "But I can't."

"Because you retired from the building game?" she asked. She held her arms out wide. "You're telling me that you're barely thirty-five and you bought this colossal waste of space and cashed out and that's it?"

"Hey!" I cried. "I happen to like my home."

"It's not home, it's a supersized mausoleum," she said. She was more on point than she knew. "I suppose it could be worse. It's mostly concrete, steel, glass, and the wood in here looks to be repurposed. At least you didn't rape the rain forest"—she paused while Jackson choked on his own spit—"for the oh-so-precious teak flooring most McMansion owners opt for."

"Um . . . thanks?" I said.

She shook her head. "No. It's still an egregious waste of resources and a ginormous drain on the power grid, all of which is heating up Mother Earth. You are one person. How can you possibly need this much space?"

"I'm seeing why the politicians and investors are not leaping on board with your development," I said. My tone was as dry as plain toast.

"Which is why I need you," she said. "I don't need your money. I just need you. Come on, Nicky, for old times' sake, help me get people excited about my development. This is my first project as architect on record. I need this."

I kept my face neutral. It was a struggle because I really loved that she was so passionate about her project and that she was taking her architectural degree in such a forward-thinking direction. I wanted to do a fist pump. Instead, I shook my head. The mere thought of getting back out there with a body that could fail me at any moment—no, I was not doing that.

"I'm sorry," I said. I kept my voice firm. "I can't help you."

She stared at me in disbelief, as if in all of her wildest imaginings my saying no had never been a part of the equation. She'd looked at me just like that when she caught me trying to be the tooth fairy slipping the change I'd found under the couch cushions beneath her pillow. I never did find the stupid tooth she'd put under there.

"Is that really how you want it?" she asked. The hurt in her voice cut through the haze of the memories with a razor's precision.

We stared at each other. Me, a shell of my former self, and her, young and vibrant with her whole life ahead of her. I was not going to be the anchor that pulled her under the water.

"That's the way it has to be," I said. I thought I sidestepped answering the question pretty well. I was in the midst of mentally patting myself on the back when she interrupted.

She leaned over the coffee table, bracing her upper body with her hands. She was pushing into my space, and it took everything I had not to back up when she growled, "Fuck that."

"Alexandra Margaret *Brewer!*" I scolded, emphasizing her adopted last name. "That language is completely uncalled for."

A slow grin spread across her face and she laughed. It was the same infectious, mischievous laugh she'd had as a kid. She pushed back to standing and propped one hand on her hip. She looked down her nose at me and said, "You're not the boss of me."

Oh, she was dragging out that old chestnut. She was playing me just like she had when we were kids. I shook my head. I was not going to get sucked in. Nope, nope, nope.

"No, I'm not," I agreed. "And I don't want to be." I turned to Jackson and said, "Do me a solid and show Lexi to the door."

Jackson looked intensely uncomfortable. He put a hand on the back of his neck like he was working out a kink. He was my physical therapist and trainer, and I paid him to live here and be available if I needed him, so he was like a bodyguard, but in more of a "one-man response team to an emergency" than a "chase away people I don't want to talk to" sort of way. I could see he was unclear as to what to do, and I decided we were going to have a conversation to clarify his position.

Lexi turned to Jackson. "You don't need to show me out. I can find my way." She glanced at me and shook her head as if she couldn't reconcile the disappointment she felt in finally seeing me again. It chafed but I knew it was better this way.

One thing niggled the back of my mind. "Wait."

Her eyes flashed with hope, which I heartlessly shit-canned immediately. "How did you get in here? Lupita said you knocked on the front door but we have a security gate."

She let out a breath and shook her head as the hope dimmed from her eyes. "I waited until someone came home and opened the gate and then I slipped in after them before the gate closed." As if she couldn't resist, she added, "Duh."

It sounded so much like the sassy child she'd once been, I huffed out a small laugh. I quickly made my face impassive and asked, "Who was it?"

"Who was who?"

"Who was it that you followed onto the property?" I asked.

She pursed her lips as if considering me.

"You're not going to get them in trouble," I said. Another lie. "I just need to know so that this sort of thing doesn't happen again."

She tipped her head to the side. "No."

"What do you mean 'no'?" I asked. I was outraged. She couldn't just refuse.

"I'm not telling you anything," she said. "Why should I?"

"Because I asked you to," I said. Yup, I'd walked right into that bear trap. I could almost feel its steel jaws snap shut around my ankle when she grinned.

"And I asked you to help me, but you said no," she retorted. She tipped her chin up. "See how that works?"

"Whatever," I said. I was not going to play this game. I had a good idea of who had let her in and I'd deal with that person next. "Where are you parked?"

"Down the street," she said. "Why?"

"It's late and it's dark," I said. "Jackson will walk you to your car."

"I don't need—" she began.

Jackson rose to his feet. It was like watching a mountain spring up spontaneously out of the couch, and Lexi's eyes went wide as she stared up at him.

"This is not negotiable," Jackson said to her. She looked like she'd argue but then thought better of it. Jackson turned back to me. "You good?"

"Yeah," I lied. I wasn't good. I was a disaster of titanic proportions, but I was not about to let anyone, especially Lexi, know.

Jackson walked to the door and opened it, waiting for her, but Lexi didn't follow. Instead, she turned to me and said, "I'm not Mom and Dad, you know, I'm not like them."

"I know." It didn't change things for me, not one damn bit.

With that, she did an epic hair toss and flounced out the door. I could hear her boots clack down the hallway.

Jackson didn't move from the doorway. His gaze met mine and he said, "You know, I never thought of you as broken beyond repair until right now."

Annabelle

10

The remainder of the week passed without my breaking any more of "the rules." I didn't see Jackson again, but I did meet the groundskeeper, Mr. Guzman. He was trimming the trees along the drive as I dashed out the door, late again, and ran by, jumping over his extension cord as I went. To my surprise, he began to sing in a deep baritone, *"And the race is on . . ."*

I hit my brakes hard, skidding to a stop. I whipped around to look at him. He was on a ladder so he seemed very tall. He had a thick head of gray hair and a bristly mustache, the kind I'd only ever seen during Movember, mustache-growing month, or on old seventies and eighties television shows.

Winking at me, he continued, *"And here comes pride up the backstretch."*

"Heartaches are goin' to the inside," I chimed in and his bushy eyebrows rose. Together we sang out the rest of the chorus, ending with, *"And the winner loses all."*

"You know George Jones?" he asked.

"My dad's a fan of old-school country." I shrugged. "After a while it sticks."

149

He laughed. "So true."

"I'm Annabelle Martin," I said. "I'm staying in the guest house."

"I know." His brown eyes twinkled, and his mustache curved up on the ends when he smiled. "I'm Juan Guzman, groundskeeper, handyman, and driver."

"That's quite a résumé."

"My wife, Lupita, is the cook and housekeeper," he said. "You'll meet her, I'm sure."

"That also seems like an awful lot of work for one person," I said.

"Mr. Daire is just one man, so it's not so much," he said. "We couldn't believe it when he said he was renting out the guest house. That place has been empty since he bought the estate."

I supposed that explained the lack of art. Maybe Daire just hadn't gotten to it yet. Curiosity got the better of me. Shocker, I know.

"What's Mr. Daire like?" I asked.

And just like that, our friendly chat was over. Mr. Guzman turned his back to me and began clipping the tree. Over the motor of the trimmer, he yelled, "I'd best get back to work. Lots to do today."

I nodded, waved, and continued on my way. It was clear I'd crossed a line—the "do not ask questions about the boss" line. Huh. No problem. This was exactly why the Internet existed.

● ● ●

I had another meeting with my chief graphic designers, Christian and Luz, where we tweaked the print ad we were confirming with a client that afternoon. It was exhilarating to be working with other people again when the ideas started popping. Before I knew it, I was eating a peanut butter and strawberry jelly Uncrustable—don't judge, those frozen sandwiches might be made for kids but they are yummy—at my desk while opening the Internet to do a deep dive on my landlord.

I started wide with a search engine using his name and city of residence. Nick Daire and Phoenix. Nothing came up, so I tried variations of Nick, like Nicholas and Nicolai, still nothing. I opted to be more specific and pulled up the website for the local paper, but there was nothing.

That seemed weird. Wealthy old guy in a premier neighborhood in Phoenix, and there was no mention of him. Hmm.

I opened up the social media apps and started searching those. Not surprisingly, there were no listings for Nick Daire in Phoenix. While every generation seemed to have an app that reflected their demographic, like Facebook for oldsters, Instagram for middles, and Snapchat for youth, it was possible that my landlord, given his decidedly introverted tendencies and being of an advanced age that required around-the-clock care, wasn't interested in any of those or in

151

social media at all. Good for him. Bad for me.

I doubled back to the newspaper. Not to have any articles about him seemed so strange. Had he never been married? Divorced? Had children? Had he done nothing noteworthy in the community all these years? Maybe he was a typical Midwestern transplant, who retired to Arizona after a full life in Iowa. Maybe I had to search out of state. Great. Which state? I had so many questions. How did a person live in this world and leave no cyber footprint? It boggled.

All too soon, my lunch hour was over and I had gotten nowhere in my quest for information. With great reluctance, I closed my browser and went to the large meeting room to prep for our presentation to a local brewery, who wanted to revamp their brand. This was one of those meetings where I needed to assess the real ask. What did they want? Sales? Recognition? What problem were they looking to solve? This was my favorite part of the work, second to the designing, figuring out how we could help our client achieve their goals. Plus, I was very interested in watching my team perform.

Not to be all braggy, but we crushed it. My designers wowed our client, who it turned out was looking for a boost in sales, with their new packaging and we were happily signing an agreement, which was handled by Nyah and

Trent, just before I walked our client out the door. It felt good to have a win under my belt, even if I'd only been operating in an advisory capacity this week. My team was ecstatic, and I was surprised by how gratifying it was to share a victory with others. I was so used to working alone, I usually just celebrated a new client's acceptance of a finished project by having a drink with Jeremy.

Jeremy. Ugh. I'd been so busy trying to acclimate to my new life that I hadn't really thought about him. I guessed that more than anything proved that he was not husband material, at least not for me. I felt an odd mixture of relief that I'd been right to end things and move away and guilt for the exact same reason. I wondered if Jeremy would ever speak to me again, but I honestly didn't know. I supposed I should have been more upset. After all, he'd been my closest friend in Boston, but I just wasn't.

Needless to say, it was a cheerful group that left work and tromped our way to happy hour. We happened to pick a place that specialized in burgers and beer and trivia. Luz, Shanna, and I grabbed a table while Booker and Christian ordered several pitchers of beer. Trent did buffet recon while Nyah went to sign us up as a team for trivia. If the questions were art history or pop culture, I was golden. Too bad we didn't have an in-house librarian; those bookish ones knew their stuff.

We scored an extra-long picnic table just as the pitchers arrived. Trent followed with a tray full of chicken wings with a disproportionately low number of celery and carrot sticks. The trivia match had just begun, and Nyah logged us in as Team V^2. The first category was movie quotes, and Trent knew them all.

It made sense. Whoever had come up with this subject hadn't moved the needle out of the eighties, which was when Trent had been a teen. There was an overload of John Hughes references, and he got every one.

Four teams were active in the bar. As the subject moved to sports, Booker became our guy with some backup from Shanna. Nyah brought it home with music, and at the end of round three, we were solidly in the lead in answers and beer consumption. My head was getting fuzzy in the best possible way.

When Christian locked down the answer to a classic television sitcom, he put us over the top. High fives were exchanged, but as I reached up to slap Luz's hand, I saw her smile dim. She was staring at the door but quickly turned her head away as if she was trying to avoid making eye contact. I glanced at the doorway, and my gaze was caught by Carson West. Mother of pearl, what was he doing here?

I reached for my beer. I had no idea what his relationship was with the staff of Vasquez

Squared, but I knew how I felt about him. I didn't trust him. I glanced back at Luz, because she certainly hadn't seemed thrilled to see him either and I wondered if there was some history there.

Luz Dominguez, who was the assistant art director, had large brown eyes and thick black hair, which she wore in a messy bun at the nape of her neck. She was dressed in a cute floral dress and a pair of pink and aqua Fluevogs with a sassy bow that tied in front. She appeared to be on the older side of twenty-five, and I had the feeling that Carson West could destroy her with one mean comment. Maybe I wasn't giving her enough credit, since she reported directly to him, but as he strode across the bar toward our table, she looked like she wanted to run. Interesting.

"Luz, would you do me a favor?" I asked. She glanced at me, looking like she hoped I was going to send her home. Not quite. "I think I've had too much beer and I'm feeling wobbly. Could you go to the bar and get us a couple of pitchers of water with ice and lemons, lots of lemons?"

It was not a total lie, I hadn't hit wobbly yet, but it was coming. The look of relief on her face told me all I needed to know. There was most definitely some bad blood there. I glanced back at Carson. He seemed completely oblivious to Luz as she slid off her seat and slipped away. Shanna, who was one of our best graphic designers, excused herself to go help Luz. Solidarity. I liked it.

"Well, hey, kids, imagine finding you here," Carson said. He grabbed a chair from a nearby table and sat down.

Nyah turned his way with a warm and friendly smile. Trent raised a fist, while still holding a chicken wing, for a bump, to which Carson obliged. Booker tipped his chin at Carson in acknowledgment while Christian was so fixated on the trivia board, which was gearing up for the next round, that he gave him a distracted wave.

Nyah leaned across the table and said, "You never join us for happy hour. What brings you by tonight?"

"FOMO," he said. He spread his arms wide. "I don't want to be left out of the water cooler gossip on Monday."

"What gossip?" Trent asked through a mouthful of chicken wing. He paused to swallow and lick the sauce off his thumb. "I mean other than V^2 kicking ass at the trivia match."

"Oh, I don't know," Carson said. He helped himself to a clean glass and filled it from one of the pitchers. "I hear Boston girls party pretty hard. I didn't want to miss it if the new creative director started dancing on tables. Sophie told us it's been known to happen."

If it had been anyone else, I would have laughed it off as a joke, but somehow, I got the feeling Carson wasn't teasing me so much as he was trying to get the others to see me in a less than flattering light.

I met his stare and forced my lips to curve up even though I didn't find him amusing at all. "It's a wasted trip for you then," I said. I fought to keep my voice light and casual. "My table-dancing days ended my freshman year in college, you know, ten years ago."

"Did they?" he asked. His eyebrows shot up in feigned surprise. "That disappoints. I bet you could give it the old college try, you know, if you really wanted to. Heck, you might even score us some free beer if you work it hard enough, flash some cleavage, or hike up your skirt a bit. Don't be shy, Annabelle."

His voice was low and calculating. Did he actually think I was going to take the bait, climb up on the table, and shake what my mama gave me to prove something to him? The man was mental. I glanced around the table to see Nyah, Trent, Booker, and Christian, who had finally turned away from the trivia board, watching us as if they sensed they were in the midst of a power play but were uncertain of how they'd gotten here and why it was happening.

I picked up my beer and took a sip. There were a variety of ways I could react. I could bristle, toss my beer at him, and call him out for being a sexist pig. No, that would likely make my new coworkers think I was oversensitive and had a temper. I could laugh, as if he were funny, which he wasn't, and pretend it was all a big joke. Nope, I was not that good of an actress. I figured my best strategy was to take the passive offensive. Bullies hate that.

"Wow, as I mentioned, those days are long over for me, but you seem to know an awful lot about table dancing, Carson," I said. My voice came out a little higher than normal, and I added a hair toss and a beaming smile to my next words, you know, to keep it friendly, when I added, "Why don't you show us how it's done."

I spread my arms wide, indicating that the table was all his. I glanced at our coworkers and with a hearty laugh asked, "Who wants to see Carson twerk for his beer?"

Trent and Christian hooted and slapped the table. Nyah laughed and clapped, and said, "Yeah, come on, that would be hilarious!"

My gaze held Carson's. I had outmaneuvered him and he knew it. He glowered. I batted my eyelashes. He tossed back his beer in one gulp and stood. Forcing his mouth into a toothless smile, he pulled a wad of bills out of his pocket, peeled off a ten, and tossed it on the table.

"Maybe next time," he said. "I've gotta bounce."

The others booed good-naturedly as he left, but I didn't, and when I scanned the table, I noticed Booker didn't either. Instead, he held up his beer to me and said, "Well played."

I clinked my glass with his, and as my gaze held his, I knew I wasn't the only one who got a hinky feeling from Carson West.

Luz and Shanna returned with the water. Shanna didn't seem to notice that Carson had already departed, but I watched Luz survey the area and visibly relax. When her gaze met Booker's, he jerked his head toward the door. I suspected he was letting her know that Carson had left. Interesting.

I switched over to water. It helped until someone ordered a round of shots, more beer, and more appetizers. It was only ten o'clock when I left happy hour but it felt like midnight. Nyah had a ride share picking everyone up, and she insisted I join them.

On the way home, Trent began to sing "Danny Boy" because Saint Patrick's Day was coming up fast, and he felt the need to practice. Not surprisingly, the rest of us joined in, much to the amusement, at least I hope it was amusement, of our driver. When he pulled up to the gate, the chorus had reached its apex, and I climbed out of the car and paused to conduct them through the last notes of the song.

I punched in the code and disappeared through the gate with a wave. On the walk up the drive to my house, I began to sing it from the top. "Danny Boy" was a favorite, after all. We'd sung it in my high school choir, and I remembered Mrs.

Bodwell conducting us with her big grin and her blond bob bouncing as she kept time tapping her foot, which was impressive because being on the petite side, she always wore spiky four-inch heels.

A feeling of victory swept over me as I climbed the steps to my house. I'd wowed a client, gotten rid of Carson at the bar, and survived my first week at a regular job. Feeling relieved that I had two days to recover before it started all over again, I sang the last line at full volume. *"Oh, Danny boy, oh, Danny boy, I love you sooooooo."*

I held the last note as long as I could. It felt as if it echoed in the trees above me and shot up into the sky and bounced back down from the stars to echo long after I had stopped singing. Heaving a sigh of contentment, I went inside to brush my teeth and pass out.

I am not a morning person. While I love a good sunrise as much as the next person, I was rarely in a position to see one as I like to sleep through the dawn, rising at the more reasonable hour of seven or, if possible, nine.

Given that the guest house had come furnished, I had to tip my hat to whoever had bought the furniture and the bedding. The sheets were buttery soft, and the comforter was like being wrapped in a fluffy warm cloud. Because I didn't close my drapes, the relentless sun kept poking me in the eyeballs and I had to pull the blanket over my head and shut out the light. This worked for another hour before my restlessness roused me.

I had decided that today's mission was to go out and hit all the thrift stores until I found some art to hang on the walls. I didn't care if it was portraits of scary clowns. I needed something to look at besides a vast expanse of Swiss Coffee–painted walls.

I'm not sure why the creamy color was called that. It seemed like a misnomer since there wasn't even a hint of brown in it, but I'd always envied whoever it was who had the sweet job of naming the colors of paint or nail polish or lipstick. In another life, that would be my dream job. Imagine spending all day coming up with new and different names for all the shades of red that have nothing to do with the color red, like *I Can't Even,* which could be an orange red or *Sorry Not Sorry,* a bluish red. Those were my favorite reds, the blue-toned ones.

Shaking off my contemplation of color hues and their names, I strode to the kitchen to make my coffee. Once I had frothed the milk and poured in the coffee, I decided to take my cup out to the front of my house to enjoy the sounds of the birds chirping, the crisp breeze, and the warm sun. I would have sat on the back patio, but I was overly conscious of the fact that I could be seen from the big house, and having been chastised about the hot tub, I didn't really want to put myself out there in my morning attire, which was not the stuff of runways. Heck, it wasn't even fit for an emergency grocery run.

I opened the front door and stopped short. Taped across both doors was another envelope. So this was going to be a fun Saturday.

I wondered if it had been Jackson who'd stuck it there. I seriously doubted it was Mr. Daire himself. I snagged the note and sat on the top step, letting the sun heat my shoulders while pondering the sealed missive. Like the others, it was business-size, white, with my name, *Ms. Martin,* written in the same blocky, exacting handwriting.

Had I taken my trash to the curb? Yes. Had I brought the bin back up? Yes. Had I used the pool or the hot tub? No. I tried to remember the list of rules. As far as I could remember, I hadn't broken any of them. Heck, I hadn't even been here much as I'd put in long days all week, getting acclimated to office life and such.

I sipped my coffee then tapped my chin with the envelope. To open or not to open, that was the question. Whether 'tis nobler in the mind to suffer the slings and arrows of my anxiety or open the damned thing and remove all doubt. Shakespeare would be proud, I know.

I decided to go with removing all doubt and

opened the letter. It was one sheet, neatly folded into thirds. I snapped it open and read.

> Dear Ms. Martin *[It started cheerfully enough]*:
> Per the rules that were delivered to you by our mutual acquaintance, Miguel Vasquez, it was stated quite clearly on page four, paragraph two, line twelve that there was to be no noise past the hour of nine o'clock at night. And yet, at approximately ten fifteen last night, a lone voice was heard to be belting out the old Irish favorite "Danny Boy."

And just like that, my stomach bottomed out. I cringed, remembering that beer-infused moment when I had been convinced I was singing with the trees and the stars. I wondered how badly I had butchered the song and if this was grounds enough to get me ousted out of my house. I had become quite fond of it over the past week and didn't really want to have to pack and move again. I glanced at the note and braced myself because there was more. Of course there was.

> Because I and my staff were all accounted for at that precise hour and because you were seen on the gate's security camera,

163

singing the same song with a carful of
people, I feel it is a safe assumption that
the source of the noise was you.

I paused to stare down the drive at the gate. Was
that the only security camera on the grounds?
I mean, it made sense, you want to see who is
swiping your packages these days, but it made
me wonder what else was on camera around here
and perhaps I needed to rethink not pulling my
drapes closed. Hmm.

In the future, please refrain from singing
after the hour of nine. In fact, if you
could curb the need to sing at all, that
would be much appreciated.
                              —Gratefully yours,
                                      Daire

Well, that last line was just insulting. Granted,
I was no Beyoncé, but I wasn't exactly an alley
cat sitting on a fence either. I sipped my coffee
and pondered my response, because of course
there needed to be a response. I couldn't let his
aspersions upon my singing go unchallenged.

I stood and stretched. I supposed I should be
grateful that he hadn't evicted me. I knew if I
could just meet the old coot, I could probably
win him over. I was a very good listener and I
genuinely liked people. Surely the old guy and I

could find some common ground. I just needed an introduction.

I ducked back into the house, and while eating my yogurt and granola, I found a fresh piece of paper and an envelope. I doodled on this one just like last time, but instead of cactus flowers and koi fish, I decided to go with a brilliant sunset over a purple mountain range, much like the sunset I'd seen upon my arrival. It took up the entire page, and only when I was finished and my fingers were cramping from holding my colored pencils did I realize I hadn't left much room for a note.

The only available space was the very narrow margin I'd left all around the paper, so I wrote in the allotted space, turning the page as I went.

Dear Mr. Daire *[I, too, can be cordial]*:
Please excuse my excessive celebration upon the completion of my first week at work. I was unaware of the time, clearly, but must point out that the rules state no loud "noise" after nine o'clock. I do not consider my singing to be noise but understand that this is a subjective opinion. I will refrain from any further displays of overt happiness.

Yours in silence,
Annabelle Martin

I found a fresh envelope and stuffed my note inside. Then I quickly showered and dressed. I went for a casual Saturday look, a navy blue and cream floral dress with a loosely crocheted shrug in ecru and a pair of cloth flats in dark blue. I brushed my hair into a ponytail and tied it with a cream-colored scarf, letting the ends hang down over my shoulders. I completed the look with mascara and pink lipstick. I was going for cute, because when I marched my note up to the house, I was determined to meet Mr. Daire once and for all, and I needed all the ingénue in my arsenal queued up and ready.

Locking the door behind me, I trekked the path to the big house. The sun was warm but the air was still cool. The enormous olive trees whispered overhead as a soft breeze rippled through them. I could hear the birds singing, and the smell of spring was on the air. It was impossible to feel low, given the beauty of the day.

The house looked as solemn as ever with all the drapes drawn. I debated taping my note onto the front door and running but decided that if I wanted to meet Daire, I needed to ring the bell and insist upon hand-delivering my letter.

I rang the doorbell. The double glass doors looked exactly like mine, except bigger, and were framed by the same planters with asparagus ferns and lavender. I could smell the pungent herb and remembered it was noted for being calming. I was unaccountably nervous and took a big inhale to see if it helped. A little. Maybe. That or I'd been holding my breath and my brain was suddenly getting oxygen again.

Not hearing any response, I rang the bell again. I wondered if this was going to get me in trouble with another note. Did Daire have rules about how many times a person could ring the doorbell or how long exactly a person should wait between each pressing of the button? Probably.

I debated ringing again when the door was pulled open. I was expecting Jackson or perhaps the crotchety old man himself. What I got was a pretty, middle-aged woman. She had to be Juan's wife, Lupita. She was softly rounded with big brown eyes, shoulder-length dark hair styled in a long bob, and a wide smile.

"May I help you?" she asked.

"Hi, I'm Annabelle Martin," I said.

"I know," she answered. She glanced me over from head to toe and her smile deepened. "I'm Lupita Guzman. I heard you met my husband."

"I did," I said. "He has excellent taste in classic country music."

"He said the same about you." Her eyes twinkled.

I glanced past her, trying to see into the dark house. Was Mr. Daire standing behind her? Could he see me? Should I call out a greeting? Would she invite me in?

It was impossible to see anything. I decided to go for it. "Is Mr. Daire in? I have a note for him."

Her smile dimmed. Much like the moment I mentioned Mr. Daire to her husband, the lightness went out of the conversation. Was the guy that bad? Maybe he was a miserable boss, and the Guzmans didn't know how to break away from him.

"I can deliver the note," she said. She held out her hand, but I didn't give it to her.

"I'd rather take it to him in person."

Her eyebrows rose in surprise. Her smile made a flickering return, and she said, "I'll go see if he's available."

"Thank you."

She closed the door, and I waited on the front stoop. I felt like a door-to-door salesperson, trying to unload my thirty-two-volume set of the *Encyclopedia Britannica* in a world where everyone just wanted to ask Siri or Alexa. I mean, who hand-delivered letters anymore? How very last century this was.

I realized that I liked that about Daire's notes, even though they were sort of grumpy. The fact that he was committing thoughts, okay, directives to paper and delivering them, or having them delivered, was so delightfully old school of him, I was charmed in spite of myself.

I wandered around the front terrace. I glanced up at the windows, wondering which room

Mr. Daire was in. I tried to look friendly and nonthreatening on the chance that he glanced out the window. Had that drapery just moved? I couldn't tell. I tried to look casual and pretended to be studying the lavender. It was an effort.

In minutes, Lupita returned. She didn't look happy, but she didn't look as if she'd just been chewed out either. It was more a look of disapproval, and if I wasn't mistaken, it wasn't directed at me, which meant she was miffy with the boss man. Interesting.

"He isn't available," she said.

"For the moment or the entire day?" I asked. "Because I can come back later."

She sighed. "For the duration of your stay, I'm afraid."

My eyes went wide. "He said that?"

She nodded.

"But my lease is for six months!"

Again, she nodded.

"He's really planning to avoid me for six months," I said. "Does that even seem possible?"

"Mr. Daire can be very . . . determined," she said. I sensed she'd revised on the fly what she really wanted to say.

I met her gaze. "So can I."

A slow smile curved her lips and made her eyes sparkle. "That's what I was hoping. I think you might be just what he needs."

I wasn't sure what she meant by that, but I

handed her my response and asked, "Would you please give him this message?"

"Of course," she said. "Happy to. It'll give him something else to think about."

"Thanks," I said. I stepped back and glanced up at the large windows on the second floor. The drapes twitched back into place.

That did it. Mr. Daire could try to avoid me for the entirety of my stay, but I was going to meet him one way or another. I waved to Mrs. Guzman as I walked down the steps and set out in the direction of the guest house.

Questions. I had so many questions, it felt as if my brain were on fire. Was it just me? Or was Daire like this with everyone? I wanted to ask Miguel and Sophie, but given their insistence that I keep my distance, I didn't want them to know that Daire and I were having issues and were struggling to communicate.

Well, I was struggling. He seemed just fine with the chastising notes and such. Me, not so much. I simply had to meet him, break through his self-imposed isolation, and make him be my friend. Newly determined, I glanced over my shoulder back at the house one more time.

This time I saw a man in the window, watching me. Surprised, I stumbled to a halt. Staring at me from the second-story window was the most breathtakingly beautiful man I'd ever seen.

11

I had barely registered his high cheekbones, square jaw, full lips, arching eyebrows, and piercing gaze when the drapes snapped shut and he disappeared from view.

I wanted to ask Mrs. Guzman who he was, but she'd already gone inside and shut the door. Who was this slice of cake in man form? Was he related to Mr. Daire? A son? A grandson? Or did he work for him? An assistant? A doctor? A nurse? I had to know.

Not that I was interested in him as anything other than a curiosity, I told myself. I mean for all I knew, he could be a lawyer, and given Mr. Daire's annoyance with me, the handsome man might come knocking on my door for a little legal chitchat. Okay, that should not have thrilled me as much as it did. Maybe I needed to reconsider Sophie's advice and get back out there.

Much to my relief—read: disappointment— the handsome man did not come knocking. Instead, I spent the rest of Saturday and Sunday attempting to make my new house look more like a home on the cheap. Plants were critical and some color. The austere interior of the house needed softening, so I bought pillows and throws in vibrant ruby reds, and some vintage ceramic canisters for the kitchen counter, also in red.

One of the plants I purchased was actually a small tree, a dracaena, that I found at Berridge Nurseries, and of course, I had to buy a deep red pot to put it in. The pot was more expensive than the plant. It weighed a ton, but I moved it in front of the largest window on the back of the house. My goal was to fill the back-facing windows with plants, thus giving me privacy without having to pull my drapes.

Now, while there had been no mention in "the rules" of whether I could decorate my place or not, I wondered if anyone from the big house would notice my plant and feel the need to comment upon it. Maybe the handsome guy would deliver the next note from Mr. Daire. Not that I was hoping for that or anything. Really.

Despite my attempts to get a glimpse at the man in the window again during the next two days, there was no sign of him. He had snapped the drapes shut as soon as our gazes met, leaving me dizzy and breathless and wondering if I had imagined the whole thing. No note came from the big house in response to mine, so I gathered that was that as far as Mr. Daire was concerned.

It was all very frustrating. Compounded by the fact that I had struck out in my quest for decent wall art and still had nothing to hang on my walls. If I didn't find something that clicked within my price range soon, I would have to invest in some art supplies and do the paintings myself. A part of me was seriously jazzed by this option so I wondered if my inability to find anything suitable had to do with my own desire to do some painting. Maybe a portrait of a handsome man staring out a window at a young woman in a garden. Small wonder what inspired that. The image of the man in Daire's house flashed through my mind but I shut it down.

I was not going to become obsessed with a stranger. Really, I wasn't. On Monday, I would casually check in with my friends, Miguel and Sophie, and see if they knew who the man I'd seen at Mr. Daire's was. They probably would, and then it would be over, because a guy that good looking simply could not be single, which was a good thing, because I would never want to date a man who was that handsome. He was likely conceited or had scores of women chasing after him and who needed that? Not me.

And so it was on Monday that I arrived at work *early*. Other than when I first started working a regular job after college, this had seriously never happened to me before. I blew through the office, the second one to arrive after Nyah. She was at her desk in front and greeted me with a grin, humming a bar or two of "Danny Boy," which made me laugh.

"Thanks again for inviting me," I said. "That was a lot of fun."

"It was," she agreed. "Mark your calendar. This Friday, same bat time, same bat channel."

"I'll look for the bat signal," I joked. She grinned. Her phone rang, and she rolled her eyes and said, "And so it begins."

I strode through the meeting room and communal work area, and arrived at my office. At a glance I knew I had gotten in earlier than Miguel and Sophie and so I sat down at my desk and fired up my computer. I figured I could get a cup of coffee from the break room and read my email while I waited.

I was just settling back into my chair when Miguel appeared in my doorway.

"Good morning, Annabelle," he said. "Could you stop by my office when you get a chance?"

"Sure," I said. I resisted the urge to do a fist pump on being seen already at work nice and early. "Ten minutes okay?"

"Perfect," he said. He turned and left, and it hit me then that he hadn't smiled once while he'd been standing there. Uh-oh.

Had Mr. Daire called him about me and the singing? I'd thought my note would have cleared that up, I mean, I did promise not to sing again. Surely if Mr. Daire had an issue with me, he could have sent me another note. He seemed to really enjoy those, after all.

With less enthusiasm than I'd started, I headed to Miguel's office. I passed Soph's space on the way. The door was open but the lights were off. She was clearly not at work yet. Hmm.

I knocked on the door frame, and Miguel glanced up from where he was standing behind his desk and gave me a curt nod.

"Close the door, please," he said.

This did not make me feel any better. It had been a long time since I'd been called to the principal's office, but I remembered the clenched feeling in my belly followed swiftly by an inappropriate urge to laugh.

I turned and shut the door. I'd worn a simple navy dress with a scooped neckline, fitted waist, flared skirt, and three-quarter-length tulip sleeves. I'd accessorized with a statement necklace of interlocking silver hoops and a hammered silver cuff bracelet. My shoes were navy loafers with silver buckles. It was a simple but professional outfit, and at the moment I was grateful because it was giving me the ability to cross the room with a confidence I didn't actually possess.

"Have a seat," he said. He gestured to the chair across from his desk, and I slid onto the cushy leather, perching on the edge of the seat like a bird ready to take flight.

"What can I do for you?" I asked. It seemed like an appropriate question, given that I had no idea what was going on.

"Annabelle, I'm going to be straight with you. I received a very disturbing phone call about you," he said. He took his seat and rested his forearms on the desk in front of him.

"Disturbing?" I asked. I kept my face blank, but I could feel my heart rate increase triple time. It must have been Mr. Daire. Damn it! I really didn't want Miguel and Soph to be mad at me, and yet I had apologized for my singing so couldn't the old coot lighten up already? Sheesh.

"Annabelle, I know you haven't worked in an office setting in a long time," Miguel said. He picked up a pen and twirled it between his fingers. I realized he was uncomfortable, which actually made me feel better.

"Yeah, it's been a minute," I agreed. I wasn't sure how this related to the "Danny Boy" debacle. Maybe he thought I was out of practice fraternizing after work and that's why I'd been singing at top volume when I got home. He wasn't wrong.

He put the pen down and met my eyes. "Which is why I feel like we can talk about this and then move past it, no hard feelings, no need to make a big deal out of it, you know what I'm saying."

I felt hopeful that he was just going to reiterate the fact that I shouldn't make noise after 9 p.m. when I'd been out carousing with my coworkers. I could handle that, especially if it meant we never had to talk about it again.

"Absolutely," I said. "I agree one hundred percent."

"Great." He sighed. "I tried to tell Carson that it wasn't personal, that you were just new to being a team player and needed to get used to it."

"I'm sorry." I held up my hand. "Carson? What does Carson have to do with it?"

Miguel gave me a confused look, and I got the uneasy feeling we hadn't been talking about the same thing. I mean there was no way Carson had anything to say about my singing as he'd already left in a snit when that happened. Besides, what business was it of his?

"Carson told me that you tried to humiliate him in front of your coworkers at happy hour on Friday night," he said.

My eyes went wide in surprise. Of all the things I had expected him to say, that was not it. Still, I needed clarification. "So this is about Carson and happy hour and not something else?"

Miguel nodded then he gave me a side-eye. "Was there anything else?"

"Nope." I shook my head. "Not a thing."

"Good," Miguel said. "So about Carson—"

He began but I interrupted, "I'm not really sure what you mean that I tried to humiliate Carson. I mean, he joined us late and, frankly, was a bit rude. He drank some beer and took off."

"He seemed to think that you'd had too much to drink and it turned you mean," Miguel said.

"Mean?" I repeated. I was caught totally off guard. I had never been accused of being mean in my entire life. Hello? Pleaser, here. Even when justified, I can't manage to be mean.

Miguel continued, "He said you tried to belittle him by repeatedly and belligerently demanding that he climb up on the table and twerk for free beer."

"What?" I cried.

"Did you say that, Annabelle?"

"Yes, but—"

"So you can see how that would be inappropriate," he said. His tone became stern when he added, "You are the senior creative director, and Carson is your senior art director. You can't single him out in front of the others like that."

I blinked at him. I took a deep breath and let it out slowly. The urge to hotly defend myself was strong, but this was Miguel, my friend, and I was certain he would hear me out.

"I'm sensing Carson left out the part of the story where he asked me to table dance," I said.

Miguel shook his head. "Carson said you'd probably mention that. He said he teased you about how you and Sophie used to go out in college and that you got defensive about his comment, which was intended as a harmless joke."

"Because sharing stories about my misadventures in my youth and asking me to show some cleavage or lift up my skirt, in front of

178

people I supervise, wasn't intended to humiliate me?" I asked.

I could feel my temper beginning to heat. When Carson's plan to diminish me in front of our coworkers had failed, it was clear he had run crying to Miguel to complain about me. At the moment I wasn't sure which one of them I was more frustrated with.

"He assured me that it wasn't, and in fact, he didn't want to say anything at all but came to me because he's concerned that your inexperience working in an office setting might cause you to mishandle your supervisory responsibilities and land us in a lawsuit," Miguel said. He looked uncomfortable and it occurred to me that he didn't want to be having this talk any more than I did. "I feel it's important that I remind you that you are in this position for a probationary period of three months, at the end of which there'll be a review."

That felt like a stone-cold slap. Not gonna lie, it hurt.

"Where is Sophie?" I asked. The connecting door to her office was open, and I could see that the lights were still out.

Miguel glanced away before he answered, "She had an appointment."

I nodded. "So you decided to do this now with just the two of us."

"Is that a problem?" he asked. One of his eyebrows ticked up.

"Not at all," I said. But it was a problem. A big problem.

Up until this moment, I had considered Miguel my friend as much as Sophie was, but now it was becoming clear that the underlying tension I'd felt between them since I arrived did exist. It had something to do with me, and I was now unintentionally caught in a power struggle between husband and wife. It seemed fairly obvious that Miguel had wanted Carson to be creative director while Sophie had pushed to bring me in and Sophie had won.

I would bet my last jelly doughnut that Miguel had only let Sophie offer me the job because he thought I would say no, but instead, I had surprised us all by accepting.

"Carson was your pick for creative director, wasn't he?" I asked.

To Miguel's credit, he owned it and said, "He has more experience in an office environment than you, he's been a member of our team for five years, and he is networked locally, whereas you are a complete unknown. It's not personal, Annabelle, but Carson just brings a lot more to the table than you do."

"Those are fair points," I agreed. "But how is his rapport with the staff? Is he a strong mentor and motivator? Is he truly getting the best work out of your designers?"

Miguel blinked as if surprised I'd questioned

180

him. "It's excellent. Everyone works really well with him."

I knew I could mention the tension I'd seen between Carson and Luz, and Booker's support of my Carson takedown, but I didn't. Instead I said, "You might want to look more closely."

Miguel frowned but I didn't elaborate. I wasn't going to throw staff under the bus to make my point, and at this moment, thanks to Carson's poison, Miguel wouldn't believe me anyway.

"Listen, Annabelle, you've been here for a week. It's understandable that you want to carve out a place for yourself, but go easy," he said.

Assuming we were finished, I rose from my chair. I strode to the door and turned back to say, "I'll keep your advice in mind. Thanks."

Miguel looked a bit nonplussed. It might have been the faint sprinkling of sarcasm in my tone. Good. It was a chickenshit move to call me into his office for a lecture without Sophie's knowledge. They were both the chief creative officers of Vasquez Squared and supposed to be equal partners. I knew Soph would have something to say about Carson's behavior at the happy hour. It had been clear at our lunch that she had her own issues with him.

I closed the door behind me and strode back to my office. Other staff had arrived while I was meeting with Miguel, and I forced myself to smile and nod with a levity I didn't feel. When

I passed Carson's office, I glanced inside and met his gaze. He looked supremely satisfied with himself.

"Good meeting with the boss?" he asked. I got the feeling he'd been waiting, probably hoping to see me cry. I wondered if Miguel reminding me that I was on probation had been Carson's idea.

"The best!" I said. I refused to look even the littlest bit flustered. If Carson thought he could derail me, he had another think coming. I sent him a beaming grin. "I love a good Monday morning pep talk, don't you?"

I strolled away from his door, leaving him looking bewildered and irritated. Yay, me. Let him wonder exactly what had been said between Miguel and me. It was a small victory but it was mine. I continued on to my office, remembering exactly why office work hadn't suited me. I would have quit right then and there, but Carson had made the mistake of making it personal. I wasn't going to leave my friend in the lurch, and I sure as hell wasn't going to let him drive me out.

Unfortunately, the meeting with Miguel set the tone for the day. There was a typo found in an ad that had already been sent to the printer. It took all my powers of persuasion to get it reprinted for free. Basically, the owner of the print company managed to get me to agree to some pro bono design work by me for his company. Whatever.

So long as the final product didn't reflect poorly on my team or blow our budget.

Another client was unhappy with the color scheme they had chosen and we had to do a mad scramble to come up with new colors and get them approved so that we could stay on schedule. This took six phone calls, several spins of the Pantone color wheel, and one thump of my forehead on my desk before it was resolved.

None of this was very different from the same sort of stuff I dealt with when I had worked for myself, but here there was a heightened sense of urgency. There were more careers at stake, more money on the line, and the reputation not just of me as a designer but of the company as well.

By quitting time, I could not wait to get out of there. I didn't see Soph all day, and when I did, she seemed distracted. I wanted to talk to her about my conversation with Miguel, but I hesitated because I didn't want to behave like Carson had, tattling to the boss about a coworker's behavior. I decided to wait until tomorrow. I was just not in the mood at the end of a long Monday.

When I arrived home, I was immediately comforted by my little house with its newly acquired red accents. The pops of color eradicated the monotonous shades of black, blue-gray, and white, and gave the place a homey feel.

I opened one of the French doors that led to the

backyard to let in the evening breeze and alleviate the stuffiness. I set to work making myself a tuna salad sandwich, and switched the radio on to the local evening jazz station and tried to shake off my aggravation with the work situation. Carson West was not going to get the better of me.

I poured myself a glass of wine and took a sip before plating my sandwich. A plaintive cry sounded from the door, and I glanced over to see a little gentleman in a tuxedo peeking around the door at me. Okay, so it was actually a kitten with black-and-white fur, but his chest and chin were white and his paws were white so in my defense, he looked like a little dude in a tux. Needless to say, my heart went smoosh.

"Hello, little fella," I said. I kept my voice soft and low at a very nonthreatening decibel.

I didn't want to scare him away, so I stood still, waiting to see what he would do. He took a tentative step inside. He sniffed the air, the floor, the open door, and then glanced at me. Could the half-full can of tuna on the counter have lured him in?

I checked the edges of the can; they were smooth. I picked it up and very slowly moved it to the ground. The little guy's nose twitched. He was clearly conflicted. Should he come closer and enjoy a delicious repast of tuna, or was it a trap? I understood his dilemma.

"I completely understand your hesitation," I

said. Coltrane was playing his saxophone in the background, and I wondered if my furry dinner guest was a jazz fan.

He took a few steps inside. He paused beside the couch. Sniffed it and then very nonchalantly approached the can on the floor. His tail swished, and he gave me an assessing glance before hunkering down and devouring what was left in the can. I'm no cat expert, but he looked on the skinny side. Life on the streets could be tough.

I had planned to eat at the table by the window but I didn't want to spook him, so I ate standing up, having a one-sided conversation with the little dude. With a few licks of his chops, he commiserated with me about office life and unscrupulous coworkers, which I appreciated.

Surprisingly, when he was finished, he didn't head out the door. Instead, he strolled into the living room and stretched, looking like a yogi assuming an asana. Then he hopped up onto the couch and began to knead my brand-new red chenille throw. Huh.

"Make yourself at home," I said.

Judging by his purr, which sounded like a V8 engine, I assumed he accepted the invitation. There were a few problems with this scenario. First, I did not own a litter box so my dude was not going to be able to stay indefinitely. Second, I was quite positive that "no pets" had most definitely been listed in "the rules."

I finished my sandwich, picked up my wine, and joined him in the living room, taking the armchair adjacent to the couch so that I didn't scare him.

"You are aware that you're going to get me in trouble," I said.

He paused his kneading to blink at me.

"Yes, I know it's a very arbitrary rule," I said. "You are by no means a 'pet.' You're more like a visiting cousin or friend."

He went back to kneading. I took this as agreement.

"Is that the argument we will present for our defense?" I asked. "Because you know, and I know, that when I leave this house tomorrow morning, there is going to be a note. There's always a note."

He yawned. He hunkered deeper into his blanket and closed his eyes. A belly full of tuna will do that to you. I yawned as well. There was something very comforting about having another living being, aside from the plants, in the house.

I picked up the romantic comedy I'd been working my way through and settled in to read. I laughed a few times, cried once, and then my head began to bob and I found myself dream reading. You know, when you're still reading but also dreaming. I had to go back and read the same paragraph three times before I realized I was actually asleep and nothing made sense. I put the book aside.

My new buddy was still snoozing. I didn't have the heart to give him the boot. Instead, I shut off all the lights and left the French door open just a crack so he could leave when he wanted and not pee on my new red area rug. Then I went to bed.

Halfway through the night, I felt the bed dip by my feet and the little guy made a soft mewling sound before he curled up into the backs of my knees. Again, I didn't have the heart to oust him. It was cold at night, dropping into the forties, and it would just be cruel to make him leave. I fell back asleep.

When I awoke in the morning, he was gone. I tried not to feel used but, honestly, no good morning nuzzle? No purr? Nothing? So rude.

Much to my surprise, when I left the house for work, there was no note attached to my door. I felt a strange pang of disappointment. There was something about those finger-wagging notes that made me feel as if I hadn't completely lost my artistic edge—my rebellious streak, if you will— as I donned work clothes and headed out to my new corporate life.

While I enjoyed working with other designers and I felt that I had a lot to contribute artistically to the company, there was no question that working in an office for me was like trying to style bangs that had been cut too short. There was nothing I could do but hope that time and growth made it look less awkward.

Having slept on yesterday's meeting with Miguel, I decided to approach Sophie in her office and find out if there was something specific going on with Miguel. I wanted to know what I was dealing with in regards to his relationship with Carson, but she and Miguel were out with a client. When they returned, I was in a design meeting, which Carson had begged out of, citing a previous appointment. By the time Booker, Luz, and I had finished, Soph was gone again, and according to Nyah, there was no telling when she'd be back.

I finished my day, feeling frustrated. It didn't help that I ran into Carson at the elevators.

"Annabelle," he said.

"Carson," I returned.

The rest of the staff had already left. It was just the two of us.

"I owe you an apology," he said.

So it was snowing in hell? Because, honestly, I had not thought Carson was the sort of person capable of apologizing for anything ever.

"Oh, really?" I asked. "For what exactly?"

Was he going to own his awful behavior toward me and try to make amends? I'm not a grudge holder by nature, too exhausting, but I wasn't sure if I was on board with that. He'd caused tension between me and my friend, and I really resented it.

"I was wrong," he said. He looked contrite and then he grinned and said, "Your office is going to be mine within three months when you blow your probationary period as we both know you will. I mean, Christ, you can barely get here on time. How much longer do you think you can fool everyone into thinking you're qualified to be creative director?"

He looked smug. For the record, smug isn't a good look on a man. I mean, it's not a good look on anyone but most especially a man, okay, this man in particular when he was looking at me.

As a typical bully, he wanted to make me react. He wanted to see me pout, cry, whine, or lose my temper. Yeah, no. I knew the best way to defeat a bully was by *not* giving him the reaction he wanted, so I squelched my urge to stomp on his instep or knee him in the junk, and instead, I just tossed my hair over my shoulder and kept my face free of any emotion.

"It's weird how you're so intimidated by me," I said. I adjusted the strap of my purse on my shoulder and reached around him to press the down elevator button.

"Me? I am *not* intimidated by this," he said. He waved his hands to encompass my whole being. I was wearing a deep purple broomstick skirt with biker boots, and a long black crocheted vest over a white cotton dress shirt, which I had buttoned to my throat, with the cuffs folded back at my wrists. It was definitely one of my artsier looks.

I glanced at him. Dress shirt, shiny shoes, creased slacks, and a power tie. He was the very definition of fragile male, trying to hide behind designer labels.

"Right," I said. I was pleased that I had executed it with the correct amount of sarcasm. Like frosting on a cupcake, the ratio was important. I stepped closer to him, getting into his personal space, or leaning in as some might say, and said, "I wouldn't start planning your move to my office anytime soon if I were you."

And then because the universe loves a fighter, the elevator arrived with a ding as if to punctuate my words. As the doors slid open, I stepped inside and turned to face him, blocking his entry. "I'll send it back up."

Nick

12

"She's persistent, you have to give her that," Jackson said. He had to raise his voice to be heard over the hippo in a tutu, singing "You Got a Friend in Me" to me. It was not my birthday; there was nothing special about this date in early March in any way, shape, or form.

"Me . . ." the hippo concluded the song. It did a pirouette and then handed me a bunch of balloons and a note.

I looked at Jackson. "Tip her . . . him . . . it."

Jackson sighed and pulled a wad of cash out of his pocket. He handed the hippo a twenty and it blew kisses at us as it jogged down the steps toward its brightly colored van.

"You were wonderful!" Lupita cried, laughing and clapping.

I handed her the balloons. There was no way I could navigate my wheelchair and the balloons and get back into the house. Plus, I was very aware that I bore a horrible resemblance to the old man in the animated movie *Up*, being in a wheelchair with helium balloons all around me, but, of course, Lexi didn't know that.

I spun around and Juan opened the door, letting

191

me through so I didn't have to hit the automatic door opener. I felt hot and itchy in my own skin. The hippo had said, "This is from Lexi," before it broke into song. At this point, as soon as the bright-colored van had shown up, I'd known it was from her. What was my little sister playing at, and why did it have my emotions rocketing all over the place? Over the past week, she'd been relentless. Every other day had brought a new message from her in some form or another.

First, she'd sent a picture of five-year-old me, holding her as a baby. I had the same picture somewhere, and it gutted me that she'd obviously kept one, too. Still, I was able to shake it off. I reminded myself that she really only wanted me in her life to help her with her project; otherwise why hadn't she shown up before?

But Lexi was playing hardball. Next there'd been a stack of comic books, particularly *Flash: The Next Generation*, which were the same comics I had read to her when I was eleven and she was six and our family was beginning to unravel. Flash had gotten us through some seriously dark days.

Frustrated by her obvious tactic to manipulate me emotionally, I had sent Jackson to tell her to cease and desist. That had been so successful, note the sarcasm, it was followed up by a cake delivery the very next day. It wasn't just any cake.

"What sort of cake is this?" Lupita asked with a frown.

She lifted it out of the box, and I felt my throat get tight. I'd seen this cake before, hell, I'd made this cake before. The recipe is quite simple. Have two junkie parents who forget it's their seven-year-old daughter's birthday. Take one twelve-year-old big brother, who loves his sister enough to risk being arrested for shoplifting for her. Have him pocket all the candy bars he can fit into his backpack along with a can of Betty Crocker chocolate frosting from the grocery store, and run like hell when the clerk spots him.

At home, find a marginally clean pan in a round shape and chop up all the candy bars, mashing them into the pan until they form a solid block in the shape of a cake. Frost the round block of candy with the stolen frosting. While the parents are out trolling for drugs, present the cake to the little sister and sing her "Happy Birthday." Have her look at you like you are the single greatest person who ever lived, and for one brief shining moment your life isn't a complete shitstorm.

"What's in that?" Jackson asked. "It looks lethal."

"And a bit lopsided," Juan said.

"Get out," I said.

The three of them snapped their heads in my direction. I couldn't blame them. The voice that came out of me sounded like the growl of a wounded animal, and in that moment I was. I was just a giant sucking wound, festering in the gangrene of my own pain. I couldn't bear to have anyone look at me.

"I said *get out*," I repeated. This time it was through gritted teeth.

Through the haze of anguish melting my insides, I saw Lupita reach for me. Juan caught her hand in his and shook his head. Thank god. If she had shown me any comfort, I would have broken down completely and assumed a fetal position on the floor. Jackson opened his mouth and then snapped it shut.

They left me, in my wheelchair, in the kitchen contemplating the ugliest cake I'd ever seen. It broke my fucking heart, and before I could push it down or hold it in, a sob tore through me, and I sat in that goddamn wheelchair and cried like I hadn't cried since the day Lexi moved three thousand miles away to start a new life.

Today, I refused to cry. Instead, I wheeled my chair into the living room. No one came to check on me, sensing, rightly, that I needed to be alone. I contemplated the note in my lap. In my sister's distinctive script—I'd gotten to know it quite well over the past few days—she'd written *Nicky*.

I expected a note inside. There wasn't one. Just a picture of me in my dad's cowboy hat and boots and Lexi in a Buzz Lightyear costume I'd made out of a box, Magic Markers, and some empty soda bottles. On the back, in Lexi's handwriting, in fresh ink, it read, *You've Got a Friend in Me.* On the bottom in faded ink in different hand-writing it read, *Halloween 1996.* It took me a second to realize the handwriting was mine.

Jackson was right. She wasn't going to go away, but I couldn't let her into my life like this. We'd been apart for twenty years. She clearly still saw me as her big brother, the one who could make everything all right, which was exactly why she was looking for my help with her housing project. I couldn't do it. I couldn't be less in her eyes now than I was then. It would kill me. But unless I took out a restraining order, she wasn't going to stop. There had to be a better solution. There just had to be.

My neurologist answered on the third ring. "Nick, how are you?"

"Not good," I said. It had taken me all of Thursday morning to work up the *cojones* to call him. "I need you to run more tests."

"Why don't you come in and we'll talk," he said.

Dr. Garth Henry was quite possibly the most patient person I'd ever met in my life. Ironically, his overabundance of patience seemed to fray the last little bits of mine.

"What is there to talk about?" I asked. "There's

195

still something wrong with me. You need to do some tests and tell me what it is. Then you can fix it."

"Eleven o'clock on Monday then?" he asked.

"Sure, or now," I said. Jackson and I were out, making a Dutch Bros coffee run. I had given up caffeine but every now and then I just needed a small hot Cocomo with whip.

There was a sigh on the other end. "Hang on." I waited while he checked his schedule. "You are in luck. I had a cancellation for an appointment this afternoon. I can see you at three."

"I'll be there."

Later that day, Jackson drove me to the office where we had logged a lot of time in over the past few months. I didn't have my wheelchair with me. It made me edgy. Jackson must have sensed it because he matched his stride to mine, walking on the side with my bum leg. I appreciated his silent understanding more than I could say.

Patty, the receptionist, smiled and waved us forward. She leaned over the sign-in desk and whispered, "Dr. Henry said for you to go right on back to his office."

We thanked her, and Jackson and I made our way through the waiting room and down the hall into the large plush office that was Dr. Henry's inner sanctum.

"Nick, Jackson," he greeted us. His thick silver hair was combed in its usual precise side part. He gestured to the chairs in front of his desk. "Have a seat."

We sat in the two leather chairs, and he leaned forward, resting his elbows on his desk and lacing his fingers together. "What can I do for you, Nick?"

"I can't live like this," I said. "There has to be something I can do to fix what's wrong with me."

He met my gaze directly. His eyes were kind, which I found annoying at present. I didn't want kind. I wanted a light of understanding to go off and then I wanted a cure, a pill, an exercise regimen, something that would alleviate my body's inexplicable fits of weakness.

"Still suffering from the sudden numbness in your leg?" he asked.

I nodded.

"And the other issues, the fatigue, anxiety, and fuzzy brain?" he asked.

I clenched my teeth. I hated all these symptoms with the fire of a thousand suns. They made me feel weak, and I hated being weak. "Yes."

"You know those are all typical conditions after an ischemic stroke?" he asked.

"Yes, but I thought they'd be gone after six months."

"There's no absolute timetable on these things," Dr. Henry said. He considered me for a moment before asking, "Have you noticed if there is a trigger?"

"Meaning?" I asked.

"When your leg gives out, are you overtired? Feeling stressed? Dehydrated?" he asked.

"No," I said. We'd had this conversation before and I was over it. I needed answers and I needed them now. "Listen, I have life stuff happening, and I just can't live like this anymore. I have to get to the bottom of why I'm still struggling to recover fully. It's been *nine* months." Nine months since the second-worst day of my entire life.

Dr. Henry nodded. He leaned back in his chair and said, "Have you considered the possibility that your symptoms are a sort of self-protection?"

"I don't understand," I said.

"Nick, you suffered a major trauma," Dr. Henry said. "It could be that your—"

"Are you about to tell me that the numbness in my leg, my heart racing, and my forgetfulness are all in my head?" I asked. I wanted to yell. I was not mental. This was not imaginary. And I resented that first Jackson and now Dr. Henry both seemed to think I had a sort of post-stroke PTSD happening.

"I want to refer you to a colleague of mine, a specialist," Dr. Henry said.

My eyebrows raised. "Why haven't you mentioned him before?"

"You weren't ready," he said. He opened the top drawer of his desk and took out a business card. He reached across the desk and handed it to me. "Give Dr. Franks a call and tell him I sent you."

I looked down at the card, expecting to see an alphabet soup of letters after the doctor's name. There wasn't. There was just a word in italics off to the side but it still hit me like a slap across the face. I glanced up at Dr. Henry. "A psychiatrist?"

"It's the only remaining avenue of help I can offer you," he said.

When we got home, I couldn't stomach the thought of food. I excused myself and disappeared into my room. I sulked in there for a couple of hours, contemplating what I should do. I was not going to a head doctor. No way. No how. Forget about it. There was nothing wrong with my mind. It was my body that was damaged. Dr. Henry had just run out of ideas. Clearly, I needed to get a second opinion and possibly a third. There had to be someone out there who understood why I had become a prisoner in my own body.

Alone, I pushed myself up to my feet. My leg felt fine at the moment, which was a relief but it was always shadowed by the anxiety of wondering when it would go out again, which caused me to spiral into a swamp of fear that I had to claw my way out of. It was exhausting.

Jackson and I had been working hard on my legs. I was convinced that if I could get them to be as strong as my arms, then I wouldn't have to worry about the left one randomly collapsing. I took a few steps toward the window. My leg held. I reached the wall and leaned against it, feeling relieved that if my leg did give out, I could catch myself or slide right down the wall. Undignified sure, but better than concussing myself on the furniture or the floor with an abrupt fall. It had happened before.

I thought about Lexi's appearance here a few nights ago. I wondered how long she had waited to get access to the inside of the estate. Even though Lexi had refused to come across with a description or a name, I knew who had let her onto the property. Annabelle Martin, my exasperating tenant. Even when she wasn't flagrantly breaking the rules, she was causing me grief. I was going to have to make sure she was more careful with her comings and goings.

The whole scene with Lexi could have been avoided if Annabelle had been paying attention and closed the gate after herself without letting anyone in. If Lexi had snuck in behind Annabelle, then a mugger, burglar, or rapist certainly could have.

The thought of my tenant being harmed while residing in my guest house made my blood run cold. Not because I cared about her, I assured myself. I'd never even met the woman, not really. No, it was just the thought of something bad happening on my property that upset me. It would be more grief that I had no desire to deal with.

I pushed aside the heavy drapes and peered down across the backyard. It was aglow from the blue lights in the pool and the violet in the hot tub. Both were vacant. At least my tenant had respected my request to stop using the hot tub. I glanced past the lemon and lime trees at the little house set amid the olive trees. The lights were on. Unlike me, Annabelle never closed her drapes. I hated to admit it, but it had unlocked a voyeuristic tendency in me, which, up until now, I'd been completely unaware of. I told myself I was just checking up on her every now and then to be certain she wasn't burning the place down, but that was a lie.

The pretty brunette was becoming a minor obsession. I looked for her in the morning, when she drank her coffee on the patio, and I looked for her again at night. She flitted around her kitchen as if listening to music and I frequently saw her working late at the desk in her bedroom. I told myself I was just keeping tabs on a single woman living alone in the city. I was looking out for her, really. That was another lie. The truth was she fascinated me, from the way she moved to the smile I saw on her lips when she sat in the sun. And truthfully, I enjoyed her sassy notes, and her pencil sketches showed remarkable talent.

Jackson was right. She really was a goddess. I shook my head. Man, I needed to get out more.

Knowing all this, I also knew that the right thing to do, of course, would be to close the drapes and walk away. I knew that. Just because my tenant left her curtains open, it was not an invitation for me to look in at her. Like right now, I could see her nestled in her chair in her living room, reading a book by the fire, and it looked so damned cozy and inviting that I—

I blinked. Once. Twice. I did not just see that. *Damn it!* Yes, I did. I squinted. Maybe I was wrong. I wasn't wrong. As I watched, a black-and-white feline sauntered from the patio outside, through the open French door, to hop up onto the red throw on the sofa of the guest house. My tenant looked up from her book and smiled as if greeting a friend. I had to be seeing things. Nope. As I watched, it lifted its hind leg and licked its butt.

There were no two ways about it. Despite my detailed list of rules, which clearly stated no pets, my tenant had acquired a cat. A cat!

Annabelle

13

Shockingly, things did not improve between me and Carson after the altercation at the elevator. Okay, it wasn't really an altercation, not even a tiff or a squabble, still every time I saw him that week, my shoulders ratcheted up around my ears. I hated conflict just like I hated tension, and Carson West was causing me to feel both. It was also why I'd been stalling talking to Sophie about Miguel's relationship with Carson. I loathed feeling uncomfortable and did not want to make anyone else feel that way either. The whole situation was exhausting, and I was so far out of my league in dealing with this sort of nonsense that I just wanted to curl up in a ball on my couch and down an entire bottle of wine.

Instead, at the end of each day, I walked home, enjoying the crisp evening air and the knowledge that I had an entire evening ahead of me that was mine all mine and I wasn't about to let Carson West take that away from me. As I walked home on Thursday night, I debated the possibilities. An online yoga class? Or I could sprawl in the chair by the fireplace and read a mystery or maybe another rom-com. I supposed I should be more productive and go to the art supply store and buy some paint and canvases. I wanted to do all these things all at the same time. Dilemma. But first dinner.

I dropped my bag as soon as I entered my house. I poured myself a glass of wine and considered the contents of my refrigerator and pantry. It looked like tonight was a fettuccine Alfredo night. This is my fallback single gal meal. All I needed to make the sauce was butter, heavy cream, a crushed garlic clove, and a cup and a half of shredded parmesan. These were ingredients that I made certain to always have on hand.

As had become my habit, I opened one of the French doors to the yard while I started cooking to allow some fresh air into the house. My fettuccine was boiling and my sauce was thickening when who should saunter in through the door as if he owned the joint? My new sleepover pal who'd been showing up every night right around suppertime. Little sir sat in the doorway, licking his chest as if making himself presentable for dinner.

"Well, come on in," I said.

I checked my pantry and grabbed my last can of tuna, realizing I was going to have to stock up on some genuine cat food if this was going to continue to be a regular thing. I turned back to find the little man at my feet. He wrapped himself around my ankle and rubbed the side of his face against my shin.

"You're going to need a name, I suppose," I said. I glanced at his tuxedo markings. He had white feet, like socks, and a white chest that came all the way up his chin and the lower half of his face, making it look like he was wearing an eye mask. "You look like quite the gentleman in your suit; how about we stick with 'Sir' for now?"

He let out a noise that was somewhere between a squeak and a meow, a squeow or a meeak, hard to say, but I took it as assent.

"Excellent," I said. "Allow me to plate your tuna, Sir."

He sat down and curled his long black tail around his body, a study in patience. While I opened the can and put half of it on a plate, I told him about my day. He blinked in sympathy. His golden eyes were ever watchful, but I was quite certain it was sympathy I saw in his gaze. When I dished my own food, I set his tuna down before him while I took a seat at the table.

It occurred to me that, without him, I would feel lonely, and I was grateful for his company. Even though he wasn't a dazzling conversationalist, he was an excellent listener, which I've always felt was a vastly underrated quality in a man.

After dinner, Sir went outside, returning a while later and making himself at home on the red throw. I didn't mind. I made a cup of tea with honey and fired up my laptop to watch a cozy British mystery. I made it through one and a half episodes before I started to doze.

Per usual, when I shut up my house for the night, I left the door ajar so that Sir could come and go as he pleased. He wasn't a pet, after all, just a dinner guest. Not surprisingly, he climbed into bed with me, and I fell asleep to the soothing sound of his purr. It seemed Sir and I had developed a lovely routine. Needless to say, I'd forgotten his presence might be unwelcome by the landlord, and it was a bit of a surprise to wake up to a note taped to my door on Friday morning.

Sir had left sometime in the wee hours of the morning. As I went to close the French door, I discovered the note taped to it instead of the front door. Huh.

I grabbed the envelope and glanced up at the big house. I stared at the curtained window where I had seen the hot guy several days ago. No, I hadn't forgotten about him. Nothing moved, nothing twitched; in fact, there were no signs of life at all. I closed my door and latched it.

I took the letter to the kitchen, where my coffee was waiting. I put it on the counter and while I sipped from my mug, I pondered the business-size envelope as if it were an incendiary device I needed to deactivate.

Finally, I put down my coffee and snatched up the note. I tore it open and a single sheet plopped onto the counter. I lifted it by a corner and shook it open.

> Dear Ms. Martin:
> At precisely seven thirty-three last evening a black-and-white feline was seen entering the guest house which you rent from me. *[Like I needed the reminder.]* Per the list of rules you agreed to when you moved in, you'll note that—on page two, paragraph four, line seven—pets of any kind are expressly forbidden. Your attention to correcting this matter is greatly appreciated.
> —Daire
> P.S. What is the cat's name?

The postscript surprised a laugh out of me. He was demanding I ditch the pet while fully acknowledging that I had likely named it. All of a sudden, I felt as if my landlord saw me with a clarity few people possessed. My determination to meet him multiplied to the tenth power. And if the hot guy was around, well, meeting him was collateral damage I could live with.

Instead of scribbling a return note to my dear landlord, explaining that Sir was not a pet but a guest, which would likely not appease his ire, I decided it was time to level up. If I wanted to actually meet my landlord, it was clear I was going to have to do something drastic. I was going to have to break *all* the rules.

Naturally, I did not include Sophie and Miguel in my plan, because I suspected they would not approve. Instead, I tapped my coworkers and convinced them that rather than going out for happy hour, they should come to my house. The added bonus of this was, of course, no Carson because it was by invitation only.

I cut out of work on my lunch hour and did a food and beverage run. Once the house was stocked, I did a quick cleanup. Then I grabbed the list of Mr. Daire's rules. I wanted a refresher so that I could hit as many as possible this evening.

It did occur to me that I was flirting with the distinct possibility of eviction, but I kept hearing Mrs. Guzman's voice in my head—*"It'll give him something else to think about"*—and I had to believe that there was a message there. The fact that he thought I would live here for six months and we'd never meet was crazy. Wait, maybe *he* was crazy.

Well, there was only one way to find out. I did a visual sweep of my house before I hurried back to work. Tonight, one way or another, I was going to meet Mr. Daire.

I arrived home from work and fired up the party playlist on my Bluetooth speaker. I had told the others that I had a pool–hot tub combo and recommended that they bring bathing suits, so they'd all gone home first. Yes, I was living quite dangerously.

Musically, I was going for a suave cocktail vibe and chose the bossa nova classic "Summer Samba." I put out appetizers and set up the bar. I was just filling the ice bucket when there was a knock on the door. I checked my cocktail party ensemble—black Capri pants with flats, and a polka dot top with a red silk scarf holding my hair back—before I answered the door.

"Hello," I cried as I opened the door. "Come on in."

It was Nyah, Booker, and Luz. Looking past them I could see Christian, Trent, and Shanna getting out of the second car in my driveway. I'd left the gate open when I got home so they could enter at will. I'd told them whoever arrived last needed to shut it behind them and I hoped they did, but if not, so what? It would be one more thing that Mr. Daire would have to complain about, but as I recalled, leaving the gate open had not been included in the rules. A shocking oversight, no doubt.

"Your place is so cute!" Nyah bounced into the house and made right for the bar. She glanced at the alcohol and mixer stash, cocked her head to listen to the music, and said, "Whiskey sours, who's in?"

"Step aside," Trent ordered. "You're too young

to know how to make a proper whiskey sour. I've got this."

Nyah raised her hands in the air and stepped back. Booker grabbed one of her hands and began to dance with her. She looked delighted and I smiled. I crossed the room and opened both of the French doors, letting our music and laughter and chatter drift out into the night. I watched the windows across the way, but there wasn't so much as a twitch of a curtain. Hmm.

We ate, we laughed, we gossiped about a few of our higher-maintenance clients. I considered asking about Carson, but I knew this would be crossing a line. He'd been there for years while I was the new girl. I was relieved that no one here seemed to begrudge me the position of creative director. Now that I knew Miguel had been hoping to give it to Carson, I wondered if any of the staff had felt the same way but no one seemed to be upset. Then again, free food and booze could buy some loyalty. Right?

We were on our third drink when Shanna stood and announced, "It's hot tub time. Who's in?"

I felt my pulse throb. I'd been checking on the big house occasionally and had yet to see any signs of life. Was it possible that I'd picked the one night to have a shindig when Mr. Daire wasn't home? *Well, hell.*

We all took turns changing into our swimsuits, except for Trent, who declared he was not hot tub material but would act as lifeguard instead. Darkness had fallen as we left my house and crossed the yard to the raised tub. It was glowing purple and emitting steam. I barely had enough towels for everyone but again, no one seemed to care.

Christian had grabbed the wireless speaker so the tunes cranked while we all sank into the glorious heat. A sing-along broke out with Lizzo's "Good as Hell," and I was enjoying myself so much, I forgot about the purpose of the evening, to draw my landlord out of his lair.

All too soon, at half past ten, Trent announced that he had to get home to the wife or risk sleeping on the couch for the weekend. The others agreed that they had to go, too. Everyone had plans for the weekend and it was time to head out.

We left the hot tub, grabbing our plastic cups as we went. I pulled on my robe, letting everyone else change first. I stood on my front patio shivering as I waved good-bye. When their cars disappeared from sight, I turned and went back into my house. It felt empty and quiet in the aftermath of the party.

I glanced at the open French doors and saw Sir. He was sitting right in the middle of the doorway, licking his chest like he always did before he entered. The boy had manners, and he didn't seem put off by the fact that I'd had a party; at least, there was no reproving look on his face.

"I suppose you're hungry?" I asked.

He stopped licking, blinked at me, and strolled inside.

I'd bought canned cat food at the store earlier. While it wasn't a huge monetary investment, it was acknowledgment that I'd become attached. I wasn't sure how I was going to convince Mr. Daire to let him keep visiting, but the truth was, I might actually move if Daire said I had to give Sir the boot.

I opened the can and dumped the contents into a bowl. It smelled fishy. I put it on the floor and then filled a bowl full of water and put that down, too. Sir did not hesitate but began to eat with gusto.

While he satisfied his hunger, I cleaned the house to a peppy Katy Perry song. There wasn't much to clean since the food and booze had been decimated. I filled the garbage, loaded the dishwasher, and saved the rest of the chores for tomorrow.

On my way to bed, I glanced up at the big house. There was no sign of life. I tried not to be disappointed that my preemptive strike had failed.

I spent the next morning wiping down my counters and floors. I was so into my chores that when there was a knock on the front door, I jumped. Could it be Mr. Daire? I glanced down. I was still in my pajamas, and I had twisted my hair up into a ball on the top of my head. This was not the look I wanted when I met my curmudgeon of a landlord.

I pulled my hair band out and fluffed my sleep-flattened hair. Realizing I had no time to change, I tightened the belt on my robe. I hurried to the door and yanked it open. I wasn't sure what I had expected. An old man with a walker? The hot guy? Jackson? It was neither of those. Instead, it was the Guzmans.

"Sorry to bother you," Mr. Guzman said. He looked pained as if being here made him extremely uncomfortable.

"It's all right," I said. "I was just cleaning."

Mrs. Guzman beamed in approval. "Excellent. I told you she was responsible."

Mr. Guzman rolled his eyes. I got the feeling I had been the topic of a disagreement for them, and I felt bad about that. I glanced at their hands. They weren't holding a letter.

"No note?" I asked, just to confirm.

"No." Mrs. Guzman shook her head. "You're wanted at the house."

"Oh," I said. She and I exchanged a look of understanding.

"Also, I brought you some muffins." She held out a small basket.

"Thank you," I said. "Very thoughtful of you. Won't you come in?"

Mrs. Guzman stepped forward but her husband shook his head.

"You're wanted at the house *immediately,*" he said.

I grinned. "Of course, but I have to change."

They followed me inside. Mrs. Guzman suggested a nice dress while Mr. Guzman raised his hands in the air as if perplexed by us both. I had been summoned. Clearly, to him, an outfit was not as important as answering the summons in a timely fashion.

I was very quick, leaving Sir, who was still on the bed, to the comforts of the house while I was gone. The walk to the main house was brisk with Mr. Guzman, striding forward as if we were late for an appointment, which I suppose we were, given that I should have met my landlord when I moved in. In my opinion, we were weeks late for this meeting but that was me.

We cut across the backyard, walked around the pool and the hot tub, which still had puddles of water surrounding it from my guests. Following the walkway through the line of citrus trees to the wide veranda, we climbed the steps and entered the house through the back door.

I was overcome with curiosity. I desperately wanted to see how Mr. Daire lived. Was his house all dipped in gold on the inside with ostentatious displays of great wealth? I wasn't so naïve that I didn't know that his house, located in the premier

Biltmore area, was worth several million dollars, and by several, I do mean double-digit millions.

There are no words to express my disappointment when I entered what appeared to be a great room and found nothing but a utilitarian gray leather couch with matching armchairs, a bland coffee table, and an enormous television. That was it.

There was no art on the walls. No art of any kind, in fact. I'd have been thrilled to see a statue, a sculpture, a drawing done in crayon by a precocious child. Truly, anything. Instead, it was as barren as a tomb that had been looted.

Mr. Guzman led me through several more rooms. All were equally plain. Black, gray, and white were the only colors, and there was nothing that signified that anyone actually lived here. No clutter, no abandoned shoes, nothing. We went down a long narrow hallway. I could hear metal clanging, and I had the sudden irrational fear that Mr. Daire was waiting for me holding a broadsword with which he planned to lop off my head. Perhaps I'd had one too many whiskey sours last night.

Mr. Guzman blew out a breath and said, "Wait here." Then he disappeared inside the room.

I stared at the frosted glass door, wondering what was happening on the other side. I could hear men's voices but couldn't make out what was being said. Maddening.

Mrs. Guzman reached over and squeezed my shoulder. "Don't let him intimidate you. He needs someone to push back at him for once."

I turned my head to look at her. What did that mean? I was about to ask when Mr. Guzman reappeared, held the door open, and gestured for me to go in. *By myself?*

I hadn't been nervous before but now I was. This was my moment of reckoning. Suddenly, my desire to meet the reclusive Mr. Daire seemed like the dumbest idea I had ever had in this life and I've had a fair few. This was like Dorothy going to meet the Wizard, except I didn't have a squad with me. Damn it.

"Go ahead. They're waiting," Mr. Guzman said. He made a shooing gesture with his hands.

I stiffened my spine. The rules Mr. Daire had requested were ridiculous. I had a legitimate case to make for being allowed to use the facilities on the property, to have a pet, and to sing if I felt so moved. I was a human being, not a robot, and I deserved to be treated like one.

I strode into the room with my back straight and my head held high. It took me a moment to realize I had entered a gym. It was full of weights and equipment and had the distinctive locker room smell of disinfectant with an underlying odor, not entirely unpleasant, of sweat. Huh. I had been expecting a study or a library, okay, or possibly a dungeon with a torture chamber.

The clang of metal on metal brought my attention around. Supine on a bench press, with Jackson spotting him, was the hot guy from the window. My gaze swept the room, looking for an old retired guy, a Tony Soprano type, who clearly felt the need to have muscle-bound bodyguards at his beck and call. I had the panicked thought that maybe Mr. Daire was in the mob. There was no one else in the room, just Jackson, hot guy, and me.

This was bad. Were they going to break my fingers or something? What sort of torture was trending these days? Maybe I shouldn't be watching crime dramas before bed. While I stood there plotting my escape—could I make it to the door?—the hot guy used the barbell he had just dropped into the rack above him, to pull himself up into a seated position. Beneath his gray sweat-soaked tank top, his every muscle was defined. Wow. I had to forcibly drag my gaze from his chest to his movie star–worthy face, where my brain sputtered like a candlewick in a strong breeze.

"Hello, Tenant," he said. His voice was a gruff growl that scraped deliciously along my spine.

Wait . . . what?

"Tenant?" I repeated like a half-wit.

One perfectly arched eyebrow rose while he waited for me to figure it out.

"Oh my god, *you're* Mr. Daire?"

14

"You expected someone else?" he asked.

Jackson smiled at me in acknowledgment and handed Mr. Daire a towel. I watched as he wiped the sweat from his brow. I resisted the urge to fan myself as I processed the fact that hot guy was my landlord. *My landlord!*

"Uh . . . um . . . no," I said. "I mean, sure, Miguel said you were retired, which using any sort of deductive reasoning would make a person assume that you were of a certain age . . ."

My voice trailed off. I was babbling. Mr. Daire was the hot guy in the window. I had not seen this plot twist coming. And now I had to defend my egregious disregard of the rules to the hot guy who rendered me mute instead of the old duff I had expected to charm silly. *Why you gotta do me this way, universe? Why?*

"You thought I was a half-dead fossil," he said.

He and Jackson exchanged a look and laughed. I was okay with the fact that they were laughing at me. I would, too, if there was anything about this that was even remotely funny. Jackson's eyes were kind when they met mine, and it was obvious that he wasn't the hard-ass that Mr. Daire was.

"In my defense, you do have a lot of rules that resemble 'get off my lawn' for a guy your age," I said.

"I like order." He picked up a water bottle and took a long drink. I tried not to stare at his throat.

"I think you mean you like control," I corrected him. Did I really just say that? Out loud?

Jackson looked at me with raised eyebrows as if he thought I had a death wish. For the record, I do not.

Mr. Daire rubbed his square jaw with the back of his very large hand. I swallowed, fully expecting him to have his minion cart me out and toss me to the curb.

"Can you give us a minute, Jackson?" he said.

Jackson glanced between us. He didn't look comfortable with this request, and I wondered what made him pause. Surely Mr. Daire wasn't a violent man. Nor did I think that I came across as the type of woman who would pull out a gun and shoot her landlord, even if he was a huge pain in the ass. An incredibly hot pain in the ass, but a pain in the ass all the same.

I meant to look at Jackson and give him my grade A ingénue smile. Instead, I couldn't manage to look away from Mr. Daire's arms. I studied his biceps and realized two things. One, it would take more than both hands for me to fully encompass those muscles, and two, I really wanted to try. I felt Jackson staring at me and I glanced up.

"I'm harmless, I promise," I said with a show of teeth.

Jackson grunted. He stepped close to me and said, in a voice even lower than Mr. Daire's, "I'm going to the kitchen, but I'll be right back."

When the door shut softly behind him, I turned to my landlord and said, "Bodyguard or trainer or both?"

"What makes you think I need a bodyguard?" he asked. He sounded offended. Interesting.

"Given the charm with which you infuse your writings—they're positively swoonworthy, really—I'm shocked—shocked, I say—that women aren't lining up outside the gate to be with you."

To my delight, he barked out a surprised laugh that made me grin in return.

"You're fearless, aren't you, Annabelle Martin?"

I ignored the way my name sounded coming from his lips. It would only cloud my already hot guy–impaired thinking. I did note the goose bumps that rose up on my skin, in the most delicious way, however.

"Not fearless," I said. "A tad impulsive and a smidgeon reckless, maybe."

"Why?"

"Why am I impulsive and reckless?" I asked.

He nodded.

"Because life is short," I said. I slipped my right thumb under my opposite sleeve and ran my thumb over my tattoo just like I always did when I thought of my mom. It used to be a nervous habit, but now it was a comfort. I felt Mr. Daire watching me and I dropped my hand.

"What is it?" he asked.

"Excuse me?"

"Your tattoo," he said. "The one on your wrist. What is it of—if you don't mind telling me?"

How had he seen it? I was certain my sleeve kept it covered. Not that I particularly cared who saw it, but . . .

"The very first day you sat on your patio, reading my rules, your sleeve fell back and I saw it," he said. "Jackson and I couldn't make it out."

"So you were both watching me?" I asked. I tried to sound indignant but I couldn't sell it. If I'd had a tenant, a stranger, moving in, I'd watch them, too.

"We were just curious about you," he said.

"Uh-huh." I pursed my lips as if considering, which was silly, because of course I was going to show him. I loved this tattoo and shared it with whoever asked. After I waited the appropriate beat to show due consideration, I walked over to where he sat and held my left wrist out to him.

My sleeve immediately slipped down, covering it. I went to push it up but he beat me to it. He brushed aside my fingers, pushed up my sleeve, and gently cradled my wrist in his large callused hand. He ran his index finger over the simple line drawing. It felt as if the tip of his finger was leaving a line of fire in its wake. I could smell his sweat-dampened hair and feel the heat pouring off his body. He smelled faintly of sandalwood with an underlying note of vanilla. It made me want to take a bite out of him. I resisted.

"It's beautiful," he said. "Did you design it?"

"Yeah," I said. My throat was hoarse, so I cleared it and focused on where he was touching me. This was a bad plan as I was finding it hard to breathe. I focused on the floor. "The big loop represents the mom and the smaller one inside of it is the child. I jazzed it up with some swirls and dots. My mom and I each got this tattoo when I turned eighteen so we'd match."

He glanced at me with a quick smile. "Is she as free spirited as you?"

"She was," I said. My gaze met his. This was the part I always hated. Telling someone my mother had passed away. People seldom handled it well. They either felt compelled to tell me about someone they lost to cancer, so more sadness to carry, or they told me how lucky she was to be in a better place. Lucky? They did *not* know my mom. Her idea of heaven was being with her family. There was nothing lucky about losing her so young for any of us. Period. "She died from cancer eight years ago."

"That sucks." His gaze held mine and I could see deep understanding in his long-lashed eyes. This was a man who knew loss.

I was about to open my mouth to agree when he glanced back down at my tattoo. He ran his thumb over it in a soothing gesture, lingering where my pulse beat. There was nothing sexual in the gesture. It was a dry, light touch, clearly meant to comfort and soothe, as if I were a child on the playground who needed a boo-boo tended, but it positively unraveled me. My insides dissolved into a hot puddle of *holy shit* with a dash of *what the hell is this?*

He let go of my hand, and it took every bit of self-discipline I'd accumulated in life up to this moment in time not to shove my wrist back at him and say, "Do it again." Instead, I decided that breathing required a few more feet of distance between us. I casually walked, at least I hoped it didn't look like I was running, a few paces away.

"You said life is short," he reminded me. "Doesn't being reckless make it shorter?"

I shrugged, pleased to note I was getting my equilibrium back. "There's a difference between calculated risks and stupidity."

"All right, I'll play," he said. "Would you say hosting a party, jumping into my hot tub, and making noise well past nine o'clock was a calculated risk or stupidity?"

"Calculated risk," I replied. "One hundred per-cent."

"How do you figure?" he asked. He looked mystified.

"Because I wanted to meet you. And I knew you wouldn't be able to let such a blatant disregard for the rules go unchallenged, and now here I am, talking to you."

He looked surprised and, if I wasn't mistaken, a little impressed. "So you are brave then."

I shrugged. I wasn't, not really, but he didn't need to know that. He took another long drink from the water bottle and wiped the sweat off his arms with a towel.

Don't stare, Annabelle, don't stare. I began to stroll around the room. There was an impressive array of equipment here. Racks of weights, all sorts of machines. Maybe my visions of a torture chamber hadn't been that far off. I was a yoga girl myself. I liked the corpse pose, Savasana, best. I always caught a good power nap there.

"You are aware that I could evict you for last night?" he asked.

"You could," I said. I kept my voice mild, never mind that my heart was pounding in my chest triple time. I decided to double down. "But you won't."

One perfect eyebrow shot high. He tipped his head as if he couldn't quite believe what he'd just heard; well, that made two of us. It must be the aftereffects of the alcohol from last night. Definitely, no more whiskey sours ever again.

"I won't?" he asked.

"Nope." I shook my head.

"And why's that?" he asked.

I paused and ran my hand over the rack of dumbbells. I wondered if I should just make room for myself among them as I'd clearly found my people. What was I even thinking in provoking Mr. Daire like this?

I turned around and flashed my most charming smile at him and said, "Because then you'll never learn the cat's name."

He laughed a big hearty chuckle that about took me out at the knees. Then he grinned at me, and it stopped my heart right in mid-pump. It just stopped. I felt instantly dizzy and overly warm. I wasn't positive but I thought I heard birds singing and the smell of freshly baked apple pie. I knew I should look away, but I had a feeling I'd only be able to see spots because looking at him was like staring at the sun.

"Which is another thing we have to discuss, Annabelle."

Oh my, I did like the sound of my name coming out of his mouth. I forced myself to focus on the conversation and not grin at him like a simpleton.

"How so, Nick?" I asked. Yep, I was going for it. If we were on a first-name basis, so be it. True confession, I liked saying his name almost as much as I liked hearing him say mine. By the way his eyes flashed at me, he either really liked it, too, or he was offended all the way to his core.

"No pets," he said. He looked quite serious now, and I knew the stakes for winning him over had never been higher. But he hadn't corrected my use of his name. So that was a win.

"Sir is not a pet," I said.

He blinked at me. "Sir?"

"That's his name." I smiled. "Because he looks like a little gentleman wearing a tux."

Nick heaved a deep sigh. "I knew you named him and that makes him a pet."

I shook my head. "No, that just gives him an identity. It'd be rude to call him 'cat,' you know, like 'landlord' or 'tenant.' "

I saw his lips twitch and took it as a solid point scored.

"Do you feed him?" he asked.

"Occasionally." Truly, it had been every night this week, but I felt this was extraneous information.

"Does he sleep in your house?"

"He's a cat," I said.

"Your point?" Again, one of his eyebrows rose higher than the other. That should not be such a hot look on a man, and yet it totally was.

I turned away, checking out a huge freestanding apparatus. It had all sorts of cables and weights. I glanced at him over my shoulder and said, "Cats sleep everywhere."

"Making that a yes, he sleeps in your house," he said. He was about to press his point but I interrupted.

"But he comes and goes as he pleases," I said. "Meaning he's more of a guest than a pet."

"Because you leave your door open at night." He said this with a look of incredulity as if even he couldn't believe what he was saying.

"Just a crack," I said. I held my hands up so they were about four inches apart.

He shook his head. "Annabelle, we're in the middle of a city of one and a half million people. You can't sleep with your door open. It's dangerous."

"We have walls and a gate," I argued. "Who is going to scale that?"

"Never mind scale it, they could slip in behind you when you're coming home, which someone did the other night," he said. "Which is another thing I wanted to talk to you about."

I felt the blood drain out of my face. "Someone slipped in behind me? Did they break in? Was there a robbery? Is everyone okay? Why didn't you tell me?" I asked. "You didn't even leave a note!"

He looked away, giving me my first glance of his profile. Even from that angle, he was ridiculously handsome with a straight nose, stubborn chin, and soft light brown curls that tumbled over his forehead in waves.

"It doesn't matter. It was taken care of," he said.

"How?" I asked.

He looked back at me with a frown. "What do you mean?"

"How was it taken care of? Did you chop them up into little bits and use them as fertilizer?"

He blinked. "That's dark."

"Sorry, I've been watching a lot of crime shows," I said.

"And yet you don't lock your door at night." He clapped a hand to his forehead.

I laughed. I couldn't help it. His overly dramatic look made me smile. When he met my gaze, he smiled in return.

"Because Sir isn't a pet, I don't have a litter box," I said. "I have to leave the door open for him so he can go about his business and not mess up the house."

"You're not going to shut your door, are you?" he asked.

I shook my head.

"You could leave a window open," he suggested. Then he made a confused face as if he couldn't believe he'd just said such a thing.

"They all have screens," I said.

He was quiet, watching me while I moved around the room. There was a heat in his gaze, and I saw him study my face as well as my body. His look was appreciative, as if he was fully aware of me without being impolite, and it made my insides hum in response.

"All right." He drew the word out with obvious reluctance. "We'll have to come to some sort of arrangement."

"Yes!" I jumped, almost as high as Soph would have, and clapped. I stepped forward to—I don't know, go hug him?—but my skirt got caught on the rack of weights. It yanked me backward and I fell against the shelf. Hard. I hit it just right, in the center of my back, enough to knock the wind out of me, and I landed on the shelves in a heap, which sent the entire structure crashing to the ground with me.

"Annabelle!"

I was fighting so hard to regain my balance and avoid getting crushed by the free weights, I barely registered my name being called. One massive arm swept into the rolling avalanche of dumbbells and plucked me out. My head was covered by a thickly muscled arm and there was a horrific tearing sound as the fabric of my skirt gave way. I clenched my eyes shut, preparing for impact, and instead found myself rolled across the floor, landing in a heap on a mat with Nick Daire on top of me, protecting my body with his.

When the horrific sounds of weights smashing

into the floor stopped, I slowly opened my eyes. And there he was. His face hovered over mine. A frown marred his forehead, but it was the first time I could really see his eyes. They were a pretty hazel, velvet brown surrounded by leaf green, and they made me think of a dewy morning hike in the thick of a forest.

"Are you all right?" he asked. He braced himself up on one elbow while he stared down at me, running his free hand over my body in a perfunctory way that was obviously looking for damage but was still devastatingly sexy.

I sucked in a breath. "Yeah, I'm okay." I flopped against the mat and gestured at the weights. "I'm so sorry about that."

"Don't worry about it." His gaze met and held mine. Our faces were only inches apart, our bodies pressed length to length. We were both breathing heavily. The urge to wrap my arms around his neck and pull him close and kiss him was so strong that I could feel the itch in my fingers just like when I saw something I wanted to paint.

Nick reached up and brushed back the hank of hair that had fallen over my right eye. His touch was gentle despite the obvious strength of his hands. I shivered. A smile ticked up one corner of his mouth as if he was registering my response and was happy about it.

"Do you always make this much of an impression?" he asked.

My throat was tight. I shrugged, which pushed my front against his sweat-soaked tank top in the most delicious way. It occurred to me that I'd be okay with lying here all day, I wasn't positive but I might have purred louder than Sir at the thought.

"All right, let's get you up and make sure you're not hurt," he said.

Noooooo. Mercifully, I only yelled this in my head.

He rolled off me and I sat up, knowing that lying on the mat and demanding that he continue to hold me would be off-putting at best and downright creepy at worst. I glanced down at my skirt. Half of it was missing. A panel had been ripped clean off. Why this caused me to blush, I have no idea. It's not like he didn't see the whole thing. So what if my underwear was visible? I could hold my skirt closed over the gap. No big deal.

I glanced over at Nick before I rolled to my feet. He had risen to a seated position. He reached out and grabbed the torn fabric of my skirt that was pinned beneath the pile of weights. His voice was raspy when he said, "You could have been killed."

Gone was the teasing note in his voice. Instead, he sounded truly horrified by what might have happened. I wanted to ease his mind and said, "Thanks to you, I wasn't."

Nick tried to push himself up to a standing

231

position, but it was clear that his leg wasn't cooperating. I could see the sweat bead up on his forehead as he tried to get a knee under him. He looked pale and shaken in the aftermath of the crash. A vein started to throb in his neck.

"Oh no!" I cried. I dropped my skirt and crouched down beside him. "Are you hurt? Should I call someone?"

"No, I'm fine, damn it," he hissed. "Just back away."

Of course, I didn't. Instead, I wrapped an arm about him and tried to help him up. He weighed a ton. I noticed his left leg was nonresponsive. I felt a burst of panic at the thought that my carelessness had somehow caused him to break a leg or sever a nerve.

"Oh my god, you are injured," I cried. "Lie back. I'll call an ambulance."

I tried to help him back down, pushing him when he resisted.

"Annabelle, stop," he said. "Just . . . leave me be."

"But you're hurt," I protested. "I can't—"

"What the hell was that noise?" The door slammed open and there was Jackson. He looked winded as if he'd run here. He took in the scene, weights scattered and us on the floor, at a glance. "Christ, I take a minute to go to the john and all hell breaks loose."

He dashed across the room and grabbed a

wheelchair. A wheelchair? He parked it next to Nick and set the brake. I backed away and Jackson swooped in. He reached down with his giant hams for arms and lifted Nick up, setting him gently in his chair.

He leaned down and met Nick's gaze and asked, "You all right, brother?"

Nick nodded. But he wasn't. He was pale, sweaty, and breathing hard. He looked rattled, and I noticed his hand shook when he pushed the hair off his forehead. Jackson turned to me.

"You good, Annabelle?"

Like Nick, I just nodded. I was trying to process too much, and I felt as if my brain was going to short out. What was wrong with Nick? Why was he in a wheelchair? Had he always been in one? Is this why I never saw him outside? I had so many questions!

Jackson's gaze flashed to my skirt. I quickly grabbed the remaining panels and pulled them tight over the gaping hole.

"What the hell happened?" Jackson demanded.

"I fell—" I began at the same time Nick said, "It doesn't matter."

Jackson and I both glanced at him. He looked broken in body and in spirit, and I felt my heart clutch in my chest.

"How can I help you, Nick?" I asked.

"You can't." He said the words with a finality that hurt.

"But—"

"Just go, Annabelle!" he bellowed. He lowered his voice when he added, "And don't come back."

15

Without waiting for a response, Nick spun his wheelchair away from me. Dismissed. I didn't know him well enough for it to hurt me as much as it did, but it did.

Not wanting to upset him any more than he already was, I began to back toward the door. Jackson cast me a sympathetic look and said, "I'll walk you out."

"You don't have to," I insisted.

Jackson didn't acknowledge my words. He simply began walking to the door. I turned and followed, only glancing over my shoulder once at the hunched shoulders of the man in the wheelchair.

We were striding down the hall, not speaking, when I cracked. "Why is he in a wheelchair?"

Jackson shook his head. "Not my story to tell."

Bro code. I nodded. I hadn't really expected an explanation, but naturally I had to ask anyway.

"Is there anything I can do?" I asked.

Jackson stopped walking. He turned to face me. He studied me for a long moment. "Don't let him retreat."

"Meaning?"

He opened his mouth, looking like he wanted

to say more, but he shook his head. He opened his mouth again and then snapped it shut. Clearly, he was sitting on the horns of a dilemma. It would have been unkind of me not to help him out.

"I can't help him if you don't give me a clue," I said. "You don't have to break his trust just help me to understand."

Jackson nodded. "Fair enough. Nick's shut himself off from the entire world. No friends, no family, no visitors, no one gets on the estate. Until you rented the guest house, it was just the four of us—day in and day out. I guess what I'm trying to say is don't disappear because of this. Be a presence he can't ignore; that will help him."

That was it. He strode forward, leaving me to follow in his wake, as if I were a dinghy trailing a yacht. He reached the back door and held it open for me to pass through.

"See you around, Annabelle," he said. He sounded hopeful.

"Later, Jackson."

"I hope you mean that," he said.

I slipped through the open door, clutching my skirt together. There was no sign of the Guzmans, for which I was grateful. I walked across the yard, through the citrus trees, to my own patio. I had the sensation of being watched, and I desperately wanted to turn around and see if Nick was looking out the window, but then I wasn't sure I could handle it if he was.

I turned my time with him over in my mind. He was devastatingly good looking. He had charm and he was clearly successful. But something had happened to him, something had caused him to lose the use of his leg. An accident? A disease? What? I was obnoxiously curious about it.

I thought about how he'd swooped in and grabbed me when I might have been flattened by the weights coming down on me. I stopped walking.

Mentally, I put myself back in the room. I'd been standing about twenty feet away from Nick when I'd knocked down the entire rack of dumbbells. Huh. I listened to the birds chirping while I drank in the scent of the sweet citrus blooms. The truth was inescapable, and the fact of the matter was there was simply no way Nick could have reached me if he didn't have the use of his legs, but I had seen his left leg all lax and dragging like it was broken. So what exactly was wrong with my landlord? Not my business. Still, I had to know.

The back door was still ajar, and I entered, scanning the house for Sir. I had a sudden need for a hug. He was curled up on the red throw right where I'd left him. I picked him up and he must have sensed my distress because he purred and rubbed the top of his head against my chin.

I felt instantly better and hoped that in light of what had happened, Nick didn't change his mind about letting me keep my furry friend.

I didn't sleep well that night. An intense pair of hazel eyes dominated my dreams. An image of Nick driving us somewhere, a formal event with him in a tuxedo and me in a gown, and we were laughing. I was happy. And then *crash*.

I jolted awake, sweaty and panicked with my heart racing in my chest and Nick's name on my lips. I knew it was my unconscious trying to figure out what had happened to Nick Daire. Sure, I knew it wasn't my concern, but that had never stopped me from trying to help a person in need before, and I doubted it would do so now.

Of course, it's a lot easier to help a person who actually wants you to help them rather than a person who is closed off in his house. A person who refuses to acknowledge your existence even when you stand in the middle of your back patio for hours on end with your new easel and canvas, painting the black-and-white cat sprawled on the limb of a lemon tree, looking very much like the Cheshire cat from *Alice in Wonderland*, except being more formal with his tuxedo coloring.

Yes, even Sir making himself at home on the grounds of Daire's estate could not draw the man out. He didn't even send one of the Guzmans or

Jackson to deliver a note or to speak to me on his behalf. I wondered if I should turn it around and send him a note. If so, what would it say?

Every time I got the prickly feeling that someone was watching me, I was doomed for disappointment when I surreptitiously checked the windows and saw no curtain twitch. It was all in my mind. I was being one hundred percent ignored and I didn't like it, not one little bit.

Even more irksome, there was no note attached to my door when I headed out for work on Monday. I'd played music, quite loudly, after nine the night before. I let Sir come and go, leaving my door open, and I even jumped in the hot tub. And what did I hear after all of this bad behavior? Crickets.

It was maddening. I was bummed out and a tad surly when I arrived for work on Monday morning. Nyah greeted me with a big smile and a thank-you for the happy hour, as did the rest of the staff, and it occurred to me that I was beginning to consider them my friends. That helped. So what if my landlord didn't like me, my crew did.

I tried to catch Soph before the weekly meeting, but she was mobbed by other staff. I had known when I took the job that her business was all-consuming. It shouldn't have hurt that she had no time for me. I was a grown-up, after all, but still, I felt as if once she'd gotten me to take the job and move here, I'd been cut loose in a sink-or-swim sort of way. Honestly, it stung.

But now that I'd met Nick Daire, she really had some serious explaining to do. Like, what happened to him that he was in a wheelchair? And why had they let me believe he was an old coot when he was clearly the hottest man alive?

We gathered in the big meeting room for an update on all of our projects. I was still learning our client roster and what projects we had in the queue, so I was caught off guard when Miguel asked me for a status update on the Schneider account.

"I'm sorry," I said. "Who?"

"Schneider," Miguel said. "You know, as in Schneider Pretzels. They're one of our biggest clients."

I blinked. "I didn't realize they were ours." In hindsight, I probably shouldn't have admitted this out loud in front of the entire staff.

Miguel frowned. Sophie bit her lip, which was her go-to anxious gesture. I could feel the eyes of the rest of the staff on me, which were sympathetic, well, all except for one. Carson West.

"Surely, you've been in touch with them," Miguel said. "They want us to design all new packaging. It was one of the projects Carson delivered to you on your first day here. I'd hoped to see the creative brief by now."

And just like that, my plans for the day and

quite probably the night went right down the toilet. Carson. I hadn't gotten anything about the Schneider account from him, but I couldn't say that without it becoming a he said/she said situation, which had the potential of causing a very unpleasant scene.

Carson had been here for years while I'd been here mere weeks. So far, I was successfully building a strong rapport with my team, and I didn't want to jeopardize it by being perceived as a supervisor who blamed others when things went wrong, even in this case, where it was definitely Carson's fault that I hadn't been in the loop about the Schneider account.

I smacked my forehead, overly dramatic, and said, "Of course, I've been working with them. Sorry. My caffeine hasn't kicked in yet. I've got meetings all day today. Would tomorrow morning be all right for me to catch you up on the account?"

Sophie visibly relaxed while Miguel looked a tad less grumpy. "It's later than I would like, but sure, ten o'clock."

"Don't we have a conference call with Bravo Pianos at that time?" Booker asked me. I stared at him. I didn't have a meeting on my calendar for Tuesday morning. What was he up to? He glanced back at Miguel. "You'd better make it midafternoon in case our meeting runs late. Mr. Bravo can be very exacting."

If it weren't totally inappropriate in the work-place, I might have kissed Booker on the mouth. We didn't have a meeting; he was just trying to buy me more time. I nodded. "You're right. Good plan."

Miguel glanced between us. "Fine. Two then."

"Looking forward to it," I lied. The tension between Miguel and Sophie visibly eased. Crisis averted, for now.

I didn't have to look at him to know that Carson was smirking. I would bet my favorite pair of Magalli boots that he'd been waiting for just this moment. What an asshat. At least now I had a heads-up and could find out what other projects he'd neglected to mention to me.

"I'm sure Annabelle's been too busy wooing her brand-new client to think too much about pretzels," Carson said. "Isn't that right, Anna-belle?"

He turned to me. His sandy hair flopped perfectly over his forehead, and I suspected a lot of product had been employed to make it seem so effortless. Had I really thought he was handsome when I'd first met him? Now I noticed that his face was too thin, his lips had a cruel twist, and his eyes held no warmth, just cold calculation.

"I'm sorry?" I asked. I had no idea what he was talking about.

"Oh, don't be so modest," he said. "You told me the other day, when you were late getting in because of an early meeting, that you were bringing in a huge account. Don't leave us in suspense!"

Oh, shit. He was using my fake phone call against me. Judging by the delight on his face, he had figured out it was bogus and was now fully prepared to humiliate me with it.

"New account?" Soph asked. She looked so hopeful that I just couldn't do it. I couldn't pretend that I'd had a client and lost them or even more outrageously admit that the entire call had been a sham to keep Carson off my back when I was fifteen minutes late.

See? This is the thing with lies; they're like the law. You can never truly escape them. This is why I never lied and why I'd been kicking myself ever since that awkward moment at the elevator. I'd have been better served to let Carson rat me out for being late that day, but I'd panicked. Well, lesson learned. Still, I couldn't disappoint Soph. I decided I'd better find a new client and fast.

I forced my face into a big grin and said, "Well, we're still working out the details but I'll loop you in as soon as there's good news."

"Excellent," Soph said.

I don't think I imagined the triumphant look she sent Miguel. I glanced at Carson. He looked annoyed. So there was that. Mercifully, the meeting ended shortly after that.

As we exited the room, I waited for Carson to

leave and then asked Luz and Booker to follow me. They exchanged a look and then nodded. Once the three of us were inside my office, I closed the door. They took the seats across from me as I sat behind my desk. I folded my hands and considered them. I wasn't sure how to go about asking them what I needed to know, but it was clear I needed information, and from what I'd observed, they were my best access points.

"Contrary to what was said in the meeting, I never received any information about Schneider Pretzels." I paused then glanced at both of them, and they exchanged another meaningful look. "From what I've observed, I don't think either of you are surprised by this."

"Carson is trying to sabotage you," Booker said.

"He wanted to be creative director and pitched a complete hissy fit when he didn't get it," Luz added.

I nodded. "He's let his feelings be known to me. That's fine. He doesn't have to like me, but I won't stand for his sabotaging the work."

"You should tell Miguel and Sophie," Luz said.

"I would," I agreed, "but there seems to be a difference of opinion about Carson in-house. Miguel wanted him for my job but Soph convinced him, sort of, to hire me instead."

"But Carson's not qualified," Booker said. He raised his hands as if imploring the gods to help him understand why Carson would even be considered. "He's not the best graphic designer, and he has terrible management skills. Being a creative director is all about solving the client's problems, new business pitches, and bringing innovative ideas to the table. He has none of that. He just wants to quaff beers on the golf course with clients and then offload the rest of the work onto his assistant."

"So exactly what he does now but for a bigger check," Luz said. "Working for him is a nightmare."

"Why haven't you told Miguel and Sophie?" I asked.

"Because Carson said he'd get me fired if I went over his head, and he's tight enough with Miguel that I think he'll do it," Luz said.

"You could leave," I said.

"No, I love my job, I love my team, and I really believe Vasquez Squared is going places. Why should I leave because of him?"

"Fair point. All right, so that I can be prepared, in what way is he awful?" I asked. "Other than what I already know?"

"Do you remember when you were in school and you had to do group projects?" Luz asked.

I nodded.

"There was always one team member who didn't do any work, but in the end took all of the credit?" Booker added.

I cringed. "He's the slacker."

"Exactly," Booker said. "But he's even worse, because he overpromises and then underdelivers, as in delivers nothing at all, and everyone else has to scramble to make it right with the client."

"What he did to you today, he's done to me, too. I almost lost my job because of him," Luz said.

"He hasn't pulled that with me," Booker said. "But if he'd been promoted to creative director, I would have quit."

"How have Miguel and Soph not noticed this?" I asked.

"Oh, Sophie knows," Luz said. "I think that's why you're here."

"As for Miguel." Booker paused and shrugged. "His bro code runs deep, and he simply can't see his old fraternity buddy clearly."

"All right," I said. "Thanks for sharing all of that with me. I know it's uncomfortable to talk negatively about coworkers."

Luz smiled at me. "In this case, it's a relief. I was a little worried you'd get taken in by him, too. Half the staff despises him—"

"The ones he's screwed over," Booker jumped in. Luz gave him a look, and he pressed his lips together.

"And the other half adores him," Luz said. "It can be hard to know where the loyalties lie in regards to him."

"Thanks for the heads-up," I said.

She nodded and I glanced at both of them. "So do either of you have a minute to get me up to speed on the pretzel company? I have to come in fully prepared with guns blazing for tomorrow."

Thank heavens they did, and we spent the next hour brainstorming. I worked through the day, taking a break for lunch, which I spent tracking down Sophie.

I did a sweep of the office, checking with Nyah first to find out if she had any meetings. She did not. Then I checked the restaurant upstairs, the staff lounge, and the break room. No sign of her. Hmm. On a hunch, I went to the bathroom.

Vasquez Squared had four unisex bathrooms, two on each side of the building. I got lucky on the second door on which I knocked.

"Just a minute," she said.

"It's me," I called. "Open up. There's nothing I haven't seen in there."

I heard a snort and then the sound of the door unlocking.

The bathrooms had all been designed as multi-purpose lounge rooms. Seriously there was a divan and an armchair in the front room, with the facilities, sink and toilet, behind another door at the back. Soph had wanted nursing moms to have a private place to pump or nurse as she and Miguel had agreed babies were welcome in the office until they were moving on their own power. And the lounger was big enough for a person to catch a nap if they'd pulled an all-nighter, which was a frequent occurrence in the graphic arts.

I followed Soph back inside and took a seat on the armchair while she touched up her makeup in the floor-to-ceiling mirror. There was a pink suit in dry cleaner's plastic draped over a chair, so it was clear she was headed off to another event.

"We need to talk," I said.

She whirled around to face me. "You're not quitting, are you?"

"No."

Her shoulders slumped in relief.

"But you have to be straight with me about a few things," I said.

She looked wary. "All right."

"Miguel only agreed to let you offer me the position of creative director because he didn't think I'd take it, did he?" I asked.

"No, he didn't," she said. "But I need you here, Belly. You've already improved our designs so much, even Miguel admitted that you bring a fresh perspective to the studio."

"That's nice," I said. And it was. "But do you remember our lunch on my first day here. I told you I had a bad feeling about Carson, and you asked me to document any problems, particularly in regards to work?" She nodded. "Well, an email will be coming your way, but you have to know

248

he totally sabotaged me at the meeting today. He never mentioned Schneider Pretzels to me, and I checked the project management list and it wasn't put on there until after our meeting today."

"I suspected as much," she said. She looked grim. "I'll talk to Miguel and tell him what Carson did."

"But you don't think Miguel will do anything about it," I said.

Sophie dropped her head and sighed before she glanced back up. "I'm sure Carson already has an excuse locked and loaded. You know, one of the things I love most about my husband is his loyalty."

"But?"

"But because he's loyal to the core, he seems to believe everyone else is. Carson and Miguel are fraternity brothers. I don't know the specifics, but Miguel told me enough to get the gist. When they were hazing, Carson saved Miguel from getting seriously hurt. Because of that, I can't seem to break the spell Carson has got Miguel under. That's why I need you here. Together, we can document every move Carson makes, and when we have enough, we can present it to Miguel as proof positive."

"I'm not gonna lie," I said. "This is stressful."

"I'm sorry," she said. She hugged me. "I'll understand if you don't want to stay."

"Don't be stupid," I said. "Of course I'm

249

staying. Carson can't have my job. He's made it personal now."

She smiled. "That's my Belly." She turned back to the mirror to finish her makeup.

"There is one other thing I wanted to talk about," I said. "Nick Daire."

Soph was applying her mascara. Something in my tone must have alerted her to the fact that I'd met Nick Daire because she met my gaze in the mirror and then slowly turned around.

"What about him?" Her voice was guarded.

"Why did you let me think he was some shriveled-up old man?" I cried. "He's, like, crazy hot. Hotter than hot. He's scorchin' hot."

"No." Soph shook her head. "No, no, no, no. You have to stay away from him. You haven't talked to him, have you?"

I opened my mouth but she cut me off.

"Don't!" she cried. "Don't talk to him. Don't go near him. Maintain a ten-foot perimeter at all times."

I frowned. "Why?"

"Because he is everything you fall for," she said.

"Charming, funny, handsome, and smart?" I asked.

"No," she said. "Broken, damaged, needy, and hot."

"You admit he's hot?"

"I'm not blind," she retorted. "He's not for you,

Annabelle. He'll use you up and spit you out, and I desperately do not want you to get your heart broken and leave. I need you. Promise me you'll stay away from him."

"He's my landlord," I said. "We live mere yards away from each other. That's a virtual impossibility."

"Is it?" she asked. "Miguel says he nevcr leaves his house. How exactly did you happen to make his acquaintance?"

"Um . . ." I wasn't sure I wanted to lead with the rule breaking. "Timing, you know, our comings and goings lined up."

"Unalign them," she said. "Seriously, you don't want a repeat of Jeremy or the BD again, do you?"

"He doesn't strike me as being anything like Jeremy or the big disappointment," I said. I remembered the feel of his fingers on my wrist, tracing my tattoo, and my visceral reaction to his touch. Yeah, neither of my exes had ever affected me like that.

Sophie heaved a breath. She picked up her mascara and resumed her touch-up. "I can't tell you what to do, I know that, but I can tell you that Nick Daire is not someone you want to get involved with, Belly. In all the years Miguel and I have known him, he's never dated a woman for longer than a season, and now he's—"

"In a wheelchair," I said.

She lowered the wand again and met my gaze. "You know then. I'm surprised. He's kept his situation private, very private, even going so far as to retire from his business, Daire Industries."

I waited for more. There was no more. Maddening!

"What happened to him, Sophie?" I asked. She didn't answer right away. I waited.

"I don't know the details," she said. "All I know is that he had a stroke last year and afterwards he withdrew completely from everyone and everything."

"A stroke," I said. "But he's so young."

"Thirty-five," she confirmed. "Annabelle, please trust me when I tell you that steering clear of Daire is for the best."

"Sure thing," I agreed. To distract her from asking me to promise to avoid him—not gonna happen—I said, "You look really beautiful."

"Thank you," she said. "We have a . . . a client meeting and then we're having dinner with the local entrepreneur group tonight, a snoozefest but the food is always amazing."

"Eat a jumbo shrimp for me," I said. I slipped out the door while she was still chuckling.

I'd been here only a little while, but I'd already noticed that Miguel and Sophie seemed to have standing client meetings at four o'clock in the afternoon a few times per week. I mentioned that Soph was a terrible liar? Yeah, every time she said "client meeting," she got a crinkle in her nose and she tipped her head. Something was up with my friends, and it took all of my restraint not to demand to know what.

It was dark when I packed up my work to finish at home. I used an app on my phone to call for a car to come collect me and left the office, switching off the light as I went because I was the last to leave.

I locked the doors behind me, feeling weary all the way to the marrow of my bones. Thank goodness Booker had been quick on his feet and stalled Miguel. It bought me the morning and I was going to need it.

The driver let me off at the gate. I used the security pad to enter, waiting until the gate closed behind me before striding up the walk. I didn't want to let any more surprise guests inside the grounds. I still felt bad about that, and knowing that Mr. Daire—he'd gone back to being Mr. Daire after he yelled at me—was in a wheelchair only made it worse.

What if something awful had happened to him, and it was my fault for letting in the perpetrator? I thought of his muscled arms and chest and realized that it was highly unlikely that someone could get the best of him, but there was something wrong with his leg. I wished Soph could have told me more.

I arrived at my house, exhausted but knowing

I needed to work well into the night to come up with a concept that really dazzled for the Schneider account. I had the work the team had already done and it was okay, but I knew if I wanted to redeem myself, it needed some wow factor. Ugh.

Once inside, I dropped my stuff, flicked on the lights, and crossed the room to open one of the French doors. There was no sign of Sir, which made me sad and a little worried. I was late; maybe he'd given up on me and gone to forage dinner elsewhere. I tried to remind myself that he wasn't a pet, but right now he was the only source of daily affection I was receiving, and given that today had been the Mondayest Monday of all the Mondays, well, a little kitten love would not have been out of order.

I cleared off the dining table and set up my laptop and preliminary sketches as I was going to need to spread out a bit. I knew I was going to be working until my eyes crossed, but that was fine. I'd had plenty of jobs just like this one in Boston. The difference, of course, was that when I was working for myself, it was only my reputation on the line. Knowing that my work was reflecting on Vasquez Squared made the stakes feel that much higher.

The old logo was a traditional pretzel outlined in a vintage seventies yellow mustard color that did nothing for the pretzels except keep the design recognizable. I had done a background check on the family and discovered the Schneiders were from the Midwest and the company had been started in the 1800s. There was a lot of family pride in their corporate message but they needed more than that. They needed to catch the eye of the younger generation.

I looked at the layouts we had. I liked them. I liked them a lot. They kept the same vibe of the old company but looked fresher. It occurred to me that one way to kick off the new logo was to let the consumers choose. I checked out the company's social media and noted that they had a solid presence. This would make my suggestion to take it to the public more viable. Cool.

I took another swing at each of the logos, making them pop. I tweaked the fonts, the size, and the color schemes. The only one I didn't touch was one that I'd worked on all afternoon, after talking to our client on the phone this afternoon, which was also my favorite. I'd taken the old logo but redrawn the letters so that the *S* and the *P* in Schneider Pretzels looked like a tasty pretzel. Then I'd stylized the *S* and the *P* so that they were a new logo of intertwined pretzel letters. Hand-drawn on Adobe Illustrator but in white with an aqua background, they popped, which would be particularly important for the thumbnail image on their social media channels.

Of course, this was the resolution of only one

of my problems. I still needed to come up with a huge client to impress Miguel and Soph and keep Carson off my back. Damn it. I was brand new to this city. I wasn't networked or connected to anyone other than the people I worked with. How the hell was I going to pull this off? I had no idea.

Frustrated, I closed up my work for the night. I glanced at the clock on the wall and saw that it was past midnight. I frowned. I glanced at the red throw on the sofa. No Sir. He hadn't snuck in while I was working. I'd left the door open but he hadn't appeared. Now I was worried. It was the first time in over a week that he hadn't shown up.

I stepped out onto my patio and searched the area for him. I took in the chilly air and pulled my sweater more tightly about me. I could hear the faint sounds of the crickets, but that was it. There was a stillness to the night, as if everyone was tucked into bed. It was so strange to find such a pocket of silence in the heart of the city. I glanced at the big house. Did Nick know how lucky he was to live here like this? Then I thought of his wheelchair, and I doubted he'd view himself as lucky at all.

I turned to go inside and get some food as incentive to lure Sir in when I heard a sound from the other side of the citrus trees. What if it was the intruder Nick had warned me about? I almost ran inside and slammed the door shut. We were in a major metropolitan area, after all, but something made me pause.

And then out of the citrus trees, he appeared, in his wheelchair. My eyes went wide as Nick propelled himself down the walkway to my house. He was wearing jeans and a hooded sweatshirt, zipped up, and I could see the muscles in his arms and chest bunch and ripple as he rolled toward me. When I glanced at his handsome face, all I could think about was the feel of him lying on top of me. Oh my.

"Hi, Annabelle," he said.

"Hi." I stood perfectly still as if he were a wild creature and I might scare him away with any sudden movements.

It didn't take a rocket scientist to realize he hadn't wanted me to see him in his wheelchair the morning he'd called me up to the house. In fact, having me walk in on him, during his workout, was likely his way of disguising any weakness. The fact that he was here now in his chair was definitely him owning his bullshit by putting it out there. I could respect that.

"I found something that I believe belongs to you," he said as he came to a stop in front of me.

"What's that, Mr. Daire?"

He tipped his head to the side. "I'm Mr. Daire again?"

"Sorry . . . Nick," I said. His hazel gaze was

direct, making me feel as if he could see not just me but what I felt and thought as well. It was unnerving and made my sleep-deprived brain flatline, so naturally, I started to babble. "Unless you'd prefer Mr. Daire because that's fine, too. Whatever you want, I'm good. I mean, name-wise whatever you want . . . oh god. Shut up, Annabelle."

He laughed. It was a delightfully deep, dark, and delicious sound. I felt my face get warm and my nervousness ratcheted up. There was something about this man that made all of my usual coolness vanish into complete nerd girl.

"Nick is fine," he said. "But 'Sir' is definitely not fine for this guy."

He set the brake on his chair and unzipped his sweatshirt. Gently he pulled the black-and-white cat out of his hoodie and held him out to me.

"Sir!" I cried. I scooped him up and clutched him close. I kissed his head, which made him meow in protest, and he batted my nose. "I wondered where you'd gone."

"He arrived around suppertime, looking quite put out," Nick said.

"I had to work late," I explained, although I wasn't sure if it was to Sir or Nick. "Poor guy. He must be hungry."

"I doubt it," Nick said. "Lupita fed him a hearty meal of roast chicken, and then he decided he needed to nap on my lap."

I grinned. "And you let him." He looked disgruntled but didn't deny it.

"I was going to bring him by earlier, but I fell asleep, too. When I woke up, he was still in my lap and I saw your lights were on so I thought I'd bring him over as you might be worried."

"Thank you, I was." I nuzzled Sir's soft fur, relieved to have him home.

"No pets," he said. But there was a gentleness in his eyes that I knew meant Sir had worked his charm on him and Nick was reconsidering.

"He's not a pet, he's a guest," I said. "A visitor. Surely we can grant him a temporary visa."

"Until a suitable home is found?"

I shrugged, which was my nonverbal answer of maybe.

"Even if he's *visiting,* he needs a better name," Nick said. "At the very least, he needs to be Sir Somebody or Other."

"Sir Somebody works," I said.

"Ack, no!" he cried in mock horror. "That's worse than plain old Sir."

I pressed my face into Sir's fur to hide my smile. We stood there for a while, enjoying the bond of affection we felt for this whiskered little ball of fluff, who chose that moment to leap from my arms and stroll into the house as if Nick were his driver and I was his butler and he was now done with us.

"Well, I can see we're no longer needed," Nick said.

I glanced at him, taking in his ridiculous good looks. Truly, one person should not be this blessed in the hotness department; it simply wasn't fair. And I said, "Thanks for bringing him by. I would have fretted all night."

Nick nodded and glanced up at the night sky. "Sir Lancelot, no, that's not it. It's too old-world and he's clearly a hip cat. I'll keep thinking on it."

"How about Sir Mick," I said. Nick raised one eyebrow in question. "You know, as in Mick Jagger."

"He does have an air of rock and roll royalty about him," Nick conceded. "We can consider it."

"Oh, *we* can?" I asked. He seemed awfully invested in naming the cat all of a sudden.

"If he's going to be visiting my house, too, then, yes, I think I should have some say," he said. His gaze met mine and then slid away, only to come right back as he continued, "Anyway, he was just an excuse for me to stop by. I wanted to apologize for the other morning. I wasn't prepared for you to see me like this." He held his hands out to indicate the chair. "But I guess that cat is out of the bag or the hoodie, as it were." He met and held my gaze. "I acted like an asshole. I yelled at you and you did nothing to deserve that. I'm very sorry."

Well, I'll be. Despite his off-putting control freak nature, Nick Daire was a good man. And truthfully, now that I knew he depended upon a wheelchair, it made the control freak thing easier to understand. He likely had to think things through, because of the logistics of using a wheelchair, much more than other people did. Simple things like going to the store, how to navigate bringing the chair, getting items off the top shelves, pushing a cart, and a million other tasks. It made sense that he had the Guzmans and Jackson to help him.

"Apology accepted," I said. "And I'm sorry—"

"Please don't," he interrupted. His startlingly pretty eyes held mine. "That's twice you've apologized when you don't have anything to apologize for."

The urge to apologize again, for apologizing no less, was right there on the tip of my tongue. As if he knew it, he slowly shook his head from side to side. Saying "I'm sorry" was my default setting. I wasn't sure of what to say without leading with an apology.

We stared at each other for a few long moments, and feeling incredibly self-conscious and fully aware that I have no sense of personal boundaries and was being peak rude, I asked, "What happened to you?" I wanted to hear the story from him.

He looked as if he was going to ignore the

question or redirect, both of which I would have expected. Instead, he shocked me. "I had what they call a cerebrovascular accident."

"A stroke?" I asked.

He nodded, looking surprised that I knew the term. I didn't feel the need to enlighten him that I hadn't until now. Instead, I studied him. How could he have had a stroke? He was only a few years older than me. A stroke or a cerebrovascular accident was an old man's condition. It simply didn't compute.

"Yes, a stroke," he said. He glanced down at the chair with chagrin. "I got lucky. I didn't lose my powers of speech, my brain was unharmed, and the side of me that went slack came back, mostly."

"Is that what's wrong with your leg?" I asked. I still hadn't been able to figure out how he'd rescued me from the falling weights. "Did it not recover?"

"Not exactly," he said. "The truth is I'm a medical anomaly. There's a residual weakness in my left leg and my left arm. It comes and goes with no warning. One minute I'm fine and the next thing I know, my left side gives out and I crumple into a heap. It's . . . very frustrating."

"I can imagine," I said.

"Other people have it much, much worse." His smile was wry. "At least that's what I keep telling myself."

"When did it happen?" I asked.

"A little over nine months ago," he said.

"I'm sor—" I bit off the words I was certain he didn't want to hear. His mouth tipped up in the corner. He was clearly amused by my propensity for apology.

"That sucks," I said. His smile grew deeper as he no doubt remembered saying the same thing to me about my mother's death. "Is that why you retired?"

"Partly," he said. "I was already getting the itch to do something else, but I'm a builder. That's who I am, that's what I do. I was considering my options when the stroke happened and changed everything."

My curiosity flared, but I felt like it would be bad form to grill him for more details about such a personal event. Sort of like when someone tells you they're getting divorced. I don't know about you, but I want all the intel, which was why, given my own past, I usually offered up the reasons for my divorces right at the start. Nick did not offer up the who, what, when, where, and why, however, so I kept my lips zipped, although it about killed me.

"Enough about that." He gestured to the window, where my work setup was clearly visible. "Still going at it?"

"I just packed it in, actually," I said. Staring at my laptop and scraps of paper, I felt all of my self-doubt bubble to the surface and added, "I'm in so far over my head."

"I don't believe that," he said. "I've seen your work."

"How?" I asked. Weary all the way down to my bones, I sank onto one of the outside chairs. Nick moved his wheelchair beside me.

"Your replies to my rules always included a drawing," he said. "You're very talented. You shouldn't doubt your abilities."

Flattered, I shook my head. "Those were just doodles, but thank you. It's not the art part. I've got that. It's the managerial stuff." Nick looked interested so I continued, "I have a coworker who, well, never mind. He's not the problem. Well, actually he is, but the bigger issue is my own stupidity."

"Not getting any clearer," Nick said. He shook his head, looking bemused as if I were a hummingbird zipping around him. I took a long breath, tried to center myself, and exhaled slowly and mindfully.

"In a moment of panic, I, quite stupidly, said I was bringing a huge new client into the business to said coworker, Carson West, who has resented me since the day I arrived," I explained.

Nick held up his hand. "Wild guess, he thinks you took his job?"

"Yes!" I cried. It felt so good to tell someone. "Which is ridiculous. I mean if it was his, it would have been his, you know what I mean?" I plowed on, not really needing a response because I was on a roll. "Needless to say, Carson's been impossible to work with, trying to make me look bad at every turn, so in an act of sheer dumbness, I told him I was bringing in a huge client to get him to back off. I'm such an idiot! Naturally, he told Miguel and Soph, who are now expecting me to deliver, and I don't know a soul in Phoenix. How the heck am I supposed to pull this off without looking horribly unprofessional, childish, and ridiculous?"

Nick pursed his lips. "You need to channel this"—he paused and waved his hands in the air at me—"insecurity—"

"I am not insecure!" I protested. I was totally insecure. "I've just been a freelancer for five or so years and I'm not used to working in an office environment with all the backstabbing and petty meanness."

"Uh-huh," he said. "That, right there, use that insec—pardon me, that frustration to give yourself momentum. Push yourself. Prove yourself. Win the job you have, leaving no question who it belongs to."

I stared at him. "So you're a motivational speaker now?"

"That depends," he said.

He glanced away, studying his house from this angle as if he'd never seen it before. From the *aha* expression on his face, it appeared he was having an epiphany of his own. I wanted desperately to ask what was happening in that big brain of his, but I didn't want to scare him off. I went for just looking cool, and asked, "Depends upon what?"

He turned back and smiled at me, a real smile full of warmth and affection, and a deep dimple appeared in his right cheek. I was charmed all the way down to my socks.

"Is it working?" he asked.

"Huh," I grunted. I didn't want to give him the satisfaction of knowing that it was working and that I did feel motivated to kick some Carson tail. I didn't want Nick to think he could roll me with a pretty speech and a dimple—a dimple, for Pete's sake! "I feel like my situation is more complex than that."

"Human behavior is complex," he said. "That's why you break it down to its simplest construct. What do you need? How do you get it? In your case, it seems pretty basic. You need to prove yourself, and you do that by bringing in a huge client."

"Did you miss the part about how I don't know anyone in Phoenix?" I asked. I flopped my head back, resting it on the top of my chair. "I'm doomed."

"Not necessarily," he said. "Again, if you break it down, you really only need to know one person."

I lifted my head and stared at him. "And who would that one person be?"

He tipped his head to the side, and the smile he sent me was one of pure undiluted hotness. "Me."

I narrowed my eyes at him. Soph said Nick had retired from Daire Industries, the business that afforded him these luxury digs. Why the heck was he willing to help me?

"Are you offering to help me to make up for yelling at me?" I asked. I drew my knees up to my chest and wrapped my arms around them, partly for warmth and partly to curb the intense longing I had to crawl right into his lap. His fault. Muscled arms like his were made for snuggling.

"Is it a problem if I am?"

"Not for me."

"Good, but I'm not. As it turns out, I need your help, too," he said.

I knew it! He was the quintessential businessman, and the only way Nick would be willing to assist me was if there was something in it for him. Okay, then.

I tipped my chin up and said, "I'm listening."

Nick

16

To be on the receiving end of Annabelle Martin's full attention, to have her big brown eyes focused on me, well, it made my head fuzzy and I had to glance away to try to reboot my brain, which had just stalled out like it had a dead battery.

I hadn't been alone with an attractive woman in so long, I barely remembered how to behave. Of course, this was all new territory for me as a man who used a wheelchair as his safe space. I'd never had cause to doubt myself with the opposite sex before, not like I did now. I glanced back at her face to see what she made of all this.

In the yellow porch light, I could just see the pulse point at the base of her throat. Was it ticking as fast as mine, or was that just wishful thinking? I sat beside her in a wheelchair. How could she see me as anything other than a broken man? She couldn't, and it was good for me to remember that.

"I need you to be me," I said.

She was quiet for a moment and then asked, "Be you? As in, you as a woman? Like you had a gender reassignment?"

A laugh punched out of me. "Uh, no, more like my representative, the face of Daire Industries."

"I'm a graphic designer," she said. "I draw things, make them pretty or interesting. I have zero skills in the business world, obviously."

"You don't have to do anything other than go to a gala and schmooze with the press, local politicians, and businessmen, assuring them that I am one hundred percent invested in the housing development for which the gala is being held to solicit money from investors."

She was quiet for a moment.

"Why me?" she asked. "Surely you must know someone from your business days who would be better suited."

"True," I said. "You aren't really qualified."

She didn't like that. I saw her shift in her seat, and her chin tipped up ever so slightly. Why was teasing her so much fun? Was it flirting? Was I flirting? My history with women had never included this sort of back-and-forth. It was always much more straightforward with me being rich and the women I dated wanting to be with a guy who could pay for the lifestyle to which they wanted to become accustomed. None of those relationships, if I could even call them that, had lasted more than three months, a fiscal quarter in businessman's terms.

"Again, why me?" she asked.

"Because this is mutually beneficial in that you need a big client, and if you do this for me, I will be delivering you one," I said.

"Delivering or coercing?" she asked.

"Does it matter?"

"I'd prefer to work with someone who actually wants to hire me," she said.

"Once they see your work, they will," I said. I gestured to her house. Visible through the window, hanging on the wall in the living room, was the portrait she had done of Sir—he really needed a better name—when he'd been lying in the lemon tree. I remembered the day she'd painted it. I'd watched from the window, noting the sunlight on her hair and her eyes narrowed in concentration. I wished I could join her and felt ridiculously jealous of the cat for having her to himself. The painting's colors were vibrant, and the likeness of Sir was incredible. "You are a major talent."

Even in the dim light, I saw her face turn pink. Embarrassment? Pleasure? I didn't know. I just had the driving urge to make it happen again.

"Who exactly is 'they'?" she asked. "You're not a mobster, are you?"

" 'They' is a woman," I said. "Her name is Lexi Brewer."

Annabelle didn't say a word, but I could feel her gaze on my face while I studied the leaves of the nearest tree, watching them flutter in the faint nighttime breeze. I don't know why I didn't tell her that Lexi was my sister. It wasn't as if it was a secret, but I was trying to maintain a boundary between myself and Lexi, and by not acknowledging our family tie, I felt as if this made the whole thing more of a business arrangement.

"A woman?" she asked. Her tone was speculative. "Huh. So this woman, is she an ex-wife?"

"Never been married," I said.

"Really?" she asked with a note of disbelief. I turned to look at her, locking my gaze on hers, and asked, "Do I really seem the marrying type to you?"

"Is there a type?" she countered. "It's been my experience that marriage just sort of happens."

"Just sort of happens?" I repeated. I couldn't keep the horror out of my voice. "It's a legally binding relationship with endless ramifications, not the least of which is losing half of your net worth if it doesn't work out."

A sigh slipped out of her. It was the sound of someone who knew the opposing argument so well that they didn't feel the need to hear it again.

"Wait a minute," I said. "Are you telling me you've been married? You have an ex-husband?"

She propped her elbow on the chair arm and then rested her chin in her hand. She regarded me steadily when she held up her other hand and wiggled two fingers. "I have two."

"What?" I was appalled. Not that she was divorced so much as that she'd ever thought marrying was a good idea to begin with. But how

271

exactly did she have two exes when a cursory glance at her rental papers had informed me that she wasn't even thirty yet?

"Shocking, isn't it?" She grinned and then she laughed. "I told you I'm impulsive."

"You also said you were reckless," I reminded her. "I feel like two marriages at your age falls more into the reckless category."

"I went through a very hard time after my mother died." She fingered the tattoo on her wrist. Her eyes seemed bottomless with sadness. It made my chest ache, and I wanted to hug her. I was not a hugger. I resisted, but it was harder than it should have been.

She was very young when her mother died. She must have felt so very alone. I knew what that sort of loneliness felt like. I supposed the two marriages made sense in light of her grief. "I'm sorry."

She nodded in acknowledgment. "The grief was so immense, like a great big black hole. I latched on to whatever, or more accurately whoever, I thought would fill the void. It took me a long time to figure out that I had to fill it myself and that it would take a long time."

"And have you filled that void yet?" I asked. I told myself I was just being polite. I wasn't asking for the seven-year-old boy who'd lost his parents to addiction, his sister at fourteen, and himself at thirty-five.

"Not really, no." She shook her head, and her dark curls bounced almost as if inviting me to reach out and twine my fingers in them. "But maybe I will someday."

"And what about your exes?" I asked. My curiosity was making me rude. I didn't care. "Are you still friends?"

"No," she said. "One of them is most definitely unhappy with me as I turned down his surprise second proposal—"

"Whoa, hold up." I held up my hand. "Explain."

"Ugh, I don't want to," she said. "I don't come out well in this story."

"And now you have to tell me," I said. I was going to be as immovable as a boulder on this.

"Fine," she said. "Annotated version only on the condition of no judgment and no laughing."

"I'd never." I put my hand over my heart.

"All right, so every year my ex and I celebrate our divorce by going to a fancy dinner, but this year signals got mixed and he thought we were in a place we were definitely not in, and he was about to propose . . ." She paused. A pained expression crossed over her face and I waited, literally on the edge of my chair, afraid to move in case it startled her into not sharing.

"Well, I caught on that he was about to propose, and I cut him off by saying I was moving here and then I downed my champagne."

"And?" I prodded. Surely, that wasn't it?

"And he'd put the ring in my glass and I choked on it," she said. She gave me a look. "Please note if and when you ever propose to a woman, do not put the ring in her food or beverage. It took three whole days for the stupid ring to pass. The last contact I had with him was a terse text from him, informing me that the professionally cleaned ring had arrived at his place."

I tried not to laugh. Hand to God, I tried. I failed. It came out my nose with a distinctive honk. I clapped my hand over my mouth to try to contain it, but how could I not laugh? Her chagrined expression was just too much. It had been so long since I'd had a good belly laugh that the sound I made into my hand was that of a barking dog, and what was worse, I couldn't stop.

"Go ahead," she said. "Let it out. You don't want to strain yourself by trying to keep it in."

The harder I tried to get it together, the worse the laughing fit became. Finally I just gave in. I laughed until I cried, actual tears. When I finally caught my breath and gave my abs a rest, I asked, "What about your other ex? No surprise second proposals there?"

"No, thank goodness. Soph calls him the 'big disappointment,' or the 'BD' for short, so that's about all you need to know there."

I chuckled. Her eyes sparkled at me, and I knew it had been her intention to make me laugh.

As I took in her big brown eyes and delicate features, I actually felt sorry for her ex-husbands. "It seems to me, any man stupid enough to lose you is going to spend the rest of his life learning exactly what disappointment is."

A faint blush swept across her cheeks, and again I was one hundred percent beguiled. If I were a different man in a different circumstance, I would make it my mission to cause this woman to blush at every possible opportunity, preferably with no clothes on. I gave myself a mental shake. There really wasn't much point in going there. I tried not to feel bitter about it and mostly succeeded.

"So this woman," she said. "If she's not an ex, then who is she?"

I thought about telling her, and for one brief moment, the idea of unburdening myself to her, telling her about me and Lexi and our parents and all of it, was so tempting, I felt my mouth open with the words right there. Instead, I said, "She's someone I knew very well a long time ago, but we drifted apart over the years. She's back in town now and I . . ."

"And you want to help her out but maintain some distance." She finished my sentence for me when I paused for a beat too long.

"Exactly." My gaze met and held hers. Much to my relief, there was no pity in her expression, no judgment, just acceptance. No wonder her first ex had wanted her back. Annabelle Martin was a rare and exotic bird.

"And what will I be designing?" she asked.

"Lexi Brewer is breaking ground on a net-zero housing development in the middle of Phoenix, and she will want you to design every bit of the identity, logo, advertising, etc., attached to it. The media is going to go bananas over this project, which I am quite certain is going to garner national attention."

Her eyes went wide. "That's huge."

"As I said."

One corner of her mouth turned up. "This would make me look really, really good."

"And I'm sure you'll do the same at the gala for me." I held out my hand. "Deal?"

She studied me for a second as if she was looking for the fine print, the hidden warnings, the buried clauses. Then she reached across the space between our chairs and took my hand in hers. So impulsive! The skin-to-skin contact sent a thrum of awareness through me. It occurred to me in that moment that Annabelle Martin was much more dangerous than I'd realized.

"Deal," she said.

"Are you sure?" Jackson stared at me as if I'd announced I was planning to skydive without a parachute.

"Yes," I said. It had taken me two days to get

the nerve up to do this thing, and my anxiety was making my impatience razor thin and just as cutting.

"Okay, I don't want to discourage you in any way, but you haven't left the house, other than to go to the doctor, in over nine months," he persisted. As if I wasn't painfully aware of this fact myself.

"Yeah, well, Lexi isn't taking my calls, so I have no choice," I said. "I'm going."

"To her office on the jobsite," he clarified.

"Did I stutter?" I asked.

Jackson shook his head. Good thing the man had a hide like a rhinoceros and was virtually impossible to insult. "Okay, I'll bring the car around front."

"Thanks," I said. I made it short, because, in truth, I was trying not to freak out, and even thinking about being out there in the world where anything could happen—okay, a stroke, a massive you're-now-a-potato stroke, could happen and I might not be able to get the care I needed in time—made me feel levels of discomfort found only at a proctologist's office.

Jackson strode down the hallway, leaving me to ponder possible death or worse in his wake. Always a good time.

Lupita arrived with a water bottle and that indefinable air that everything was going to be okay. In the days following my stroke, she'd been there in the hospital advocating for the best care for me. She'd never left my side, and I'd never forgotten how reassuring it was to wake up and find her there, day or night. I didn't know when I'd hired her and Juan that she would come to mean so much to me, but she had. Lupita was the only person on earth who could mother me and I accepted it. I knew her concern was genuine, so I believed her when she reassured me that all would be well.

"You're doing the right thing, Nick," she said. She straightened the collar of my shirt and smoothed the fabric on my shoulders. "Family is the most important thing, and your sister needs you."

I glanced down at her and nodded. She was right, I knew that. It was why I was going on this fool's errand for a sister who suddenly wouldn't take my calls. Stubborn brat. Sure, I hadn't acknowledged any of her overtures, and it had likely hurt her feelings. Okay, I'd been a total jerk and I was sure she was paying me back, so mature, but she could have saved us both a lot of trouble if she'd answered any of my calls over the past couple of days.

Lupita stood beside me as I leaned against the wall, trying not to obsess about every little twinge in my leg. *I am not going to collapse,* I kept repeating in my head like a mantra. I began to sweat and my heart was racing. Somehow I had to get through this meeting without Lexi catching on to my true condition. Sure, it was a pride thing, and too much pride was bad, but when I'd been scrambling to survive on my own in the city, not even a legal adult yet, my pride had been the one thing that kept me going.

Jackson pulled up and I nodded at Lupita, hoping the next time I saw her, I was still walking under my own power. I climbed into the passenger's seat, stored my water in the cup holder, and buckled up. I had left my house a million times to go to the doctor. Surely this would not be that different, or so I tried to tell my racing heart.

"So why the sudden change of heart about your sister?" Jackson asked.

I sighed. "Are we going to talk the entire drive?"

"Yes," he said. "Come on, it'll keep your mind off of things."

I appreciated that he said "things" instead of the more accurate "being an anxiety-ridden basket case."

Why had I changed my mind? It was simple really. Neither of the two women currently crowding my life was going to go away. Annabelle would be living in the guest house for five more months, and all the rules in the world were not going to push her out. And Lexi, sure, she was pissed at me now, but I knew my sister.

Once she got over giving me the cold shoulder, she'd double back trying to convince me to help her get local support for her project. The perfect solution was, of course, to have the two women work together.

It was genius, really. Annabelle would have her super huge client, and Lexi would have Annabelle, a hell of a lot better-looking representative for Daire Industries than I'd ever been. A little coaching and Annabelle would be able to handle the gala and anything else Lexi and the construction world threw at her.

"I don't need to keep my mind off of things," I said. "I have everything under control. I merely need to get some things in play, namely get Lexi and Annabelle working together on this huge project, which will get both of them out of my hair, and then I can step back into my blissfully reclusive existence and be left alone."

"Couple of problems with that theory, brother," Jackson said. I had repeatedly told him not to call me that. It indicated a closeness that we did not share. He continued to ignore the request, however.

"Name one," I scoffed. It was a perfectly well-thought-out solution. I dared him to find a problem with it.

"Annabelle lives on the estate," he said. "How can you possibly avoid her? Never mind, why would you want to?"

"She's about to get very, very busy," I said. "Next."

He looked at me from under his bushy eyebrows and scratched his chin. "What about your sister? The woman sent you a singing hippo. Do you really think she's just going to crawl off because you've got a stand-in helping with the gala?"

"Lexi hasn't been my sister in the real sense in almost twenty years," I said. "Don't you find it the least bit telling that she didn't look me up until she needed my money?"

"It's not your money that she needs," he said.

"Yeah, you're right," I said. "She needs my contacts, which are worth more than gold."

"You really think she only came to you for your connections? She's in town for this job; of course she took the opportunity to look you up," Jackson said. His tone made it crystal clear that he thought I was an idiot.

"Yeah, it's all very convenient." I refused to accept any other explanation for her sudden appearance. It was easier this way.

Jackson sighed but I continued speaking to stave off another lecture about my brotherly duty to my sister.

"Listen, this is a win-win. Everyone gets what they want, it will help both women, and give me some peace and quiet," I said. "I just need to get everyone on board."

Lexi was the unknown quantity in the equation,

but I was positive I could get her to see things my way. I was going to bankroll my sister's gala on the condition that she hire Annabelle to design her corporate identity for the development and anything that included, such as advertisements, brochures, a website, you name it. The idea had come to me while talking to Annabelle in the yard. Now I just needed to get it in motion.

"Oh, speaking of the ladies, we're picking up Annabelle at her office," I said.

Jackson's head whipped in my direction.

"Relax, she knows," I said. He didn't look reassured but it did shut him up, which I took as a victory.

Annabelle was waiting by the curb when we pulled up. She was wearing a tailored blue suit and matching heels. Her long curly hair had been restrained into a smooth knot at the nape of her neck. She looked all buttoned up and not in a sexy librarian way but more like trying to be someone she wasn't. I didn't like it. Not that it was for me to judge. It just didn't suit her personality.

The Annabelle I had come to know was bright colors, flowing fabrics, and unrestrained curls. She was hot tubs on starry nights, singing at the top of her lungs just because she felt like it, and giving sanctuary to strays that had no place to go. That Annabelle made me think about things I shouldn't, like burying my fingers in her hair and holding her still while kissing her senseless. Of having her body pressed up against mine while I—

"You okay over there?"

Jackson interrupted my erotic thought stream and I blinked. Yeah, it was clear. I needed to keep my tenant as far away from me as possible if I didn't want things to get complicated, which I didn't.

"Yeah, I'm fine." I was not fine.

Jackson parked and hopped out of the car. He greeted Annabelle and then opened the passenger door behind the driver's door for her. A part of me was irritated that I hadn't beaten him to it, but I knew I was on borrowed time with my body so I sat, feeling useless and lame. Always a solid kidney punch to the old self-esteem.

"Hi, Nick," Annabelle said.

I turned in my seat to glance at her over my shoulder and noticed that a single curl had escaped her hairdo like a loose spring. It made me smile. Annabelle was still in there, behind the pressed linen and product-tamed hair. The curl spiraled just over her ear by her temple. The urge to twist it around my finger was almost more than I could stand.

"Good morning," I said. "How was the new pretzel packaging received?"

"They loved it," she said. Her grin was contagious.

I held up my hand and she high-fived it with

enthusiasm. I smiled and asked, "You brought what we discussed?"

She patted the laptop bag beside her. "Of course."

"Excellent," I said. I don't think I imagined the faint blush that filled her cheeks.

"Everyone ready?" Jackson asked, climbing back into the driver's seat. Annabelle and I both nodded. "Then we're off."

Jackson steered us out into traffic, and we headed west until we reached Central Avenue and then he turned left and we were headed south. The city no longer resembled the rough-and-tumble place where I had grown up. Downtown, which used to be a wasteland inhabited by the down-and-out, was now a thriving art and food scene. The nearby university had revitalized the several city blocks by building a large portion of its campus in the center of the city. I knew all of this because I had built many of the new apartment complexes that now filled the district.

I used to feel a heady surge of pride every time I drove through the area, as if I'd left my thumbprint on every beam and brick, but now all I felt was futility. What had been the point of it all? Money? Power? None of that mattered when your body shit the bed.

Had I made anyone's life better by banging up these overpriced monstrosities, or were the residents now bogged down by paying for a home they couldn't really afford? Meanwhile, the stress of the years I'd worked like a demon had given me an old man's case of hypertension and likely caused my stroke and would probably bring on another. I knew, in that moment, that I'd give away every last dime I had if I never had to sleep another night with that black cloud of worry hovering above me.

A chain-link fence cordoned off the construction site, but a section had been left open. Convenient. Since I hadn't been able to reach my sister, to say this was a surprise visit was an understatement. We'd be lucky if she didn't greet us all with a nail gun strapped to her hip and the attitude to match. If I remembered right from when she was a kid, she could hold a grudge.

I glanced at Annabelle to see what she was making of the situation. She looked as if she was concentrating on taking it all in.

Jackson parked right in front of the stairs that led up into the trailer, which was the temporary office of the builder and where I knew my sister maintained a work space so she could oversee her project. The smell of the place, plowed-up dirt, damp from the water being sprayed to keep the dust down, and the underlying smell of gasoline fumes and exhaust from the construction trucks filled my nostrils, and just like that I was back on my first jobsite. It was intoxicating stuff.

I opened my door and stood. My leg felt

solid, no numbness as yet, and I was grateful. My mission was to get in and out as quickly as possible with Lexi none the wiser to my condition.

As I'd explained to Annabelle the night I made my proposal, under no circumstances did I want our client to know about what had happened to me. She'd looked like she was going to argue, but I'd wrapped up her compliance by reminding her that she needed this account.

I started up the steps using the handrail. Annabelle and Jackson fell in behind me. I could feel Annabelle's stare on my back. I wondered what she was making of my ability to navigate the steps. The two times we'd seen each other, I'd been seated. How could I explain that post-stroke my life was a constant loop of being fine and then landing flat on my face for no diagnosable reason? I couldn't. And I didn't want to try as the very last thing I wanted from her was pity.

When I reached the landing, I rapped on the metal door. I heard the sound of a chair scraping back on a hard floor and the door was pulled open. Standing in the doorway was Lexi, and unsurprisingly, she did not look happy to see me.

"What the hell do you want?" she snapped. "Are you here to say 'I told you so'? Because if you are, you can shove it right up your behind, I have nothing to say to you, big bro—"

17

"Good to see you, too," I interrupted. I knew if I looked over my shoulder at my companions, I'd see two things, Jackson most definitely trying not to laugh and Annabelle looking alarmed, and possibly trying to flee the conflict zone.

"Problem, boss?" An enormous black man, who rivaled Jackson in size and width and who also had his head shaved down to the scalp, appeared behind Lexi. Being a few inches over six feet tall, I wasn't used to looking up at people. This made two men in the vicinity that I had to crane my neck to look at. I didn't like it.

"No, I'm fine," she said. "Stand down, Micah."

He didn't. Instead, he crossed his arms over his chest and continued to loom.

"I'm here to talk about the gala," I said. "We can do it on the front steps or you can invite us in and be civilized about it."

Lexi squinted at me. Her expression was suspicious and at odds with the fresh-faced Rosie the Riveter look she was rocking with her honey-colored hair tied up with a blue bandanna, baggy jeans, flannel shirt, and work boots. She didn't look old enough to buy alcohol, never mind be in charge of building a housing development.

"Micah, do me a favor and walk around the site and make sure nothing else has been tamp . . . er . . . um, make sure everything is okay," she said.

He looked us over. "You sure?"

She nodded, flashing him a quick smile. "Yeah, I'm sure."

They both stepped aside, allowing us to enter the trailer, which looked just like every other construction office I'd ever been in with desks, tables, chairs, and a refrigerator all crammed in, forcing people to walk sideways to get from one end to the other.

As Micah passed Jackson, I saw them size each other up. Standard gym rat behavior. I hid my smile when Micah jerked his chin at Jackson in acknowledgment and left the trailer, letting the door bang shut after him.

I glanced at Annabelle to see if she was okay. She looked bemused, taking in the interior of the trailer while casting surreptitious glances at my sister. Another of her curls had escaped, making my fingers itch to catch it and pull it taut just to see if it sprang back when I let go.

Clearly, it was a damn good thing that she was going to be very busy in the near future. I needed her out of sight until she moved out, for both of our sakes. I was in no place to have anyone in my life who wasn't on my payroll. Period.

"I'm really busy," Lexi said. She glanced at her

watch. "So if you could make this less than five minutes, I'd be super grateful."

It was weird to be out of my house after so many months and not sitting in a waiting room. I wondered if I was becoming a touch agoraphobic. My tension ratcheted up and I felt vulnerable not having my wheelchair nearby. A jolt of electricity shot up my leg, followed by a numbness that made my knee wobble. Oh, hell no. I was not doing a face-plant in front of Lexi.

I took a deep breath as I walked past her, feeling anxious with every step. I slid gratefully into a chair at the lone table, clearly used for meetings and, judging by the random ketchup and mustard packets, also lunch. I gestured for my sister to take a seat. Heaving a put-upon sigh, she stomped over to the table and sat down. Annabelle followed while Jackson motioned that he was going to wait outside. A part of me wanted him to stay close in case something went wrong, but I just nodded. I was going to make this quick.

"Lexi Brewer, this is Annabelle Martin," I said.

"Nice to meet you." Annabelle smiled. She didn't offer Lexi a handshake as if sensing she might get bit. Smart woman.

"Same." Lexi's voice was flat. She turned to me and asked, "One more time, what do you want?"

I studied her face. She was furious. I knew my nonresponsiveness must have pissed her off, but this seemed like something else. I got the feeling something big, something not about me, was wrong.

"What's happening?" I asked. I leaned forward, holding her gaze with mine. "Why did you think I was going to say 'I told you so'?"

"Just tell me you didn't do it," she said. Her voice wobbled a little, and I could see a sheen of tears in her eyes.

"Do what?" I asked. I steeled myself. My sister's tears had always gotten to me.

"Chased off my crew," she said. "When I arrived at eight this morning, Micah, my construction manager, was the only one here. Everyone else was a no-show."

I leaned back in my seat. "Shit."

Her features were pinched and her face pale when she turned to me and asked, "Was it you?"

"What?" I cried. "How can you even ask that? I would never. I'm the one who—" I bit off the words before I confessed that I had invested in her career by paying for her education. She didn't need to know that.

"Who what?" she asked.

"Who is committed to the development of my city," I said. It sounded ridiculous but I had to pivot somewhere and that was all I had. "I would never sabotage any project, especially yours."

I held her gaze, and finally, she nodded. "Okay, then." She exhaled a short, tight breath. "So why are you here?"

"I've been thinking about what you said," I began. I chose my next words carefully. I wanted to be clear that the support I was offering was financial only. "I'd like to help you—"

"Oh, Nicky!" she cried, interrupting me. "Do you mean it? This is so great!"

"Nick," I corrected her. She ignored me, and I saw a speculative look in Annabelle's eye. *Nicky* sounded much more familiar than a business acquaintance. Damn it.

Lexi turned to Annabelle. "I'm sorry if I was rude before. It was a rough morning. Do you work for Nicky?"

"No!" "Yes!" we answered at the same time. We glanced at each other. I wanted to correct her and point out that she did work for me in the sense that she would be representing Daire Industries, but it was clear Annabelle didn't see it that way.

"I'm Nick's tenant," Annabelle explained. "But I'm also a graphic designer, and he seemed to think you might have need of one."

Lexi looked from Annabelle to me, raising one eyebrow in question.

"If you're going to woo investors, get the city's support, and get the public on board, you have to get ahead of the project with the right packaging," I said. "Whenever I started a development, I already had the angle I was going to use to sell it."

Lexi's face grew grim. "I already have the

angle. *Green Springs* is all about renewable resources and being self-sustaining."

"Still sounds like a place where people go to die," I said. Lexi let out a bleat of protest, but I steamrolled right over her. "Annabelle is one of the best graphic designers in the country. She'll work with you to rename your project and design your logo and the necessary accompanying materials."

Lexi's head dropped to her chest. "While I appreciate the offer, I have bigger issues than the name and logo. In case you didn't hear me, someone drove off my crew."

I shrugged. "Then they weren't worth having."

"Easy for you to say," she said. "Without your public show of support, Nick, I'm doomed."

She looked so defeated. It reminded me of the time we were vacationing in Lake Tahoe before our parents flaked on us, and she was determined to catch a crawfish but they were quicker than her chubby four-year-old fingers could manage. She'd stood in the cold water until her lips turned blue, her eyes as sad and lost as any I'd ever seen. Needless to say, I found a bucket and helped her catch loads of them.

"I know plenty of general contractors. I'll hire you a new crew," I said. "Just like I'll pay Annabelle to design your corporate identity."

Lexi's lips thinned. "I don't want your money. I want your support. There's a difference."

"Well, now you're getting both," I said. "And I'm not giving you the money. It's an investment. I'm buying in and I fully expect to double my money if not triple it when the properties start selling. Your project will get done and on time, and you can use my name however it will benefit you."

And just like that, her eyes shone. Her smile lit up the room, and she threw herself across the table to hug me tight around the neck. "You mean it? You'll help me? You'll go to the gala and talk up the project and help me with the city council?"

"Whoa," I said. I unhooked her arms and pushed her gently back into her seat. "I said you can use my name. Annabelle will be the face of Daire Industries at any public functions you require."

Her shoulders slumped. "But not you?"

"My name will be on the checks," I said. "In construction, that speaks louder than any fancy shindig."

"But—" she protested.

"Take it or leave it, Lexi," I said.

I could feel Annabelle's eyes flitting between us. She was obviously trying to determine the relationship between us. I'd say estranged sibling with a side of distrust at least on Lexi's side of things. While I was more in the "estranged and trying to keep it that way" category.

"I'll take it," Lexi said. "But I'm not going to

stop asking you to come to the gala. It's going to be the biggest event in Phoenix. Anyone who is anyone is going to be there."

"How is that?" I asked.

She grinned. "Are you kidding? When word gets out that you're supporting a net-zero housing development, I won't be able to keep them away."

"I'm not going to the gala, Lexi."

"So you say." She tipped her chin up and turned to Annabelle. "What has Nick told you about this project?"

"That you're going to revolutionize home building," she said.

Lexi barked out a laugh. She patted my arm and said, "Same old Nicky. You always did believe in me more than I did myself."

I felt my throat get tight at her words. It was jarring to have her back in my life. I didn't know how to feel about it. I'd intentionally not reached out to her for twenty years so that she could have a better life with a good family, and yet here she was.

Why now? Why when I was feeling like a poor imitation of my old self? I didn't want her to see me as broken or weak. I wanted her to remember me as her hero. And I definitely didn't want her to get attached just to have me punch out early and leave her brotherless again. What would that do for her? Nothing good.

An awkward silence filled the room as I didn't know what to say. Annabelle seemed to understand, and she jumped in and said, "Lexi, I love the art you have in here."

She gestured to the walls, and I noted that there were architectural drawings covering every surface. Lexi grinned. "Thanks. I've been working on this project for years so I have plenty of renderings in various degrees of completion."

"Maybe you could loan some to Nick. He has no art on his walls. As in none."

"That's not—" I began to protest but stopped. Her statement wasn't entirely accurate, but if I corrected her, I'd have to explain what art I had, and admit that I'd had her drawings framed and they were now hanging in my bedroom. Yeah, awkward.

"See?" she said to Lexi. "None. He doesn't have any in the guest house either or he didn't before I moved in. How does a person not have any art on their walls?"

More curls had sprung free from her bun. Her face was flushed and her eyes sparkled. Now she was rocking the sexy librarian look, because of course she was. A hot spear of desire, something I hadn't felt in forever, made my brain blink out. All I could do was stare at her while she talked art with Lexi. I felt as awkward as a middle school boy with a crush on his hot math teacher. Toenail fungus, soap scum, a fly found in an ice cube, I tried to think of things to squash the lust rocketing through me like a pinball. It was a struggle.

When they finally wound down from their love of every artist from Monet to Haring, I had myself under control although it took me a second to realize they were both staring at me. Shit, was I supposed to answer a question?

"So what is it?" Lexi asked.

"What is what?" I shifted in my seat.

"What are you thinking about that has you looking so—" Annabelle began but Lexi interrupted.

"Weird," she said.

I sent her a look and she grinned. Same old Lexi. It made my heart clench in my chest.

"Brussels sprouts," I said.

They both made expressions as if they'd just tasted something bad.

"Why?" Lexi asked.

"Because there has to be some way to make them taste good," I said. I almost laughed at their matching expressions of confusion. I clapped my hands together and glanced from one to the other. "Okay, so are we done here?"

"If you're in, I'm in," Lexi said to Annabelle.

"Oh, I'm in!" Annabelle beamed, and even though it wasn't directed at me, I felt it shoot through me all the way down to my feet. But then she turned to me, still grinning, and I forgot how to breathe. "And I'll stop by your place after work and we can come up with a plan."

"Plan?" I asked, utterly bemused. I had no idea what she was talking about and I didn't really care.

"Yes, for the art," she said. She gestured between her and Lexi. "We agreed that we'd repay you for all that you're doing for us by making your house look less like a Motel 6. I take that back, even a motel has better art than you."

"Hey!" I protested.

"Don't thank us," Lexi said. "We're happy to do it."

"What if I like bare walls?" I asked.

They looked appalled.

"No one likes a naked house," Annabelle said.

And just like that, my inner adolescent boy lost his powers of speech. The word *naked* coming out of Annabelle's mouth ruined every hard-on-squelching image I'd been able to think of, plus I'd just lost my argument for barren walls. So now it looked like I would be acquiring some art.

Lexi glanced between us with a shrewd look that I ignored. Mercifully, the trailer door opened and Jackson poked his head in. "Nick, a word?"

I noticed the tight line of his jaw. Something was bothering him. I glanced at Lexi and said, "Why don't you give Annabelle some idea of what you're looking for in a logo, and I'll be right back."

Annabelle was already hauling out her laptop, looking delighted, and her enthusiasm was contagious as Lexi scooted her seat closer to see what Annabelle had already come up with. I wanted to just sit there and stare at them, appreciating how everything was coming together even though it meant keeping them both away from me, but I could feel Jackson's looming presence like a bootheel poised to drop.

I crossed the trailer, being mindful of every step I took, and went outside onto the narrow platform. Jackson jerked his head to where Micah was standing on the ground a few feet away. I took a deep breath and strode down the short staircase like the man I used to be.

"What is it?" I asked.

"Your sister has made some enemies," Micah said. "She would kill me if I told you this, but there is more going on than the contractors not showing up today."

"What do you mean?" I felt my insides tighten.

"In the past month, she's had her tires slashed," he said. "Someone called in a bomb threat, and the office was broken into not once but twice."

"Shit," I swore. "Did she call the police?"

"Yeah, they said it was junkies likely looking for easy money or something they could sell, but these were pros. No evidence was left behind," he said.

My stress level started rising. I could feel the tingle in my fingers and my toes, indicating my system was going into overload. I crossed my arms over my chest and casually leaned against the side of my SUV. If my body went numb, as it occasionally did, this would keep me from falling. I hoped. Micah didn't seem to notice but I saw Jackson's eyes narrow. I'd never appreciated him as much as I did right now. I knew he had my back, or my leg and arm, as the case may be.

"Do you think she's safe on her own?" I asked. My voice was tight. Turned out you could take the little sister away from the big brother, but you couldn't subtract the big brother from the big brother. Every protective instinct I'd ever had about Lexi roared to life.

"I don't know, man," Micah said. "Whoever is behind the incidents wants this development stopped and they are not playing."

I nodded. I knew there was only one solution. I didn't like it. Lexi was going to hate it, but so sad too bad.

"Are you going to stay on?" I asked.

"Are you going to get me a crew?" he countered.

"It'll be done by the end of the day," I said.

His smile was a slash of white teeth and he

nodded. "Well, all right, all right. I'll make sure we're ready to work at sunrise tomorrow."

"Thanks, Micah," I said. He met my gaze and I knew he understood, but I felt the need to say it anyway. "For looking out for her, I appreciate it."

"Are you kidding? She's one of my best friends," he said. He turned and scanned the barren lot. "She's got a vision, and this development is going to change this entire neighborhood."

His tone was full of respect, and it occurred to me that Micah was a man of vision as well. With a wave, he walked across the lot toward an excavator parked on the far end. I had no doubt that he'd have the work assignments ready tomorrow, and I was going to have to scramble to get a crew ready in time.

"How do you feel about taking on an extra job?" I asked Jackson.

He pulled at his chin hair. "Depends upon what it is."

"I want someone I trust to keep an eye on my sister," I said. "I know Micah can keep her safe here, but it's the to and from home I'm worried about."

"You want me to shadow her or actually escort her?"

"Escort," I said.

"Ooh, male escort." He laughed. "Can't wait to add that to the old curriculum vitae." He glanced around the jobsite, as if scanning for potential danger. "Of course I'll do it."

The door to the trailer opened, and Annabelle and Lexi stepped outside. They were both smiling so I assumed the meeting of the minds had been a success.

"I'll stop by your office tomorrow," Lexi said. "We can finalize the details with your bosses."

"Excellent," Annabelle said. She glanced at me and Jackson, and I could see she was positively vibrating with excitement.

"Are you finished?" I asked. "I need to make some calls if we're going to be up and running tomorrow."

The relief and gratitude in Lexi's gaze was a look I was going to cherish forever. "Thanks, Nicky."

She was never going to curb that habit. I sighed. I spun to face Jackson and said, "Don't even think it."

He shrugged right before a grin appeared out from behind his face hair and he said, "Sure thing, Nicky-oli."

"You're an idiot," I said.

His big bark of a laugh drowned out my words, and I noticed Annabelle and Lexi were laughing, too. Whatever.

I walked toward the steps. Might as well get the next battle over with. "Lexi, I have an additional condition on my support."

The laughter was wiped clean from her face replaced by a wary look. "What's that?"

"While this development is under construction, Jackson here is going to act as your bodyguard," I said.

"Oh, hell no!" she snapped.

Jackson looked at her in surprise. "That seems an overreaction."

"Nothing personal," she said. "But I'm thirty and I can take care of myself." She shot me a dark look as she stomped down the steps with Annabelle following. "I've had a lot of practice."

"What the hell does that mean?" I asked. I knew a dig when I got hit with one.

"It means that just because I'm your little sister, you do not get to manage my life," she said. "I don't need a bodyguard."

"Little sister?" Annabelle asked. She sounded surprised. Her gaze cut between us as she compared our features.

"Yes, Lexi is my sister," I said.

"Not really," Lexi said. She sounded a tad bitter. "We're siblings, but we haven't seen each other in almost twenty years."

I frowned at Lexi. "I've seen you."

She planted her hands on her hips and glared. "When?"

"I saw you graduate from middle school, high school, and college," I said. "And I've followed you on social media for years. You really need to make your settings private."

She gasped. "You've been stalking me?"

"Stalking?" I raised my hands in the air in a *what the hell* gesture. "I'm your brother. I had to make sure you were okay, didn't I?"

"But that's not fair," she cried. She sounded so much like little Lexi, I expected her to stamp her foot just like she used to do. "I didn't know. I . . . you . . . you should have reached out."

I looked at her. "And how would that have worked out for me?"

She glanced away. We both knew her adoptive father would not have tolerated that.

"Still, you should have . . ." Her words trailed off. It was a woulda, coulda, shoulda situation that I couldn't have won. Anger made her mouth tight, and she snapped her head up. "Fine. Whatever. I still don't want a bodyguard."

"Listen, not that anyone is asking for my opinion," Jackson said, "but I don't like it either."

Lexi opened her mouth to speak, but he boomed right over her as Jackson tends to do. "But it's clear someone does not want you to build this place, and until we know who it is and how far they're prepared to go, I'm going to be stuck to you like glue."

Lexi's eyes widened as she took him in, and then her gaze flitted away. Was that a spark of interest? Well, hell.

303

"I suppose I could put up with you *very temporarily,*" she said.

"Good enough," he said. "I'll be here at quitting time to pick you up."

"Excellent," I said. And then, a genius idea struck. I gestured to Annabelle and Lexi. "You can come to dinner, both of you, and we'll nail down the required pieces of art in my house. We'll make it a project and be done with it tonight. Be there at seven."

The two women exchanged a look. Now they both crossed their arms over their chests and stared at me with the exact same expression of displeasure.

"What?"

"Wild guess, but I think they were looking for an invitation to dinner instead of a command appearance," Jackson said.

Both women nodded.

"Fine," I said. "Would you two care to join us for dinner tonight?"

Again, they exchanged a look. How had these two women bonded so tight, so fast? How did women do that? I mean, Jackson and I had been living in the same house for months, and I could no more read his mind than I could tell you what was in the back of my refrigerator.

"I think I'm available," Lexi said. "How about you, Annabelle?"

"I'll move some things around," she said.

Her gaze met mine, and it was full of unspoken challenge. I had a feeling I was in trouble for not telling her Lexi was my sister. I smiled before I could stop myself. There was just something about that look that called to me; it made me want to put my hands on her hips, pull her close, and kiss her stupid.

I forced my gaze away and said, in the driest tone I could muster, "Excellent. I'll let Lupita know."

"Should we bring something?" Annabelle asked. "I don't want to put Lupita to trouble at the last minute."

"Uh, no," Jackson said. "Lupita's going to be thrilled. She's been begging this one to have a dinner party so she could show off. She's an amazing cook, you know."

"I didn't know, although she brought me some muffins that were out of this world," Annabelle said. She walked toward the car and Jackson opened the back door for her.

I glanced at Lexi. "Thanks for agreeing to this." I motioned to Jackson with my thumb. "It's just until we get a handle on things."

She nodded. She reached up and tightened the bandanna that held her hair in place before she met my gaze. "Micah told you everything, didn't he?"

"About the slashed tires, bomb threat, and break-ins?" I asked.

"Yeah."

"He's worried."

"I know," she said. "That's the only reason I'm not mad at him. Well, that and the fact that he and his wife, Monique, are invested in this place. They already bought the first home." A frown line appeared between her eyebrows, and her voice was gruff when she said, "I don't want to let them down."

"You won't," I promised.

She nodded. "Thanks, Nicky."

I turned and opened my door. "Call me if anything—"

"I will," she said. "I promise."

Reassured, I climbed into the car and closed the door. Jackson hit the gas and we left the jobsite behind us. I immediately took out my phone and began working my contacts. I was going to have to pull out every favor I'd ever been owed to make this happen, but if it kept my sister safe, it was worth it.

Annabelle

18

So many questions! I had so many about Nick and Lexi, I was surprised they didn't overflow out of my eyes and mouth and ears, drowning anyone in the vicinity. Sadly, none of my questions were answered at dinner, because how could they be when I didn't even know how to pose those questions without seeming intrusive? Instead we talked about sports, films, politics, weather, and how many paintings it would take to fill Nick's barren house.

The lack of information was problematic, causing my fascination with Nick to become a borderline obsession. He and his sister had been estranged, and I had to know what had happened. Not my business, to be sure, but still, I *had to know*. Neither of them, however, were talking.

I knew Soph wouldn't approve of my having dinner with Nick, but what she didn't know wouldn't hurt her, right? Right. Besides, it wasn't as if we were alone. Pity.

Jackson and Lexi arrived for dinner right on time. So frustrating. I had attempted to get there early, but only managed to show up on time as well. There was no opportunity for just the two of us to talk. Maddening. The meal was amazing. Lupita had really outdone herself with the food. Given that microwavable ramen had become my go-to dinner, her homemade guacamole with pomegranate seeds, chicken and cream cheese taquitos, and machaca beef with fresh tortillas and homemade salsa were to die for. We had margaritas on the side, but I stopped myself at two, not wanting to risk making an ass of myself.

I noted that Nick wasn't using his wheelchair. In fact, it had been parked out of the room. He didn't get up and move very often, preferring to sit on the couch after dinner, and I suspected it was all part of his effort not to let Lexi know that there was something wrong with him. While we enjoyed dessert, homemade flan, and coffee, and discussed the possible art for his walls, I realized I wanted, quite desperately, to be alone with him.

I wanted him to look at me the way he had that night, the one where he caught me in his arms and saved me from being crushed to death by the free weights. Yes, it had taken on that soft focus romantic glow in hindsight, erasing the details that my skirt had been ripped open and he'd been covered in sweat from his workout. Sue me.

He hadn't looked at me in anything more than a perfunctory way ever since, his gaze friendly but distant. I wanted the intensity back. I wanted the zip and sizzle. I wanted him to notice me, thus,

I stayed at two margaritas lest I do something desperate for his attention like strip down to my undies and cannonball into the pool. Impulse control not being my strength. So yay me for not doing that. Yet.

"You could go with some Arizona art," Lexi said. "Something that pulls together your color scheme but evokes a certain feeling."

Jackson gave her side-eye. "His color scheme?" He gestured to the room. "Black, gray, and white. That's all we've got going on here."

Lexi tapped her spoon to her lips as she considered. "Ansel Adams. An enormous print of his *White House Ruin, Canyon de Chelly*, would be amazing on the big wall. It's Arizona, it's historical, and you have the space. Back me up, Annabelle."

"You can never go wrong with Ansel Adams," I said. I stared at the big blank wall. "Unless, you want to bust out and have some color. There are so many amazing Arizona artists, like Jimmy Todd or Frederick Sommer. Or if you want a contemporary, how about *Silent Soliloquy* by Dorothy Fratt? She was an Arizona artist and I just love her work."

Lexi gave me an approving grin. "You know your local artists."

"I studied up before coming here," I said. "I like to familiarize myself with the art scene in places before I visit."

"Visit?" Jackson asked. "You're not planning to stay then?"

I could feel Nick's gaze on the side of my face. I wanted to see his expression, but I was afraid I'd lose my train of thought if my gaze was caught by his. It was clearly his superpower.

"I'm here for six months, well, more like five now," I said. "And then we'll see."

"You're going to make a decision at the height of the summer heat?" Lexi asked. "That's a terrible idea. Any sane person would flee once the temperature hits one hundred and fifteen."

"I heard it's a dry heat," I said.

All three of them laughed. I tried not to be offended.

"Sorry," Nick said. He grinned at me. And there was that dimple! "It's just that once you get past one hundred and ten degrees, does it really matter if it's a dry heat? It's hella hot and miserable."

"Oh, goody," I said.

"Don't worry," Lexi said. "Nicky has a pool. You jump in that and you'll be just fine."

"Are you planning to have a pool at the development?" Jackson asked her. She answered, but I wasn't listening.

Instead, I turned and gave Nick a pointed look. He grinned at me, clearly not in the least repentant about banning me from the pool.

"There's always room to negotiate, you know,

like awarding visas to visiting cats," he said. He looked amused. It charmed me silly but I fought it off.

"Is there?" I asked. "Because if it gets that hot here, we are most definitely going to have to adjust the rules. I will die—die!—if I don't have a pool during that kind of heat."

"Are you being overly dramatic in an attempt to win?"

"No," I said. "I can assure you this is not hyperbole. Need I remind you, I am from New England. We can't handle temperatures above ninety. Everyone freaks out and loads up on the iced Dunkin' Donuts coffee. Then we're all overcaffeinated and locked indoors, clutching our window AC units for dear life. Truly, it's ridiculous."

"Well, then," he said. He pressed his lips together in an obvious attempt to not laugh. "We can't have that. We'll discuss."

I gave him a sly look. "And put it in writing?"

"Of course," he said.

I turned back to see Lexi yawning. She looked like she was fighting it off, but Jackson shook his head when he started to yawn, too.

"Stop that," he said. Then he nudged her with an elbow, pushing her to her feet. "Come on, I'll take you home before we both pass out."

She looked like she'd argue but then another yawn slipped out. "All right. Morning does come early and since I'm going to have a crew tomorrow . . ." She glanced at Nick.

"Not just a crew," he said. He stood and I rose with him. "The best crew."

"Oh, Nicky." Lexi stepped close and then, as if bracing herself for rejection, she threw her arms around him anyway.

I held my breath, waiting to see what would happen. Nick lifted his arms and put his hands on her upper arms as if he'd peel her off him. Instead, he slid his hands to her upper back and hugged her close. The look on his face, as if he couldn't believe she was here and he was hugging her, about broke me. My throat got tight and my heart went sploosh, and I felt a suspicious pricking in my eyes as if the tear ducts were just firing up.

Nick cleared his throat and patted Lexi's back. She released him with a watery smile of her own and then turned to Jackson. "Well, come on. Places to go. People to see."

He exchanged a nod with Nick and followed her to the door. Before she disappeared, Lexi spun back around. "I'll see you at your office tomorrow, Annabelle. Ten o'clock, okay?"

"Perfect," I said.

"Just remember when you meet Sophie and Miguel Vasquez to leave my name out of it," Nick said.

Lexi squinted. "You said that before, but you didn't say why."

"It's for me," I said. "Nick is trying to let me take the full credit for landing a huge account. Sophie and Miguel know he's my landlord, so if they know that you're his sister and that he's paying for the work, then—"

"It looks like your landlord gave you the job instead of you earning it?" Lexi asked. Nick and I both nodded. "Well, just so we're all clear, if your designs had been garbage, I wouldn't have agreed to hire you even if it did mean losing Nicky's support."

I grinned at her. "Thank you. That means a lot."

Lexi nodded, cast one last look at her brother, smiled, and left.

I began to gather the dessert dishes from the coffee table. Nick started to help but I shook my head. "I've got it."

He ignored me and followed me into the kitchen, carrying the remaining dishes and coffee mugs. We set them in the sink. When I would have started to rinse them, he reached across me and shut off the tap.

"I can do that later," he said. "Come on, I'll walk you home."

"Oh, you don't need to," I said. *What?* What had just come out of my mouth? Why? Why was I telling him no? Hadn't I wanted to be alone with him just a few minutes ago? Yes. But now that I was, I was actually nervous. So stupid.

313

"Probably not," he said. "But I'm going to anyway."

"Do you want your wheelchair?" I asked. "I can go get it."

He stood still as if trying to decide. Then he shook his head. "No, I think I can do this."

We strolled through the enormous house and stepped outside into the backyard. The scent of citrus blossoms was heavy in the night air. It was chilly and very quiet. The only sound was the soft bubbling of the hot tub. I almost asked if he wanted to go in with me, but I thought that might be pushing it.

We crossed his patio and followed the path along the line of trees that circled the pool until the path broke off to my house. My back door was open just a few inches. I had fed Sir before arriving for dinner and left the door open for him if he wanted to leave. I glanced at Nick to see if he was taking all this in. If he was, he didn't show it.

I thought about Lexi and wondered how she'd react when she discovered that he'd been keeping his stroke and subsequent issues secret from her. It had been my experience that secrets didn't like to be held. They were like wiggly toddlers that way, and the harder you held on to them, the more of a fuss they made until they were loose.

"Are you going to tell Lexi?" I asked him.

"Tell Lexi?" he asked.

"About your . . . issues."

"Issues?" He stopped walking and turned to face me, forcing me to stop, too. "That's a helluva euphemism for a stroke and the residual fallout."

"I was trying to be delicate," I said.

"No need, I'm not that fragile. Truthfully, I don't have any plans to tell her anything," he said.

"Why not?" I asked.

"It's complicated."

"Really? Seems to me you just need to 'break it down to its simplest construct.' "

A slow smile lifted one corner of his mouth. "Very clever, using my own words back on me."

I shrugged. "Just sharing some very wise advice."

"The difference being you had a situation you wanted to change, and I don't."

"No?"

"No," he said. He began walking again. "Lexi is only in Phoenix for this project, and then she'll go back to the East Coast and on to her next job. I'm not going to bog her down with my stuff. She's better off not getting too attached."

"How do you figure?" I asked, falling into step beside him.

"Because before the stroke hit, I was on my way to being a supremely arrogant, narcissistic asshole," he said. "And while the stroke was a reality check for me to change my life, it doesn't mean I'm okay with being a burden to Lexi in its aftermath."

"How are you a burden?" I asked. I was genuinely mystified.

He stopped again and stared at me. "Annabelle, you saw me. I went to save you from those falling weights and damn near got us both crushed."

"You protected me," I said. "And put yourself in harm's way to do it."

"You don't understand. The doctors can't figure out what's wrong with me," he said. Frustration made his tone sharp. "I'm fine one second and then everything goes sideways and my heart rate accelerates and I can't breathe, and then my left side starts to go numb. It's like there's another stroke lingering beneath the surface just waiting for me to let my guard down." He shook his head. "And no one can tell me why it keeps happening."

"They'll figure it out," I said. I had a theory about what was happening. I'd seen this sort of thing before, with my sister, Chelsea, after our mother died, but I kept that to myself, for now.

"There's no guarantee of that, but even if they do . . ." He paused. His gaze held mine, and he reached up with one hand to grab a stray curl that the evening breeze had tossed across my face. He rubbed it between his fingers as if absorbing its texture before he gently tucked it behind my ear.

I held perfectly still. I wanted to press my cheek into his palm, but I didn't.

"Even if they can fix it," he continued, "there's no guarantee that I won't have another stroke tomorrow, next week, next year. Did you know that twenty-three percent of people who have a stroke have another? How could I let Lexi sign on for that? One second she has her long-lost brother back, and the next she has a big old useless bedridden, drooling potato for a sibling. I won't do it. I won't risk it."

"Shouldn't you tell her what's going on and let her decide?" I asked.

"No, because I know what she'll choose," he said.

We reached my patio and he stopped on the path before it as if there were an invisible boundary he would not cross. To heck with that. He might succeed at keeping his sister at arm's length, but I wasn't going to let him do it to me. The awareness between us wasn't going away. In fact, it was only getting worse with every second I spent in his company. I liked him. I really liked him.

He was interesting and complicated, smart and funny, and strong. Plus, I saw kindness in him. He was a man who'd been on top of the world and had it all crash down around him, but he survived. There was a strength in him he didn't recognize in himself, but I did.

Of course, I couldn't ignore the fact that he was

as hot as a house on fire, but that wasn't what made me respond to him. What really drew me to him was how he tried so hard to protect everyone around him from caring about him. As if he could push them away and save himself the heartbreak of caring for them in return if he just kept them at a distance. Ridiculous.

I saw how he joked around with Jackson. He pretended to be irritated by the big man, but I knew that if anyone crossed Jackson, Nick would destroy them. He had the same protectiveness toward Lupita and Juan. They were fiercely loyal to him as well. I knew the truth was that Nick Daire was a good man, even if he didn't see it himself. As for his sister, Lexi, it was clear he'd never stopped looking out for her. It didn't take any great powers of deductive reasoning to realize that the college scholarships she'd talked about at dinner, the ones that she didn't recall applying for, hadn't just appeared. They were from Nick.

"So it's okay for you to help her but not for her to help you," I said.

"I don't need any help."

"Really?" I asked. This was my moment. I knew it as surely as I knew my potential to crash and burn was at an all-time high. I didn't care. My heart was pounding hard in my chest. Holy banana balls, I was about to make a move. "Seems to me, you could use an assist."

He frowned. His eyes moved over my face as if he was trying to read my intent. "In what way?"

Moment of truth. I tossed my hair over my shoulder, because I'd picked up on the fact that he liked that. It was dark out and hard to see, but I was certain his pupils dilated just a little bit. Then I reached out and took one of his hands and put it on my hip. He didn't move. In fact, I wasn't sure he was even breathing.

I glanced up. His nostrils flared just the teensiest bit, and I wanted to do a fist pump in triumph, but I kept it cool. I didn't want to scare him off. Ever so slowly, I took his other hand and wrapped it around me, moving into the circle of his arms, so that his palm sat on the base of my spine, right above the curve of my derriere.

Tipping my head up, I noticed our faces were now just inches apart. Then I licked my lips and said, "How's this—helpful?"

"Only if your goal is to make me insane or to be certain I kiss you," he said. His voice was deep and gruff and made me shiver in the best possible way.

"Definitely, the kiss—" That was all I got out before his lips were on mine, and I abruptly had no idea how words were even formed.

He pulled me in high and tight until my body was pressed against his. The hand on my hip slid up my side and he buried his fingers in the hair at the nape of my neck, holding me as if he was afraid I'd get away. I would have told him not a chance, but I was too undone by the sandalwood and vanilla scent of him that surrounded me, the press of his lips against mine as he traced the seam of my mouth with his tongue, deepening the kiss as I opened to him.

I slid my hands up his arms, pausing to squeeze his powerful shoulders, then I twined my arms around his neck, locking him in while I kissed him back with equal fervor. I broke the kiss, because oxygen, but after two gasps I was ready for more. Nick had other ideas, however, as he slid his lips down my neck, kissing the pulse point at the base of my throat before sliding back up to kiss me just behind the ear. *Guh*.

Stars went off in my vision, my core liquefied into a hot puddle of desire, and I was certain I was having a nuclear meltdown of epic proportions. I let out a low moan and then his mouth was back on mine, and he doubled down on the rampant lust between us, nipping my lower lip and then soothing it with his tongue. Mercy, this man could kiss.

"Impulsive," he muttered, his lips against my skin. "Reckless woman."

I dug my fingers into his hair, wanting him to feel how much I desired him and wanting him to suffer the same acute need I was feeling. If the man did not spend the night with me, I would not survive until morning. I was sure of it.

"Come inside," I whispered in his ear.

His body went rigid and not just the obvious part pressed up against me. He let go of me, moving his hands to my upper arms as if he was going to push me away. I was not having it.

I ran my hands from his shoulders, down his sides to his waist. My fingers slid under the hem of his thermal shirt, and I reveled in the feel of his hot skin under my palms. He let out a hiss of breath as I traced his insanely defined pectorals, slowly lowering my hands to his abs. He froze so I went for the bold maneuver and slid my fingers over the front of his jeans.

"Fuck," he cursed. He managed to make it a three-syllable word.

"Yes, please," I whispered before gently biting his earlobe.

He pulled away from me, and for a moment I feared I'd been too aggressive or had gone too far. Nope. He yanked me back in and kissed me as if I were the last bit of air he'd breathe before going under water for good. I was happy to drown along beside him. Abruptly, he pulled back, breaking the kiss, and his hot gaze met mine.

"I don't do long relationships," he said. "Three months is my max. No exceptions."

Just like Soph had said. I was glad she'd told me so I wasn't caught off guard.

Every muscle in Nick's body was taut, and

I suspected he wanted to fight off this crazy attraction between us, but instead of denying it, he threw up obstacles, or more accurately, because it was him and he was all about control, he made rules. Like the length of a relationship could be determined at the start. I ducked my head so he couldn't see me smile as I felt a surge of pleasure that I had pushed him to this tipping point.

"I'm not going to be in Phoenix for much longer than that," I said. This was not a sure thing, but he didn't need to know that.

"When it ends, it ends. No crying, no fits, no stalking, no weirdness," he said.

"I'm sure you'll try to control yourself." I batted my lashes at him.

That surprised a laugh out of him. He looked at me as if I were already naked—so hot!—and then he asked, "Are you sure, reckless one, because there's no turning back after tonight."

"I'm sure." I wasn't but when was I ever sure of anything? I operated on instinct and intuition. All I knew, for certain, was that this man made me feel things no one ever had before, and I was damned if I was going to leave Phoenix and not indulge myself in him as if he were a rare top-shelf sipping tequila.

He nodded and spun me around. With his hands on my hips and him right behind me, we walked through the open door of my house. As soon as we stepped inside, Nick shut the door behind us and drew the seldom-used drapes closed. Then he pulled me back in and kissed me.

It wasn't just a kiss. It was a promise of rumpled sheets, sweaty bodies, and orgasms, yes, multiple. I dug my fingers into his hair and held him still while I sipped at his mouth, slid my tongue inside, and then kissed him so deep, his only response was a groan and some muted swearing.

When we broke apart, we were both breathing heavily. I glanced at the couch and noted that Sir was curled up in his blanket, oblivious to the porn scene we were acting out right in front of him.

Nick spun me around again and nudged me toward the bedroom. As soon as he stepped in after me, he kicked the door shut with his foot. He backed me up to the bed. When the backs of my knees hit the mattress, I went down and Nick pounced. Lying full on top of me, he kissed me and kissed me and kissed me some more, fitting his mouth to mine and plundering me like a pirate seeking treasure. He didn't stop until my ears were ringing, my lips were puffy, and my chin sported whisker burn. I didn't care. I would have kissed him all night long if that was all he offered.

He cupped my cheek and ran his thumb over my lower lip. His eyes were gentle when he looked at me with tender affection and said, "You are a feast and I am a starving man. Sorry."

"Don't be," I said. My voice was breathy when I added, "I'm yours."

A low hum was his only response, and then he was kissing me again. I'd told the truth. I was totally his. He could make love to me or suggest we play Scrabble. I did not care. I just wanted to be with him. There was something about him that called to me. As if he was a lonely voice, crying out in the distance, and I was trying to find him.

In unspoken agreement, we attacked each other's clothes. My dress went one way, his shirt another. We paused to kick off our shoes, and they dropped to the floor with loud thuds. Then we peeled off our remaining clothes until we were both down to our skin. I hardly got a chance to look at him when he rolled me. Pressing his entire body the length of mine, he settled on top of me. His hands roamed over my curves with delicious abandon, and I could hardly process the sensations rocketing through me. I arched against him, feeling him lock into place exactly where I wanted him. My blood felt hot and sluggish in my veins. The need I felt was so sharp, it made me gasp.

"Easy, Goddess," he said. "We have all night."

Goddess? How was I supposed to resist that? I couldn't. I rolled us so that I was on top. My hair formed a curtain, cocooning us in.

I was breathing as if I'd run a marathon. He was right. I needed to slow it down. Savor it, us, him. He stared up at me, his eyes intense but with a glint of humor. His lips curved up on one side so I leaned down and kissed the corner. His smile deepened and that wicked dimple appeared, taunting me. I kissed it and then his eyebrows, his nose, the line of his jaw. I felt his body move beneath mine, and I realized he was laughing. I pulled back to admire him. I loved it when he laughed. I suspected he hadn't laughed near enough in life. He took the opportunity to roll us again, so that I was on the bottom.

"You're a playful one, aren't you?" he asked.

"Me?" I blinked innocently. Then I pinched his side. He yelped and laughed again.

"Yes, you," he said. He caught my hands in his, laced our fingers, and held them by my head. Then he began to kiss his way down my body.

"Reckless," he murmured. He drew a nipple into his mouth and sucked hard, nipping the tip, making me grunt, and then soothing the sting with his tongue. My eyesight went fuzzy. He repeated the process with my other breast, making me hiss.

"Impulsive," he whispered. He kissed his way down my belly, swirling his tongue around my belly button. He chuckled when I squirmed and giggled. I tried to pull my hands free to block him, but he wasn't interested in tickle torture.

No, he was focused on another goal entirely.

Not letting go, he pulled my hands down so that they were beside my hips, his fingers still laced with mine. The soft light in my bedroom illuminated the planes of his face, and I was again caught breathless by how incredibly handsome he was. His gaze met mine, and it was ripe with intent. He was the predator, and I was the prey, and I was happy to be so.

He released my hands and turned them so that my palms were facing down. He curled my fingers around the bedsheets, indicating that I should hang on, then he moved my thighs wider apart as he settled in.

"Goddess," he hummed into my most personal private space before he put his mouth on me. It was everything. He used his lips, teeth, and tongue in a sensual assault that had me arching my back and begging for something that sparkled just out of reach.

"Please, I need—" I stopped, unable to form a fully coherent sentence.

"Let it come, Annabelle," he demanded.

"What about you?" I asked. I felt myself going under but clawed my way back. It didn't seem right. I was the initiator; I should be making him fall apart first.

"Don't worry about me," he said. "We have all night." Then he put his mouth on me again and wooed me with an undeniable skill. The feeling was so exquisite; I couldn't fight off the ripples of pleasure that started low and deep and spread through my entire body from my toes to my hair in delicious wave after wave. I closed my eyes and rode out each one until, satisfied, Nick planted one last kiss on me and slid back up my body, settling his hips in the cradle of my legs.

He was watching me with a self-congratulatory grin, and I would have balked but, really, what would be the point? The man had wrecked me, positively wrecked me, and he knew it.

I looped my arms about his neck and pulled him down so I could look him in the eye. Then I kissed him, long and lingering. When I ended the kiss, I pressed my forehead to his and asked, "Can an orgasm make you stupid?"

He chuckled low and deep, pressing his face against the side of my neck. Feelings were bubbling up inside of me, and I wrapped my arms around his shoulders, holding him close while hiding my face. I felt a tear prick the corner of my eye, hot and wet and full of all the emotions I was feeling but couldn't say. It wanted to spill, but I blinked it back. He'd said no crying at the end, but I believed it would be a deal breaker even now.

"I've never experienced that symptom," he said. "But I'd be willing to give it a go, so I could weigh in with some empirical evidence."

This time, I laughed. I rolled out of his arms and

opened the top drawer of my nightstand. A girl should always be prepared. I grabbed a condom out of the box and tossed it over my shoulder. He caught it in midair. The grin he sent me was positively wicked, and I felt an answering thrum in my core. Oh, this man.

He made quick work of putting on protection and then he was rolling me back under him. I could sense he was looking for a signal from me that I was ready. I didn't know how to wave him in any clearer than to wrap my legs around his waist and decisively invite him in. He looked down at me in surprise and I grinned. He sucked in a breath.

"Definitely a goddess," he growled and then slid into me, pushing against the muscles that were still swollen and flushed. The pressure felt glorious, and I let out a gasp and arched into the feeling of him, filling me. I readied myself for a wild ride with him setting us in motion. There was none, however. Instead, he held himself perfectly still as if he was afraid to move.

"Nick?" I whispered. He was so still, I was afraid he'd hurt himself.

"Sorry, I just . . . I can't breathe," he said. He shook out his left hand as if trying to get the feeling back in his fingers. "I just . . . damn it . . . I don't know if I can—"

I could hear the anxiety in his voice. I knew that if Nick bailed on me now, I would likely never get him naked again. Also, it would become one more obstacle on his path to recovery.

Obviously, I wasn't a doctor, so I hesitated to say what I suspected, but I genuinely believed that the symptoms Nick was exhibiting weren't precursors to another stroke but rather he had a case of severe anxiety manifesting in panic attacks.

I'd seen it before. Several times in the months following my mother's death, my sister, Chelsea, had been convinced that she was having a heart attack. After several doctor's visits, including a few trips to the emergency room, we discovered she was having panic attacks.

"How can I help?" I asked. I ran my hand up and down his spine, hoping to soothe him.

He heaved a deep breath. He pulled back to look at me. His hazel eyes practically glowed with unsatisfied lust. He looked like a man standing at the edge of a cliff, wanting to jump but terrified of what was in the deep dark water below. Understanding hit me with the precision of a hammer.

"This is your first time since . . ." I trailed off, not wanting to kill the mood by using the *s* word.

"Yeah," he said through gritted teeth. "I'm trying to get my bearings."

I smiled. He was trying so hard to keep his cool. I leaned up and kissed him quick.

"It's okay," I said. "Let's just breathe together and see what happens. Come here."

We stayed entwined, but I pulled him down so his weight settled against me. I looped my arms about his neck, holding him close, and Nick pressed his forehead against mine. Together, we began to breathe. I had done breathing exercises with Chelsea, so I knew to inhale for eight, hold it for four, and then exhale for eight. Nick matched his breathing to mine, and I felt the tension ease out of his body. He settled in against me, his nose pressed against my neck, his hands cradling me gently as if I was the most precious thing in the world to him.

I don't know how long we stayed like that. Time ceased to mean anything. My entire world became him, just him.

When he pulled away, his face was clouded with a feeling I knew all too well. Shame. I had suffered bouts of it after both of my divorces, feeling like something was wrong with me. That I was defective. I could see the same self-loathing in his eyes right now. I couldn't let him feel that way. Not about this. Not about me. Not about us.

Before he could get away, I dug my fingers into his hair and kissed him. Then I rolled him, so he was on the bottom and I was on top.

"What if you just relax and I do all the heavy lifting?" I asked.

He looked uncertain but his gaze was all heat. "Well, I can't argue with the view."

There was something incredibly powerful

about being the one in control, much like he had been with me before, and I reveled in it. I splayed my hands on his chest and I made love to him as sweetly and as gently as I could until I noticed a sheen of sweat on his brow and his teeth were gritted.

"How are you feeling now?" I asked.

"Like I'm about to die the sweetest of deaths," he said. "Totally worth it."

He sat up and pulled me in tight, then he put one hand on my lower back while the other slipped in between us and with his thumb he caressed me in an insistent circular motion that made everything zero in on that pressure point. I lost my sense of rhythm, my powers of speech, and my balance.

Nick took full advantage and lowered me to the bed, regaining the top position. He took over, lifting one of my legs and pushing in deeper and deeper still. In a matter of thrusts, we were both lost to the bliss that rocked through us from the place where we were joined. Like a shout into the void, it echoed on and on and on.

Nick rolled onto his side and pulled me up against him, locking me in place with his arms, while he placed kisses on my hair. This time, I was certain I would never be able to string a full sentence together again. Neither of us spoke for a long while.

"So that's a yes," he said.

"Yes, what?" I murmured, still wrecked.

"The evidence clearly suggests an orgasm can make you stupid as fuck," he said. He ran a hand over his face. "What's my name? Where do I live?"

I laughed out loud, delighted that he felt the same way I did. He laughed, too, and in that moment I felt as if we'd achieved a perfect connection. Impulsive and reckless, I might be, but I believed he was worth it.

19

He didn't spend the night. I was all right with that. Tonight had taken an unexpected turn, and I knew we were both processing.

Besides, not spending the night in this case was really him leaving me after we fell asleep together for a few hours and then woke up to that delightful half-awake sex, you know, when you're barely conscious but your body has very specific demands that need to be met.

We dozed after that with me splayed across him like I was a blanket. I wanted his heat, his strength, his comforting presence. I slept the sleep of an innocent child when there'd been nothing innocent about our time together.

And then when the sky was murky, not yet sunrise but no longer night, he kissed me long and deep and tucked me in. *He tucked me in!* He pulled the blanket over my shoulders, making certain none of the night's chilly air could reach my skin. His fingers lingered on my body with a tenderness I'd never received from a lover before. Then he planted a kiss on my head and quietly slipped away.

I wanted to call him back, but I didn't. Given his rules and boundaries, I was going to have to take my cues from him. Besides, today was the day that I introduced Lexi as my big client to Miguel and Sophie so I needed to have my game face on. You'd think this would have given me at least a mild case of insomnia. Nope. I fell into the sleep of the utterly sated and naturally overslept. Way overslept.

Late. Later. Latest. That was me. I downed the scalding coffee. It burned. I spit it out, not sure I'd ever have feeling on the roof of my mouth again. I ran in and out of my shower, barely getting wet. I yanked on a long navy dress, brown ankle boots, and a floral scarf with the same blue and brown and some sassy pink tones. I threw my mascara and lip gloss into my shoulder bag to put on at the office, twisted my hair up into a ball on the top of my head, and ran for the door.

I yanked the door open and found a note. The blocky handwriting told me right away who it was. Nick. I pulled it off the door, feeling my heart flutter in my chest. I wanted to rip it open right there, but—*shit!*—I was so late. I stuffed it into my bag and made a run for it.

I wondered as I was dashing to the gate if Nick was watching me from the house. If he was, he was probably laughing his butt off at me, knowing that this was his fault, having worn me out the night before. I could just picture him, his chest puffing up with male pride. As I skidded past the keypad, where I knew there was a security camera, I paused to stick my tongue out, then I grinned before breaking back into a run.

A glance at my phone while waiting for the crosswalk light to change and I saw I was almost an hour late. *An hour?* This was a new personal best for me. I tried not to freak out. Soph was always pretty chill about my tendency to be late, but at this rate I'd be lucky to get there before Lexi. I pulled out my phone to see if there were any messages from her. There was nothing. Maybe I was okay.

I dashed across the street and rushed into the building. I strode across the rose quartz floor, waving to the security guards, Curtis and Hector, as I passed by.

"Morning, Annabelle," Hector called. He was ninety if he was a minute, and he reminded me of a peanut in the shell with his bald, wrinkled head and big ears. His grin was brilliant, however, and it managed to light up the lobby.

"*Buenos día, mis amigos,*" I called. Hector had been coaching me with my Spanish, and his grin widened at my effort, which I'm sure was terrible but he seemed pleased. Curtis, who never spoke, waved. He didn't have to speak. He was young and had the solid build of an armored car. No one messed with Curtis.

"*Pasa buen día,*" Hector called after me.

The elevator doors opened and I ducked inside.

I turned and hit the button for the fifth floor, moving aside for the person I felt stepping in behind me.

"Late again, Annabelle? Tsk tsk tsk. I've already had two meetings this morning while you're sprinting in an hour late. What will the bosses say?"

Crap. Of course it was Carson who stepped in behind me. Sadly, no one else did, leaving me to ride all the way up to the fifth floor trapped with him.

"You really don't seem to value this job very much," he said.

I ignored him. Bullies hate that. I pretended to be looking for something in my bag. I was doing such a good job, I missed it when he put his hand on the wall behind my shoulder and leaned in, forcing me back.

"You're going to fail probation," he said. "You're always late, you forget clients and accounts. Face it, your work is subpar and you're not cut out to be creative director." His eyes had a mean glint in them. "And you lied about bringing in a major new client, admit it."

Don't show any emotion. Don't show any emotion. I repeated the words in my head like a mantra. I just had to get to the fifth floor, so I could get away from him. He reeked of a high-end cologne, the sort that suffocated, and his shiny shoes, creased slacks, and crisp shirt all sported designer labels as if he needed the names of others to assert his own worth.

"Well? Nothing to say for yourself?" he taunted.

I kept my face bland and pretended I just noticed his presence. "I'm sorry, did you say something?"

A derisive smile crossed his lips. Then he leaned in, crowding me but not touching me. He lowered his mouth to my ear and hissed, "Bitch."

I don't intimidate easily, but I'd be lying if I said that the hate pouring off of him didn't rattle me. I was the ultimate pleaser, everyone liked me, but not this guy. The urge to lift my knee in a sudden defensive strike almost overrode all common sense. Carson West was a weak man, and I had no doubt that he'd charge me with assault, especially because it would get me fired and he'd finally get the office that he felt was his.

Nope, the absolute best way to win was to show no reaction. No fear. No anger. No emotion of any kind. I tilted my head to the side, away from him, and said, "I'm sorry, what was that? I didn't catch what you said."

His eyes narrowed and his lips thinned and he snarled, "You heard me."

"No, I'm afraid I didn't," I said. I shrugged and used the gesture to move away from him. I glanced at the numbers on the elevator and saw that we had arrived. The ding of the elevator had never been such an appealing sound. I glanced at him over my shoulder and added, "Perhaps it's because I don't speak asshole."

The doors slid open and I stepped into the lobby, taking an enormous inhale. I hadn't realized I'd been holding my breath, but with his cologne giving off an olfactory assault and his menacing presence crowding me, it was small wonder I'd forgotten to breathe.

"Annabelle, you're here!" Lexi bounced up from the couch where she was seated.

She was dressed in a charcoal gray skirt and blazer with a black blouse underneath. Her jacket was unbuttoned and she was wearing very high, spiky-heeled pumps. Her hair was fastened in a loose bun at the nape of her neck, and she wore just enough makeup to accent her eyes and lips. She had a laptop bag on her shoulder, completing her woman-of-business look.

I immediately felt like a jerk for being late, especially given that my extracurricular activities with her brother were the reason I was tardy. I felt my face get warm as she opened her arms and gave me a quick hug.

"I'm sorry. You weren't waiting long, were you?" I asked.

"Not at all. I just arrived," she said with a shake of her head.

"I was going to get Lexi a cup of coffee, can

I get you one, too?" Nyah asked from her spot behind the reception desk.

"If it's no trouble, that would be amazing," I said. Caffeine in any form including a solid would be more than welcome at the moment.

"No trouble," Nyah said. "It gives me an excuse to get one for myself. Should I bring them to your office?"

"Yes, thanks," I said. I glanced back at Lexi. "I'm going to have Soph and Miguel, the owners of Vasquez Squared, pop in to meet you while we figure out our initial timetable."

"Sounds good," she said.

"Whoa, who's this?" a voice asked from behind me. I didn't have to turn around to know it was Carson.

I also didn't have to acknowledge him, especially after his intimidation tactics in the elevator. "Come on, Lexi. I know your time is valuable, let's get to it."

"Hey, how about an introduction?" Carson called after us.

I ignored him. I walked through the lobby with Lexi at my side, casting me furtive glances. We pushed through the meeting room and cut into the main work area. There were several people in the room. I smiled at Christian and Shanna, but I could feel Carson behind us, closing in. I didn't want to have to introduce him to Lexi. I'd spare her that if I could.

"Ms. Creative Director, I'm talking to you." Carson raised his voice as he entered the room after us. I felt the gaze of everyone in the room swing from Carson to me and back. He managed to say my job title with just the right amount of contempt to make me grit my teeth.

"Everything cool, Annabelle?" Lexi asked in a low voice.

"Yup, everything's fine," I lied. I was still rattled by my time in the elevator with Carson, and I was trying to rally but he was not making it easy. I pointed down the hall. "My office is this way."

We passed both Soph's and Miguel's offices. The lights were on and their doors were open, signaling that they were here. This would make things much easier. In fact, I decided to slow down just outside their offices and let Carson catch up. Naturally, he decided to shoot past me and then stopped, turning around and blocking my access to my office. Predictable.

He crossed his arms over his chest and stared at Lexi, then he turned to me. "No introduction? I thought a Boston girl would have better manners than that."

I stared at him.

"What? It's just a joke," he said. He made an exasperated face. "You need to lighten up, Annabelle."

I did not take the bait. This would have been

a fine moment to ask him if his calling me a bitch in the elevator had been a joke, too, but I knew better and I didn't go there. Shocking, I know.

"How can I help you, Carson?" I asked. I crossed my arms over my chest, mimicking his stance, and met and held his gaze. "I assumed you said everything you needed to say to me in the elevator."

I saw his eyes flash at that. Let him wonder if I was going to make a thing of it.

He turned to Lexi with charm oozing out of his every pore. "Hi, I'm Carson West, the senior art director, and you are?"

He held out his hand. I wanted to slap Lexi's hand away from his. I didn't want him to contaminate her. Instead, I watched as she shook his hand.

"Lexi Brewer," she said. "New client."

She gave him nothing more. I could have hugged her right there, but it would have been awkward so instead I gestured to my office behind him and said, "Lexi's on a very tight schedule, so if you'll excuse us."

Unfortunately, Carson didn't take the hint. Instead, he looked from Lexi to me and asked, "And what is it we'll be doing here for you, Lexi? As the senior art director, I'd like to be in the loop."

I blinked. Was he insane? Was he actually

standing there, including himself in my meeting with my client? That was . . . no, just no!

"Um." Lexi looked at me, obviously sensing the bad vibe between us and uncertain of how to answer.

"As the creative director, I'm the key client point person, so I'll be managing Lexi's account," I said. I hoped my voice came out firm, shutting down any idea he had of jumping in on this project without being invited. "When we're ready for your input, I'll let you know."

"I know the collaborative thing is a struggle for you, Annabelle," Carson said. He glanced at Lexi and added, "She's new. But that's how we do things here. We're not solo units. We work as a team. Right, Miguel?"

I glanced over my shoulder to see Miguel standing in his office door, watching us with a speculative stare. I realized Carson had said what he did to make me look bad in front of Miguel. Argh.

"That's right," Miguel agreed. He glanced at me. "New client?"

"Yes," I said. To my relief, Sophie came out of her office as well. Finally, I had some backup. Sophie's eyes met mine, and I could see the question in them. *Is this the big client?* I nodded and she ran with it.

"Annabelle, is this the client you mentioned at our staff meeting?" she asked.

I gave Soph my brightest smile. "Yes. Sophie and Miguel Vasquez, this is Lexi Brewer." I paused while they shook hands. "She's the architect of a groundbreaking net-zero housing development that's going up in the middle of Phoenix. Using tax-reverted lots, she's designing small homes for middle- and low-income families that will eliminate energy costs as they are completely self-sustaining. Lexi's project will change the residential building industry in Phoenix as we know it."

They looked suitably impressed, so I continued, "As you can imagine, the news outlets are clamoring to interview her so we have a lot of materials to create, the development's brand identity, including the logo, colors, fonts, and photo direction. And that's just to start. We'll also be designing the brochures, ads, social media graphics, website, landing pages, and email marketing templates."

"Don't forget the gala," Lexi said.

"Gala?" Sophie asked. She bounced on her toes, just once, and I could tell her inner cheerleader loved where this was going.

"Yes, there is also a fundraising gala happening, to get the community actively invested in the development, which is to be held at the Phoenix Country Club and we're designing the invitations for that, too."

"Impressive," Miguel said.

Lexi flushed with pleasure, and I felt a surge of satisfaction that I was going to be working with her on something that actually mattered. It was thrilling.

"So this is a done deal?" Carson asked Lexi. "You're not looking at any other design studios?"

"No, Annabelle came out to the construction site yesterday and sold me on working with Vasquez Squared," Lexi said. "I had some free time this morning, so we decided to nail down the details."

I could have kissed her, which would have been weird since I was now sleeping with her brother but still. She had just rocketed to the top tier on my list of favorite people.

"Lexi and I are going to review the creative brief that I wrote up yesterday afternoon," I said. "Trent is drawing up the working agreement, and we'll review that as well when he's done. If you want to sit in?"

"Absolutely," Soph agreed.

"Unfortunately, I have a meeting with another client," Miguel said. He looked conflicted.

"I'm happy to take your place," Carson offered.

Miguel gave him a sharp look. While I was sure Carson had meant it in an ingratiating way, I didn't think Miguel heard it that way. Soph and I exchanged a glance and I knew she'd caught Miguel's expression, too.

"I don't think that's necessary," Miguel said.

344

"As creative director, Annabelle's got this."

For a second, I thought I might faint. I had no idea what was happening but Miguel had clearly backed me—probably because I had landed a huge project with an incredible amount of exposure for the studio—and judging by the pinched look on Carson's face, he didn't like it one little bit.

I opened the door to my office and gestured for Soph and Lexi to go ahead inside. I turned to follow them, and Miguel called after me, "Nice work, Annabelle."

"Thanks." I flashed him a huge grin. When I turned around, my first thought was that I could not wait to go home and hug the stuffing out of Nick Daire for giving me my best working day to date.

The meeting went well. Lexi outlined what her needs were, from the naming of the housing development to all of the subsequent materials, including the invitations to the gala, which was happening in six weeks. Soph looked mildly panicked at the tight turnaround on that, but I promised that it could be done. I remembered Booker saying that Carson overpromised and underdelivered. I did not want to get slapped with that label, too. I didn't care what I had to do; we were going to be ready for the gala.

By the time Lexi headed back to work and Soph left my office with the newly inked working agreements in hand, my coffee was cold and the late night was catching up to me, making me yawn and try to figure out where I could wedge a catnap into my day.

It was after lunch before I remembered the note that had been taped to my front door. I grabbed my shoulder bag out of the desk drawer where I kept it and found the envelope.

It occurred to me, in a flash of panic, that this could be something bad.

I'd assumed that it was a love note, well, probably not a *love* note this soon in the game, but a "thanks for the awesome night" note wouldn't have been out of order. I had been sure Nick would have penned something sweet or sexy about our night last night, but maybe it wasn't that at all. Maybe now that we'd slept together, he wanted me gone from the premises. Perhaps in hindsight, he was freaked out that he'd slept with his tenant. Uh-oh.

My fingers shook when I opened the note, which was ridiculous. A single sheet of paper fell onto the top of my desk. I picked it up and slowly unfolded it.

Scrawled in Nick's bold hand were the words: *My place? Seven.*

Was this an invitation? There was a question mark, but it still felt more like one of his mandates. Hmm. Was I going to go? As if that were a real question. Of course I was. My curiosity would kill me if I didn't. That being said, I thought it best to keep my guard up and be prepared for whatever was coming my way. Good or bad, happy or sad, hot or not, I was ready. I hoped.

Nick

20

"Holy shit!" Jackson startled me out of my nap on the workout bench.

I lurched upright, clutching my chest. "What the hell, man?"

Jackson was looming over me so I slid down the bench. A normal person would have grasped the subtle cue that I was putting some distance between us. Not Jackson. He sat down next to me.

"You slept with Annabelle, didn't you?" he asked.

My eyes went wide. I had assumed that when he got back from driving Lexi home, he would think I'd gone to bed.

"What are you talking about?" I asked. I could feel my face get hot so I tried to cover it by looking pissed off. I was good at pissed off.

"Lupita said you didn't sleep in your bed," he said. "And look at you, you're unconscious at nine o'clock in the morning. That, my brother, is a night well spent."

Usually, I corrected him when he called me "brother," but today I was straight up too exhausted to call him on it. Besides, while I'd never admit it to him, I kind of liked it. It gave me a feeling of belonging that had been sorely missing in my life.

"I'm not talking about this," I said.

"Sure, I get it, a gentleman doesn't talk about his lady." He nodded in understanding but his grin was literally from ear to ear. The big idiot.

I felt myself return his smile. I just couldn't stop it. That was definitely Annabelle's fault.

"She's not my lady." I don't know why I felt compelled to correct him, but there was a part of me that resisted staking a claim on her, because if I did, I was sure I'd lose her just like I'd lost everyone I'd ever considered my own.

His smile vanished. He raised one eyebrow at me and said, "A man waits a lifetime for a woman like Annabelle. For your own sake, do not fuck this up."

"There's nothing to fuck up," I said. "I don't do long term and Annabelle knows that."

He stared at me for a moment and then shook his head, saying what he thought without actually saying it. In Jackson's opinion, I was too stupid to live.

I thought about defending my position. The old me would have. I would have insisted that no relationship was meant to last more than a season, but it hit me then that I wanted this one to last the three months and possibly more. I had a feeling it would take me at least that long to get enough of whatever this crazy energy was between us. I felt a flash of anxiety at the note I'd left for Annabelle this morning.

It had lacked finesse, endearments, or any sort of charm whatsoever. If I were her, would I show up here at seven, not knowing what to expect? I thought of her with her carefree smile, gypsy eyes, and goddess body. Yes, she would show, because she was reckless and impulsive and I really lo—liked, I really liked that about her.

"Don't worry," I said. "I've got this." I didn't have shit. I knew it and I knew Jackson knew it, too. Naturally, I did what all damaged men do when faced with uncomfortable emotions. I ignored them. I rose to standing, pleased to see that my leg felt stronger than it had in ages. Had sex been what was missing? I liked that theory. "Come on, let's get to it."

We spent the morning working out, and I pushed myself harder than I had ever dared before. I only caught myself smiling stupidly at nothing once or twice, okay four times but that was it. I swear.

At seven minutes past seven, I glanced at the clock for what must have been the hundredth time. She was seven minutes late. I glanced down at the guest house, looking for any sign of Annabelle. The lights were out. The place was empty. It could be she hadn't gotten my note.

Or maybe she was blowing me off. Perhaps for her, last night had been a one and done. The amount of unhappiness I felt at the thought was unbecoming, to put it mildly.

I had given the Guzmans and Jackson the night off, assuming that Annabelle would be here with me. When I'd asked Lupita to make a dinner for two that I could heat up later, she had beamed at me, like I hadn't just asked her to do extra work, and set right to it.

Directions on an index card in her neat hand sat on the quartz countertop, while the prepped food had been stored in the refrigerator until it was ready to be cooked. Salmon on a bed of rice with asparagus, melt-in-your-mouth Parker House rolls, and a papaya mousse for dessert. I really didn't deserve that woman despite how much I paid her.

I glanced at the clock. Seven ten. She was standing me up. I was sure of it.

I paced, not caring if I had another stroke and my leg gave out and I fell on my face. It would just be a physical manifestation of the emotional angst I was in. In the living room, I slumped onto my couch, feeling defeated and a little depressed. Had last night not meant the same thing to Annabelle that it had to me? What did it mean to me? I slapped that thought away as soon as it flitted into my head.

I was debating what to have with my double

351

portion dinner for one, whiskey or beer, when there was a soft knock on the front door. I bolted upright, did a quick finger-comb of my hair, and smoothed down my shirt.

Christ, I was nervous. I hadn't been nervous around a woman since I was in middle school and had the misfortune to be in Ms. Madison's algebra class. There wasn't a heterosexual boy in that class who didn't crush on her. It was a wonder any of us were able to pass a class where our hormones ran rampant, leaving us scrambling to find x while wondering y we even had to. Punny, I know.

I strode to the door, not even thinking about my leg, my arm, or my potential for another stroke. I just wanted to see her.

I yanked open the door and there she was. Breathtakingly lovely in a navy dress with a pretty scarf, her hair twisted into a knot on the top of her head.

"Hi." Her voice was soft. "Just so I know, is this the moment when you kick me out for fraternizing with my landlord?"

"Uh-huh," I said. I had no idea what she said. I was too busy staring at her, taking in every bit of her from the stray curls that framed her face to her cherry red lipstick to the dress that hugged her curves the way I wanted to.

"What?" She looked stricken.

"Huh?" I shook my head. "No, wait, oh hell . . ."

I couldn't stand it, the whole two feet of space between us, anymore. I reached out and snatched her close and then I kissed her. Everything in my world clicked right into place the moment my lips met hers.

She was sweet, effervescent Annabelle, and if I could drown in her, I would. I slid my mouth down the side of her neck, tugging her scarf out of the way. Her fingers dug into my hair and she pulled me back and kissed me as if she'd been waiting for this moment all day. A low moan sounded in her throat. It was the same sound she'd made last night, and it hit me like a trigger.

I pulled her into the house and pushed her back against the closed door. I had no idea if we kissed for minutes or hours or days. If I could have spent eternity like this, I would. When she finally broke the kiss, we were both breathing heavily, and I could feel my heart racing in my chest. For once, it didn't cause me any panic. I knew why it was beating so hard. It was because of her. It just wanted to be near her. I totally understood.

"Come on," Annabelle said. She grabbed my hand with hers. "We have to go."

"What?" I asked. "But I have dinner."

"Is it already cooked?" she asked.

"No, just prepped," I said.

"Good, then it can wait," she said. "Come on."

She grabbed my hand in hers and dragged me out the door.

"But where—"

"Trust me," she said. She didn't give me a chance to think it over. She pulled me through the door and into the night.

She walked beside me down the steps as if afraid I might collapse and fall at any moment and she'd be there to catch me. I glanced at her. She was on the tall side but she was not muscular. I would squash her like a bug. When we got to the bottom of the stairs, she stopped in front of a black Jeep. She opened the passenger door and said, "Sorry I was late. I was out picking this bad boy up. Get in."

I balked. Leaving the safety of my house was not something I did lightly. "Where are we going?"

"It's a surprise," she said.

"I'm not really a surprise kind of guy," I said. This was me, trying to be diplomatic. The truth is, I don't like surprises; in fact, I hate them. "And I don't go out in public anymore."

"Trust me," she said. She stood with the door open as if she had every confidence that I would just climb into the passenger seat like a damn sheep. So I climbed into the Jeep, natch. She ran around the front of the car to the driver's side.

"Did you buy this today?" I asked.

"Borrowed it," she said. "Hang on."

I buckled up and grabbed the armrest on the door. The woman drove like she did everything else—at top speed, all in, giving it one hundred percent.

"Where are we—" I began but she interrupted.

"I'm not telling you," she said. "But I am confident you're going to like it."

She blew through the open gate and headed east on Camelback Road. The city lights whipped past us, and a tingle of excitement crept into my veins. How long had it been since I'd been out of my house in the evening? Ages. I'd been so determined to get my health back to optimum, I considered sleep one of the best things I could do for myself. Subsequently, I was rarely up past ten, last night being a major exception, and I was usually hunkered in for the night by seven. I glanced at the clock on the dashboard. It was seven thirty and I hadn't even eaten.

I glanced down at myself. When exactly had I become an eighty-five-year-old man? But I knew the answer. My stroke had changed everything for me.

It was cold out. The cloth top of the Jeep kept most of the night air out but not all of it. Annabelle had the heat cranked up, and it blasted over my feet so my bottom half was hot while my upper half was chilled. She must have registered my discomfort because she grabbed a fleecy throw from the back seat and shoved it at me. I wrapped it around both of our shoulders, and she flashed me a grateful smile. It occurred to me

355

that there wasn't much I wouldn't do to be on the receiving end of that smile.

As she drove us through Scottsdale and the Fort McDowell Yavapai Nation Reservation, I tried not to panic, thinking about how far I was from a hospital if I suddenly needed one. My anxiety spiked and I did some of the calming exercises that Jackson had taught me. We were flying up the Beeline Highway into the Tonto National Forest, and the air was getting cooler, the night darker, and the world quieter.

She peeled off on an exit that was one lane of loose dirt and then she flicked on her high beams. We followed the pitted road into the rocky terrain for several miles. There were no other cars, no other signs of life, and I tried very hard not to have a complete freak-out.

Annabelle consulted her phone two or three times until, satisfied, she pulled into a small dirt lot. A posted sign announced that it was the trailhead for a hike. Sweet baby Jesus, she did not think we were going night hiking, did she? That was a hard no.

She switched off the engine and cut the headlights. Then she began unfastening the cloth top of the Jeep by the light of her phone.

"What are you doing?" I demanded. I was getting impatient.

"Wait for it," she said. I saw her flash of a smile in the darkness, and I wasn't sure if I wanted to throttle her or kiss her. Oh, who was I kidding? I was only here because I wanted to kiss her until the end of time. Damn it.

When she had the top completely dismantled, she reached over me and pulled the lever on my seat. I went down hard into a full recline and she landed on top of me. My arms went instinctively around her and pulled her close.

"Hi," she whispered.

"Hi," I said. Before I lost my train of thought, I asked, "If you won't tell me what we're doing here, will you tell me why we're here?"

"Light pollution," she said. "We had to get out of it, so we could see."

"See what?" I asked. We were in the middle of nowhere in the dark. What were we supposed to see? Cactus? Coyotes?

Again she grinned and said, "Wait—"

"For it," I said. "Yeah, I got that. Is it all right if I kiss you while I'm waiting?"

She glanced at her phone. "Yes, we have a few minutes before it gets good."

And that, my friends, was how I came to be making out in a borrowed Jeep in the middle of the desert at night. I had just gotten to the point where I felt clothing needed to be removed when Annabelle pulled back and reclined her own seat. She had more blankets that she pulled from the back seat as well as a flask of whiskey, which she handed to me.

"Okay, get ready," she said.

Get ready for what? My prurient brain had a host of scenarios run through it, and I was about to give her a dirty multiple-choice pop quiz when she grabbed my hand and gasped, "Look!"

In the darkness I could just make out her profile and I noticed she was watching the sky. I turned my head and glanced up. The stars were a million times brighter out here and I had to admire how many there were and how they sparkled like a fistful of glitter that had been thrown across the dark night and stuck.

And then a flash caught my eye. It was gone before I registered what it was. I stared, trying to figure it out. And then, there was another and another. It was as if the sky had come alive, and I marveled at the natural wonder as bright sparks kept flying off in all directions.

"Is that . . . ?" My voice trailed off. I had no words to describe it.

"Shooting stars," she said. "Aren't they beautiful?"

"I've never seen anything like it," I said. I was whispering as if a loud noise might interrupt the magic.

Annabelle reached between our seats and grabbed my hand in hers and gave my fingers a gentle squeeze. "I know they're not really shooting stars," she said. "It's actually a meteor shower."

Her hand felt right pressed into mine. It occurred to me that I'd never had this natural rapport with a woman before. It was astonishing and rather delightful.

"I heard about it on KJZZ today," she explained. "They said tonight was the best night to view the meteors because the moon is just a crescent, but that you had to get out of the city to really be able to see. I've never seen one before, and I didn't want to miss it, so I borrowed Nyah's Jeep."

"Who is Nyah?"

"One of my hot tub friends," she said. There was mischief in her voice, and her grin was a slash of white in the night. Irresistible.

I rose up out of my seat and leaned over her. Then I kissed her. She responded immediately, wrapping her arms around my neck and returning my kiss measure for measure. The taste of her, the scent of her, which reminded me of apple blossoms and honey, filled my senses and sent them swimming, mostly south. Reluctantly, I pulled back and collapsed into my seat.

"You know, you didn't have to drive us all the way out here to see the stars," I said. "Every time I kiss you, I see stars."

"Oh, Nick." She sighed. "I feel the same way."

We were both silent, as if processing the truth that whatever was between us was something special. It occurred to me that it needed to be

359

handled with extra care. I wasn't sure I was up to the task, given my history of short unemotional hookups, but I knew that for Annabelle I wanted to try.

"Hey, Nick," she whispered. "Have you made a wish yet?"

"No, have you?"

"I've made a dozen," she laughed. "Your turn."

I glanced up and sure enough, in a matter of seconds, a skinny blaze of light shot across the sky. I closed my eyes. I knew exactly what I wanted. I wanted to be normal again, I wanted my body to stop giving out on me, I wanted to be who I used to be . . . my thoughts stopped right there.

Would the old me have let Annabelle drag him out of his house and drive him out into the desert to look at shooting stars? Nope. The old me would have been busy making deals, working angles, getting what I wanted when I wanted it with a piece of arm candy hanging on me that was as much a testament to my success as the Rolex I wore or the sports car I drove. It hit me then, like a closed fist to the temple, that I didn't want to be that guy anymore.

Instead, I found myself wishing for something wholly unexpected. I wished that I could be a better man for Annabelle, for Lexi, and most important, for myself.

"Well?" she asked. "Did you make a wish?"

"I'm working on it," I said. I glanced at her, catching sight of her profile, the slender nose, full lips, and stubborn chin, barely visible in the dark, and yet still so lovely.

"Is astronomy a hobby of yours?" I asked. It wouldn't have surprised me if it was. In fact, I was getting to the point where I expected nothing but surprises from Annabelle.

"No, but I follow NASA on their social media, and I love the pictures they share of deep space," she said. "Looking at star clusters, galaxies, nebulas, and supernovas makes everything down here seem, I don't know, overwrought and ridiculous, like pesky coworkers or rude sales-clerks—"

"Or overbearing landlords," I added. She laughed, which had been my intention, and it made my chest thrum with pleasure.

"Yes, well, I don't really know any overbearing landlords," she said. I snorted and she laughed some more. "All of that"—she gestured up at the sky—"it makes me feel like I'm just a teeny tiny speck of cosmic dust and that all of the things I worry about are even less than that, you know what I mean?"

"It doesn't make you anxious, being so tiny in this enormous universe surrounding us?" I asked. "It doesn't make you feel insignificant?"

"No." She shook her head. I saw her smile again. "It makes me feel relieved, like no matter how badly I screw up—and boy, have I—it's okay. When I look out into the vast universe, I realize that a lot of stuff is really not that big of a deal."

"You're breaking my brain, Goddess," I said. I was trying to keep it light, but in all honesty, she was challenging me in ways I hadn't expected.

She laughed again. "Sorry, my dad's a mathematician so my sister and I were frequently encouraged to go big in our thinking."

"Well, you don't get much bigger than this," I said. I opened the flask of whiskey and took a big sip. I handed it to Annabelle, who did the same. It fought off the chill, and as its heat coursed through me, I settled back into my seat, pulled my fleecy blanket around me, and stared up at the sky.

Annabelle handed the flask back to me, but I didn't drink any more. I didn't want anything to take the edge off this time with her. As I watched the falling stars—I didn't care if it was technically a meteor shower—I made wish after wish, and they all began and ended with her.

Annabelle

21

"Thank you all for making Lexi Brewer's project a priority," I said. "I know it's a tight turnaround, but I'm confident we can do amazing things. We're Vasquez Squared."

Christian, ever the competitor, let out a roar and raised his fist in the air. This was greeted by laughs from the rest of the staff.

I was standing in front of the whiteboard in the meeting room at the office. I glanced around the big table and smiled at my coworkers. Their enthusiasm for Lexi's project was off the charts, and I was genuinely excited to see what they all came up with.

Because there was so much to be done, we'd broken everyone into teams. So Christian, a graphic designer, and Shanna, a copywriter, would prioritize working on the materials for the gala, while Booker and Luz took on the overall branding of the housing development with their team of designers. Carson and I would oversee the execution of the deliverables in our capacities as art director and creative director. Sophie and Miguel as chief creative officers and owners of the studio would act in an advisory capacity as needed.

I handed out the creative brief as well as packets of information to the teams that explained what Lexi's project was all about. As a net-zero housing development, the goal was to create a self-sustaining community that required little to no support from the utility companies for power or the city for waste management or water. Lexi was utilizing fascinating technologies in her structures like gray-water harvesting for irrigation and toilet flushing, and green roofs for insulation and temperature management. She even planned to use electrochromic glass, which tinted as needed like sunglasses. Composting both food waste and human waste were to be incorporated as well. I saw Luz make a face when she read about that, and I had to hide my laugh.

"If there are no more questions—" I began but Carson interrupted me, because of course he did.

"I have one," he said.

I felt the entire room watching me. I pasted a smile on my face and said, "Sure, what is it?"

"How did you meet Lexi Brewer?" he asked. He was reclining in his seat in a casual pose, but I could see the tension in him as he fidgeted with his pen, twirling it between his fingers.

"I'm sorry, what?" I asked.

"I just find it interesting that you're brand new to Phoenix, don't know a soul, and yet here you are, bringing in a huge new client with quite the generous budget." He paused to tap his pen on the proposed budget for our work for Lexi, the budget Nick had signed off on under her name, and then back up at me. He was smiling but it left me cold.

I supposed I should have expected this. My bringing in a huge client threatened all of Carson's plans to oust me. He was going to do anything he could to undermine me, including questioning the Golden Goose I'd brought to the table.

I had a moment of uneasiness. Did he know? Did he know about Nick and Lexi? About me and Nick? I could feel my face get warm and my heart was racing. This was crazy. I hadn't done anything wrong. There was absolutely nothing suspect about my landlord introducing me to his sister and her hiring me to do design work for her.

Except Nick didn't want anyone to know that Lexi was his sister or that he was paying for the work, and I definitely didn't want anyone to know that I was sleeping with Nick. Fair or not, I knew it would damage my credibility in bringing in this client. I knew that I'd have gotten the job whether Nick and I had hooked up or not, but it wouldn't appear that way from the outside looking in and there was nothing I could do to curb the speculation.

I glanced around the room. Everyone was watching me, some wanting to see how I handled

Carson and others looking for an explanation.

Miguel glanced at Carson, looking irritated. He was about to say something but I jumped in, knowing that if I didn't answer Carson, his question would linger in people's minds. I was not about to let him sow seeds of doubt about me.

"I know, it's crazy, right?" I asked. I decided to brazen it out. As has been noted before, I am a terrible liar so I stuck as close to the truth as possible. I forced a laugh and hoped it didn't sound like I was choking on it. "Lexi and I have a friend in common who introduced us and we clicked. I guess it was sheer luck, being in the right place at the right time."

Carson stared at me. He looked like he wanted to push for more details, but Sophie interrupted him.

"It was lucky for Vasquez Squared, that's for sure," Soph said. "But then Annabelle has always made connections so easily. I'm not surprised at all."

She brushed a speck of lint off of her suit coat. Everyone was watching her, but I was looking at Carson, and I saw his eyes narrow with a blast of hatred that made me catch my breath. For the first time, I wondered if Carson's problem wasn't with me so much as it was with Soph.

The thought made me very uneasy, but not as uneasy as the summons I received later. Trent called me into his office just after lunch. I left the

366

preliminary mockups for the logo for Lexi on my worktable and hurried to his office. I was feeling very connected to the project and had some ideas I wanted to flesh out before bringing them to the team, but when the business department called, I answered. This reminded me of why I had liked working for myself. No interruptions.

I knocked on the doorjamb and waited for Trent to call me into the room. He was seated at his desk, and a frown marred his usual jovial appearance. I wondered what was up.

"You wanted to see me?" I asked.

Trent waved me into the chair across from his. "Come on in, Annabelle, this should only take a moment."

I sat, and Trent smiled at me, but I noticed it didn't reach his eyes. I started to get a bad feeling.

"I just need to go over some expenditures with you," he said.

"All right." As far as I knew, I didn't have any. We were all issued company credit cards for taking out clients, but I hadn't used mine as yet.

Trent handed me a sheet of paper. I looked at it and blinked. It was an itemized list of expenses billed to the credit card that had been issued to me. The sum at the bottom made me gasp. It appeared I had charged over a thousand dollars' worth of food and drink at several restaurants in Phoenix. Restaurants to which I had never been.

"I don't understand," I said.

"This is your billing statement for the past few weeks," Trent said. "Looks like you've been working the client connection hard." He laughed as if trying to make light of it, but I didn't return it.

"But I haven't used my card," I said.

Trent stopped laughing. "Are you sure? You're not in trouble. It's just that we try to keep the monthly totals to a quarter of what's listed here, but with the client you've brought in, I'm sure Miguel and Sophie will be okay with it."

I nodded. "Soph told me that when she gave me the card, but I'm telling you the truth. I haven't used my card. Not once."

Trent's eyebrows drew together. He glanced down at the copy of the bill that was in front of him and said, "On March seventh, you weren't at Durant's on Central Ave?"

I shook my head. "I've never even been to Durant's."

"Oh, you should go," he said. "It's like walking back in time. You enter through the kitchen and the chefs all greet you. And the dining room is totally vintage with red leather booths, paneling, and red velvet wallpaper."

"I'll keep it in mind," I said. I glanced down at his desk and Trent glanced down, too.

"Right," he said. "Okay, how about Tarbell's on Camelback on March ninth?"

"Nope."

"Pizzeria Bianco downtown on the thirteenth?"

"Never been there."

"That's a pity. You should check it out. Do you still have your card?" Trent asked.

"As far as I know, it's in my wallet," I said. "Do you want me to go get it?"

"Yes, please."

I hurried from Trent's office back to my own. I opened the door and rushed to my desk. Even knowing I hadn't made those charges, I felt sick to my stomach. How could this have happened? Had I lost it? Had it been stolen? I opened my wallet. Sitting right in its place was the business credit card. I thought I might throw up.

I took the card back to Trent. Sheepishly, I handed it over and he examined it against the balance sheet as if he thought it was an imposter.

"It's your card all right," he said. He scratched his head as if boggled. It was clear. Somehow I'd been hacked.

"Annabelle, it's not that I don't believe you—" he began but I interrupted.

"But it seems weird since I've never used it," I said. "How did someone get the number?"

"Good question. Do you remember where you were on those evenings?" he asked.

I tried to remember. "Home alone, out in the desert watching a meteor shower, and—" I paused. I'd been having mind-blowing sex with

369

Nick on that third date. This was not something I planned to share for a variety of reasons. "Again, home."

"Can anyone corroborate your whereabouts during those evenings?" he asked. He sounded hopeful then quickly clarified. "For the credit card company."

"No," I said. I was not dragging Nick into this. Full stop.

"It's clear someone made fast and loose with your card, repeatedly," Trent said, and sighed. "I'll cancel this card and have them issue you a new one."

"No," I said. I studied his face, wondering if he'd hear me out. "Listen, I don't know what happened but I promise you, I haven't used my card, not once, so there's no way a stranger hacked my number."

"What are you saying, Annabelle?"

"I think it was someone in-house," I said. His eyes narrowed. He didn't like that any more than I did. "Is there any way we can put an alert on it, so that when it's used, it will tell us when and where?"

"I can track it online," he said. "The credit card company will flag suspicious charges, but you'd have to be in Paris or something to trigger that."

I rather wished I was in Paris at the moment. Paris is always a good idea, after all.

"What if we leave it open just to see if we can catch them?" I asked.

"I don't know, they could rack up thousands in debt," he said. "I don't want to risk it."

"Could we put a cap on the amount?"

One eyebrow went up higher than his eyeglass frames. "Meaning we make your maximum low enough that whoever wants to run up a huge bill gets rejected and has to use another form of payment?"

I nodded. "I hate to even suggest this, but if it's someone in the office, then they'd likely use their business card to cover it, tipping us off to who it is."

Trent handed my card back to me with a calculating look. "There's going to be an email, announcing to the staff to be more conscientious with their business expenses. It would help if you look duly chastened by it."

I smiled at him. "We're going fishing?"

"That's right, shark bait."

I laughed. I had my suspicions about who had hijacked my card, but I was willing to wait until he was outed for certain before I threw any confetti in the air.

"One question," he said. "How would you feel if there was a security camera installed in your office temporarily?"

"Whatever it takes is fine with me," I said.

I arrived back at my office and stored my card

back in my wallet. I hadn't been in the habit of locking my door, although I usually kept it shut when I wasn't here. I was going to have to rethink that while still giving the thief access to my office. Hmm.

I glanced at the room and noted that something was different. The mockups on my worktable weren't as I had left them. I crossed the room and studied them. Nothing was missing, but it was clear they'd been moved, as if someone had picked them up and studied them. I felt a chill run down my spine. I had no doubt it was Carson West. Now I just had to prove it.

My raft floated by Nick's, and I felt as if I were caught in a dream, floating around a gorgeous aqua pool with a hot guy on a Sunday afternoon as if I didn't have a care in the world.

Ha! If only. Despite the margarita in my hand, I was not relaxed. Anything but. The gala for Lexi's housing project was coming up fast, and I was being hypervigilant about every single aspect of it. With so much work to be done, it was exhausting, but I didn't dare take my eyes off the prize.

Carson West being on the design team was a stressor I did not need, but I couldn't figure out how to get rid of him without a truckload of office drama. The pleaser in me didn't like making waves, but I didn't trust him not to sabotage the project intentionally and make it look like my fault. Add in my suspicion that he was also the one tampering with my corporate card, and tracking his every move at the office was becoming an obsession.

I was still unsettled by his questions about how I'd met Lexi and managed to bring her in as a client. The man gave me bad vibes, and they were creeping into my off time, too, which I mightily resented.

"All right, what's going on?" Nick asked.

He caught my raft as it came alongside his, keeping me from floating by.

"What do you mean?" I asked. I sipped my margarita, playing it cool.

"You keep making these exasperated little noises while you're staring off into space so it seems something is bugging you," he said. He closed the paperback book he had in his hand and gently tossed it onto one of the lounge chairs beside the pool. "I thought you'd consider it a victory to have the tenant ban from the pool lifted."

I grinned at him and made a V for victory with the index and middle fingers of my free hand. I had been quite stoked when he told me the pool and hot tub were at my disposal whenever I wanted.

"Which is much appreciated," I said. "I'm just having a hard time leaving work at the office."

"Can I help?"

I considered him. "That depends. Do you have any experience with disgruntled narcissists?"

"Carson West?" he asked.

I was impressed that he remembered the name from our conversation on my patio the night he'd turned up in his wheelchair with Sir.

"Yeah," I said. "I don't trust him and he's maneuvered himself onto Lexi's project and my instincts are telling me he's going to do something to sabotage it. He's already started questioning how I, a new resident to Phoenix, managed to bag such a big client. I suspect he's talking about me behind my back to other staff members, because there were just a few instances where I felt like something was off with colleagues that I normally get along with just fine. He's trying to undermine me, and I genuinely don't know what to do about it."

I didn't mention the corporate card because I didn't have proof, but also I suspected Nick would be mad enough to talk to Miguel and I didn't want anyone to know we were a thing. If we were going to last only a few months, then there wasn't much point in going public.

"What's your strategy been so far?" he asked.

"Watch him," I said. "And try to anticipate what he might do to sabotage the project."

"That's got to be exhausting," Nick said.

I let my head flop back on my raft. "Yes. I'm

so tired. Although most of that is your fault."

Nick let out a self-satisfied chuckle that warmed my heart. The same heart I had deep packed in ice so that it wouldn't smash to bits when this fling was over.

"Okay, you're playing a solid defense, but what you really need to do is move to an offensive position," he said.

"Man-to-man or zone?" I asked. He lifted an eyebrow in surprise. "What? I played basketball."

"Then you should know how to establish a fast break offense," he said. "You need to soften Carson into thinking he's got you figured out and then you kick into high gear and charge right around him. Nothing but net."

"Our sports analogy is no longer working for me," I said. "Is this how you managed your business when you were a builder?"

"Absolutely. I gave people enough work to break them. They either got it done or they got a new job," he said. "Fast break offense means fast. You need to keep Carson off balance all the time. How much work are you putting on him?"

"The absolute bare minimum," I said. "I don't want his sticky fingers making a mess of things."

"That's a mistake," he said.

My mouth dropped open. "Mistake?"

"Yeah. From what you've described, Carson is a user. He's the Tom Sawyer of the office, getting everyone to do his work for him."

I nodded. I'd seen it in action.

"He doesn't have enough to do. That's why he's always looking for trouble. You need to bury him," Nick said.

"In what way?" I asked.

"In all the ways," Nick said. "Give him every assignment you can think of in regards to Lexi's development."

"Ah! But what if he messes it up?" I asked. "I'm quite certain he'll try."

"He can try, but since you'll be doing the real work and he'll just be doing busywork, who cares?"

I stared at him. It had never occurred to me to take control of the situation like this. I was in charge of Lexi's project. I called the shots. As senior art director, Carson was on the team, but he reported to me. Ever the pleaser, I'd tried to placate him by having him oversee the creation of the logo but gave him nothing substantial to keep him occupied, guaranteeing that he had plenty of time to mess things up.

I was an idiot. I had to rethink everything. Nick was right. I could give him so much work, Carson wouldn't have a minute to spare.

Nick was watching me while I turned this idea over in my mind. "I think you might be a genius," I said.

He shrugged. "Best-case scenario, he actually comes up with something usable. Worst case, he messes up, but it doesn't matter because you've got it covered already anyway. Besides, imagine his face when you dump a load of work on him."

I laughed. The mental picture of Carson being forced to work instead of prowling the office looking for trouble brought me great joy. I reached out and placed my plastic margarita glass on the cool deck. Then I slid from my raft into the water. I popped up on the side of Nick's, and he smiled down at me.

"Would this be considered a fast break offense?" I asked right before I kissed him. His hand cupped the back of my head and held me still while he returned my kiss with enthusiasm. When we broke apart, we were both breathing heavily.

Nick slid off his raft, and we stood in the waist-high water, facing each other. There was so much I wanted to say to him but I didn't know how. The weeks were slipping by so fast, and our three months would be over before I knew it. How would I manage to live here when we were no longer together?

"What are you thinking?" he asked. His hazel gaze was intent on my face, which I was desperately trying to keep blank. I didn't want him to see my angst.

"Nothing," I said. I shook my head. I wasn't going to ruin the time we had by wishing for something more.

"You look pensive," he said.

I felt like ducking under the water to avoid his scrutiny. Instead, I went right to my default setting.

"I'm sorry," I said.

He shook his head. "No apology necessary."

"It's just work on my mind."

"Is it?" he asked. "Are you sure there's nothing else?"

I got the feeling he knew. My heart started to beat really hard. Did he know that I was having *feelings* that would complicate things? Should I admit it?

"Canonball!"

The universe saved me from my own stupidity in the form of Jackson, leaping into the air and tucking himself into a ball, before he splashed down into the pool beside Nick and me, sending a sheet of water over us and breaking the moment, saving me from probable disaster.

As water dripped off the two of us, I heard Nick mutter, "I definitely need to fire him."

Nick

22

The following weeks were the most singular of my life. I woke up with Annabelle in the morning and fell asleep curled up around her at night. It was the safest I had felt since I was a child, before my family fell apart. I tried not to dwell on a month passing so swiftly, assuring myself that we would start to get sick of each other before the three months were up. *Right.*

It was Annabelle who convinced me to let in the light. She drew open all the drapes in my house, letting the warm March sunshine in. I don't think I imagined the lift in the spirits of Jackson, Lupita, and Juan at this abrupt change. Either the light made them happy, or possibly, the haze of happy I was looking at them through made them seem happier, or perhaps it was a bit of both.

Annabelle was like having an exotic being from another dimension around. She saw things I missed like the way a hawk rode the thermals over the construction site for Lexi's development or how the leaves in the trees turned upside down before a rain.

She sat completely still on a chair in the backyard for hours, watching the birds interact, and then she made up voices and conversations for them. My favorite was a big black cowbird that she called "the Masshole," a mash-up of Massachusetts and asshole, and she voiced him with a thick Boston accent, saying things like, *"The grub heah's a wicked pissa."*

I'm not sure at what point I became one hundred percent smitten with her. It might have been when she voiced the birds, or maybe it was the night after I'd made love to her, twice, that she announced she needed pancakes right then and there or she was going to perish. I'd obviously lost brain cells during the orgasm portion of the evening, proving once again her theory that orgasms made you stupid, because instead of refusing I said, "Okay."

I never left my house at night. Hell, for the previous nine months I had practically never left my house at all. This was madness.

But Annabelle didn't live within the tight boundaries of my very narrow comfort zone. She was new to Phoenix, and she wanted to do *all the things* and experience every nook and cranny of life in the Southwest.

Over the past few weeks, she'd dragged me and Jackson to the Phoenix Art Museum, the Heard Museum, the Desert Botanical Gardens, and we'd even toured Tovrea Castle. When I say toured, what I mean is I found a quiet place to sit while they walked through the various places. If

Annabelle resented that I didn't participate fully, she never said so. I was doing my best to meet her halfway but I'd be lying if I said I enjoyed it.

The truth was that leaving the safety of my house was torture. I think she believed that if I kept doing it, it would get easier, but it didn't. The anxiety and panic bubbled just beneath the surface, and I didn't draw a full breath until we were back home. With any other woman, I would have just said no, but I found that being with Annabelle overruled my need to stay within the cocoon of my safe space. As for tonight, at least a midnight pancake run wouldn't take long and I'd be sitting down, and so it was that I found myself in the passenger seat while she drove us to the neighborhood Denny's.

"I miss diners," she said. "There just aren't that many diners in Phoenix. Back East, every town has two or three diners usually in those weird, silver tube-like buildings, you know, so you feel like you're eating in an old railroad car. The coffee is hot, the food is plentiful, and the grease is thick enough to write your name in."

"That may be true," I said. It was true. There really weren't that many authentic diners in Phoenix. "But we do have Mel's Diner from the show *Alice*."

"No, suh," she said in full Boston mode.

"Yes, suh," I countered. "It's over on Grand Avenue, but it's only breakfast and lunch. We should go sometime." I couldn't believe I'd just said that.

The smile she sent me about stopped my heart. "I'd love that!"

Of course she would.

We parked at the Denny's and walked in. The place was hopping for one o'clock in the morning, and as I glanced around the restaurant, I felt woefully underdressed.

"Did we crash a party?" I asked.

"No, sugar, we always come here after a show." A deep voice spoke from behind me. I turned to find a very tall black man, dressed in a glorious blond wig and a gold lamé dress, with full makeup and in heels. While I gaped and pretended not to, Annabelle extended her hand and said, "Hi, are you a performer?"

"Phoenix's finest female impersonator, at your service." He curtsied and then struck a sexy pose. "Did you recognize me?"

"No, I'm sorry," she said. "I'm new in town."

"You're forgiven then, cutie," he said. He batted his long purple eyelashes at her. "I'm ManDee. You can catch me at Club Twenty-One every Friday at nine thirty."

"I'll definitely check it out," she promised.

"Bring this handsome fella with you, too." ManDee winked at me and sauntered away as if the industrial flooring beneath his enormous high-heeled feet were the red carpet.

Annabelle and I watched him for a moment and she said, "I sure wish I could walk like that."

I glanced down at her, noting that she still wore the afterglow of our evening's activities, and I felt a ridiculous burst of pride that I'd given her that sleepy-eyed sated look.

"If you walked into a room like that, I'd probably keel over dead of a heart attack," I said. She laughed but I'd only been partly kidding.

We ordered piles of pancakes, eggs, bacon, and orange juice to wash it all down. Annabelle kept up with me in the food department, and I started to look forward to going home so we could work it all off.

We were slumped in our seats on either side of the booth, waiting for the waitress to bring the check, when I happened to glance out the window. The usual midnight fare of drunks, hipsters, and dates that didn't want to end filled the area, but amid all of that, I still saw them.

I felt the hair on the back of my neck stand on end as I watched the family drama play out in the parking lot. A feeling of déjà vu hit me so hard, I couldn't breathe.

The man appeared strung out, and the woman was crying. The children—oh god, the children—a boy standing beside his mother, visibly trying not to cry, and a baby in the mother's arms, fussing because she looked exhausted. I watched as the husband threw his hands in the air and started to walk away. The mother shoved the baby into the boy's arms and ran after the man. I watched the boy comfort his baby sister, looking scared, lost, and confused. I thought I might throw up.

"Nick, are you all right?" Annabelle reached across the table and patted my hand. I realized she'd been speaking but I'd missed it.

"Yeah, come on," I said. I slid out of the booth, and with a surprised look, she followed. I grabbed our waitress on the way out and shoved a fistful of bills at her. "Will that cover it?"

"More than," she said. She went to hand me back a twenty but I shook her off.

"Keep it."

Her eyes went wide. "Thank you!"

I barely heard her as I was already shoving my way out the door, past the line of people trying to get in.

"Nick, wait, what's going on?" Annabelle asked from behind me. "Are you all right? Do you feel okay? Should I call Jackson?"

"I'm fine," I said. The night air was chilly and not appropriate for two little kids to be out in. I strode across the parking lot. The husband was gone and the mother was coming back to her children. She was crying but she opened her arms and they clambered into the safety of her embrace. I felt the panic inside me ease, just a little.

"Hi," I called out to her. Her eyes went wide and she looked in both directions as if searching for an escape. She started to pull her children in the direction of the bus stop. "Wait. You look like you could use some help. Can I help you?"

"No, we're fine," she said. Her voice shook. "Go away. Leave us alone."

It was clear. She was terrified. She probably thought I was social services, coming to take her kids.

"Do you have a safe place to sleep tonight?" Annabelle asked as she stepped up beside me.

The woman ignored her and continued to pull the boy, still holding the baby, away. He wasn't having it. He locked his legs and said, "Mom, wait."

"Not now, Elijah," his mother hissed. "Abigail needs—"

"Daddy's gone and we have no place to go," Elijah interrupted. His voice was wobbly, and he sounded so very tired. "Please just listen to him."

My throat got tight. I knew this boy. I'd been this boy. I swallowed hard, blinked twice, and forced a gentle smile.

"Have you heard of the Sunshine House?" I asked.

The woman stopped pulling her son and nodded. "They help women and children . . ."

"When their spouse or parent has an addiction problem," I said. I reached into my pocket for my wallet and she flinched. "I'm just going to get my card."

Thank goodness I had one on me. I didn't do outreach; in fact, I didn't do anything with the Sunshine House except read their monthly report and cut them a check accordingly. I held it out to her. She looked from it to me to Annabelle, then she snatched it as if afraid I was using it to trap her. She looked at it and then me. Her gaze was suspicious. "You work for them?"

"Yes," I said. I wasn't about to explain that I was just the money behind the program. I felt Annabelle staring at me, but I kept my gaze on the woman. "We can help you. We'll find you housing and get you some job training and child care. You don't have to be trapped in this."

She shook her head as if I were as dumb as a brick. "Don't I? We were kicked out of our apartment yesterday. All this time I thought my husband was working, but it turns out he lost his job two months ago and he's just been sitting in a bar every day, drinking. Everything we had, everything we worked so hard for, he just drank it all away."

She broke down then, sobbing. I thought again that I might be ill. It was too much. I glanced at the boy. Tears were coursing down his cheeks. He was me. I'd lived his life, but I'd be damned if I'd walk away and leave him to live mine.

"What's your name?" Annabelle asked with a

gentleness that wouldn't even cause a ripple on still water.

"Emily," the woman choked out through her sobs. It broke me.

"See that hotel, Emily?" I asked. I pointed to a standard businessman's travel hotel across the street. "We're going to get you set up there for the night or for however long it takes for the Sunshine House to find you something more permanent. Would that be all right?"

She sobbed some more then she gave me a suspicious look. "Why? Why would you help me?"

I glanced down at Elijah, who was openly crying in relief as he pressed his cheek to the top of his baby sister's head.

"Because I've lived your life. I've walked in your shoes," I said. She gave me a doubtful look, and I pushed aside my usual reluctance to talk about my past. I knew Annabelle was listening, and I didn't even have the capacity to feel the usual shame I harbored about my childhood. It was nothing compared to the moral imperative I felt to get this family to safety.

"When I was his age." I jutted my chin in Elijah's direction. "My parents were junkies, and they abandoned me and my sister, leaving us to fend for ourselves most days. I was homeless, scared, hungry, because my parents were more interested in their next fix than they were in being parents. I was completely alone and there was no one reaching out to help me or my baby sister."

I paused to shove aside all the memories that were so thick, they were suffocating me. "I'm telling you, you can climb out of it, but you're going to have to be very brave. Can you do that, Emily? Can you do that for them?" I asked.

That got through. Emily glanced at her children and nodded. Annabelle stepped forward, herding the mother and her children to the crosswalk. I brought up the rear, hoping my body didn't decide that this was the perfect moment to collapse like a wet noodle. I didn't have Jackson. I didn't have my wheelchair. I started to feel the panic rise. Instead of dwelling on it, I stared at Elijah, still carrying his baby sister. I would not fail him. Not now.

The hotel associate was happy to take my card and keep it open. We walked the family of three to their small suite, and I scrawled my personal number on the back of the Sunshine House card and told Emily and Elijah to call me if they needed anything. Meanwhile, Annabelle managed to finagle the kitchen into sending some food up to their room.

When they were all safe and sound, Annabelle and I left them to rest. We were walking to the bank of elevators when Elijah came tearing out of their room. My first thought was that something bad had happened and I started forward, prepared to call an ambulance, but that wasn't it.

Elijah threw himself at me with all the strength in his scrawny little boy body. He wrapped his arms about my waist and buried his face against my shirt. Sobs wracked his frame, and I reflexively hugged him close while making soothing sounds, just like I used to do with Lexi when our parents were out getting stoned, leaving us home alone, hungry and terrified.

"Thank you," Elijah said. He lifted his face to look at me. His brown eyes glistened with tears, and the tip of his nose was pink. "Thank you for saving us."

My heart cracked in two right then and there. As fast as he'd arrived, he turned and ran back to their room, slamming the door behind him. It was too much. I was gutted. I leaned against the wall, feeling the shock waves of the evening ripple through me. My breath was shaky, my heart was pumping hard, and I could feel the tingles start in my fingers and toes. Wouldn't it just be fitting to stroke out on Annabelle right here, right now?

"Nick, are you all right?" she asked. "You look pale."

"I'm fine," I lied. "Let's get out of here."

I wasn't fine. As we crossed the street, I felt the entire left side of my entire body give out. One minute I was walking, and the next, my leg couldn't support me, I felt like my heart was going to explode out of my chest, and I was going down.

"Nick!" Annabelle screamed, and reached for me.

But the pavement got me first, and my face bounced off the hard ground like a cantaloupe.

I woke up, lying on the curb with Annabelle and, improbably, ManDee crouched over me.

"Ambulance is on its way, pumpkin, don't you worry," ManDee said. He patted my arm. "I saw you from the window, and I thought, *What the hell is wrong with that guy?* And the next thing I knew, you went down, right in the road. I ran over to help your girlfriend get you up on the curb." He fanned himself with a prettily manicured hand, sporting several very large rings. "I think you scared a year off me."

I could hear a siren increasing in volume and assumed it was for me. I glanced at Annabelle. Her eyes were enormous in her face. She was shaking. I wanted to comfort her and assure her that I was fine. I fully expected not to be able to find the words or to be able to speak them, but aside from the thumping pain of my forehead, I found I could speak.

"What happened?" I asked.

"I don't know," she said. "One minute you were beside me and the next you went down hard. Oh, Nick, I—"

Whatever she was about to say was cut off by the arrival of the ambulance. Damn it. I would have given a lot to hear what she had to say.

ManDee and Annabelle made room for the paramedics. When I realized I hadn't had a stroke and could, in fact, move all of my limbs, I let them look me over but refused to go to the hospital. I wasn't going to take a bed from someone who needed it because I'd had a fainting spell and bumped my noggin, for fuck's sake.

The EMT who checked my vitals let it be known that he didn't approve of my decision and said, "You lost consciousness when you hit your head. You really should go to the hospital."

"No." I shook him off.

The guy looked annoyed but resigned. He cracked a cold pack to activate it and handed it to me to hold on my forehead. He glanced at Annabelle, who was standing behind me, and spoke loud enough for her to hear. "You need to watch for a headache, ringing in the ears, vomiting, nausea, fatigue, blurry vision, and if you go to sleep, have someone wake you up every few hours to check that your pupils aren't dilated."

"Got it." I'd say anything for them to go away so I could go home. Cars slowed down to see what was happening, pedestrians paused while walking by. It was a nightmare.

"You need to follow up with your regular

doctor. From what you've described, I think you had a massive panic attack and hyperventilated."

"Panic attack?" I asked. I knew I frequently got stressed and anxious about having another stroke, but this seemed like a new level.

"They can be pretty dramatic," he said. "You probably felt weak like you were going to faint but you wouldn't have. Fainting rarely happens during panic or anxiety." I glared at him. Did he really have to keep saying that? "You did manage to knock yourself out on the pavement, though, and you really should have that checked out."

"That" was a bump the size of an egg on my forehead. I promised that I would. He clearly didn't believe me as he glanced at Annabelle to confirm that she'd heard him. She nodded and gave me a steely-eyed stare that let me know she wasn't going to let me off as easily as he did.

ManDee left us when the ambulance took off, clearly appreciating that the show was over. Annabelle drove me home. We were silent for most of the ride with me reclined in the passenger seat and holding the cold pack on my head.

I was caught between feeling terrible that I'd clearly frightened her and horribly embarrassed that I'd had a panic attack. *A freaking panic attack.* What Jackson and Dr. Henry had gamely called post-traumatic stress, which I had rejected, really was just me having a huge freak-out. They were right. I was a head case. This was not my finest hour.

Annabelle parked in front of the house, and I'd never been so grateful to be home in my life. As if by stepping over the threshold, I could leave this vulnerable version of myself behind.

"You don't have to stay," I said. I climbed the steps, pulling out my keys. "I'm fine."

I didn't want her to lose sleep waking up every few hours to check on me. Also, there was a part of me that was certain she must see me differently now. She'd learned more about my past than I'd ever planned to tell her, she'd found out about the Sunshine House, and she'd witnessed me having a complete and total nervous breakdown, culminating in knocking myself out. I'd never felt like such a complete loser in my entire life.

That was the moment that I knew that this crazy thing between us was done. It had run its course and we hadn't even hit the three-month mark. But there was no way I was going to keep her tied to me, a broken guy with mental issues, when she deserved so much more. I turned to face her.

"Go home, Annabelle," I said. I felt ridiculous, like a kid yelling at a stray puppy to stop following him, but I did it anyway for her sake. "I don't need you to look after me. I've got this."

"Shh," she shushed me. "Don't be an idiot. And you have exactly two choices here, I can stay with you and check on you every few hours or I can call Jackson, tell him what happened, and we'll put you back in that car and go to the hospital."

The fierce light in her eye told me she was not playing. Okay, then. I'd let her tuck me in, which was galling, but then she was out of here.

I unlocked the door and we slipped into the house in full stealth mode, not wanting to wake anyone up. That lasted all of three seconds when the moonlight caught Annabelle's delicate profile, and the longing for her, to be inside her, hit me so low and deep, I couldn't think of anything else.

She turned to walk to my bedroom, but I grabbed her hand and tugged her into my embrace, then I brought her down to the floor, surprising even me. I was so not an impetuous guy when it came to women, but Annabelle was different. She let out a startled gasp, and I braced for her to push me away. Naturally, she flipped the script, and pulled off her dress in one sweeping motion, leaving herself mostly naked beneath me.

"Are you sure?" she whispered.

"Positive." Since this would be our last night together, I planned to commit every inch of her to memory.

Without even a pause, she unsnapped my jeans and drew the zipper down. She shoved them aside until they rode low on my hips, setting my dick free. It jutted forward, obviously seeking its favorite place in the known universe, and Annabelle accommodated by pushing aside her underwear and then she looped her legs around my waist and pulled me deep inside her. Fucking bliss.

I drove into her, again and again, as if in the euphoria of her, I could obliterate the fact that after tonight, I was letting her go. She made hot sexy noises in her throat that drove me right to the edge and then she whispered in my ear, "I love you, Nick. I love you."

I was undone.

Annabelle

23

I watched him sleep. His face was relaxed but the chiseled cheekbones and stubborn chin remained, making him ridiculously attractive even while unconscious. There was no drool or snoring or even a case of bedhead to diminish his good looks. It simply wasn't fair.

His breathing was deep and even. It calmed me a little. The truth was my head was spinning. Had I really told Nick I loved him? Oh man, he was going to shake me off like a bad case of fleas.

I couldn't blame him. Getting attached had not been a part of our deal. We had agreed, three months and then we went our separate ways. I'd thought I'd be okay with that but—damn it—how was I supposed to walk away from a guy who made me feel all these feelings?

He was so much more than he let anyone see. When he set up Emily and Elijah and the baby with temporary lodgings, I knew it was personal for him. I knew he was the money behind the Sunshine House, and I knew it was his cause because as he'd said he saw himself in Elijah. The things he'd said about his childhood had left me cold. He'd never mentioned his past to me before, but I'd known it was troubled, just like I knew that right now he needed his sister.

I reached out and pushed his hair off his forehead. The bump was still there, it had turned a deep shade of blue, but it hadn't gotten any bigger. I pondered the self-made man in front of me and acknowledged that what I was about to do would likely finish off everything between us. Given that we were a little more than halfway through our three months, I supposed I'd have to be content with the time I'd been given.

The fact of the matter was, Nick needed someone to watch over him if I was going to be kicked to the curb in a matter of weeks. I knew he had Jackson, Lupita, and Juan, but he needed someone more. Someone who wouldn't leave his side when he arbitrarily decided the relationship was over. He needed family. He needed his sister, Lexi.

Decision made, I climbed out of bed, grabbed my phone, crept down the hallway, and called Lexi. I told her that Nick had fallen and cracked his head. I didn't mention the panic attack or the stroke. I could respect his privacy that much. I told her that he needed to be watched, and I told her that I couldn't stay with him and she needed to be here to take care of him. I'd barely finished speaking before I could hear her running to her car, where she hung up on me. I texted her the code to the gate to get in.

I went back to Nick's room and got dressed. The soft glow from the gas fire in the fireplace illuminated his face, and I tried to commit it to memory because I had a feeling that by letting Lexi into his world, I was losing Nick for good. Who was I kidding? I was going to lose him in a matter of weeks anyway. This way at least I knew someone would be taking care of him, and I could protect the tattered remains of my poor heart in the meantime.

Before I was ready to say good-bye, I heard Lexi's car in the drive. I went downstairs to meet her. She dashed up the front steps. Her hair was in disarray, she was wearing glasses, and she had on two different shoes. She threw her arms around me in a hug that strangled.

"Is he okay? What happened?" she demanded. Then her face scrunched up and tears fell. "I can't lose him, not now. I just found him."

"He's okay," I said. I put an arm around her and tried to calm her down before she woke the whole house. I continued in a whisper. "He's resting right now, but come on in and you can wait with him if that will make you feel better."

She nodded. I led her inside and up the stairs, telling her what to look for with his head injury. Nick was still asleep when we entered his room. Lexi very quietly pulled one of the two armchairs from in front of the window on the far side of the room over to the side of the bed. I went to get her a blanket. As I tucked her in, she glanced up at me.

"Thanks, Annabelle," she whispered.

I nodded. No matter how this played out, I knew I'd made the right decision. I left Lexi with Nick and went home to find Sir waiting for me. It was good to have company, because I didn't plan to sleep. Not at all.

"You had no right!"

I snapped awake, finding myself on my couch with Nick seated in the armchair across from me. He was still in his flannel pajama bottoms and thermal shirt. He was barefoot. His hair was mussed and the bump on his head was now deep purple. I lurched upright, dislodging Sir, who leapt to the ground with a plaintive meow.

"Nick, are you all right?" I asked. I made to reach for him but he leaned back.

"No, I'm not."

"Your head," I said. "Let me get you some ice. How about pain medicine? Have you taken any recently?"

"Stop," he snapped. "Stop taking care of me like I'm some injured bird you're trying to rehab back into the wild. I'm fine."

I pushed my hair out of my eyes. Fine? He was not fine. He had a knot on his head, he was pale with dark circles under his eyes, and he was so agitated, he was practically vibrating in his seat.

"I'm making coffee," I said. There was no way I could handle this conversation without coffee. "Can I get you some?"

"No." He paused. "Thank you."

Manners. Maybe he wasn't as mad as I thought.

"Where's Lexi?" I asked. I knew it was the equivalent of hitting a hornet's nest with a stick, but I figured we might as well get it out of the way. Nick followed me into the kitchen, where he slid onto one of the barstools.

"I sent her home," he said. He watched me make the coffee. Neither one of us spoke. When it was finally ready, I poured my first cup, and he continued, "You knew how I felt about keeping my distance from Lexi, but you called her anyway. Why?"

He sounded genuinely confused. I sipped the hot brew, trying to figure out how I could answer him in a way that would make him understand.

"Because she's your sister." I went for the simple truth. My sister, Chelsea, was my first best friend and the person I always reached for in a crisis. Nick needed to have the same in his life even if he didn't realize it yet.

"So what if she is?" he asked.

"She's your family, Nick. She had a right to know."

"No, no, no," he argued. "She was my family once, a long time ago, but she moved away and I moved on, and that's the way I want it. Just like I don't know where my parents are and I don't care. I have kept my life on lockdown for a reason."

"Is that why I couldn't find anything about you on the Internet or in the news?" I asked.

"You looked?"

"Yes, back when I thought you were a grumpy old codger." I resisted adding that I hadn't been wrong, which I thought showed remarkable restraint.

He huffed out a breath. "I paid a lot of money to have any trace of me wiped clean from the Internet. I've never granted interviews with the press or been on social media. I even had nondisclosure agreements for anyone I got involved with—until you." He paused and I knew he was thinking what a mistake that had been. Ouch.

"Assuming they're not dead, I never wanted to risk my pa . . . past showing up and demanding a handout. Nice to know it worked. Mostly," he said.

"Lexi isn't your parents," I said. I braced for his ire.

"I know but it changes nothing. I don't want her in my life."

I felt myself get furious. "What about what she wants?"

"She's better off without me."

"How do you figure?" I asked.

"For the same reason that you'll be better off without me," he said. He gestured between us. "I'm damaged goods, Annabelle. I'm no good to anyone."

"Bullshit," I said. "So you had a stroke, so what? I have high cholesterol and asthma when I catch a cold. We all have stuff, Nick."

He glared at me. "It's not that simple."

"Yes, it is actually." I stood my ground.

"You had no right to call Lexi in when I was unconscious," he said. "You didn't even wake me to ask permission. You made a decision that wasn't yours to make."

I knew he was right, and my voice came out a bit more defensive than I would have liked. "I was only trying to help."

"I don't want your help. I don't want to be with a woman who thinks she's my mommy," he said. "What's next? Are you going to start cutting my lunch into adorable little shapes, picking out my clothes, and making sure I eat all of my vegetables?"

I flinched. He had no idea that he was recounting what had gone wrong in both of my marriages. According to my exes, I tended to suffocate them, although in Jeremy's case, I suspected he liked it that way.

"You're supposed to be my partner, not my nanny," he continued. "*You* don't get to decide what I need, or how I'm supposed to live my life.

It's my life, not yours, and not anyone else's."

We glared at each other. This was not going to work for me. Maybe I did hover. Perhaps I was too invested in the men I loved. And sure, I probably was a lawnmower wife/girlfriend who tried to remove obstacles from the path of those I loved. So sue me!

"Is that it then? Is that your ultimatum and I'm supposed to fall in line?" I asked. "I'm just a secondary character in your life? Or are we going to talk about last night? About the Sunshine House or why you felt so compelled to help Emily, Elijah, and the baby? How about why seeing them triggered a massive panic attack for you?"

He looked taken aback as if it had never occurred to him that I might want to talk about this stuff. *Men!*

"No, we're not talking about it," he said. "None of that is relevant to us."

"Really?" I asked. "I think it's pretty damn relevant when the guy I'm seeing collapses in the middle of the street. I heard the EMT, Nick. He said you had a panic attack. It's not just going to go away, and you can't continue to live like this." I gestured to the house. "You are so freaked out about having another stroke that you're having panic attacks. You need to talk to someone, and if it isn't going to be me, then maybe it can be your sister."

"Is that how you see me?" he asked. "Some

broken guy that you want to foist onto his sister because he's too much to deal with?"

"I never said that," I said. "But it's pretty clear you have a lot of damage from your childhood that you need to figure out."

"Says the woman who was married twice by the age of twenty-eight," he said.

I sucked in a breath. That was a low blow.

"So now you're going to weaponize my past and use it to hurt me?" I asked. His scorn cut more deeply than I was willing to show him. I'd thought we were better than this.

"I'm sorry," he said. "That was out of line— much like you calling my sister."

"If you're expecting an apology, you're in for a long wait," I said. "She deserved to know."

Yes, this was the hill I was prepared to die on. It was more important to me that Nick have someone in his life for the long term than to have me in the short term.

"Fine," he said. He stood and walked to the door. He paused to scratch Sir between the ears and then he straightened up. "I guess we're done here."

"I guess we are," I agreed. He closed the door very gently behind him.

I didn't need it spelled out for me that we had just broken up. It was clear from the way my heart had just crinkled up like a piece of paper over a flame that we were through.

• • •

"You can't be serious," Carson said. "You're going with *that?*"

I glanced at him from where I was standing in front of the whiteboard. My entire team was in the meeting room, finalizing our materials for Lexi's approval. She'd had input along the way, but this was a run-through of our final presentation to her and the investors of the development. It was a very big deal.

I had followed Nick's advice and buried Carson in work. He'd managed to fob off a lot of it, but there'd been enough that he'd actually had to put in some hours because Miguel and Sophie had made the material for Lexi's housing development priority number one.

"Is there a problem, Carson?" I asked. I knew he was making a scene because Miguel and Sophie weren't in the meeting, and he thought he could get away with it. Also, it was possible his ego was feeling a bit dinged. I hadn't chosen his design for the logo, and since he was the art director, that probably chafed a bit.

"I busted my tail on the logo for New Dawn," he said. He gestured to the artist rendering in front of him. "And you're choosing this one?"

"Yes, I am," I said. I glanced behind me at the whiteboard, where the chosen logo filled the entire screen. "I think Luz's design captures the spirit of a net-zero development in the desert perfectly."

405

"It looks like a child drew it," he said. His voice dripped with condescension.

"That's uncalled for and extremely unprofessional," I said. I glanced at Luz, who had worked with me on rendering the logo: a bright yellow sun rising over the desert with a stylized mid-century modern vibe. I loved it, and most important, Lexi and the investors loved it even more.

"What are you going to do, tell on me?" Carson sneered. He rose, pushing back his seat so forcibly that it slammed against the glass wall. I saw staff members in the room beyond whip their heads in our direction.

"She won't have to," a voice said from the doorway. We all turned to see Trent standing there. He looked pissed. Trent never looked pissed. "A word, Carson?"

"Sure," Carson said. "Whatever."

He grabbed his materials and stalked from the room. Trent met my gaze as he waited for Carson, and he made the tiniest nod. Then he turned and followed him.

My heart started to pound in my chest. Had Trent tied Carson to the bogus charges on my card? I wanted to run after them, but I forced myself to play it cool. It had been weeks since my meeting with Trent about my credit card. Frankly, I'd been so consumed with the New Dawn development and Nick, I hadn't given it much thought.

The meeting broke up, and I pulled Luz aside. "I hope you won't let what Carson said bother you. He was wrong. Your design is brilliant."

She flushed with pleasure. "No, it's all right. His ability to hurt me dried up a long time ago."

"Good," I said.

I was walking back to my office with an armful of materials when Carson stepped out of Trent's office. He began to clap slowly. It was the sort that let you know the person doing the clapping really despised you.

"You must be so proud of yourself," he said. "You did it. You got rid of your competition. Well done, by the way."

Of all the things I had expected Carson to say, that was not it. I squinted at him.

"What?"

"It took me a second, but I finally figured it out while sitting in there being accused of things I didn't do. You're threatened by me," he said.

A surprised laugh burst out of me. "I'm sorry, what are you talking about?"

"Forget it, Annabelle," he said. "You're not that good of an actress. When the truth comes out, and it will, everyone will know exactly what sort of cold, calculating bi—"

"Is there a problem here?" Sophie appeared in the doorway to her office.

If Carson had been angry with me, his temper dialed up to volcanic when she appeared.

"It was you, wasn't it?" he raged. "You put her up to it."

Sophie frowned at him. "Up to what exactly?"

"You've hated me from the first moment we met," he said. "Probably because I didn't fall at your feet like Miguel did."

Sophie looked bored. "Carson, you are—and I can't emphasize this enough—making an ass of yourself."

"Who cares?" He raised his arms in the air. "Tell me, Annabelle, did you think the whole scheme up by yourself, or did she tell you to do it? Is that how you got your job here?"

As Carson's voice rose, people were poking their heads out of their office doors. The workroom had come to a complete standstill as everyone watched the unfolding drama. I was only surprised I didn't hear the sound of popcorn being made.

"I'm going to my office now," I said.

Carson stepped in my way. He was taller than me and decidedly more muscular. It occurred to me that he could definitely do me some damage if he chose.

"Oh, no you're not," he said. "I want answers. Were you so threatened by me that you set up a whole *'Oh my god, someone's been stealing my company card out of my wallet and charging expensive dinners to it'* scenario so that you could falsely accuse me in an attempt to get me fired?"

408

"That's enough, Carson," Sophie said. We both ignored her.

I stared him down. His gaze flitted from mine, hardly keeping it. He was lying. He was projecting what he had done onto me and acting like the victim. I wasn't having it.

I looked shocked. I dropped all the materials in my arms for dramatic effect. "Carson West, are you telling me you stole my company card out of my wallet and charged expensive dinners to it?"

"No!" He denied it. "It's all a lie. You faked it to set me up."

I looked at him in confusion. "What possible reason would I have to do that?"

"Because you're threatened by me," he insisted. More projection.

"How would I be threatened by you?" I asked. I made a point of looking him up and down. "Is it my higher salary? No. Bigger office space? No. Being the creative director? No. I'm not really seeing why you think you have anything happening that I would consider a threat."

"Because I'm . . . Miguel and I—"

"Correction, there is no 'Miguel and I.'" Miguel stepped out of his office. He moved to stand beside his wife. "You're fired, Carson."

There was a collective ripple of shock in the office, and I have to admit I was right there with them. I had never seen Miguel look so furious.

"You think you're so clever," Carson spit. "Miguel Vasquez, owner of a design firm, married to the hot girl, living the big life, but you're not. You're just a whipped—"

"We have video, Carson, of you taking Annabelle's company card out of her wallet," Miguel said. He sounded so disappointed. Carson's chin jutted out like he was still going to deny it, but Miguel didn't give him a chance. "How was Beckett's Table last night?"

Carson opened his mouth to speak, but Miguel held up his hand.

"Never mind. We have video of you putting the card back this morning as well. There's no wiggle room here, Carson."

"This is a total setup," Carson cried.

Everyone stared. It seemed no one believed him.

"We'll escort you to your office to pack up your desk now. We'll want your keys to the building when we escort you to your car," Hector said. I hadn't even seen the security guards arrive, but as they shouldered their way past me, I knew their timing wasn't a coincidence. Someone had expected Carson to handle this badly. I glanced at Miguel and realized it was probably him.

Carson opened his mouth, but Curtis, who was as wide as he was tall, stepped forward. He shook his head and crossed his arms over his chest in a fair impression of a brick wall. Thinking better of whatever he'd been about to say, Carson turned and stomped down the hallway to his office. I wasn't sorry to see him go.

24

"Belly, where are you?" Soph asked. "I feel like I've been talking to the side of your face for the last fifteen minutes."

I turned from my Sunday brunch people-watching to face her. We were enjoying Bloody Marys at Matt's Big Breakfast on Camelback Road, and Soph had been talking about how amazing the materials for Lexi's development, New Dawn, had turned out.

"What's wrong?" Soph asked.

"Nothing," I said. She didn't know that Nick and I had ever been together so I couldn't exactly cry on her shoulder now that we'd broken up, could I? "Just thinking about the gala."

"It's so exciting," Soph said. "I heard that the mayor is going to be there, and she's bringing several prominent local politicians with her. I'm just thrilled. We have to get our hair done and shop for new dresses. It's my treat."

"Oh no, I can't let you—"

"Yes, you can. Annabelle, I'm going to be straight with you," she said. She took a big sip of her drink. These were not lightweight beverages, so I wondered why she felt she needed liquid courage. Needless to say, she now had my full and undivided attention.

"Okay," I encouraged her.

"Miguel and I have been in marriage counseling," she said.

"So that's what the meetings at four o'clock are," I said. I didn't mean to say it out loud but oops.

She nodded. "We've been going for a few months."

Months? My eyebrows rose. I reached for my drink. I had a feeling I was going to need it.

"Go on." I took a big chug.

"We've been having some issues," she said. "Mostly I felt betrayed that when we started the company, we were on equal footing, but over time, Miguel seemed to respect Carson more than me. Carson spent years slowly creating a wedge between us. It was so subtle, *I* didn't even notice. You coming to work for us was a tipping point. I knew Carson wouldn't handle not getting the promotion very well, and I knew he would try to turn Miguel against me completely, but I felt as if I had nothing left to lose. The situation had become untenable."

She took a huge breath, and I asked, "So you used me?"

"No!" she cried. "At least not totally. I really wanted you to be creative director because of your diverse skill set, and look, you've brought out talent in our staff that they didn't even know they had, you've got everyone working together on a huge project, and you managed to keep Carson from sabotaging the whole thing by outmaneuvering him every step of the way. You are totally management material. Still, I knew Carson would react badly, I didn't know how badly and I'm very sorry for that, but fortunately he was enough of a jerk that Miguel finally saw his true self, too."

"So are you guys going to be okay?" I asked.

"I think so," she said. She smiled and it was hopeful. "I love my mother-in-law, but there is no question that as a single mother, she raised her family with an iron fist. Our counselor has helped Miguel realize that when he disagrees with me, he tends to respond to me as if I'm her, and he becomes defiant like a child instead of listening to me and talking about it like a grown-ass man. We're working on it."

I had no idea what to say. Sophie looked vulnerable and nervous. I reached across the table and grabbed her hand, giving it a squeeze. "I think the fact that you're both invested in working on it means you're going to be all right."

"I hope so," she said. "I love him like crazy, but I am *not* his mama. Now, promise you're not mad at me."

"Nah, I'm flattered, I think," I said.

I took a moment to consider what Soph had said. I *had* done all those things. I had managed a team, and we were crushing it. Maybe I wasn't the lonely freelancer I'd always thought I was. I had to admit that I was grooving on the office vibe. I genuinely enjoyed the collaborative work and the challenges that came with being part of a large studio. I glanced at my friend and knew I owed her the truth as well.

"I'm relieved that it's all worked out for the studio. Also, I have a confession of my own to make, too."

Soph met my gaze. Whatever she saw in there must have warned her of an incoming bombshell, because she raised her finger in a wait gesture and downed half of her drink.

"Hit me," she said.

"Lexi Brewer is the estranged younger sister of my landlord, Nick Daire," I said.

"Shut up!" she said. "How did you come to know her—wait, through him?"

"Yes, she approached him about helping her with the housing development because she was getting squeezed on all sides from other developers, utility companies, and local government, and Nick agreed on the condition that she hire me to design all of the materials for the development, you know, the name, logo, brochures, etc. She was calling it Green Springs before I got involved."

"Sounds like a place you go to die," Soph said.

I laughed. "You're not the first to say that. Anyway, Nick is bankrolling a lot of the project, including the gala, and I thought you should know."

"Nick, huh?" she asked.

"Uh-huh. Also, we slept together," I added.

Soph blinked at me, slowly, as if it was taking great effort to absorb my words.

"That is way more than one confession," she said. She reached for her drink and finished it. Then she raised it in the air and signaled to our waiter to bring two more. "And now everything is ruined because he is going to break up with you after three months, then you're going to leave me—*oh my god*—I told you to stay away from him. Why didn't you listen to me? Why doesn't anyone ever listen to me?"

"Breathe, Soph," I said. "For what it's worth, our fling is over and I'm not leaving."

"You're not?" She sounded doubtful.

"No, I need to see this project through the gala at the very least," I said.

"That's two weeks away." She reached across the table. "If you need a new place to stay, we'll find you one. Please don't leave, Annabelle. I feel as if your life here has just begun. You can't leave."

My phone buzzed, and I picked it up with an apologetic smile. If it was Nick, I didn't want to

416

miss him. It wasn't Nick. I stared at my phone in astonishment.

"Are you all right?" she asked.

"Oh, sure, I'm fine," I said. I wasn't fine. "The BD just texted that he's blowing through Phoenix and wants to see me."

Greg DeVane, ex-husband number two. It had been a few years since I'd seen him, and we hadn't parted on the best of terms. Meaning I'd hauled his stuff to his mother's house and let her deal with his five bass guitars, two amps, and a fish who wouldn't die.

In my defense, I had just discovered that he was cheating on me, and I didn't handle it well. After that, it was a swift visit with our attorneys and our marriage of two years was—*poof!*—over.

Greg was as opposite from my first husband, Jeremy, as a person could get. While Jeremy was an engineer with OCD tendencies, Greg was a long-haired musician who always maintained a chill vibe. He played bass with an up-and-coming band, Breaking the Curve, who'd spent the last few years on the road as the opener to several national touring acts. As far as I knew, the BD lived on a tour bus ten months out of the year, and just what the heck was he doing in Phoenix anyway? I had no idea.

We weren't enemies. I have an inability to stay mad at my exes. But we had never really recovered from our breakup, mostly because he'd cheated on me, and while I could forgive him for falling in love with someone else, because that just happens sometimes, what I couldn't forgive him for was not doing me the courtesy of ending things with me first.

I mean if he knew he wanted to leave, and clearly he did, then he should have left me before he had his tawdry fling with the groupie girl. Oh, that sounds like I'm bitter about her. I'm not, not really. I just never understand women who hook up with married men. By sleeping with him, you just proved to yourself that the guy is a cheater; why would you then want him? It makes no sense.

As for Greg's fling, it lasted all of two weeks after I'd thrown him out and before he got the call that the band was hitting the road. Shelby, the girl he left behind, showed up at our apartment a few weeks after that, looking for him. We shared some Ben and Jerry's Cherry Garcia, cursed him, and then burned the last of the stuff he'd left in our apartment. It was wonderfully therapeutic, and I still get Christmas cards from Shelby, who went on to marry a firefighter and now has twin baby boys.

After a very stern lecture from Sophie, where she basically told me to ignore the BD, I sat on the text message from Greg all morning. Did I want to see him? Kind of, sort of. It had always bothered me that we'd never made up like Jeremy and I had. Of course, I had no interest in making up quite like that, but still, it would be nice to be able to call the BD my friend again. I blamed the pleaser in me.

By midafternoon on Sunday, having heard nothing from Nick, I answered Greg's text. I kept it brief, said I'd love to see him if it worked out, and that I hoped he was enjoying the glorious weather in Phoenix. Since I was from New England, it was practically mandatory that I mention the weather.

His response came back like he'd been sitting on his phone just waiting to hear from me. I didn't really think that but was flattered nonetheless. After a flurry of back-and-forth messages, we agreed he'd come to my place that evening and I'd cook dinner. He said he'd missed my fettuccine Alfredo. See? It really is my signature dish.

I took a shower, scrubbed all thoughts of Nick, or at least I tried to, from my mind. It was clear he was still angry about Lexi, and as much as I hated it, I had to respect his boundaries and give him time.

The gala was in two weeks, and I'd been hoping that I could convince him to go. I wanted him to be there for his sister on her big night. Heck, I wanted him to be there for me as it was my night, too, in a lesser but still really important way.

For the thousandth time, I stared up at his house. The curtains were drawn again. Had I actually managed to get him to let in the light? At the moment, I felt as if I had just moved in and was befuddled by the old codger in the big house. I thought about the moment I realized Nick was my landlord and then remembered how it felt to have him make love to me and hold me all night long. I wanted to cry with frustration but I didn't.

Instead, I dried my hair and put on some makeup. I didn't want the BD to think I'd gone completely to seed. Then I assessed my wardrobe. What was a woman supposed to wear when entertaining an ex-husband she hadn't seen in a couple of years? I needed to look good but not too good. I didn't want to give out any mixed signals here. Despite the good times between me and Greg, I had no wish to rekindle anything. I had learned my lesson with Jeremy.

Besides, despite my cavalier attitude with Soph, I was crazy in love with Nick. And even though I was the only one who'd said it, I really thought he might love me, too. Otherwise why would he get so mad when I was trying to help? The man had built a fortress around his heart if ever I'd seen one.

The evenings were getting warmer so I opted for my favorite snap front denim dress with my leopard print ankle boots. Nothing says sassy like a leopard print boot. I kept my hair loose, my makeup light, and my jewelry minimum.

I texted Greg the code to get through the gate, and then I sat down to do some work while I waited. I had several other projects I was working on aside from Lexi's, and I didn't want to fall behind just because the gala was so all-consuming. The Schneider Pretzel people had been ecstatic about their redesigned logo so at least I could scratch that one off my list.

While I worked, I tried not to think about Nick. It was impossible. In the time we'd been together, he'd permeated every square foot of my apartment. The kitchen where he'd stood drinking his morning coffee, the couch where we'd snuggled while watching old movies, the bedroom where . . . I shook my head . . . best not go there.

There was nothing in this guest house that didn't bear an imprint of Nick in some way. I realized if he couldn't forgive me, I was going to have to move. The sooner the better. Maybe I'd put some feelers out at work to see who knew of a place that was available. I hadn't brought that much stuff with me; surely it wouldn't be that hard to move. I glanced at the French door that was open just a crack. I wondered what Sir would make of my departure. Could I take him with me? The thought of never seeing his inquisitive little face again about did me in.

My eyes watered up, but my therapeutic cry

sesh was interrupted by the sound of someone at the door. "Annabelle!" *Knock, knock, knock.* "It's me, Greg."

I sat up straight and swiped at my eyes, which were damp. Just like that, my tears evaporated because the BD was here, and I was not about to have my ex-husband find me in such a state over a man and a cat.

I took a deep breath and told myself to get it together. I fluffed my hair and smoothed my skirt and then I hurried across the living room to answer the door.

I pulled it open and there he was. With his thick black hair falling in waves just past his shoulders, his beat-up black leather jacket, worn jeans, and biker boots, he looked exactly as I remembered him.

"Hi, Greg," I said.

He shook his head. "What sort of lame-ass greeting is that? Come in for the real thing." He opened his arms wide and I stepped in for a hug. This was one of his genuine talents. He was an excellent hugger. He managed to make you feel safe and secure without squishing you and he never held on overlong.

He let me go, and I glanced past him at the Harley parked in front of my house. "Yours?"

"Rental," he said. "I'm just in town to visit my dad."

"Carl's living here?"

"In Sun City." Greg nodded. "We had a week in between gigs so I drove here from California to see him. He said to say hi, by the way."

"Did he?" Carl had never liked me. He felt I wasn't sexy enough to keep Greg interested, which he told me the very first time I met him, and it was galling to have him proven right two years later. Although Greg swore it wasn't his lack of attraction to me that had driven him to cheat, his father's words still chafed.

"Be sure to tell him I said I hope he chokes on Meredith's cooking," I retorted.

Greg burst out laughing. "He'd love that. He always admired your spunk. Unfortunately, he's no longer married to Meredith."

"What?" I gestured for him to come in, closing the door after us. "She was his fifth wife. I thought for sure he'd found his soul mate there."

"You have to have a soul to find a soul mate," Greg said. It was clear he still had father issues.

I made a sympathetic noise. I wasn't sure I wanted to spend the evening unboxing Greg and his father. "Has he remarried?"

"No," he said. "He's discovered that in assisted care, the ratio of women to men is so unbalanced that he now has a roster of Bettys."

"Bettys?" I asked.

"He calls them all Betty, whether it's their name or not, and he has them on a schedule, so there's Monday Betty and Tuesday Betty, etc."

I gaped at him. Carl DeVane was a bald-headed, potbellied, miserly old man, who frequently smelled like onions. How could he possibly be this much of a Casanova?

"Sometimes the internalized misogyny in women exhausts me," I said. I held up a beer in question, and he nodded. "Why would any woman put up with that shit?"

Greg shrugged out of his leather jacket and draped it on the back of a stool at the counter. "Because they're lonely and they were raised at a time when women were taught to believe that their worth was wrapped up in their ability to bag a husband."

I shook my head. "What a load of horseshit." I twisted the cap off the bottle and pushed it and a glass at him.

"Says the woman who's been married twice and is not yet thirty," he said. He ignored the glass and drank out of the bottle.

"Why does everyone keep reminding me? And . . . ouch," I retorted. "Did you come all this way to insult me because I can do that myself."

"No, I know you didn't get married to prove your womanly worth," he said. He sent me a sympathetic glance. "You did it to avoid dealing with your mom's death."

You didn't have to be a psychiatrist to know that, but I thought it spoke well of Greg that he understood I'd been operating out of a place of pain for our whole marriage.

"Yeah, well, that didn't work with you or Jeremy."

"Speaking of Jeremy," he said.

"Are we?" I asked. I heard an alarm bell clanging in my head. Jeremy had hated Greg, while Greg always seemed ambivalent about him. Why now would Greg want to talk about him? It was unsettling. I led Greg into the living room, where we sank onto the couch facing the fireplace, settling in for a nice catch-up.

"We are now," he said. He took a long sip off his beer. "He called me."

"What?" I spluttered beer all over myself. Mercifully, I had a cocktail napkin to dab it up with. I hacked until my throat was clear and asked, "Why on earth would he call you?"

"He thought you came back to me," he said. "As if that would ever happen."

Was he fishing for a denial? Because he wasn't going to get one. He was absolutely right. That would never happen.

"Your abrupt departure to Phoenix. He thought it was all too coincidental with my touring schedule being in the Southwest," Greg said. He rested his arm along the back of the sofa and put his ankle up on his knee. He looked perfectly at home. It was weird but it also grounded me.

"I can't believe he called you," I said. I hadn't

spoken to Jeremy since I'd left for Phoenix and was planning to give it a few more months before I reached out to him to see if we could be friends.

"I know, he hates me," he agreed.

"He doesn't, okay, yes, he does," I said.

Greg stared at me for a moment, and I sensed he had a lot more to say, but when he finally did speak, it was short, to the point, and devastating. "You know he's in love with you, right?"

"He's not," I protested.

"He is," he said. "Or more accurately, he *thinks* he is."

I felt my stomach twist into a hard knot. "I feel terrible about how things ended. What did you say to him?"

"That he needed to grow the hell up and stop being such a damn mama's boy."

"You didn't!" I stared at him with my mouth hanging open. How many times had I wanted to say that very thing to Jeremy? "I don't imagine he liked hearing that."

"He didn't. He swore at me. Then he hung up on me."

I narrowed my eyes at him. "You enjoyed that, didn't you?"

He held up his thumb and forefinger, holding them about an inch apart. "Maybe about this much."

I laughed. "You're a horrible person." I kept

my voice light so that he'd know I was mostly joking.

He laughed. "At least I know that about myself, and I'm not pretending to be something I'm not. Jeremy pretends he's a grown-up, but he's just a child looking for someone to make all of his problems go away, which is why he's so attached to you. You're his fixer. It's what you do."

I had a flashback of Soph telling me that exact thing that night she called me in Boston to offer me the job. I stared at Greg and took in his long dark hair, his blunt features, the scar that split one of his eyebrows. He was handsome in a knuckle dragger way. He was the guy you wanted at your back in a bar fight or when fleeing the law. He had never needed me the way Jeremy did.

"Why didn't it work out between us?" I asked.

His eyebrows rose.

"No, I am not looking to start anything here, I'm just curious," I explained.

"It didn't work out between us because I wanted a partner, not a mommy," he said.

The words were harsh and I tried not to cringe. I failed. It was painfully close to what Nick had said to me, and I didn't like hearing it any better this time.

"Listen, Annabelle, I love you. I always have and I always will, but you were never comfortable with that," he said.

"What do you mean?" I protested. "I was very

comfortable with being loved. I was crazy about you."

"You tried to manage me," he said.

"No, I didn't," I argued. I was coming in hot. There was no way he was going to blame his infidelity on me.

"Annabelle, as soon as we got married, you became a completely different person," he said. "You started pestering me not to stay out too late, not to drink too much, you even started packing my lunch when I went into the studio to record."

"I was worried about you and I thought you might get hungry," I said. *Oh god, Nick had been so right. I was only steps away from cute-shaped sandwiches.*

"Annabelle, I am a fully realized adult male who can make himself a sandwich or not if I want one," he said.

"I was just trying to show you how much I loved you," I muttered.

"Were you?"

"What do you mean?"

"Once we got married, you stopped painting and all of that creative energy that made you such a free spirit started to fade. You became this Stepford wife who was determined to take care of me whether I liked it or not."

"Why was it so wrong that I wanted to take care of you?" I asked. I was genuinely mystified.

428

If you cared about someone, shouldn't you want to help them in any way you could?

"Annabelle, you never needed to do that," he said. He ran a hand over his eyes. "I never wanted you to become less than what you are. It felt at the time like you found me lacking and you were trying to fix me. Of course, because I was so mature, I chose to push back and stayed out later, drank more, and then cheated on you. I'm very sorry about that, by the way."

I could tell that he meant it, and I felt something shift inside me. I think it was forgiveness pushing to the front of the crowd. I reached over and put my hand on top of his. "It's okay. I forgive you."

"Thank you." He blew out a breath. "That means a lot to me. No matter how much of a jerk I was, and I know I was a big one, I never wanted to hurt you."

"No, you just wanted to get away from me."

"I was suffocating," he said. "I didn't feel like I could be what you wanted me to be."

"I wanted you to be happy," I said.

"Did you?" he asked. He took a long pull off his beer. "Because it felt like you wanted me to be someone else, and I just couldn't be anyone but myself. I didn't want you to fix me into some lesser version of myself."

My mouth dropped open. Is that the message he'd gotten from me trying to take care of him?

"I never thought you needed fixing," I said. "I

just wanted . . ." I frowned. What had I wanted? "I just wanted you to need me so much that you would never leave me."

There it was. The truth that I had never uttered before. I hadn't taken care of Jeremy or Greg or Nick because I loved them, although I did in their different ways. I did it for me, to make them need me, so that they wouldn't leave me. Whoa. Was that what I had been doing with Nick?

I'd dragged him out of his house when he didn't want to go, I made him open his curtains, buy art, and I pushed him to let his sister into his life, all against his wishes, so I would be his savior and he'd love me forever and ever. I slumped against the couch. This epiphany felt like a punch in the gut. It completely winded me.

"You okay?" he asked.

"Not really, no," I said. I tipped my head, resting it on the back of the couch. There were tears bubbling just under the surface, but I didn't want to cry. I knew that I tended to jump in and fix things for people. I'd always thought that it was because I was a giver. I'd never realized that it was because I thought I could bind them to me that way.

"Why do you suppose I do that?" I asked. "Do you think I have bad self-esteem?"

Greg leaned back, resting his head against the couch, too. "No. I don't think that's it. But you do seem to have an issue with your self-worth.

You have a pattern of picking guys who are broken or damaged or whatever you want to call us, and then you throw yourself into trying to make everything better, which is lovely but—"

"But what?"

"You can't fix other people, honey. They have to want to fix themselves. You need to stop settling for the diamonds in the rough, Annabelle. You deserve so much more. You deserve someone who is willing to fix their shit for you."

We were quiet for a while. My brain was reeling. This new self-awareness changed everything.

"So are we good?" he asked.

"We will be," I said. "Now that we've figured out what's wrong with me, let's do you."

"Not necessary," he said. "I already know what's wrong."

"Oh, really," I said. "What's that?"

"I'm an asshole." He said it as if it was the most obvious thing in the world, and I burst out laughing. For the first time since we'd split, I realized I'd missed him.

"Sophie's wrong, you know," I said.

"About?"

"You."

"You told her I was in town?" he asked. I nodded. "Does she still call me the big disappointment?"

"We shortened it to the BD," I said. He laughed

and shook his head. I reached across the couch and patted his hand with mine. "But I think maybe you've outgrown it."

"Well, I'm kind of partial to the initials," he said. "I'll just tell people they stand for something else." He wagged his eyebrows at me, and I shook my head. Musicians.

We sat side by side for a long time, reminiscing about the good times we'd had and sharing news about our mutual friends and acquaintances. I made dinner and we laughed all the way through the meal, especially when Sir arrived and looked at Greg with his whiskers twitching as if he'd taken his seat.

When it was time for him to leave, I was genuinely sorry to see him go.

"Stay in touch?" he asked when he hugged me good-bye.

"Definitely," I said.

He tipped his head to the side as his gaze met mine. "It was good to see you, Annabelle."

"You too, Greg," I said.

He put on his helmet and climbed onto his motorcycle. With a roar of the engine, he shot out of the drive. I waved until he disappeared from sight.

I turned and went back into the house, feeling exhausted and nostalgic and a little weepy. As soon as I stepped inside, I felt a change in the air. There was an electricity to it. I glanced around and then started. Standing in the open French door was Nick with his arms crossed over his chest as he leaned against the doorjamb. Sir was twining himself about his ankles and purring. Traitor.

Startled, I put my hand to my chest. Before I could offer a word of greeting, his hazel eyes snapped to mine and he asked, "Who the hell was that?"

25

"Well, hello to you, too. Damn it, Nick, you scared me," I said. I felt a flash of guilt for the time spent with Greg but then shook it off. I hadn't done anything wrong, and I was not going to feel as if I had.

"Who was he, Annabelle?"

"What do you care?" I asked. Yes, I was clearly spoiling for a fight. "I haven't heard from you in days. As far as I know, whatever was happening between us is deader than dead, meaning I do not have to answer to you . . ."

He crossed the floor toward me with a predatory grace that made it hard for me to concentrate. Those hazel eyes of his were positively wicked. He was wearing an unbuttoned dress shirt over a tank top that looked as if he'd just thrown it on. Jeans and sneakers completed the look. I glanced down and noted that the sneakers were untied, so it was clear he'd been in a hurry to get over here.

"Who was he, Annabelle?" he asked.

He was standing right in front of me. I refused to give up any ground, so I crossed my arms over my chest and stared up at him. "Why do you care?"

His eyes flashed. He started moving forward.

This time I did back up. Damn it. Until I felt the wall at my back. He immediately braced a hand on each side of me.

"I am not a very good sharer," he said. His voice was low and deep and scraped across my senses, making them raw with want. "And until this thing between us is dusted and done, you're mine."

Okay, so we weren't done? That sent a thrill through me that my independent, liberated self was totally appalled by. I decided the only way to enjoy it fully was to own it and make it mine.

I pushed off the wall, pressing myself against him while I twined my arms around his neck and said, "Which means you're mine."

"Duh," he replied. I would have laughed, but then he kissed me and it was everything.

We'd been apart only a few days but it felt like a lifetime. We latched on to each other with a fierceness that was almost violent. I was mad at him for shutting me out, and I'm sure he was furious with me for meddling in his life. None of that mattered at the moment.

We kissed hard and hot with teeth and tongue. My entire body broke out in a sweat, and I yanked his shirt off and tossed it aside. I let my hands glide over his shoulders—*my gosh, his muscles had muscles*—and down his arms. When I would have reached for his waist to pull off his tank top, he brushed my hands aside and in one ferocious tug he unsnapped my dress from top to bottom. *So hot!*

A soft meow sounded and Nick glanced over his shoulder to see Sir, lying across the top of the couch watching us, the end of his tail flicking as if he couldn't decide if this was a game or something that required an intervention. Nick chuckled and then turned and tugged me toward the bedroom. We fell on the bed in a tangle of limbs and half-undone clothes.

It felt so good, so right, to be with him again. I wanted to touch and taste him everywhere, but he was ahead of me. He tugged off my dress, unfastened my bra, and pulled off my undies before I'd even gotten my bearings.

When I glanced down, I realized I still had my leopard print boots on. When I would have kicked them off, he shook his head. "Those stay."

He sat on the edge of the bed and pulled me into his lap, positioning me so that I straddled him. The feel of his jeans beneath my bare thighs was incredibly erotic, and my head started to buzz with lust.

From this vantage point, his hands could reach every part of my naked person and he took full advantage while I dug my fingers into his hair and kissed him as if he were offering me the breath of life.

His wicked fingers pinched my nipples and then he lowered his head, forcing me to arch my back while he soothed the ache with his tongue. His hands moved to my thighs, and he gently nudged my legs farther apart. His thumb stroked the very center of me, and I almost leapt right out of his lap, so sensitive was my body to his touch.

He whispered soothing words while he continued to stroke me, then he ran his mouth from my breasts to my throat and up to linger in the sweet spot just behind my ear. I felt as if I were on fire. I couldn't remember my name or the date or even what country I lived in. I was just a frenzied ball of need. Unable to take much more, I reached between us and unzipped his pants, pushing the opening apart until he was fully accessible.

I reached into my nightstand for protection, and slid the sheath over him, feeling him arch as he became even thicker in my hand.

"Now, Nick, now," I pleaded. I sensed he was trying to resist me to make it last, so I leaned in close and whispered in his ear. "I want you inside me *now*."

A grunt was his only response as he lifted me up and then entered me on one spectacular thrust. Perfection.

This. This was like nothing I had ever known with anyone else. We fit perfectly, we moved together instinctively, and when he wrapped his arms around me and pulled me in tight while still rocking his hips up against me, I tightened into a knot of sensation that with just the flick of his thumb, he unraveled in a thousand directions all at once. It was a pleasure so intense, it was almost painful, and when he joined me, the sensation doubled and left me gasping as I rode out each shock wave until the end.

In the aftermath, I rested with my head on his shoulder with his arm around the small of my back. His fingers traced patterns on my hip, and I thought I might purr as loudly as Sir if Nick kept it up.

"So who was your dinner date?" he asked.

"Greg DeVane," I said.

"Ex-husband number two?" he asked.

I was surprised he remembered his name and tried to gauge how he was feeling by his tone, but his voice was even, betraying no emotion other than mild curiosity.

"His father has retired out here, and he was in town to visit him," I explained.

"Ah." He pressed a kiss against my hair. It was a comforting gesture, and I wondered if he thought I was upset about seeing my ex again.

"It was good to see him," I said. "We didn't part on the best of terms before."

"I'm sorry," he said. "I'm also sorry that I showed up in the doorway, looking like a jealous lunatic."

I smiled, feeling the heat of his skin beneath my cheek. "It's okay. I would have felt the same if the situation was reversed. And I'm sorry about Friday night. I didn't mean any harm."

"I know," he said. He rolled so that he was on top of me. He looked down at me and smiled. That rogue dimple of his winked at me and I was done for. "Can we just put it behind us? All of it?"

"Yes," I said. "Except there's one thing I want to put out there for your consideration."

He stilled. His hazel eyes held mine, and a wary look came over his features. "All right."

"I want you to consider going to the gala with me," I said.

He rolled back on the bed and stared up at the ceiling. "Public events aren't my thing. I would think after the Denny's debacle you'd understand."

"I do but this is different. It's important. As Lexi's brother, you need to give her your full support," I said.

"I've been giving her my full support, and I'll continue to do so."

"I meant in public," I said.

"Why? What difference does it make if I cut a check or show up at a party?" he asked. "Either way, she's got a crew, her net-zero development is under construction, and it's known in the community that Daire Industries is supporting her."

"The gala is a pretty big night for me, too," I

439

said. "All of our—my—work will be on display. I don't know if you know this, but I'm a pretty big deal."

The teasing made his mouth curve up on one side, but I could see he was resistant to the idea of going to the gala. I knew I should let it go, but suddenly I heard Greg's voice in my head—*stop settling for the diamonds in the rough, Annabelle, you deserve so much more*—and I knew he was right.

"It's important to me that you go to the gala, Nick," I said. I felt very brave and equally nervous. I wasn't great at asking for what I wanted in a relationship—thus my default mode as a pleaser—but if Nick and I were going to have anything worth having, I needed to ask for what I needed, too.

He went still. "Are you telling me that the gala is a deal breaker?"

I thought about it. Did I want to be in a relationship with a man who barricaded himself on a huge estate, who didn't engage with the world? No, I didn't.

I met his gaze and said, "Yes."

A flash of hurt crossed his face, and I almost recanted right there. It caused me physical pain to see him hurting, but I just lay there unable to move. With a sigh, he rolled away from me and sat on the edge of the bed. He ran a hand over his face as he slowly pulled on his clothes.

"I can't be what you want, Annabelle," he said.

So there was my answer. It shouldn't have gutted me, but it did.

"You don't want to think it over?" I asked. "Mull the possibility of going?"

"No," he said. "I can't. That world, those people, they all know me as an unstoppable force in this city. Everyone thinks I retired, hell, even my own sister has no idea that I've had a stroke, and I don't want her to. Annabelle, I could keel over dead from another stroke at any moment, and the lack of control I have over it eats me alive, every waking moment."

He shook his head as if he couldn't believe this was his life.

"I have to live with that every day. I'm not going to ask my sister or you to live with it, too. And as for the world at large, I do not need their pity. Can you even imagine going to a black tie event not knowing if you were going to fall on your face? Christ, the humiliation would kill me."

I sat up. I wrapped the bedsheets around me to keep warm, but I didn't think anything could ward off the chill that was creeping through my veins. It felt as if icicles were forming on my heart, and I wondered if it was some self-protection mechanism of which I'd been unaware until this very moment. As if my heart knew that if it was encased in ice, it couldn't be broken.

"So your image of yourself is more important

to you than having your sister back in your life?"

"That's not what I said," he snapped.

"Yes, it is," I argued.

He stood and started to walk away.

"You don't understand," he said. "And I can't explain it to you."

"Oh, I understand," I said. The ice around my heart was suddenly being consumed by the fire of my temper. "You're afraid."

He snapped back around as if I'd struck him.

"Hell yes, I'm afraid," he said. He spread his arms wide. "I almost died. One minute I was on top of the world and then *wham!* Everything was taken from me like that." He snapped his fingers. "And it could happen again and there's not a damn thing I can do about it."

He strode from the room, and I hopped off the bed and followed. We were not done. Not until I had my say. "That's not what you're afraid of."

He whirled around and looked at me with one eyebrow higher than the other. "You're joking, right?"

"No, I'm not," I said. He picked his shirt up off the floor and shrugged into it. Sir was asleep on the red throw and didn't even pop his head up at our raised voices.

"You're afraid to let anyone in," I said. "You say you were on top of the world but you were alone up there, Nick."

He put his hands on his hips and stared at me.

It felt like yelling at a brick wall, but I did it anyway because I'm thick like that.

"Now you have people in your life who care about you and what terrifies you even more than that is that you care about them, too."

He shook his head, and I knew it was more him shaking me off than disagreeing. I kept going.

"Yes, you do," I said. "You think I don't know that Emily and Elijah and Abigail are better off for having you in their life. You think I don't understand that the Sunshine House is yours? That it's your way of trying to save kids from the same childhood trauma you suffered?"

"Why isn't that enough?" he asked. "Why can't I just make a difference in my own way, from a distance?"

"Because that's not how being alive works. You have to stand up for the people you care about," I said. "And not just as a checkbook. Lexi needs you. She needs her big brother at the most important event in her life. And I need you, too."

"No, you don't," he said. He gestured to his body and said, "What can I possibly do for you, for any of you, Annabelle, if I drop dead tomorrow?"

"You could be with me today," I countered. Then I decided to go all in. "Listen, I get that you're scared. We're all scared. I'm terrified by how much I love you, but I'm standing here, loving you anyway."

"I never asked you to love me," he growled. "Three months, that's all this was supposed to be, and now it can't even be that. I can't be the man you want me to be, Annabelle. I just can't."

He turned and strode out the open door without looking back. Not once.

Nick

26

"Two more reps," Jackson said. "And two and one."

I used the last of my arm strength to set the bar in thc holder over my head. Jackson grabbed it, probably to make sure I didn't drop it on my head. The knot on my forehead had gone down, but he'd been tracking me like a hawk the last few days, probably to make certain I didn't do any more damage.

He handed me a towel, and I wiped the sweat off my face before taking a long drink of water. I could feel him watching me, but he didn't say anything. It was annoying.

"What?" I asked.

"Nothing." He shrugged. "I haven't seen Annabelle around is all."

"Are we going to braid each other's hair and talk about our relationships now?" I asked.

Jackson ran a hand over his bald head. "You could try." He laughed that big booming laugh of his that made the walls shake.

I glared. He stopped laughing then and studied my face. "Did you fuck it up?"

"No!" I said.

"You did, didn't you?" he asked. "You fucked it up."

"Stop saying that." I rose to my feet, checking to see how steady I was. My heart rate felt fine, I didn't feel any tingling in my hands or feet, and my leg seemed to hold. "It's complicated."

I walked over to the treadmill. I knew if I was jogging on it, he couldn't expect me to talk to him. I stepped up and hit the start button.

"What's complicated?" He moved in front of the treadmill so I had to look at him while I walked. "You like her, she likes you—although God only knows why—and now you're a thing."

"We're not a thing," I said. "And even if we were, I don't do long-term things, so we'd be ending in a few weeks anyway."

"Are you terminally stupid?" he asked. "I mean, is it like a chronic condition for you?"

I ignored him and turned the machine up, breaking into a light jog. Jackson wasn't dissuaded and just yelled at me over the treadmill's steady hum.

"Is this why you pushed your sister away?"

Ignore him, I told myself.

"You made her cry, you know."

I didn't know. I slapped the stop button on the machine and hopped off it. I moved to stand in front of him. I normally hated looking up at him but I did it now.

"What are you talking about?"

"Lexi," he said. His voice was full of disapproval. "The morning after you came home with that"—he pointed to my forehead—"she was here, but you told her that you didn't need her to watch over you. Do you have any idea how much that hurt her? I saw her in the driveway when she left. She was crying."

My stomach twisted. The thought of Lexi crying about me made my gut twist. Why was protecting the people I loved from the burden of caring about me making me feel like total shit?

Worried that I might succumb to another panic attack, I took a seat and hung my head.

"Annabelle called her to keep an eye on me after I cracked my head," I said. "She shouldn't have done that."

"Why not?" he asked. "Lexi's your sister."

I glanced up at him. "She hasn't been in my life in almost twenty years. We're not close. I hardly even know her anymore."

Jackson shook his head. "Bullshit. I've seen you two together. Even a deaf, dumb, and blind man would pick up on the fact that you're siblings. You're so much alike. You have the same long-legged walk. You both talk with your hands. You actually enjoy arguing. Weirdos. And you have the same way of tipping your chin out when you're mad."

"Whatever," I said. I didn't want to know any

of these things. "Annabelle had no right to call Lexi without asking me."

"Maybe not," Jackson said. "But who else do you have?"

I sat up straight and stared at him. "You."

"Sure, until you get pissed off enough to fire me."

"Which is becoming more likely every second," I said. "Even then, I'll still have Lupita and Juan." Even I could hear the note of desperation in my voice, trying to convince myself that I wasn't completely alone like I had been in my teens.

"They will be retiring soon to spend their time with their grandbabies, my brother," he said.

No more Lupita? I hated the very idea that she might retire on me. Still, I wasn't going to play this game. Annabelle had been wrong, and Jackson was not going to sway me on this point.

"I'll hire replacements," I said. "For all of you."

"So you'll have staff tending to your needs for a paycheck," Jackson said. He wrapped his enormous arms around his middle and shivered. "That just gives me the warm fuzzies. How about you?"

"Your point?" I asked. I really was going to fire him.

"That Annabelle was right to call the only available member of your family to come check on you when you were injured," he said. "That's what family is for, and you owe Annabelle an apology."

I gaped at him. "I owe her an apology? How about she owes me an apology for crossing boundaries she had no right to cross?"

"Was she your girlfriend?" he asked.

I hated that he used the past tense. "Something like that." Shit, we hadn't even been together long enough to determine if we were boyfriend and girlfriend, which seemed an awfully lightweight way to describe my feelings for her. For the first time in my life, I'd fallen hard.

"Then let's litmus test this," Jackson said. "If Annabelle had gotten hurt, cracked her head or broken her arm, and her—let's say brother just to keep the genders matched—her brother was here in town, and you knew him, would you have called him?"

I opened my mouth to say, "No, absolutely not," but Jackson held up his hand, stopping me. "Slow your roll, really picture it. Annabelle, lying in her bed, broken, hurt, rejecting a visit to the hospital when she has a history of medical issues."

I could see it, and it gutted me. I hated the mere idea of her being injured.

"Now her brother is in town. You know him because you've been working with him," he said. "You know that Annabelle is keeping her brother at arm's length, because they've been estranged by life circumstances, but you also know that your relationship with Annabelle is temporary and ending soon. Who can you call that you know will take care of her when things are over between you?"

"Her brother," I said. And just like that, I understood exactly why Annabelle had done what she did. She cared. She cared about me, and she didn't want me to be alone.

"Damn it," I said.

Jackson sat down beside me. He fished a card out of his shorts pocket, and he handed it to me. I recognized it as the card Dr. Henry had given to me when he referred me to Dr. Franks.

"It's not too late to fix things, but you're going to need some professional help," Jackson said. "Call him."

The fierce teenager who had struck out on his own, refusing any help from anyone, was still inside me. I could feel him rejecting the doctor, Jackson, Annabelle, and Lexi. He didn't want to have anyone in his life whom he might care about. He didn't want to be vulnerable. He didn't want to get hurt. And he most definitely didn't want to be abandoned again.

Out of fear, I'd let him have his way for a very long time. Annabelle was right. I was afraid. I'd kept everyone at a distance. Relationships lasted only a season. I paid people to take care of me instead of leaning on friends or, in Lexi's case, family. I'd spent the past twenty years working myself into the ground so that I was safe, untouchable, but what I hadn't realized was that I was lonely.

It wasn't until after my stroke when I was vulnerable that I discovered I not only needed Lupita's mothering, Juan's steadfastness, Jackson's friendship, and Annabelle's affection, but also wanted all of those things. And I wanted my sister. I wanted Lexi back in my life. I didn't want to be so alone anymore.

I looked at Jackson, knowing that there were tears in my eyes and for once not feeling ashamed of seeming weak.

"You're right. Will you help me?" I asked. I met his piercing gaze and said, "Please . . . brother."

Much to my horror, Jackson watered up. He looked like he was going to full-on cry. Instead, he hugged me tight. It was like being hugged by a bear. Then he laughed his booming laugh and slapped me hard on the back. *Ouch.*

"Let's do this," he announced.

For a second, a nanosecond really, I wondered what the hell I had just done.

Annabelle

27

The day of the gala roared up on us with the speed of a breakaway locomotive. The days prior were spent in a frenzy of last-minute details. Because Lexi was hip deep, working onsite with Jackson still acting as her driver/bodyguard, Sophie took it upon herself to pry Lexi away from the development to get cleaned up for the big event.

The afternoon found us at Benz Hair Design, being blown out and styled by Barb and Ben Fimbrez, the owners of the salon, of which Soph was a longtime customer. Barb, a pretty woman with a thick mane of beautiful black hair and a contagious smile, took one look at Lexi and hustled her into a chair, clearly realizing she had her work cut out for her. I waited while Ben sat Sophie down in his chair and began to work on styling her hair in the updo she wanted for the gala.

I thumbed through a magazine and listened to them talk. Soph was telling Ben the latest happenings at our office. He was a good listener and knew exactly when to crack a joke when

Soph started to get too uptight about the business. The fact that he could do that while wielding five different hair implements at once made him a wizard in my book.

When Soph was finished, it was my turn in the chair. Barb was still working on Lexi as they'd decided to give her hair a little boost since it had been sorely neglected for the past few months. Ben asked me what I wanted to do with my hair. I had no idea. Honestly, the thought of going to the gala without Nick being there depressed me to no end.

I hadn't seen him since the night he left my house. The curtains remained drawn, and there was no sign of life coming from his home. I hadn't even seen Lupita, Juan, or Jackson. I almost wondered if everyone had moved out and I was there on the property by myself.

I shrugged and Ben, in his dress shirt and jeans and perfectly cut silver hair, studied me from behind his glasses for a moment. "Are you willing to trust me, Annabelle?" he asked.

"Sure," I said. I figured I had nothing to lose; besides, Soph's hair had come out perfect. The man clearly had skills.

"All right then," he said. The wizard set to work, and I tried not to think about the coming evening and how I was going to have amazing hair, an amazing dress, and no boyfriend to share it with. It made me mad all over again. Damn it.

• • •

We dropped Sophie off at her house to get ready as she was driving to the gala with Miguel. Then Lexi came with me to my house, where she and I would get dressed. Given that neither of us had dates, we'd decided to go together.

We were just getting dressed when there was a knock on the door. It was a big thumper of a knock, and my heart leapt into my chest with the crazy hope that it was Nick, that he'd changed his mind, that he'd be there for Lexi's big night regardless of his stupid pride. I yanked the door open. It wasn't Nick.

Jackson stood there, looking amazing in a tuxedo with his beard trimmed and the smell of bergamot pouring off him in waves like he was a walking air freshener called scent of man.

"Hey," I said. I'm a dazzling conversationalist, I know.

"Hi, Annabelle. I'm here to drive you and Lexi to the gala."

"You are?" I asked. I did not know about this. I turned toward the bedroom, where Lexi was getting ready. Did she know about this? "Lexi, your driver is here!"

She came out of the bedroom with her newly highlighted and curled hair, carrying a flirty pink lipstick that she had applied only on her upper lip so far, and wearing her body-hugging sky blue trumpet gown, which plunged in the front and had a slit up to mid-thigh on the side. It showed off all of her curvy assets to their best advantage. Soph had picked it out, natch.

"My what?" she asked.

"Driver," I said. I gestured to Jackson, who was standing there in his tuxedo, a stunned expression on his face as if I'd just smacked him upside the head with a rolling pin. It wasn't a great look.

"What the hell are you doing here?" Lexi asked.

"I'm your escort," he said.

"Says who?"

"Says Nick."

"The same Nick who's not going tonight?" she asked. She held up her hand. "Forget it. I changed my mind."

"What?" Jackson and I asked at the same time.

She looked at us, and her pretty hazel eyes were anguished. "I can't do this. The New Dawn development was never supposed to be about me. It was supposed to be about me and Nick, about the two of us doing something together, but he just keeps pushing me away. This whole thing has been for nothing and I . . . I just can't! I'm sorry!"

She whirled around, her skirt flaring, showing off her long lithe legs, as she dashed back into my bedroom and slammed the door.

Panic began to thrum through me. Everyone who was anyone was going to the gala tonight.

The freaking mayor would be there! If Lexi didn't show, we were so screwed. Damn you, Nick Daire! As if I wasn't mad enough at him on my own behalf; now I was devastated for Lexi and everything we had worked so hard for over the past few months.

"Do you mind if I . . . ?" Jackson gestured to the closed door.

I waved him on. "Go for it."

Moving with a grace that always surprised me for such a large man, he disappeared into the bedroom, closing the door softly behind him.

I didn't want to eavesdrop so I went to the kitchen and poured myself a medicinal glass of white wine, which I sipped while I waited. I checked my reflection in the mirror. My hair was holding its long stylized curls, thanks to Ben, and my makeup was finished. My gown was a vintage number from 1962 that I had picked up in a thrift store in the Melrose district. It was off-the-shoulder and dipped low in the back, made of a form-fitting crimson lace over cream-colored satin that boasted a matching deep red satin bow, which perched above the slit at the back of my knees, making it flirty and fun and, more practically, possible to walk.

I could hear murmurs coming from behind the closed door. The low one was Jackson's, punctuated every now and then by a higher tone, which was obviously Lexi. I wondered if the two of them had formed a friendship or more during the time he'd been driving her to and from the jobsite. I wondered if Nick knew. I wondered if he cared. The thought depressed me, and I tried to wash it away with a gulp of wine.

I glanced at the clock. If Jackson didn't work his magic quickly, we were going to be late. Yes, even I, the chronically late one, knew that when you hosted the party, it was best not to be the last to arrive. I began to pace.

The murmurs stopped. I wondered if that was a good sign or a bad one. I drank some more. I could feel the wine buzzing through my veins. I pushed the glass away. I was about to go knock on the door when it opened and Jackson stepped out.

He met my gaze from across the room, and a faint pink blush appeared just over his neatly trimmed beard. He cleared his throat and said, "She'll be right out."

I nodded. Then I grinned. "You have some lipstick in your beard."

He looked horrified and swiped at his face. I laughed and held out a paper napkin to him.

"So," I said. "Driver or boyfriend?"

His blush deepened. "Boyfriend."

I laughed, delighted. "Good for you. She's a keeper."

He grinned in return as he dabbed at the section of beard I indicated. "I think so, too."

"Do you think she's going to be okay to do this tonight?" I asked.

He cast a dark look toward the big house. "I hope so."

That was not as reassuring as I'd hoped, but I appreciated the honesty.

When Lexi reappeared, she looked calmer and her lipstick was fully applied. She glanced at us and said, "All right, let's do this."

It took us only fifteen minutes to arrive at the country club. Situated downtown on Seventh Street and Thomas Road, the club had been founded in 1900 by twelve of Arizona's most prominent citizens. It had a very mid-century modern vibe with stylized permanent overhangs and exposed stonework.

Jackson handed his car keys to the parking valet, and Lexi and I stepped out of the vehicle as soon as our doors were opened for us. A glance at Lexi's face, and I noticed she was looking pale and, frankly, petrified. I looped my arm through hers and said, "Come on, let's find Sophie. She'll know exactly what's what."

Jackson stepped up to Lexi's other side, and I saw her visibly relax. I wondered if Nick had any idea that his friend and his sister were clearly a thing. Probably not. As far as I knew, he hadn't seen Lexi since the night I'd called her to check on him. I felt like this was a fail on my part. Had I not been so consumed with him, with us, maybe he would have gotten closer to his sister on his own.

I shook my head. No, probably not. The demons Nick was fighting were keeping him from letting anyone get too close, and that included me, Jackson, and Lexi. Someday I would probably look back at our relationship and feel sorry for him, but at the moment, I was just too damn angry.

There was a huge sign, which I'd had made, and it featured Luz's mid-century modern bright yellow sun rising behind two stylized purple mountains with an aqua and orange sky. The sign welcomed us and indicated the room where the New Dawn gala was being held. I took a second, just a second, to appreciate our work. It was a nod to the Arizona state flag, but also celebrated Phoenix's heyday, the fifties. I was proud of it and knew it was going to become a premier piece in the studio's portfolio.

"There you are!" Sophie came darting out of the room at the end of the hall. She was wearing a silver sheath dress with cap sleeves and matching silver platform sandals. On anyone else the dress would have overwhelmed, but Soph had such a vibrant personality, she and the dress were a perfect fit.

She stopped in front of us and pressed her hands to her cheeks. "You two are beautiful." She looked at Lexi. "No one is going to hear a word of your speech; they're just going to bask in your beauty."

Lexi blushed bright red and glanced at Jackson. He winked at her and said, "It's true."

"Come on." Soph grabbed Lexi and me by the hands and pulled us toward the room. "I have a million people for you to meet. You should see the architectural rendering in the middle of the room. It's lit perfectly and people are agog! Lexi, you are going to come out of this as one of the most innovative architects in the country. My god, it's thrilling."

I glanced at Lexi. She was looking a sickly shade of green. I leaned close to Soph and said, "Dial it back a little. We've been battling a case of nerves for the past hour."

Soph glanced at Lexi, noted her pallor, and immediately threw an arm around her. "Don't you fret. You've got this. Just speak from your heart."

Lexi swallowed. I thought she might lose the vomit battle, and I wondered if there was a place I could stash all the items in my clutch in case we needed it as an emergency barf bag. I needn't have worried. Soph hit the room, dragging us in her wake, like a cyclone of meet and greet.

Drinks were pressed into our hands, small talk was made, as we worked the room from one end to the other. My crew, Nyah, Trent, Booker, and the others, were there, and it was a relief to see their friendly faces. The crowd became a blur, I had no idea if I was just repeating myself, and from the looks of it, neither did Lexi.

When we'd been going hard for an hour, she leaned close and whispered, "Make it stop."

I glanced around the room, looking for Jackson, who had been discreetly shadowing us the entire time. I waved him in and said, "I think Lexi could use some air."

He nodded and took her elbow, leading her through the open doors and out onto the patio that overlooked the golf course. I envied her even as I turned back to the banker who was regaling me with his triumphs on the course that day. Not knowing a thing, and caring even less, about golf, I smiled and nodded until I was sure I resembled a well-heeled bobblehead doll. The man did not seem to care.

When Soph appeared at my elbow, I could have kissed her in gratitude. The perturbed V in between her eyebrows checked that impulse.

"What's up?" I asked.

"It's time for Lexi's speech," she said. "But I can't find her."

I turned back to my golfing banker, who was still talking, and excused myself. He gave a quick nod and turned to the person on his left and continued his monologue. Okay, then.

"She was stepping outside for some air," I said. "I'll go grab her."

"Meet me at the stage," Soph said.

I nodded and hurried outside. I searched the patio and almost retreated until I heard a suspicious moan coming from behind a potted orange tree.

"Lexi? Jackson?" I called. There was no response. I did not have time for this. I circled the tree and found them in a clinch. "Really? You're doing this now?"

They broke apart. Jackson was rumpled and Lexi looked dazed. Jackson said, "I was trying to take her mind off her nerves."

"Mission accomplished," I said. The sarcasm in my voice could have sliced through steel. "Come on, let's get you ready."

I took Lexi's hand and hauled her to the ladies' room. The attendant and I helped fix her mussed hair and she reapplied her lipstick. She looked lovely and fragile and completely petrified.

"I take it you're afraid of public speaking," I said.

"Afraid?" she asked. "Try I'd rather jump out of a plane, swim with sharks, or be forever lonely, like live alone in a tower with no Internet lonely."

"You might have mentioned this before," I said.

She raised her hands in the air. "I thought Nick would be here. I thought he'd come around. Whenever I've needed him, he's always been there. Always." She was shaking all over, and she looked like she was going to cry. "Until now."

Fury bubbled up inside me. I was mad at Nick, I was mad at Lexi, I was mad at Soph for convincing me to come to Phoenix, and mostly, I was mad at myself because, no matter how hard I tried, I couldn't shut off the feelings I had for that man.

"Listen," I said. "It doesn't have to be a long speech. All you really need to do is go up there and say thank you to everyone for coming out and supporting New Dawn. I'll have Jackson stand front and center and you just talk to him. And I'll be right there with him. You can do that, can't you?"

Lexi stared at me. She took a deep breath. "Yeah." She nodded. "I think so."

"Okay, let's get it over with," I said. I figured we'd better move while she was in the right frame of mind. The old "rip off the bandage quickly" strategy.

As we stepped out of the ladies' room, Jackson was waiting for us. His face was scrunched in concern and he stepped toward Lexi. I shot up a hand and held him off. "Later, Romeo. Right now she has a speech to give and you're going to help her."

"Whatever you need, babe," he said. The smile Lexi sent him was a stunner, and if they weren't so darn adorable, I'd have been consumed with jealousy. I glanced at my watch. Yeah, there was no time for that.

"Let's go," I said.

We swept into the reception and headed for the stage. Soph was at the podium, and she was addressing the crowd. Her inner cheerleader was turned up to full spunk as she charmed and disarmed the guests. I saw Miguel, standing off to the side, watching her with the same mix of awe and pride I'd seen on his face on their wedding day. Well, it looked like they were back on track, so that was something.

When Soph saw us, she beamed. "And now, ladies and gentlemen, I'd like to introduce the incredible woman whose vision has brought us all here tonight, Alexandra Brewer."

There was a commotion at the center of the room and suddenly over the applause a small but loud chant began. It took me a second to realize that this wasn't an approving crowd noise but rather it was taunting.

"Ban New Dawn! Ban Gentrification!"

Jackson and I exchanged an alarmed look. In a flash, I knew this was the group responsible for the slashed tires and bomb threats that had stalled Lexi's building site before Nick got involved.

"Take her," Jackson said. He pushed Lexi at me and spun around, marching into the fray.

"Jackson, wait!" Lexi cried.

The murmurs and commotion continued. I

looked at Lexi. "What do you want to do?"

Her hazel eyes were enormous and she glanced up at the stage where Sophie was waiting.

"I can't let them ruin the gala," she said.

I glanced over my shoulder to see Jackson, holding two of the male protesters by the scruffs of their necks. They were young, twenty-somethings with neckbeards and glasses. I thought Jackson would toss them out. He didn't. Instead, he dragged them forward front and center beneath the stage.

The applause grew louder, and I wondered if it was for Lexi or Jackson. I glanced at the rest of the protesters. They looked to be college-aged as well. Two of the hotel's security guards brought them, three women and a man, forward.

"Sit and listen," Jackson barked at the students. They all sat. It was the wise choice.

As the applause grew in volume, Lexi navigated the steps to the stage. I moved to stand front and center beside Jackson just like I promised her.

The glare of the spotlight shone on her new highlights. She was so lovely, she looked like she'd walked out of a story about fairy princesses. Her smile was nervous as she waved to the crowd, and I could see that her hands were shaking. I saw Jackson stiffen out of the corner of my eye, and I knew he likely wanted to go and snatch her off the stage and smuggle her to safety. I didn't blame him a bit as I felt the exact same way. Seeing her so petrified was absolutely excruciating.

"Hello," she said into the mic. It boomed around the room, and she yelped. Her eyes went wide, and she put her hand over her heart as if to make sure it was still beating.

"Um, hi," she said, trying again. Her voice was softer when she continued, so soft it was almost impossible to hear her, and we were right in front.

I glanced at Soph, who was standing off to the side with Miguel. They glanced from the students to Lexi and had matching looks of *What the hell is happening?* on their faces, and I quickly glanced away because there was no way I could answer them at the moment.

"I want to thank you all for coming," Lexi continued. Her gaze was zeroed in on Jackson. Her voice was little more than a mouse squeak. Conversations started up around the room, the protesters started to get restless, and I was certain that what was being said was not flattering. I glanced at Soph again and our gazes met. She looked like she was about to storm the stage and take over. I shook my head. Lexi had to do it.

"This project, New Dawn, i . . . it . . . it's more than just a . . . um . . . an . . ." Lexi looked at Jackson. Her face was a mask of horror. It was clear she had gone completely blank and had absolutely no idea what to say.

"Oh, shit," Jackson muttered. I was right there with him.

"Ban—*ouch!*" One of the protesters started to chant but Jackson stepped on his hand. When the man shot him an accusatory look, Jackson flexed and the guy settled down.

A restlessness swept through the crowd, and the murmurs and whispers took on a fevered pitch. Lexi visibly paled, and I stared at Sophie. Okay, now we had to do something.

I was about to step forward when I saw the curtain behind Lexi twitch. A little boy in a suit appeared. He looked familiar, and I narrowed my eyes, trying to see against the blinding light on the stage. *Elijah!*

Now I thought I might faint. I leaned hard against Jackson, and we watched as Elijah yanked the curtain aside with all his might and a man in a wheelchair rolled forward through the opening. Looking impossibly handsome in his tuxedo, he propelled his chair forward until he was beside his sister. Nick had arrived just in time.

Nick

28

"Nicky?" Lexi gasped. She gestured at the chair I was in. "What happened? Is it your head? Are you all right?"

I locked the chair and then pushed myself to standing. I could feel the hot glare of the lights and hear the murmur of the crowd. I knew most of the people in this room. I had worked with many of them in some capacity or another. Having them all staring at me like they were seeing a ghost, because I'd become a ghost, was unsettling to say the least. But this moment wasn't about me.

"I have some explaining to do, but first." I held out my arms, and Lexi stepped into them for a hug. She looked lovely, just like the princess she used to pretend to be when she was little, and I was so proud of her, I thought I'd bust.

"I'm sorry I was late," I whispered against her hair. "I've never missed the big moments in your life, and I shouldn't have thought it was okay to skip out on this one."

"Oh, Nicky," she cried. Tears coursed down her cheeks, and I handed her my pocket square. Isn't that what they're for? She laughed and dabbed her eyes and her nose.

"Do you want me to step in?" I asked, gesturing to the podium.

She looked at me as if I'd just saved her from the guillotine. "Yes, please." Then she grinned. "But first, I'll introduce you."

She spun away from me and approached the mic. She looked poised and pretty, and she cleared her throat and said, "I'm sorry, ladies and gentlemen, there's been a change of plan." Her voice wobbled, betraying her nerves, but she soldiered on. "Speaking to you tonight about the New Dawn *net-zero housing development*"— she emphasized the words as she glared at the protesters—"is the man who made this gala possible, and he is also my big brother, Nicholas Daire."

The applause started slowly, and then as Lexi stepped back and I stepped forward, the applause grew louder and louder. I tried to speak, but when I looked down, Jackson, the big idiot, was standing there, clapping his enormous hands together with a dopey grin on his face, and beside him was Annabelle.

She was breathtakingly beautiful, and for a second, I forgot everything except her and how much I loved her. Yes, it had taken me two weeks to come to terms with the fact that what I was feeling for her was not going to go away, but with the help of my new psychiatrist, Dr. Franks, I was figuring it out. Among other things.

Annabelle was clapping and laughing and crying, and my heart about clawed its way out of my chest to get to her. In fact, I wanted to jump off the stage and go to her, but now wasn't the moment for me to fall to my knees and beg her to forgive me for being a fucking idiot. That would come later.

I raised my hands, hoping to get the crowd to settle, and slowly they took it down a notch. I saw faces I hadn't seen in over a year. Builders, bankers, investors, city officials, all of the people who cared about Phoenix, who were invested in its growth and development, and I was surprised that instead of feeling like the outsider I'd always thought I was, I felt like one of them. One of the people committed to making our city the best place in the world to live, to raise a family, and to pursue dreams.

"Good evening," I said. The applause started again, but I shook my head. I had a lot of ground to cover and no idea how long I'd be able to stay upright. "It's been a while since I've seen most of you, so I'm going to give you a quick catch-up."

The room grew deadly quiet. I knew it was because the wild speculation about my abrupt retirement had included theories from I was a mobster and in the witness protection program to I was dying of cancer.

470

"Eleven months, three weeks, four days, and seven hours ago, I suffered what they call a cerebrovascular accident." There were a few gasps from people who knew what that meant. One of which was my sister. I glanced at Lexi, and she put her hand over her mouth. Elijah, who was standing next to her, patted her arm and said, not in a whisper, "That's a stroke. Don't worry, he's okay now."

I smiled. It was always so much simpler when kids explained things. I looked back at the crowd and continued, "Yes, what my young friend says is correct. I had a stroke."

Now the crowd was murmuring and muttering. I ignored them and looked at Annabelle. Just the sight of her centered me.

"As you can imagine, I didn't handle this well, especially when it appeared that I had suffered residual damage from the stroke that impeded my ability to walk or think," I said. "For the first six months after my stroke, I spent half the time picking myself up off the floor; thus, my wheels." I paused to look at my wheelchair, the thing that had been my security blanket for so long. "I also struggled with severe fatigue and a bit of fuzzy brain."

I looked back out at the crowd. This was my chance to make things right, and I wasn't going to blow it. "Unsurprisingly, I became reclusive and withdrawn. I was consumed with the fact that the doctors had no idea why I'd had a stroke and therefore couldn't tell me if I'd have another. The odds were not in my favor. In short, I was afraid and I let that fear consume me, but then a funny thing happened."

I paused, giving the audience a moment to catch up, to appreciate the twists and turns of the story. "This brilliant architect, my sister, whom I hadn't spoken to in almost twenty years, showed up at my doorstep and she needed me."

A restlessness hummed through the crowd. The protesters Jackson had corralled, undoubtedly the ones who made the threats against Lexi, were shifting where they sat probably looking for the exits about now. Good.

"My sister, Alexandra Brewer—" I began but Lexi interrupted.

"Alexandra Daire," she said. Then she whispered, "I've made it legal and everything."

Oh crap, I felt the tears well up in my eyes. I would rather have my leg give out and fall on my face than burst into tears. I blinked several times, willing them back, and cleared my throat.

"Alexandra Daire," I said. I savored the sound of it for just a moment. "She needed me because she was trying to do something so big, so extraordinary, so out of the box, that the big thinkers of the city didn't know what to make of her and neither did the younger crowd who believed this was just another gentrification project."

The student protesters turned embarrassed shades of red. Good. I gestured to the different displays around the room. The architectural model of the twenty small houses currently under construction took up the center space. It was massive and it was extraordinary, but Lexi had also brought models of the solar, wind, and water generators that were the main sources of power for the development. They sat around the room, chugging away as if this were a science fair.

"That's all right," I said. "It took me a minute to appreciate it, too. But as the founder of the Sunshine House, a local nonprofit committed to helping families torn apart by substance abuse start new lives, I have recently acquired several tax-reverted lots in the city on which Lexi will be designing more net-zero small house communities for low- to middle-income families who need a new start."

I heard Lexi gasp. I turned to her and said, "That's assuming you're willing to stay for a while."

She was crying. It looked like happy tears since she was grinning at the same time. I laughed and grabbed her hand, holding it in mine.

"Excellent. With the commitment of those in the community with the ability to look forward to the future, Lexi has broken ground on the first development that will revolutionize urban housing, and secure Phoenix's ranking as the most innovative city in the country. Now it's up to us to keep it going."

It was a good little speech, if I do say so myself. The applause was deafening as people were swept up with the idea of being the hub of innovation. The world was changing, renegades like Lexi were going to lead the way, and this was the moment when the powers that be needed to get with it or get out of the way. I led Lexi around the podium, and we stood side by side, the Daire children, together again. I held out my other hand to Elijah. He leapt forward to take it.

His mother and sister were in the crowd, and I'd return him to them soon, but I wanted to give Elijah what I had never gotten as a child. I wanted him to know that he belonged wherever he damn well decided he belonged in the world. And even more important, he wasn't alone. I was always going to look out for him and his sister just like I had Lexi.

When the applause died down, Sophie Vasquez came back on stage and invited everyone to mingle, take pictures, and ask questions.

While she spoke, Lexi, Elijah, and I made our way off the stage. Elijah pushed my wheelchair down the ramp, and Lexi and I followed. I glanced at her. She had a sparkle in her eyes, and the color had returned to her face. She leaned against me and said, "Thanks. You saved me again."

"Yeah, well, sorry I was late."

She looked at me, and her eyes were filled with confusion. "Why didn't you tell me about the stroke? I would have understood."

"I was in a very dark place, Lex," I said. "I was consumed with anxiety and fear. It made me selfish and stupid, but a certain someone has challenged my negative outlook."

"Annabelle?" she guessed.

I started in surprise and she grinned. "You can't keep your eyes off her."

"Yeah, well, I might have screwed that all up," I said. "I have amends to make there, too. I'm actually seeing a professional who's helping me sort through my issues." I paused. The next part was the hardest bit. "Actually, I was wondering if you'd go with me to a session sometime."

I held my breath, waiting for her answer.

"Oh, Nicky, of course," she said. "You know I'd do anything for you."

Then she hugged me. It was the same full-tilt, hug-the-stuffing-out-of-you stranglehold she used to hit me with when we were kids, and it made me laugh just as it had back then. For the first time in forever, I felt like things might be okay.

"Did you see me, Mom? Did you?" Elijah asked.

Emily arrived with Abigail. All dressed up, Emily hardly resembled the sobbing woman in the parking lot, whose life had been in ruins just a few weeks before. We talked regularly since that night, and when her husband had resurfaced, not a big surprise, she told him he needed to get help before he was welcome back in the family. He had opted to keep drinking. I listened while she cried, and I made sure with the help of the Sunshine House staff that she could stand on her own. It was my intention that she get one of the houses in the new developments that Lexi and I were going to build.

"I did," Emily said. She was grinning at Elijah. "You looked amazing up there, being Mr. Daire's helper."

"Nick," I corrected her.

"Nick," she said with a nod. She glanced down at her son. "Want to go see the exhibits before your sister falls asleep?"

"Yeah," Elijah said. He turned to me and gave me a hearty high five. "See ya, Nick."

"See ya, buddy."

"Thank you," Emily said, but it ended on a yelp as her son pulled her away. I had a driver waiting to take them home whenever they were ready, but I appreciated that they were here. They grounded me.

"Time to own your bullshit." Jackson's voice boomed, and I was about to snap back that I was

476

when I noticed the leader of the protesters I had seen from backstage was standing in front of Lexi.

"I . . . I'm sorry, Ms. Daire," he said. He was tall and thin with a scraggly beard. He looked to be about nineteen. "I didn't know . . . I didn't realize—"

"Idiot," one of his fellow protesters muttered.

The young man turned a deeper shade of red, blushing all the way to the roots of his dark brown hair.

"I grew up in that neighborhood, and I saw the construction happening, and I just assumed it was going to be more of those overpriced town houses that are horrible for the environment and the economy."

Okay, now it was my turn to get red-faced as I was responsible for a lot of the poorly planned gentrification of the city. Annabelle joined the group, and I saw the wicked twinkle in her brown eyes when she heard what was being said.

"Your heart was in the right place, err, what's your name?" Lexi asked.

"Jacob."

"Come visit me at the jobsite," Lexi said. She grinned. "We can formulate a plan about what to do about those horribly cheesy developments."

Jacob grinned. "I'd like that." He shook her hand and then departed, signaling to his squad that it was time to go.

"Impressive speech," Jackson said to Lexi as we watched them leave.

"Wasn't Nick amazing?" Lexi cried. She hugged Jackson tight and stared up at him. "I was so nervous. I made a mess out of it, didn't I?"

"Nah, you were great, babe," Jackson said. He looked down at her in complete worship.

Babe? I felt my eyes go wide. "Now wait just a second—" I began but the mayor approached Lexi with a wide warm smile and began to pepper her with questions about the development. As the two women walked toward the architectural model with Jackson following them like a puppy, I felt Annabelle step up beside me.

"They're a thing," she said. "I'm not sure how serious of a thing but definitely a thing."

I turned to face her. It was the moment of truth. Scale of one to ten, how much did she hate me—with one being "Hate-shmate, let's kiss and make up" and ten being "I wouldn't spit on you if you were on fire"? I almost wished I would catch on fire because then I'd know.

"Hi, Goddess," I said.

"Hi."

She was so achingly beautiful in her curve-hugging dress that I wanted to whisk her away from everyone and everything and have her all to myself. Selfish? Probably. Did I care? Not a bit.

"Well, well, well, now it's all coming into focus." A man's voice interrupted whatever I'd been about to say, which was probably a good thing because all I could think of was *Guh* and then I'd likely drool on myself. Still, it was annoying to be interrupted, and I turned to see a thin-wristed, sandy-haired guy standing there in an Armani tux and shiny shoes, looking at Annabelle with unchecked hatred.

It didn't take a big brain to figure out that this was the guy who'd been making her miserable at work. Objectively speaking, he had a very punchable face.

"I'm sorry, Carson, did you say something?" Annabelle asked. She was all poise and grace, and I wanted to kiss her until I passed out.

"This. You. Him." Carson sneered. He wobbled on his feet, spilling the whiskey in his glass. He didn't seem to notice. "You didn't get the creative director position because you deserve it; you got it because you're banging him, the rich guy with the stroke." His voice was slurred and the word came out "shtroke," which frankly sounded like more fun.

"How much did he pay Miguel to give you the job? Was it worth it?" Then he waved his hands in the air and moaned like he was mimicking me having a seizure and an orgasm at the same time. His whiskey went everywhere, and I pushed Annabelle back behind me before she got soaked.

"You all right?" I asked. She nodded, but her lip was curled in disgust.

"Oh, isn't that precious?" Carson asked. He mimicked me stepping in front of Annabelle.

I hissed a breath and stepped forward. I was going to rip this asshole apart, not for mimicking me, because . . . whatever. But how dare he diminish Annabelle's talent that way?

Annabelle must have read my intentions because she looped her arm through mine, holding me back from reaching the dickhead. Still poised, she shook her head and said, "I don't know what you're implying, Carson. I was hired for the job before I even met Mr. Daire."

"Really?" Carson sneered. "So divorced-twice Annabelle Martin had to move across the country to find a man. Looks like you found the only sort that would have you. A lame duck."

I clenched my teeth and my fists. I wasn't going to punch him; really I wasn't. Okay, maybe I was but I never got the chance. In the blink of an eye, Carson was standing in front of me and then he wasn't.

Jackson had zipped up behind him with my wheelchair and clipped him in the back of the knees, causing Carson to reel back into the chair. He was sprawled in the seat like he'd knocked back a few too many at the open bar, which judging by the sight and smell of him, was not too far off the mark.

"Pardon me," Jackson said. "I'm just going to take out the trash."

"And now I'm really glad I didn't fire you," I said.

That made him laugh, his big, booming, shake-the-rafters guffaw. It also startled Carson, who started to rise. Jackson stopped that by rolling out, forcing Carson back against the seat. Annabelle and I watched as they disappeared. I knew Jackson would dump Carson in a cab, making certain he left and couldn't do any more harm.

"Good riddance," Annabelle said. She turned back to me and smiled. "It seems everyone's timing is on point tonight."

The sight of her took my breath away, and suddenly that was all I wanted—to be far, far away with her.

"Any chance we can get out of here?" I asked.

"Let's go," she said.

We ghosted out of the gala to the curb outside. The valet ran to get my car, and when he returned, I gave the keys to Annabelle. Given the dramatic events of the evening, I had no idea how much longer I could go without my constant companion, anxiety, making an appearance. Dr. Franks and I were making progress, but I knew we were playing the long game in regards to my ability to cope.

Annabelle drove through the city streets, and I sat happily beside her, just watching her. I didn't know how tonight was going to play out, but since she had agreed to leave with me, I was feeling hopeful.

When we arrived at home, I directed her to drive to her place. She cast me a concerned look as if she thought I was just going to dump her off. Fat chance. Little did she know that if things went according to plan, she was going to have to scrape me off her from this moment forward.

She shut off the car and we climbed out. I reached over and took her hand, stopping her on the bottom step. I had some things I needed to say before we reached the door.

"I'm sorry," we said at the same time. I shook my head at her and she pursed her lips.

"What are you apologizing for?" I asked.

She shrugged. "It's my default setting. I'm working on it. Also, I felt that I was perhaps a bit harsh the last time we spoke."

"No, you weren't. You just said what I needed to hear. I'm the one who has to apologize," I said. "I was so wrong. Wrong to walk away, wrong to shut you and everyone else out. I can't believe I let my pride and my fear of intimacy cause me to lose the people I care about most in the world."

Her brown eyes got wide and then turned soft as if she was hoping this was going to go her way but she wasn't sure yet.

"You were right to demand that I be there tonight, that I stand up for my sister," I said.

"And you did," she cut in. "Spectacularly."

"I would never have done it without you," I said. "Thank you."

She hugged me then. A tight squeeze around my neck that gave me more hope that perhaps all was not lost.

"There's more. I've been seeing a psychiatrist," I said. I figured I'd better double down while I had her in a good place. She stepped back and looked at me in surprise.

"I spent months railing against anyone who told me that I had suffered a trauma and that I was having a psychological reaction to it," I explained. "In my narrow-minded view, I wrote that off as being weak and convinced myself my problems had to be physical in nature. They're not. And I'm not. Suffering from anxiety, depression, and panic attacks isn't weak, and it isn't any different than suffering from heart disease or diabetes. These things just exist, and they have to be dealt with."

She smiled at me and it was everything. I had to look away for a second to stay focused.

"So Dr. Franks and I are figuring out my issues with my panic and how it manifests in my body with a racing heart and my leg going numb. Turns out Dr. Henry was right, there isn't anything wrong with me physically, but my brain just doesn't want to believe it."

"Nick, that's wonderful," she said.

"Maybe." I shrugged. "I have a lot of work to do.

I'm on an antidepressant, and I've committed to counseling. I'm going to have to reprogram myself, and I might not always be easy to be around."

She didn't say anything for a moment, and I was certain she was going to give me the old heave-ho. Why wouldn't she? She was bright, beautiful, and full of life. Why would she want to be with a broken guy like me?

"Is your body giving out on you your way of dealing with loss?" she asked. "As in, it gives you a reason to push people away and protect yourself from more loss?"

I stared at her. Shocked. "How did you figure out in a matter of weeks what I've been trying to figure out for months?"

"I understand loss," she said. "It makes you do crazy things when you're trying to cope, you know, like marry anyone who asks."

I smiled at her self-deprecation. "Yeah, well, my crazy thing was to have my body give out so I could hide in my house for months." My voice was bitter with self-disgust.

She shook her head. "You weren't hiding. You were regrouping. In a way, you could look at it as your anxiety protecting you by giving you the solitude you needed to heal."

I blinked. I had never considered it from that angle before.

"Besides, who am I to judge?" she asked. "You've made me do some thinking, too."

"I have?" My heart thumped in my chest. *Oh god, please don't let it be that she was better off without me.*

"You were right about me, too," she said. "I *was* trying to manage you. I was trying to make you dependent upon me, by being the bridge between you and your sister, so that you would never leave me. That's *my* damage, and it took you refusing to put up with it for me to see it."

"So what you're saying is I'm good for you?" I asked, only partly kidding.

"Yeah." She laughed.

I glanced up at the night sky. It was a vast expanse of darkness with just a few pinpricks of light. No shooting stars. Pity. I really needed some celestial magic at the moment.

"Now that we've acknowledged how good we are for each other." I cleared my throat. "Does this mean you're willing to give us another go?"

"Yes," she said. Just like that. No hesitation. No second-guessing. My god, I loved her.

Before she'd even finished saying the word, I kissed her. Her mouth fit perfectly under mine, and I wasn't sure how I had survived without this for two whole weeks. I kept my hands on her hips as I pulled her in tight and plundered her lips with mine. As I'd told her before, I didn't need any shooting stars in the sky because she made me see them every time she kissed me.

She broke the kiss and grabbed my hand. With

a swish of her hips, she led me to the door. She stopped cold when she saw the envelope taped to the double doors. She turned to look at me with one eyebrow raised.

"Is this an eviction notice?" she asked.

"I did write it before we made up," I said. "It occurred to me that if you were going to continue living here, we were going to have to renegotiate the rules."

She weighed it in her palm. "It feels thick."

I took her keys and unlocked the door. "We can talk about it inside." I opened the door and led her inside, switching on the lights and noting that one French door was open a crack and Sir was asleep on his red blanket. He really needed a better name and a litter box.

Annabelle followed me into the living room. Her steps were slow as if she were walking to her doom. I felt terrible. What had seemed like a good idea while we were estranged suddenly felt like the stupidest thing I'd ever done in my life.

I held out my hand and said, "You know what? Why don't we just destroy that? We can burn it. Pretend I never wrote it."

She shook her head. "No, I need to see it."

Uh-oh.

She slid her thumb under the flap, tearing it open. The sound seemed inordinately loud, and I started to sweat.

The sheets of paper fell to the floor, scattering

around her feet. We both dropped into a crouch to retrieve them.

Annabelle snatched up two before I could stop her. She scanned the pages then she looked up at me, smiled, and burst into tears at the same time.

Then she read it out loud.

> Goddess: Be advised that the
> following is a list of rules that I
> encourage you to read with an
> open heart and mind:
> Rule number one: I love you.
> Rule number two: I love you.

Her voice wobbled and tears coursed down her cheeks. She glanced up at me and then at the second page she held.

She read more. *"Rule number three hundred and ten: I love you.* Oh, Nick, how many times did you write it?"

My throat was tight, my voice gruff, when I said, "One thousand."

She sobbed. I glanced at the pages in my hands until I found the last one. I handed it to her.

She dropped one of the pages, wiped the tears from her face, and took it. She scanned the tail end of the nine hundred and nineties and then the one-thousandth *I love you*. Then she gasped. She tried to speak but she couldn't get the words out, so I took the page and read it to her.

Rule number one thousand: I love you.
Your besotted landlord, who hopes you'll consider him for the role of devoted husband.

She dropped the note and stared at me. Her eyes were enormous.

"Too soon?" I asked. "We can wait. It was just an idea, you know, because I'm a mess and you're a mess and our messes really seem to complement each other—"

"Nick," she said. "Shut up."

Then she kissed me, and it was perfect and lovely just like her.

When we broke apart, I asked, "Is that a yes?"

"Yes," she said on another sob.

That did it. It was all too much, my heart was pounding, my hands were tingling, and my breath was tight. I landed on my ass on the floor, but it didn't matter because Annabelle went down with me. She wrapped me in her arms and kissed me, and I realized in a flash of clarity that everything that had gone wrong in my life had given me everything that was right, namely her, Annabelle. I was in the arms of my reckless, impulsive goddess, and every bit of pain and hardship that had brought me to this place with her was worth it.

Acknowledgments

It takes a village to write a book, and I am fortunate to have a village of amazingly bighearted, smart, creative people, who give me so much support from the initial idea through the finished product. To that end, I'd like to thank my editor, Kate Seaver, and my agent, Christina Hogrebe. I am ever grateful to have your wisdom and talent with me every step of the way. You're both amazing. Thank you to Mary Geren for finessing all the details.

This book was gifted with so many talented editors who really made it sparkle and shine. Thank you Joan Matthews, Christine Legon, and Jennifer Myers for helping me get the details right. I'd also like to thank the cover artist, Vikki Chu, and the book designer, Alison Cnockaert, for making such a spectacular package for this story. For helping me release this book out into the wild, I could ask for no better crew than Jessica Mangicaro, Natalie Sellers, Brittanie Black, and Dache Rogers. I feel so fortunate to work with all of you. You're simply brilliant!

And here's a giant high five to my author assistant, Christie Conlee. For your positivity, enthusiasm, sassy GIFs, and cupcake baking skills, you are just a bright shining light, and I'm thrilled to have you in my life.

An author is nothing without readers, and I truly have some of the best. Thank you McKinlay's Mavens and Fans of Jenn McKinlay for your kindness, support, enthusiasm, and refreshingly delightful presence on social media. I adore you all. And for every reader who demanded Annabelle's story after meeting her in *Paris Is Always a Good Idea*, this one's for you!

On a personal note, I had to lean on several truly amazing people in my life to help me get the details right. For architectural information, particularly about net-zero building, thank you architect extraordinaire and cuz-in-law, Nancy Clayton. For graphic design information, I am ever grateful to my creative genius cuz, Brad Collins, and my extremely talented friend Bob Diercksmeier. I took all of the information you three gave me and twisted it to suit my own purposes. I take full responsibility if I messed anything up—it's been known to happen—but, hey, it's fiction!

Because this book was written just as the world was entering lockdown and I suddenly had two Hooligans and a Hub also online at home all day long (chaos!), I want to thank Leslie and Dale Thomas for the use of their beautiful home as my office. Truly, the book never would have gotten written without this area of temporary refuge.

One of my greatest challenges as a writer is to craft characters who travel difficult paths. I struggle with torturing them! I want to thank three people who have shared their personal journeys with me and by doing so have given me greater insight into the inner lives of my characters. Sheila Levine, Natalia Fontes, and Chris Hansen Orf. You are three of the strongest people I know, and I love you dearly.

On a lighter note, but equally important, much thanks to my nephew Austin McKinlay for showing me how to view the world through an artist's eyes with your brilliant photographs. Annabelle's artistic temperament definitely came from you.

I suppose I need to thank my Hooligans, Beckett and Wyatt, for getting me to the gym and working out with a trainer. For the record, I still hate it, but I love you very much.

Authors will tell you that everything is material. It's true. Thank you to my nephew Phoenix McKinlay and his number one, Bailey Boutiette, for introducing me to their adorable tuxedo kitten, Giuseppe Socks. I'd never met a tuxedo before! Thanks to my nephew Chase Johnson, who nicknamed Otto—my salt and pepper schnauzer—"Sir" while dog-sitting him. It just happened to be the perfect name for the cat (a tuxedo!) who appears in *Wait For It*. Yes, this is how an author's brain works.

This book wouldn't exist without the time (i.e., happy hours) I spent with my dear friend and neighbor, Howard Adams. You taught me so much about life and resilience and compassion. Being a wheelchair user never slowed you down, in fact, you learned how to gain speed. I'll always remember our *X-Files* marathons, where you hid under your hat, and I'll forever be your Ave Maria.

Lastly, I want to thank my brother, Jon McKinlay, for never letting me quit, but also for giving me the nuts and bolts of the city he helped build—his beloved Boston. All that I am I owe to you, Bro. Love you forever.

Questions for Discussion

1. Annabelle is a fixer. She feels her role is to take care of those she loves. Why does she feel this way? Are you a fixer? Do you know someone who is?

2. Nick is afraid to show any weakness. Why? How does he change? Why does he change?

3. Nick and his sister, Lexi, have a complicated relationship, but the sibling bond is too strong to be denied. Do you have siblings? What is your relationship like? How would it be affected by a twenty-year estrangement?

4. Annabelle chooses to run away from her current situation in Boston. Have you ever wanted to run away and start over?

5. Nick feels trapped. Fear has him living as a shut-in. Have you ever wanted to shut the door on life?

6. Who are you more like? Annabelle who runs away or Nick who hides?

7. When Nick and Annabelle are watching the meteor shower—the shooting stars—they

have very different reactions to the vastness of the universe. Nick feels panicked and powerless, but Annabelle feels relieved to be part of something bigger. What do you feel when you contemplate the stars?

8. Both Nick and Annabelle are forced to step out of their comfort zones and take risks. What is the biggest risk that each of them takes?

9. Having a stroke in his mid-thirties, Nick has suffered a terrifying setback in life. Does he handle it well? How would you have handled it?

10. Annabelle is challenged by a rival at work. How does she cope? Could she have managed it differently? How would you deal with someone who tries to undermine you professionally?

11. The tragic circumstances of their lives shaped Nick and Annabelle. Have you ever suffered a loss or a tragedy like theirs? How did it change you?

12. What do Nick and Annabelle find in each other that helps them heal?

JENN MCKINLAY is the award-winning, *New York Times*, *USA Today*, and *Publishers Weekly* bestselling author of several mystery and romance series. Her work has been translated into multiple languages in countries all over the world. She lives in sunny Arizona in a house that is overrun with kids, pets, and her husband's guitars.

Books are produced in the United States using U.S.-based materials

Books are printed using a revolutionary new process called THINKtech™ that lowers energy usage by 70% and increases overall quality

Books are durable and flexible because of Smyth-sewing

Paper is sourced using environmentally responsible foresting methods and the paper is acid-free

Center Point Large Print
600 Brooks Road / PO Box 1
Thorndike, ME 04986-0001 USA

(207) 568-3717

US & Canada:
1 800 929-9108
www.centerpointlargeprint.com